FICTIO

Translated by Ja

Each disparate subject described in this book—a species of tiger, a villa in Rome, a Greek love poem, an island in the Pacific—shares a common fate: it no longer exists, except as the dead end of a paper trail. Recalling the works of W. G. Sebald, Bruce Chatwin, or Rebecca Solnit, AN INVENTORY OF LOSSES *is a beautiful evocation of twelve treasures that have been lost to the world forever.*

In these exquisite stories, Judith Schalansky, the acclaimed author of ATLAS OF REMOTE ISLANDS, *adopts many different tones and burrows into the language of contemporaneous accounts while interrogating the very notion of memory and extinction.*

JUDITH SCHALANSKY, *born in Greifswald in 1980, lives in Berlin and works as a writer, book designer, and editor (of the prestigious natural history list at Matthes und Seitz). Her book* ATLAS OF REMOTE ISLANDS *was an international best seller, and was called "magnificent" (Robert Macfarlane, The Guardian) and "charming, spooky, and splendid" (The New Yorker).*

JACKIE SMITH *is a German translator. Her translation from Hans Platzgumer's novel* AM RAND (*On the Edge*) *won the Austrian Cultural Forum London Translation Prize in 2017.*

AN INVENTORY OF LOSSES

Judith Schalansky

AN INVENTORY
OF LOSSES

*Translated from the German
by Jackie Smith*

A NEW DIRECTIONS BOOK

First published as *Verzeichnis einiger Verluste* by Suhrkamp Verlag, Berlin, in 2018. This edition is published
by arrangement with MacLehose Press, an imprint of Quercus Publishing Ltd.

The translation of this work was supported by a grant from the Goethe-Institut.

First published in cloth by New Directions by 2020
Manufactured in the United States of America

Library of Congress Cataloging-in-Publication Date
Names: Schalansky, Judith, 1980– author. | Smith, Jackie (Translator), translator.
Title: An inventory of losses / Judith Schalansky ; translated from the German by Jackie Smith.
Other titles: Verzeichnis einiger Verluste. English
Description: New York : New Directions Publishing Corporation, 2020.
| Includes index. | Translated from the German.
Identifiers: LCCN 2020004722 | ISBN 9780811229630 (cloth ; acid-free paper)
| ISBN 9780811229944 (ebook)
Classification: LCC PT2720.A63 A2 2020 | DDC 833/.92—dc23
LC record available at https://lccn.loc.gov/2020004722

2 4 6 8 10 9 7 5 3 1

New Directions Books are published for James Laughlin
by New Directions Publishing Corporation
80 Eighth Avenue, New York 10011

CONTENTS

PREAMBLE

While I was working on this book, the Cassini spacecraft burned up in Saturn's atmosphere; the Schiaparelli Mars lander crashed in the rust-colored rocky landscape of the planet it was supposed to be exploring; a Boeing 777 disappeared without trace en route from Kuala Lumpur to Beijing; in Palmyra, the 2,000-year-old Temples of Baal and Baalshamin, the facade of the Roman theater, the Monumental Arch, the tetrapylon, and parts of the Great Colonnade were blown up; in Mosul, Iraq, the Great Mosque of al-Nuri and the Mosque of the Prophet Jonah were destroyed and in Syria the Early Christian Monastery of St. Elian was reduced to rubble; in Kathmandu an earthquake caused the Dharahara Tower to collapse for the second time; a third of the Great Wall of China fell victim to vandalism and erosion; unknown perpetrators stole the head from the corpse of Friedrich Wilhelm Murnau; Guatemala's Lake Atescatempa, once renowned for its blue-green waters, dried up; the archlike rock formation on the coast of Malta known as the Azure Window collapsed into the Mediterranean; the Bramble Cay mosaic-tailed rat, native to the Great Barrier Reef, became extinct; the last-known male northern white rhinoceros had to be put to sleep at the age of forty-five, survived by only two specimens of this subspecies: his daughter and his granddaughter; the only existing sample of metallic hydrogen, obtained after eighty years of fruitless efforts, disappeared from a laboratory at Harvard University, and no one knows whether the microscopically small particle was stolen or destroyed or simply reverted to a gaseous state.

While I was working on this book, an archivist at New York's Schaffer Library found in an almanac dating from 1793 an envelope containing several strands of gray hair belonging to George Washington; a hitherto unknown Walt Whitman novel and the lost album *Both Directions at Once* by the jazz saxophonist John Coltrane came to light; a nineteen-year-old intern discovered hundreds of Piranesi drawings in Karlsruhe State Museum's collection of works on paper; a double page of Anne Frank's Diary which had brown paper pasted over it was successfully deciphered; the world's oldest alphabet, carved on stone tablets 3,800 years ago, was identified; image data were successfully reconstructed from the photographs taken in 1966–67 by the Lunar Orbiters; fragments were discovered of two hitherto unknown poems by Sappho; ornithologists recorded several sightings, in a Brazilian tree savanna, of blue-eyed ground doves which had been presumed extinct since 1941; biologists discovered the wasp species *Deuteragenia ossarium*, which builds multichamber nests in hollow tree trunks for its young, placing a dead spider ready in each chamber as a source of nutrition; in the Arctic the wrecks of H.M.S. *Erebus* and *Terror* from the ill-fated 1848 Franklin Expedition were located; archaeologists in northern Greece unearthed an enormous burial mound, the final resting place probably not of Alexander the Great but possibly of his companion Hephaestion; Mahendraparvata, the first Khmer capital, thought to have been the largest settlement of the Middle Ages, was discovered close to the Angkor Wat temple complex in Cambodia; archaeologists working in the necropolis of Saqqara happened upon a mummification workshop; in the Cygnus constellation, 1,400 light years from our sun, a celestial body was found, in a so-called habitable zone, on which the average temperature is similar to that of Earth, meaning there may be or may once have been water there, and hence also life, such as we imagine life to be.

PREFACE

On an August day a few years ago I visited a town in the north. It lies on one of the innermost bays of a marine inlet that has extended far into the interior of the land since a prehistoric ice age, and whose brackish water is home in spring to herring, in summer to eels, in autumn to cod and in winter to carp, pike, and bream, hence fishermen ply their trade there to this day. For centuries these men and their families have lived in a neighborhood that can only be described as quaint, consisting of little more than two cobbled streets, a drying place for the nets and a monastery now occupied only by two aristocratic old ladies. In short, it is one of those seemingly timeless places that might very well tempt one to believe that some bygone age as vague as it is appealing is still alive today. Yet it was not the flowering rose-bushes and leggy hollyhocks in front of the squat, whitewashed houses, nor their brightly painted wooden doors or the narrow alleys between the buildings, most of them leading straight down to the stony shore, that particularly lodged in my memory, but rather the peculiar fact that, in the village center, instead of a market square, I found a graveyard, shaded by the green foliage of young lime trees and enclosed by cast-iron railings, in other words the fact that, in the place where normally goods would be exchanged for money, instead the dead and buried were doing what, out of entrenched wishful thinking, is generally termed "resting in peace." My astonishment, which I initially took for unease, was considerable and was further compounded when someone pointed out to me the house of a woman who, while she cooked, was able to look out from her kitchen upon the grave of her prematurely deceased son, and it became clear to me that the centuries-old tradition of the guild that takes care of the funeral rites here had resulted in the dead and the living of the same family ending up in the kind of close proximity I had previously only heard of in the case of the inhabitants of certain Pacific islands. Of course I had visited other notable burial sites before: the cemetery island of San Michele, for instance, which, with its high red-brick walls, looms up out of the turquoise water of the lagoon of Venice like an impenetrable fortress, or the garish stalls in the Hollywood Forever Cemetery to mark the *Día de los Muertos* celebrated annually by the Mexican people, with graves decked out in orange and yellow, and skulls made from brightly colored sugar and papier-mâché, doomed by their advanced state of decay to grin in perpetuity. Yet none touched me as deeply as the fishing community's cemetery, whose peculiar shape—a kind of compromise between a circle and a square—struck me as the very emblem of the remarkable utopia I saw embodied there: a life where death was always in view. For a long time I was convinced that in this place, whose Danish name means "small island" or "surrounded by water," one is closer to life, precisely because its inhabitants had literally brought the dead into their midst instead of—as is otherwise the norm in our latitudes— banishing them from the heart of the community to beyond the city gates, although these burial sites often became reintegrated into the urban environment only a short time later, the result of unchecked urban sprawl.

Only now, having almost finished work on this book in which the diverse phenomena of decomposition and destruction play a central role, have I realized that this is just one of myriad ways of dealing with death, one that is fundamentally no more crude or caring than that of the Callatiae tribe whose custom, as Herodotus attests, was to eat their deceased parents, and who were horrified when they learned of the Greeks' tradition of cremating theirs. Indeed opinions differ as to who is closer to life: someone constantly reminded of his own mortality or someone who manages to suppress all thought of it, and likewise on the question of which is more terrifying: the notion that everything comes to an end, or the thought that it may not.

There is no disputing, though, that death and the associated problem of how to deal with the sudden absence of a person at the same time as the presence of their legacy, from the corpse to the abandoned belongings, have, over time, demanded answers and prompted actions that have had a significance beyond their strict purpose and mark the elevation of our early ancestors from the animal to the human sphere. Not simply giving over the mortal remains of the fellow members of our species to the natural processes of decomposition is generally regarded as something peculiar to humans, although similar behavior can also be observed in other higher animals: elephants, for instance, gather around a dying member of their herd, touch it with their trunks for hours on end, trumpeting in distress as they do so, and often try to push the lifeless body back upright before eventually covering the corpse with earth and twigs. What's more, they return to the place of death regularly, even years later, something that undoubtedly requires a good memory, and possibly even a certain conception of the afterlife that, it is fair to imagine, is no less fanciful than our own and just as unverifiable.

The caesura of death is the point where legacy and memory begin, and the lament the source of every culture by which we seek to fill the now gaping void, the sudden silence with chants, prayers, and stories in which the absent one is brought back to life. Like a hollow mold, the experience of loss renders visible the contours of the thing mourned, and it is not uncommon for it to be transformed by the transfigurative light of sorrow into an object of desire or, as the Heidelberg professor of zoology put it in the foreword to a slim volume published by Neue Brehm-Bücherei: "It seems to be one of the characteristics of western man that defies rational understanding that he prizes the lost more highly than the existing. There is no other explanation for his curious enduring fascination with the Tasmanian tiger."

All manner of strategies are used to keep hold of the past and ward off oblivion. If tradition is to be believed, our historiography begins with a series of devastating wars between the Persians and the Greeks, while the now almost forgotten art of memory starts with an accident in which many perished: it was in Thessaly, where in the early fifth century B.C. a collapsing house buried an entire party of festive revelers and the only survivor, the poet Simonides of Ceos, succeeded, with the aid of his trained memory, in reentering the destroyed building in his mind's eye and recalling the seating arrangement of the guests, thus enabling the bodies crushed beyond recognition by the falling rubble to be identified. It is one of the numerous paradoxes inherent in the either-or of life and death that, by labeling the deceased as something irretrievably lost, the sorrow at this loss is at once doubled and halved, whereas the indeterminate fate of a person missing or presumed dead keeps the relatives trapped in a confused nightmare of anxious hope and denied sorrow that makes it impossible either to come to terms with it or to get on with one's life.

Being alive means experiencing loss. The question of what the future holds is presumably nearly as old as the human race itself, given that one feature of the future, as inevitable as it is disquieting, is that it defies prediction and hence gives no clue as to the timing and circumstances of death. Who can deny the protective magic of bittersweet anticipation, the fatal urge to forestall the feared event by mentally preempting it? We picture the cataclysm ahead of time, imagine possible disasters, and believe this renders us immune to nasty surprises. In ancient times, dreams promised consolation: the Greeks said of them that, like oracles, they prefigured what was to come and thereby rid the future not of its immutability, but at least of the terror of the unexpected.

Quite a few people take their own life out of fear of death. Suicide seems perhaps the most radical means of conquering the uncertainty of the future, albeit at the cost of a curtailed existence. It is reported that the gifts presented by the Indian delegation that Augustus once received on the island of Samos included not only a tiger and an armless youth who was able to use his feet as hands, but also a man named Zarmarus from the Brahmin caste who was intending to end his own life for the very reason that it had turned out the way he wanted. To make quite sure that no calamity could ever befall him, he leaped onto the pyre in Athens, naked, anointed, and with a smile, was burned alive, undoubtedly in excruciating pain, and in staging his self-determined death, went down in history, if only as a curious anecdote in one book of Cassius Dio's once eighty-volume *Roman History*, the content of which happened to be passed down to us. In the end, all that remains is simply whatever is left.

A memory that retained everything would essentially retain nothing. The Californian woman who, without the aid of mnemonics, can recall every single day since February 5, 1980 is trapped in the echo chamber of the memories that constantly overwhelm her—a modern embodiment of that Athenian general Themistocles, who knew the names of every single citizen of his native city and who told Simonides, the father of mnemonics, that he would rather learn the art of forgetting than that of remembering: "I remember even what I do not want to remember, but am unable to forget what I want to forget." However, the art of forgetting is an impossibility because any allusion represents a presence, even when it refers to an absence. Encyclopedias claim to know the names of almost every person condemned to *damnatio memoriae* under the Roman Empire.

To forget everything is bad, certainly. Worse still is to forget nothing. After all, knowledge can only be gained by forgetting.

If everything is stored indiscriminately, as it is in electronic data memories, it loses its meaning and becomes a disorderly mass of useless information.

The organization of every archive may, like its prototype, the ark, be guided by the desire to preserve everything, but the undeniably tempting idea of transforming, say, a continent like the Antarctic or even the moon into a central, democratic museum of the Earth in which all cultural products are accorded equal status is just as totalitarian and doomed to failure as the re-creation of paradise, a tantalizing primal object of longing kept alive in the beliefs of all human cultures.

Fundamentally, every item is already waste, every building already a ruin, and all creation nothing but destruction, and the same is true of the work of all those disciplines and institutions that claim to be preserving the legacy of humanity. Even archaeology, however cautiously and soberly it may profess to probe the debris of past ages, is a form of devastation—and the archives, museums, and libraries, the zoological gardens and nature reserves are nothing more than managed cemeteries whose stored specimens, as often as not, have been plucked from the life cycle of the present to be filed away, allowed to be forgotten even, like those heroic events and figures whose monuments populate urban landscapes.

It should probably count as a good thing that the human race is not aware of all the great ideas, the poignant works of art and revolutionary feats that have already been lost to it—willfully destroyed or simply vanished over time. What we do not know cannot weigh us down, we might think. It does seem surprising, though, that quite a few European thinkers of the modern age saw the periodic demise of a culture as a reasonable or even beneficial occurrence. As if cultural memory were a global organism whose vital functions could only be maintained by a brisk metabolism in which each intake of food was preceded by digestion and elimination.

It was this world view, one both limited and autocratic, that enabled the uncontrolled occupation and exploitation of foreign territories, the subjugation, enslavement, and murder of non-European peoples and the obliteration of their scorned cultures to be regarded as part of a natural process, and the evolutionary principle misunderstood as meaning the survival of the strongest to be used as justification for crimes committed.

Naturally we can only mourn what is absent or missing if some vestige of it, some whisper, perhaps little more than a rumor, a semiobliterated trace, an echo of an echo has found its way to us. How I would love to know what the Nazca lines in the Peruvian desert mean, how Sappho's Fragment 31 ends, and why Hypatia was considered such a threat that not only her complete works but even she herself was hacked to pieces.

Sometimes certain remnants seem to be commenting on their own fate. For instance, all that remains of Monteverdi's opera "L'Arianna" is, of all things, the *lamento*, in which the eponymous heroine sings in despair: "Let me die! What do you think can comfort me in such harsh fate, in such great suffering? Let me die!" The picture by Lucian Freud that now survives only as a reproduction since it was stolen from a Rotterdam museum and incinerated in a Romanian stove by the mother of one of the thieves, shows a woman with her eyes closed, and one cannot tell for sure whether she is just sleeping or is actually dead. And of the work of the tragic poet Agathon only two aphorisms have found their way to us, because they are quoted by Aristotle: "Art loves chance and chance loves art" and "Not even the gods can change the past."

That which is denied the gods is something that despots through the ages all seem to aspire to anew: the destructive drive to make their mark is not satisfied by inscribing themselves in the present. Anyone who wants to control the future must obliterate the past. And anyone who appoints himself the founding father of a new dynasty, the source of all truth, must eradicate the memory of his predecessors and forbid all critical thinking, as Qin Shi Huang, the self-appointed "First Sovereign Emperor," did when in 213 B.C. he ordered one of the first recorded book burnings and had anyone who opposed the measure executed or sentenced to forced labor, working on the expansion of the imperial road network and the Great Wall of China—or otherwise on the construction of that colossal mausoleum whose megalomaniac funerary art includes the Terracotta Army of life-size soldiers along with their chariots, horses, and weaponry, copies of which now tour the world, thereby both fulfilling and undermining the purpose of the memorial its patron had so craved by untold profanation.

The dubious plan to make a *tabula rasa* of the past often springs from the understandable desire to start afresh. Apparently, in the mid-seventeenth century, the British parliament seriously discussed burning the Tower of London archives to extinguish all memory of the past and start life over again, at least according to Jorge Luis Borges in a passage I have been unable to locate.

The Earth itself is, as we know, a heap of rubble from a past future, and humanity the thrown together, bickering community of heirs to a numinous yesteryear that needs to be constantly appropriated and recast, rejected and destroyed, ignored and suppressed so that, contrary to popular belief, it is not the future but the past that represents the true field of opportunity. That is precisely why its reinterpretation is one of the first official acts of new governing regimes. Anyone who, like me, has experienced a historical upheaval, the iconoclasm of the victors, the dismantling of monuments, will readily recognize every vision of the future as effectively representing a future past in which, say, the ruins of the rebuilt Berlin City Palace will have to make way for a replica of the demolished Palace of the Republic.

At the Paris Salon of 1796, in the fifth year of the Republic, the architecture painter Hubert Robert, who had captured the storming of the Bastille as well as the demolition of the Château de Meudon and the desecration of the royal tombs in Saint-Denis, exhibited two paintings in the Palais du Louvre. One depicted his proposed design for the transformation of the royal palace to create the *Grande Galerie*—a room packed with paintings and sculptures, teeming with visitors and flooded with light thanks to its glass roof—while the other painting showed the same room in ruins. The skylights visible in the first vision of the future are replaced in the second by an uninterrupted view of a cloudy sky: the arched roof has caved in, the walls are bare and unadorned, broken sculptures lie on the floor. Only the Apollo Belvedere, a trophy from Napoleon's Italian foray, is left standing among the rubble, sooty but unscathed. Disaster tourists wander among the ruins, salvage toppled torsos, warm themselves by a fire. Weeds sprout from the cracks in the vault. The ruins are a utopian place in which past and future become one.

The architect Albert Speer went even further with his speculative theory of a "ruin value": decades after the end of National Socialism, he claimed that its plans for, literally, a thousand-year Reich would not only have made use of exceptionally durable materials, but would even have taken into account the future appearance of each building once it fell to ruin, so that, even in a dilapidated state, it could still compete with the grandeur of the Roman ruins. Auschwitz, on the other hand, was referred to, for good reason, as a case of destruction without ruins. It was the utterly dehumanized architecture of a minutely organized industrial annihilation machine whose workings left no trace, which by exterminating millions of people, left behind the biggest void in Europe in the twentieth century, a trauma still not fully processed in the memory of the survivors and their descendants on either the victims' or the perpetrators' side, one which forms a dissociated foreign body that resists integration. The genocides committed have lent added urgency to the question of the extent to which loss can ever be made tangible and have led many from later generations to the frustrating yet understandable conclusion that what happened eludes all representation.

"What do historical sources preserve? Not the fates of the violets trodden underfoot in the Battle of Liège, nor the sufferings of the cows as Leuven burned, nor the cloud formations on the approach to Belgrade," writes Theodor Lessing in his book *History: Making Sense of the Senseless*, published during the First World War, in which he exposes the chapters in any history that advances in a reasonable way as retrospectively giving form to the formless— stories of beginnings and endings, of ascendancy and downfall, of blossoming and decay which tend to follow narrative rules.

The fact that faith in progress, the legacy of the Enlightenment, persists virtually intact, even though the principles of evolution have shown that what survives for a certain time is determined, rather, by a disturbingly complex interplay of chance and adaptation, is perhaps due to the simple appeal of the nerdy historical timeline and its equivalents in the linear scripts of western cultures—which make it all too easy to fall prey to the naturalistic fallacy, despite the loss of significance of the divine entities, of perceiving everything that exists as intended and meaningful. In the simpleminded yet compelling script of ceaseless advancement, the only use for the past consists in it being inferior to the present, whereby history—the history of one's own life or of a nation or of the human race—is imagined as representing necessary, or at least not random, progress. It has been proved however that, as every archivist knows, chronology—the allocation of sequential numbers for each new addition—is in its banal logic the most unoriginal of all organizational principles, being only a simulation of order.

In a sense, the world is a sprawling archive of itself—and all animate and inanimate matter serves as documentary evidence forming part of a monstrous, highly tedious inscription system that attempts to draw lessons and conclusions from past experience, while taxonomy is merely the retrospective attempt to index the muddled archive of biological diversity by keyword and impose an apparently objective structure on the sheer inexhaustible chaos of evolutionary legacy. Fundamentally, nothing can be lost in this archive, because its overall energy level is constant and everything seems to leave a trace somewhere. If there is truth in Sigmund Freud's perplexing dictum—reminiscent of the law of energy conservation—that no dream and no thought is ever really forgotten, then not only could past experience—an inherited trauma, two random lines from a poem, a hazy nightmare from a stormy night in early childhood, a pornographic horror scenario—be exhumed from the soil of human memory by an effort akin to an archaeological dig in the same way as bones, fossils, or fragments of pottery. It might also be possible to wrest from the underworld the actions of countless lost races, if only one started to look for traces of them, in which case the truth, even that which has been suppressed or obliterated, recast as a mistake or consigned to oblivion, could not be denied and would remain ever present.

Yet the laws of physics offer only limited consolation. For the principle of energy conservation with its triumph of transformation over the finite fails to mention that most conversion processes are irreversible. What use is the heat of a burning artwork? Its ashes will retain nothing worthy of admiration. Those billiard balls fashioned from the recycled, desilverized material used to record early silent movies roll over the green felt-covered table with indifference. The meat of the last Steller's sea cow did not take long to digest.

True, the demise of all life and endeavor is a condition of its existence. It is naturally only a matter of time before everything has disappeared, disintegrated, and decayed, before everything is annihilated and destroyed, even those peculiar products of the past whose existence we owe entirely to disasters: the only documents written in the long unfathomable, pictogram-style ancient Greek syllabic script, Linear B, which have been preserved only because the major fire that destroyed the Palace of Knossos in around 1380 B.C. at the same time caused thousands of clay tablets on which the palace's income and expenditure were recorded to harden, thereby preserving them for future generations; the plaster casts of people and animals buried alive in Pompeii when Vesuvius erupted whose corpses, having decomposed, left fillable cavities in the set stone; or the silhouettes left like ghostly photographs on walls and road surfaces in Hiroshima by people vaporized when the atomic bomb went off.

To acknowledge one's own mortality is painful, and the vain urge to defy the transience of life and leave traces for unknown future generations, to remain in memory, "unforgotten," according to the valiant declaration of intent chiseled into the granite of gravestones, is understandable.

The poignant desire to draw attention to the existence of an intelligent species is also manifest in the messages carried by the two time capsules on board the *Voyager I* and *Voyager II* space probes as they drift further and further into interstellar space. The two identical gold-plated copper discs contain images and diagrams, pieces of music and sounds, as well as spoken greetings in fifty-five different languages, the intrepid awkwardness of which—"Hello from the children of the planet Earth"—reveals much about humanity. There is a certain appeal in imagining that all that will one day remain of humanity is Mozart's "Queen of the Night" aria, Louis Armstrong's "Melancholy Blues," and the blare of Azerbaijani bagpipes, assuming the extraterrestrial finders succeed in both deciphering and following the instructions for playing the analog-encoded record, which are engraved on the disc in diagrammatic form. The likelihood of this, as the authors of this space-age message in a bottle themselves conceded, is so slim that this undertaking can be viewed as the product of a kind of magical thinking that lives on in the scientific community, which, in this project, has staged a ritual that serves first and foremost as a means of self-reassurance for a species unwilling to accept its own utter meaninglessness. But what use is an archive without a reader, a time capsule without a finder, an inheritance without inheritors? Experience shows that it is the discarded trash of past ages that proves most enlightening to archaeologists. Forming a geological layer of technological junk, plastic, and nuclear waste, it will stand the test of time without our assistance, provide genuine information about our habits, and burden the planet for generations to come.

It may be that, by then, our descendants will have long since relocated to that second Earth we have yearned for since time immemorial, which would enable us to turn back time, put right past mistakes and if need be painstakingly recreate all that was thoughtlessly destroyed. And perhaps by then the cultural legacy of the human race will actually be stored as artificial DNA in the genetic material of a particularly resistant strain of bacteria.

There exists a papyrus roll dating from the middle years of the first Egyptian dynasty in around 2900 B.C. that, owing to its precarious state of preservation, has not been opened to this day, so we cannot know what message it contains. Sometimes I imagine the future thus: generations to come standing baffled in front of today's data storage media, strange aluminum boxes whose contents, owing to rapid advances in platforms and programming languages, file formats and playback devices, have become nothing but meaningless codes, and moreover ones that, as an object in themselves, exude less of an aura than the knots of an Inca quipu string, as eloquent as they are mute, or those mystifying ancient Egyptian obelisks that may commemorate triumph or tragedy, no one knows.

Although nothing lasts forever, some things do endure longer than others: churches and temples survive longer than palaces, and written cultures outlive those that got by without complex semiotic systems. Writing, which the Khwarezmian scholar Al-Biruni once described as a being propagating itself in time and space, was from the outset a system for passing on information in parallel with inheritance and irrespective of kinship.

By writing, as by reading, one can pick one's own ancestors and establish a second, intellectual hereditary line to rival conventional biological heritage.

If you want to regard the human race itself, as is sometimes suggested, as the world-archiving faculty of a deity, one that preserves awareness of the universe, then the myriad written and printed books—with the exception, of course, of those written by God himself or his numerous emanations—appear as attempts to discharge this futile duty and capture the infinite nature of all things within their finite bodies.

It may be due merely to my inadequate powers of imagination that the book still appears to me as the most complete of all media, even though paper, in use for several centuries now, is not as durable as papyrus, parchment, stone, ceramic, or quartz, and not even the Bible—the most commonly printed, most widely translated collection of writings there is—has been handed down to us in its entirety, though its multiplicity of versions increases the chances of its being passed down for the duration of a few human generations, an open time capsule in which the traces of the time that has passed since it was written and printed are recorded as well, and in which every edition of a text proves to be a utopian space not unlike a ruin in which the dead communicate, the past is alive, the written word is true, and time is suspended. The book may be inferior in many ways to the new, seemingly incorporeal media that lay claim to its legacy and overwhelm us with information, and may be a conservative medium in the original sense of the word, but it is the only one which, by the very self-sufficiency of its body, in which text, image, and design dovetail perfectly with one another, promises to lend order to the world or sometimes even to take its place. The theological division of being into a mortal and immortal part—the body and soul—may be one of the most consoling strategies for overcoming loss. However, for me, the inseparability of form and content is the reason why I like not only to write but also to design books.

This book, like all others, springs from the desire to have something survive, to bring the past into the present, to call to mind the forgotten, to give voice to the silenced, and to mourn the lost. Writing cannot bring anything back, but it can enable everything to be experienced. Hence this volume is as much about seeking as finding, as much about losing as gaining, and gives a sense that the difference between presence and absence is perhaps marginal, as long as there is memory.

For a few precious moments during the long years of working on this book, the notion that all things must pass struck me as just as consoling as the image of all the copies of it gathering dust on the shelves.

Südliche Cookinseln

TUANAKI

also known as *Tuanahe*

* *The atoll was situated around two hundred nautical miles south of the island of Rarotonga and around one hundred nautical miles southwest of the island of Mangaia.*

† *Tuanaki must have sunk in a marine earthquake in late 1842/early 1843, for in June 1843 missionaries could no longer locate the island. Not until 1875 was the atoll erased from all maps.*

It was on a bright, perfectly windless April day exactly seven years ago that I discovered, on a globe in the map department of the National Library, an island by the name of Ganges that I had never heard of. The solitary isle was located in the empty expanse of the northeastern Pacific Ocean, in the wash of the mighty Kuroshio, that blue-black rippling ocean current that sweeps great bodies of warm salty water tirelessly northwards from the island of Formosa along the Japanese archipelago, and formed the imaginary northern vanishing point of the Mariana and Hawaiian Island chains, the latter of which still bore the name of John Montagu, the Fourth Earl of Sandwich, at least on that sphere of plaster and elaborately printed papier-mâché roughly the size of a child's head. Intrigued by the familiar name and unusual position, I embarked on a bit of research which revealed that, close to the coordinates 31°N 154°E, there had been two sightings of a coral reef and no less than four sightings of land. Its existence, however, was repeatedly called into question by various authorities until, on June 27, 1933, a posse of Japanese hydrographers, after a thorough search of the region in question, announced the official disappearance of Ganges, though the world at large paid little attention to this loss.

Indeed, old atlases record scores of phantom islands. The more accurate the maps became and the less scope they left for uncharted territory, the more frequently seafarers claimed to have sighted such islands, excited by the latest white dots, inspired by the desolation of the fathomless sea, fooled by low-hanging clouds or drifting icebergs, nauseated by briny drinking water, maggoty bread, and stringy salt meat, thirsting so eagerly for land and fame that, in their boundless greed, everything they desired coalesced into a cluster of gold and glory, tempting them to note wondrous names in their logbooks alongside prosaic coordinates, to cut through the monotony of their days with would-be discoveries. And so names like Nimrod, Matador, and the Auroras started to appear on charts in bold cursive lettering next to the sketchily defined outlines of scattered chunks of land.

Yet it was not these long-unchallenged claims that piqued my interest, but the islands whose one-time existence and subsequent disappearance are vouched for in numerous accounts, and especially the testimonies referring to the sunken isle of Tuanaki, owing in some part, no doubt, to its sonorous name, which has the ring of a long-lost magic word, but above all to the strange reports about the inhabitants of this island stating that fighting was entirely unknown to them and the word "war" was not familiar to them in any of its unpleasant shades of meaning, something that, out of some deep-seated remnant of childlike hope, I was immediately disposed to believe, even if at the same time it reminded me of the wishful utopian dreams outlined in countless treatises that went so far as to claim that another world was possible, but that—as the often verbose descriptions of their increasingly elaborate and hence inhospitable social systems went to show—it was generally only preferable to the existing world in theory. So against my better judgment, I, like so many before me, set out on a search for a land that knew no memory, but only the

present, a land in which violence, hardship, and death were forgotten, being unknown. And so Tuanaki appeared before me—
every bit as magnificent as the sources suggest: an atoll of three
islands rising only slightly above sea level in the shallow milky-
blue waters of a shimmering lagoon teeming with fish, protected
from pounding breakers and relentless tides by a coral reef, home
to slender skyward-reaching coconut palms and lush fruit trees,
inhabited by a peace-loving people of unrivaled friendliness, in
short, a delightful place which, for simplicity's sake, I pictured
in my mind's eye as paradise, differentiated from that much-
vaunted archetype only by the subtle yet significant fact that no
knowledge whatsoever was contained within the fruits of its trees
besides that truism that it was more of a blessing to stay here
than to go, for, as I soon discovered to my astonishment, in this
part of the world the Garden of Eden was held to be a place of
refuge rather than one of banishment.

The reports describing this improbable patch of land were just
detailed enough to plausibly prove that it did indeed once exist, even if the chronometer never determined its exact position,
for neither Tasman nor Wallis, neither Bougainville nor even a
captain of some wayward whaling ship ever sighted its gentle
shores. Again and again I studied the routes of the major South
Sea expeditions, followed the dashed and dotted lines across the
graticule and through the paper ocean, and compared them with
the presumed position of that island that, in a rush of imperial
sentiment, I had marked in the bottommost empty square.

There was no doubt about it: the explorer celebrated to this
day by a small continent as the greatest of all its many seafarers
to have crisscrossed the globe, must have only narrowly missed
Tuanaki on his third and final voyage. Indeed it must have been
only just out of sight when his two vessels, launched originally
as colliers in the Whitby fog, passed by it on March 27, 1777—
with sails billowing, proud as frigates, in full regalia. It was more
than a month since James Cook's long-serving flagship *Resolution*

and her newer, more maneuverable consort ship *Discovery* had weighed anchors in their customary bay in Queen Charlotte Sound, New Zealand, as a slight breeze blew up, and traveled through the strait named after their captain, after two days finally leaving behind them the hills of Port Palliser, which shimmered blackish-green in the mist, and heading out to the open sea. But the winds were not in their favor. Fresh, changeable breezes were followed by miserable windless spells, and rain-swept squalls by torturous lulls. Even the drift of the westerly winds, which should have carried them with familiar constancy northeast into the same circle of longitude as Otahaiti, failed—contrary to all seasonal forecasts—to materialize, leaving an ever more worrying distance between them and the next anchorage. A lot of time had already been wasted. And with every passing day, hope faded further of still being able to sail along the coast of New Albion during the approaching northern summer in search of the entrance to that much-attested passage which, on the incomplete charts, promised the long-awaited shortening of the maritime route between the Pacific and Atlantic oceans. For the dream of that corridor, fringed with pack ice yet still navigable, was old and stubborn like all cosmographers' dreams and had become all the more pressing since the vision of a vast southern continent had had to be abandoned after Cook, in his quest for this legendary land, had plowed the southern seas in huge, sweeping zigzags and discovered nothing but mountains of ice.

So the two ships drifted along with limp sails, and that booming silence began to settle on them, so fundamentally different from the peaceful hush of my library existence. Sometimes, though, I could hear the rolling, long-drawn-out groundswell, the taunting of the fine weather, the endless litany of waves forever welling up and subsiding that once seduced Magellan into describing this ocean as the "peaceful" one, a ghostly harmony, the remorseless sound of eternity, more terrifying than the most violent storm, which at least is bound to blow over in time.

Yet this ocean was neither peaceful nor placid, for in its dark-est depths lurked indomitable forces that were certain to return. Its seabed was fissured and furrowed, the earth's crust riven with submarine trenches and peaks, unhealed scars from that prehis-toric age when the as yet undivided continents, adrift as a single mass in the global ocean, were torn asunder by colossal forces and rammed up against the earth's mantle until their plates were forced, some over, some under each other, down into plunging abysses, up into clear daylight, surrendered to the laws of nature, which know neither mercy nor justice. Water submerged the vol-canic cones, and myriads of corals colonized the rims of their craters, building reefs in the light of the sun, the skeletons of new atolls, on whose fertile floors the seeds carried by washed-up branches flourished, while the extinct volcanoes sank down to the dark seabed far below—on the timescale of infinity. And in the midst of this even now still inaudible din, below decks the livestock—the bull, the cows, their calves, the rams, ewes, and goats—bleated and lowed with hunger, while the stallion and the mares whinnied, the peacock and his hens screeched, and the poultry clucked. Never before had Cook carried so many ani-mals on board, but on this voyage, at the king's express wish, he had brought along half an ark, which, like the menagerie of the original model, was assembled with reproduction in mind, and he wondered how Noah had contrived to feed all the hungry mouths, which devoured as much in the way of provisions as an entire ship's company.

On the fifteenth day on the open sea, way off their intended course, the captain, who, as the ship's cooper records in his jour-nal, was particularly concerned about the welfare of the horses, gave the order for eight sheep that were supposed to have pop-ulated a South Sea island with their kind to be slaughtered in order to save on hay, supplies of which were steadily dwindling. But some of the meat disappeared from the mess even before it could be prepared, a petty act of theft that had been repeated once too often. The captain sensed insubordination, he sensed betrayal and even—as he docked the meat ration for the entire crew until the culprit was turned in, at which the men refused to touch even that meager meal—mutiny. The word, an unlit match under the scorching sun, its sole purpose to ignite sparks, hung in the air for a few interminable days during which the wind veered around once more, now blowing from a southerly direction, and seemed to tip the commander from his characteristic aloofness into pure rage. Cook stamped and ranted, a tall, lonely figure, and his curses resounded all the way down to the munitions store. Suspicion rather than worry was now gnawing at his heart, and the image many of the men had of him as a strict but fair father figure darkened during those days to that of an aging despot, as unpredictable as the winds. Anyone so inclined may see in the disquieting events of that passage, and in the fact that Cook himself made not a single mention of these episodes in his diary, the seeds of that chain of events that, two years later in a bay on Owyhee, would put a violent end to his life.

But for now the remaining days of a month that seemed to go on interminably ticked by, a month in which time had long since transformed itself into that eternity verging on standstill, in which a single hour and a single day no longer counted for anything. Albatrosses and petrels circled the ships, flying fish flitted through the dry air, porpoises and dolphins swam past, as did a swarm of tiny globular jellyfish about the size of musket balls. Once a large white bird with a red tail appeared, promising land nearby though none could be made out, and on another occasion a thick tree trunk, which had been floating in the water for so long that it was covered in a pale layer of barnacles resembling oozing pus.

Then finally, at 10:00 a.m. on March 29, 1777, the *Discovery*, traveling ahead on the leeward side, hoisted the red, white, and blue flag of Holland, the signal for a sighting of land. At almost the same moment the gray-blue shimmering coast became visible on the northeastern horizon from the masthead of the *Resolution* as well, barely more real than a mirage. The ships headed for the unknown strip of land twinkling in the distance until the sun went down, and tacked all night until the break of day, approaching to within a distance of about four miles of the island, whose south side must have presented an almost painfully enchanting image in the light of the sun as it rose out of the water. Profoundly moved by the heavenly sight, several of the crew members immediately took up quills and brushes, using watery colors and brushstrokes displaying varying degrees of skill to capture the auspicious panorama somewhere other than in unreliable memory: the hills of moderate height shimmering purple in the morning sun, their wooded summits with their many-hued trees and scattered palm crowns, the lush dense green vegetation of the hillsides, the coconuts, breadfruit, and plantain visible through the bluish-pink haze.

I studied those pictures, which still conveyed a sense of the longing that had inspired them, in a stuffy room in the cartography department, whose milky windows, as I discovered on inquiry, could not be opened as the pictures had to be protected. Among the sketches was also the chart drawn by the *Discovery*'s navigator, to whom the task had fallen of recording the dimensions of the island and sketching its cartographic outlines insofar as was possible from the sloop in which he circumnavigated the modestly sized land. The sheet showing the island, whose peaks, indicated with bold strokes, might just as easily have been a whorl of hair on a person's head, was framed with a double line and headed with a doubly absurd name, the chancery script solemnly labeling this as a depiction of "Discovery's Island." One more name, I thought, one more untenable assertion, as presumptuous and vain as the age-old custom that gave rise to it.

For gathered for some time now on the beach were the people who, though they did not realize it themselves, had been discovered and were to be assigned the role—essential for the purpose of any report from far-off lands—of the Natives. Accordingly, the islanders had already taken up position, clubs on shoulders, spears at the ready, and the more of them emerged from the shade of the wooded embankment into the morning light, the louder and more urgent their guttural singing grew. They swung their weapons, hoisted them in the air over and over in time with their shouts—whether with threatening or welcoming intent it was impossible to say, even after much peering through the telescope. For although the crowd of now some two hundred was brought markedly closer by the eyepiece, the wood, brass, and glass instrument proved useless for clarifying any matters of real consequence. Despite the genuine curiosity, despite the eloquent descriptions of their language and gestures, physique and clothing, even down to the way they wore their hair and the decoration on their skin, and despite the undeniable precision with which this tribe could then be compared with others in these respects, their view of these people, formed before a single word had been uttered, missed all that was truly of the essence, since it recognized only foreign versus familiar, similar versus different, since it separated that which was one and the same and drew boundaries where there were none, like the overly distinct ragged coastlines on the nautical charts which purported to know where the water ends and the land begins.

I spent a long time thinking about who is truly capable of interpreting signs, the language of muskets and swivel guns, the numerous right and left hands, be they raised or extended, the wild or controlled behavior, the skewered limbs over an open fire, the touching of nose against nose, a vertically held banana or laurel branch, gestures of greeting, symbols of concord, of cannibalism. What was peace and what was war, what was a beginning and what was an end, what was mercy and what was guile, I wondered as I slumped down on one of the dark-red velvet-upholstered seats in the cafeteria, and observed the people around me preoccupied with their food. The sharing of the same food, the nightly sitting together in the glow of a fire, the exchanging of a thirst-quenching coconut for ironwork and trinkets?

So people stood on the shore, teetered through the shallow water, and reportedly waded out to the reef, dancing and with shrill cries. But what was going through their minds? Who was I to decide that? At the time, although I had no shortage of invitations from abroad, I was leading the life of a home dweller, of a library frequenter, permanently on the lookout for new research subjects to shed light on some hidden source of my existence and lend some kind of meaning to my life by the semblance of a daily work routine. So once again: they thought what they thought, and they saw what they saw, and they were right.

This much, though, is as good as certain: that two islanders paddled out to the ships in a canoe with a high, forked stern and did not touch a single one of the gifts tossed in their direction, neither the nails, nor the glass beads, nor the shirt of red cloth. It is also established that one of them was fearless enough to take hold of the rope ladder and climb aboard the *Resolution*, where he introduced himself as Mourua of the island of Mangaia. He and the captain must have stood facing one another in his cabin for a while, eye to eye, appraising each other, like two animals encountering each other for the first time: two men, the smooth round skull of Mourua versus Cook's birdlike head; the mild facial features, bright eyes, and full lips of the one, the austere countenance, with a strong nose, thin lips, and penetrating deep-set eyes, of the other; the long black hair bound into a thick bunch on the crown of the head, the already sparse hair concealed beneath a silvery-gray wig; the olive skin marked with black tattoos from shoulder to elbow, next to the pale skin; the knee-length, ivory-colored garment fashioned from bast fibers on the stout, well-fed body, the light-colored breeches paired with the open, gold-braided uniform jacket of navy-blue cloth on the tall, angular figure. Yet the huge scars that disfigured both men seemed to me like a sign of secret affinity, even if the numerous paintings and prints depicting Cook, and the portrait of Mourua produced by the ship's artist that afternoon, have the good grace to omit them: the long, poorly healed wound on Mourua's forehead, acquired in fighting, and the bulging burn scar running from between Cook's right thumb and index finger to his wrist. And as if to seal this moment of unexpected closeness, an iron was handed over, and the Mangaian took it with him when he was ferried back to shore in one of the ship's boats. The surf was still as rough as ever, and soon all hope of mooring or anchoring was abandoned, for no matter where the plumb line was dropped, it always indicated that the seabed lay too deep and moreover was encrusted with sharp coral. And so the ship's company was beset by a sense of sorrowful regret at having to leave the island without setting foot on it, a feeling that turned to agonizing disappointment when, in the evening hours, gentle drifts of ambrosial scents were carried over to them on the breeze.

And it was here that I was abandoned by the eyewitness accounts which, though inviting contradiction, had nevertheless brought me to this point, under the English red ensign on board those blue and yellow ships that would recede into the distance at daybreak the following day. I suddenly found myself all alone on deck, or rather on the shore of an island known to me only from a rough outline on a map, and for a moment I forgot that it was not Tuanaki, but its neighbor Mangaia on which I had been cast up, a rayfish-shaped atoll standing five kilometers above the ocean floor, encircled by a broad calcium carbonate reef with numerous inner cliffs and excavations made by the beating of the waves, while in the interior, an undulating landscape of damp peaks with dry flanks on the leeward side overlooked uncultivated land and swampy lakes. Mangaia's own sources also proved eloquent. They detailed who was or became the son of whom, and who had inherited or snatched what title from whom, ever since the days when their forefathers had paddled out eastwards in log boats and canoes, guided by the Dog Star, and settled on these scattered patches of land. But those stories, rather than following the flow of time, traced the paths of blood, which fanned out into different branches and lines of descent, before being repeatedly spilled on the battlefield.

So I could only conjecture as to how Mourua was received on his return to shore, though, for some probably dubious reason, I had a precise picture in my mind of how his fellow islanders pressed him with questions about the nature and provenance of the pale visitors and came to the unanimous conclusion that they had been sent by Tangaroa, the god once worshipped on Mangaia, who, eons ago, had been defeated in battle by his brother Rongo and had fled out to sea. And I saw in my mind's eye how, recalling that fateful combat, they made their way together to the stone statue of Rongo a little way inland and gave thanks to him for having put the enemy and his followers to flight one more time. In my feeble imagination it was Mourua who stepped before the idol first and launched into the song of praise with the pride of an honorable man whose powerful physique revealed the veteran warrior. A long time had passed since, as an uncircumcised youth armed with an ironwood club, he had joined the back row of combatants, before working his way forward, battle by battle, fearlessly filling the gaps left by his forebears, and had exchanged his weapon for axes and chiseled basalt spearheads. It was on the ground of the old lagoon, windswept cliffs towering over it like the terraces of a huge amphitheater, that the battle had played out again and again through the ages between the warriors of different clans, the descendants of hostile gods, continuing until the hollow sound of the war drum signaled the battle's end, and the dancing began, its shrill sounds drowning out the groans of the dying, a bloodcurdling victory chant that reverberated through the night, superseded only as dawn was breaking by the beat of the peace drum. As his prize, the victor could claim the ruler's title "Mangaia," no less. Mangaia meant peace, Mangaia meant power, a temporary power that was nevertheless solid enough to allow the titleholder to rule on everything: who was allowed to cultivate and live on which patch of land, and who would be banished to the barren, karstic rocky reef where nothing prospered but dry foliage. It was not uncommon for the losers to remain there in the clammy limestone caves until they were nothing but skin and bone—or had reproduced in such numbers that they were hopeful of winning victory over their one-time conquerors in the next battle. I saw the whites of their eyes flashing in the semidarkness, heard the water dripping from the stalactites onto their heads and necks, tasted the musty air.

Power, as I discovered during those weeks in which the rites and customs of that island were revealed to me in the ethnological reports of the first missionaries, was not passed down through the generations on Mangaia, but won—seized in battle or snatched in a nighttime spree that, more often than not, degenerated into a massacre in which the betrayed, anesthetized with ground kava root, were dumped in a pit, covered in hot stones and left to stew in their own juices until they were fit to eat.

Now, though, Mourua's hands clasped the strangely gleaming ax, and anyone regarding it as nothing but a lump of iron on a wooden shaft, a well-meant gift, fails to do justice to its power. From then on, this ax was conferred upon whoever emerged victorious on Mangaia, since it was more useful than any other tool, allowing wood to be split with the same ease as the skull of a doomed man on Rongo's altar at the start of the reign of each new ruler.

Mangaia was not just one island among countless thousands in this fathomless ocean but a whole world in itself, in which it made no difference whether you were condemned to starve to death in the labyrinth of moldy grottoes or to perish in a rotten pirogue under the scorching sun. The loser forfeited everything, his name, his land, his life, and those who contrived to save themselves harbored no thought of returning. Some managed to escape, and evidence suggests that those lucky few found refuge on the island of Tuanaki, two days' voyage away. On Mangaia, though, one ruler followed another until the cycle of victory and defeat was brought to an abrupt end. It's the same old story, in its various versions: strangers came, invaders who needed to be repelled, whalers bearing a mottled seashell in their chapped hands, its toothed opening like a hungry mouth; missionaries and their wives who, barely had they reached the shore, cast themselves back into the surf in mortal fear, leaving all their worldly goods behind on the beach: a boar and a sow, which henceforth, dressed in bast, would be revered as a pair of divinities, thick books filled with black characters resembling tattoos, whose torn-out, wafer-thin pages made a rustling adornment for the dancers, and lastly an unnamed plague that claimed more victims than all the battles put together. That was the beginning—and what then followed was the end, a long process of parting company with the gods. Their ironwood images were stripped bare, their sacred groves desecrated, their shrines burned down. The protests of the last pagan tribe went as unheeded as their pleas for mercy in the final battle. Those who would not be converted were killed with axes made of American steel, and from the rubble of the Rongo statue soon a church was built. Cook's ax was now no more than a rusty relic of past times and past rulers which, now that it had served its purpose, was presented to a second-generation English missionary, whether with pride or in the vague hope of thereby strengthening or rupturing the bond once forged I could not discover. Since it was not clear to the missionary either, he promptly dispatched the lump of iron to the British Museum.

I found myself thinking about the forces in the Earth's interior. Wherever they prevail, the age-old cycle of rise and fall, blossom and decay is cut short. Islands emerge and are submerged. They have a shorter lifespan than the lands of the continent; they are temporary phenomena—compared to the lifetime, running into millions of years, and the endless expanse of this ocean represented in turquoise, azure, or light blue on the reverse sides of all the globes on display in the cartography department, which I now ceremoniously patrolled, convinced I had finally found the thread, the thin umbilical cord binding Mangaia and Tuanaki together: it was the might of a marine earthquake that one day lifted Mangaia up from the seabed and out of the water, a ring of dead coral and basalt lava, a mountain summit rising steeply out of the depths. And it was the might of a marine earthquake that one day dragged Tuanaki down into the depths and submerged it beneath the water masses of the Pacific Ocean, not long after missionaries had started looking for the atoll. The gray shadow of a giant wave must have approached from the horizon almost without a sound and engulfed everything in one go. The next day, so I imagined, there was nothing in the place where the island had been but dead trees floating on the glassy surface of the ocean.

Only a year earlier, a small schooner with a crew of seven had found the entrance to the reef and made it to the deserted shores of Tuanaki. One of the sailors, at the behest of the captain, had set off, armed only with a sword, towards the interior of the island, made his way through the jungle of banana trees, coconut palms, bougainvillea, and wild orchids, breathed in the air perfumed with frangipani, hibiscus, and white jasmine, and finally discovered, in a clearing, a meeting house in which a number of men were gathered. All of them, I read with endless satisfaction in the one and only report describing that encounter, wore the Mangaian poncho and spoke the Mangaian dialect.

One of them, no doubt the eldest, motioned to the visitor to enter, and when he complied, the old man inquired as to the whereabouts of the ship's captain.

"He's in the boat," the sailor replied truthfully.

"Why doesn't he come inland?" the man asked, without altering his expression. A shell horn dangled from his neck.

"He is afraid you might kill him."

Silence fell, and for a brief moment the breakers seemed ominously close. The old man gazed at the forest foliage. At last he said, with utter calm: "We don't know how to fight. We only know how to dance."

My gaze alighted on the pale-blue globe one last time. I soon found the location. Right there, to the south of the equator, between a few scattered islands, this perfect patch of land had stood, remote from the world, having forgotten everything it had ever known about it. The world, though, only grieves for what it knows, and has no inkling of what it lost with that tiny islet, even though, given the spherical form of the Earth, this vanished dot could just as easily have been its navel, even if it was not the sturdy ropes of war and commerce that bound them one to the other, but the incomparably finer-spun thread of a dream. For myth is the highest of all realities and—so it struck me—the library the true theater of world events.

Outside, rain had set in, a damp monsoon, unusually warm for these northern latitudes.

Ancient Rome

CASPIAN TIGER

Panthera tigris virgata, also known as *Persian*, *Mazandaran*,
Hyrcanian and *Turanian* tiger

* *It was the separation of their territories, less than ten thousand years ago,
that led to the split into two subspecies, the Siberian and the Caspian tiger.
The Caspian tiger lived in the upper reaches of the River Aras, from the
forested slopes and plains of the Talysh mountain range to the Lankaran lowlands, on the southern and eastern shores of the Caspian Sea, on the northern
side of the Alborz mountain range up to the River Atrek, in the southern
part of the Kopet Dag mountain range as far as the Murgab River basin, as
well as along the upper stretch of the Amu Darya and its tributaries, in the
Amu Darya valley to the point where it reaches the Aral Sea, and in the
lower reaches of the Zeravshan, upstream of the Ili, along the River Tekes
and into the Taklamakan desert.*

† *Direct hunting, a dwindling habitat and a decline in its main prey populations were the reasons for the extinction of the Caspian tiger. One was
shot in 1954 in the Sumbar River valley in the Kopet Dag range, on the
Iran-Turkmenia border. Other reports suggest the last tiger was killed in
1959 in the Golestan National Park in northern Iran. Caspian tigers were
last sighted in 1964 in the foothills of the Talysh mountains and the river
basin of the Lankaran lowlands near the Caspian Sea. In the early 1970s,
biologists from the Iranian Department of Environment spent years scouring
the remote, uninhabited Caspian forests for them, in vain. None survived
in captivity. A handful of preserved cadavers found their way into natural
history collections in London, Tehran, Baku, Almaty, Novosibirsk, Moscow,
and St. Petersburg. A stuffed Caspian tiger was on display in the Tashkent
Museum of Natural History until the mid-1960s, when it was destroyed
in a fire.*

In the evening they are hungry and restless. No meat for days. No hunting since they themselves were captured. Instincts worn down by captivity until they lie bare like gnawed bones. Fire blazes in the cats' eyes. It is the reflection of the torches. These herald the arrival of the handlers who, each time they pass by on their rounds, peer through the bars, listen into the darkness for signs that their cargo is still alive.

The cage opens. Yet rather than a meal, it is a den that awaits them. Torches guide the way. Spears force them into a black, windowless hole, two wooden crates barely higher than their withers. These are rolled onto the waiting wagons. Senses sharpened by hunger. Commotion, movement, a clamor of voices: the barked orders of the handlers, the piercing whistle of the driver, the jangling of the bridles, the clunking of the corn barges against a far-off quay, the clatter of the wheels, the flick of a rope.

The convoy jerks into motion, sets out on its preordained path. To the innermost heart of the city. To the outermost reaches of being. The axles creak at every turn.

The two animals are separated by a single partition. They crouch in the darkness. They know everything and see nothing. Not the moldering docks and the steaming knacker's yard, not the Praenestine Gate, which they pass, not the buildings of marble and Tiburtine stone that gleam even at night. They are animals. Animals like us. Doomed like us.

It is still night when they are taken into the catacombs. During the last hours of darkness they turn in tight, aimless circles, strangers to one another—whether equally matched remains to be seen. The cells are musty; dungeons hidden from the sun. And when it finally rises, not one ray filters down here, into this underworld of passageways, ramps, and lifts, of traps and doors.

Far above them a sail is now unfurled until it arches like a second sky over the stone bowl that is gradually filling with people: consuls and senators, vestal virgins and knights, citizens and freedmen, discharged legionaries—and at the very top, around the edge, the women. They have all come to see. They have come to be seen. It is a feast day, a spectacle, and anyone calling it a game has failed to appreciate the holy order inherent in it and the deadly seriousness that attends it.

The day is still young as the emperor steps into his box, pushes back the hood of his robe, shows off his tall sturdy physique, his stout neck, his imposing profile that everyone knows from the coins. When finally he sits down, the dungeon is unlocked, a chasm opens at ground level and a colossal animal of a kind never before seen emerges from the pit, bursts into the ring, races around the enclosure, leaps high against the parapet separating the public from the arena and, with a thunderous din, beats its mighty paws against the iron gate, stops, looks around, and for an infinite moment stands still.

This beast is preceded by a reputation that transcends oceans and mountains: it is said to originate from the depths of the forests of Hyrcania, the wild, rugged, evergreen land that borders the Caspian Sea. Its name is at once a curse and an incantation. It is reputed to be swift as an arrow, wild as the Tigris, the fastest flowing of all rivers, from which it takes its name. Its fur blazes red as an open fire, the sooty stripes akin to branches in the embers, the facial features finely drawn, the ears upstanding, the cheeks powerful, the muzzle bristling with white whiskers, the eyes glowing green beneath heavy brows, and on its forehead a dark symmetrical marking, the meaning of which no one knows.

The creature shakes its huge head, reveals its large, terrible teeth, its two pointed fangs, its fleshy maw. It runs its tongue over its bare nose. A growl rises up from its throat; a hoarse snarl unlike anything heard before echoes through the terraces—a bloodcurdling sound, after which every word becomes a whisper. And a rumor circulates, half lore, half poem: that there exist only females of its species, for the animal is savage, as savage as only a mother can be when robbed of her offspring. Chance alone bears out the assertion: beneath the tail with its brown-black rings lies concealed a fertile womb that will bear no more cubs.

The animal moves off again, paces the ring with silent steps, clings to the shadow cast by the walls, looks for a spot offering refuge, quiet, and shelter—and finds none. There is only the greasy gray of the palisade, the barred openings, the white dazzle of the billowing togas, patches of brightness, naked faces frozen into masks.

When, in fact, had they first set eyes on this animal? Not in a nightmare, as a man-eating manticore with the sneering face of a child, its bared jaws full of powerful teeth, its tail armed with stings, but in the flesh, part of an Indian delegation on the shores of the island of Samos. On that occasion too it had been a female, the only one of the group of solitary beasts to have survived the desperately long, torturous journey. It was paraded before Augustus on a wrought-iron chain as a gesture of reverence—and as a hideous wonder of nature, as rare and horrifying as the herm-like boy who had been made to stand beside it: half-naked, his whole body dusted with spices, with no arms, these having been cut off at the shoulders when he was still an infant. There they stood, the snarling animal and the mutilated human—two wondrous beings, a bizarre pair, a cue for poets to pen epigrams about the majesty of the abominable.

It was six years later that this creature was first seen in Rome. On the Nones of May, it was paraded at the long-awaited inauguration of this theater, together with a rhinoceros and a patterned snake ten cubits in length. The beast was changed beyond all recognition, for it could be seen licking its handler's hands with its rough tongue like a dog.

The empire of the Romans was vast, extending raggedly in every direction under the sun. Not only had they subjugated the Latins, the Volsci, the Aequi, the Sabines and Etruscans, they had also conquered the Macedonians, the Carthaginians and

Phrygians, even claimed victory over the Syrians and Cantabrians—and had now tamed this monster as they would a barbarian people, driving out its wild nature with whips and crowbars, winning its trust with goat and rabbit meat, and in return granting it protection, as they did all their subjects. It seemed almost as though this tigress, who blinked away every ray of sunshine yet did not flinch from the intrusive glances of the humans, were about to be declared a citizen of this empire, like a slave about to be set free. But then from somewhere, more out of whim than conviction, came the call for revenge, which never fails to resonate, the unchanging shrill chorus of budding suspicion and sudden distrust. It was suspected that their submission was merely feigned, their gentleness but a ruse. The predator may have hidden its claws, rolled on its back and, with its belly fur exposed, asked the handler for a caress, yet it lost none of its terror. Almost nothing stokes fear as surely as having won power over an enemy to whom one still feels inferior despite the victory. For as always, there was no denying the truth: nature was not vanquished, the wild remained untamed. Every breath the animal took served as a reminder of long-held fears and impending doom—and rendered its swift death as necessary as the sacrifice of thanksgiving after victory in battle. The verdict was unanimous: the tame beast was to die in combat, like all enemies of Rome. Yet when they set about choosing an adversary, no one could be found who dared to take up the challenge. So they killed it in its cage.

Chains rattle, swords clatter, a wooden hatch drops onto the sand. The ground opens. A murmur passes through the tiers. Out of the darkness a tan head appears. A lion steps into the arena, calm, composed, his head held high, framed by the cloak of his rusty-black mane. The dark wool extends down over his shoulders to his underbelly, a shaggy coat. He sees the unfamiliar feline, takes in her perfect predator's build. The two animals stand there and eye each other for the first time—from a safe distance.

Beyond the gates, a horse whinnies, a whip cracks. Otherwise all is quiet. Everyone is leaning forward to try and interpret the beasts' expressions, their mute demeanor, their motionless stance. But nothing gives them away. No hint of superiority, nor any trace of that understanding that binds predator and prey out in the wild.

The lion now sits, enthroned, showing no sign of agitation, with his shoulders drawn in and his chest proud, rigid as a statue, a long-serving monarch. No one can say which came first: his noble status or his heroic appearance. A world that does not venerate him is unthinkable. A fable that does not make him the ruler not worth telling. His mane shimmers reddish in the sunlight. His gaze is frozen. His eyes gleam amber. The furry tassel of his tail whips the grainy dry sand. He opens his jaws, wider and wider, reveals his big yellow teeth, pushes his head forward, pricks back his ears, narrows his eyes to a thin slit—and starts to roar, a groan issuing from the depths of his chest, again and again, followed by a terrible rumble that seems to rise from an even deeper abyss each time, growing ever louder and more breathless, ever more urgent and menacing. It is the howl of a raging tempest, say the Indians, the roar of a charging army, the Egyptians, the thunder of Jehovah's fury, the Hebrews. But it might also be the elemental sound of creation announcing the end of the world.

The tigress drops low, tenses her long narrow body like a bow-string, presses her straggly white beard into the sand, stretches her hind legs in feline fashion, the sheer power of her muscles smoldering beneath her shoulders. With infinite caution she advances one paw, then the next, creeps and sidles closer and closer, pauses—the lion in her sights.

He sees her coming, but remains calm. The lion's proverbial bravery is borne out. Fear has no hold over him. He stays stock-still on his spot and awaits whatever may come. Only his tail swishes back and forth, describing the same curves over and over in the dust. Destruction blazes in his eyes. And perhaps there is truth in what is written: that his blood is hot enough to melt diamonds.

There comes a breeze; a pigeon is briefly trapped beneath the sail and flutters in search of open sky. In this instant the tigress launches herself, springs through the air at the lion. He rears up, the two animals collide with a dull thud, and a tangle of bodies and fur writhes in the sand, turning lightning pirouettes until flashes of bare wooden boards show through. A hissing, panting, and roaring fills the theater, mingles with choruses of hooting and bawling, swells to a deafening racket that embodies everything: the plaintive cries of an exhausted lion in a dark pit, the hoarse yelps of a tiger cub caught in a net, the weary trumpeting of a wounded elephant, the groans of a hind pursued to the point of exhaustion, the pitiful squeals of an injured pregnant sow.

They come from the furthest reaches of the empire; panthers, lions, and leopards from Mauritania, Nubia, and the Gaetulian forests, crocodiles from Egypt, elephants from India, wild boar from the banks of the Rhine, and elk from the Nordic swamps. They come in ships with sails and oars, in torrential rain, heat and hailstorms, wretched from the swell of the sea, with bloodied paws and teeth filed blunt, in crates of rough elm and beech wood, like prisoners of war or condemned criminals, on some ponderous conveyance drawn by oxen which, when they turn their bowed necks beneath the yoke and catch sight of their cargo, immediately shrink back from the drawbar, snorting, their eyeballs white with terror.

Under towering skies the wagons cross the shimmering plains and dark forests, the barren or fertile terrain, stop and rest in the shabbiest parts of towns and villages, which are required by law to provide for the animals and their keepers. All this for Rome, that temporary, fragile center of an empire that nourishes itself from its peripheries. But most die along the way. Carcasses thrown overboard, bloated by the water, dried out by the sun, a meal for dogs and vultures. Theirs is a cruel fate, though it seems kinder than that of the survivors.

They roll into Rome on high-wheeled wagons alongside the military equipment, receiving an enthusiastic welcome like all rare and precious goods, their names and places of capture emblazoned in large lettering.

They are kept outside the city walls, near the docks, crammed into cages, prepared for the arena where every hunter becomes prey, and those found stoical are stirred to hatred. If an animal is overly docile, it is left to starve for days on end, pelted with sharp thorns and burning brushwood, festooned with bits of jangling metal or teased with straw dolls dressed in red. Any animal that refuses to fight in the amphitheater, that is reluctant to play the role assigned to it by others, has lost its life. The games are serious. As serious as the deaths of those men and women whose memory they honor: victorious generals, heirs of Caesar who perished before their time, the emperor's father and mother.

The fight is sacred. To force the spectacle, tormentor slaves chain the animals to one another: aurochs to elephants, rhinoceroses to bulls, ostriches to boars, lions to tigers, so that animals that would never come across each other out in the wild face each other in the semicircle of the arena—forced into hostility, robbed of their habitat, driven to a state of terror and frenzy, exposed to everyone's gaze, tethered to existence by invisible cords, condemned to die the painful and entertaining death for which they have been kept alive. The verdict may be unequivocal, but the crime of which they are guilty remains obscure to the last.

It may be an old ritual, but here no one pulls their toga over their head to spare themselves the sight of death. No god will be appeased by these steaming entrails. No dirge will extol these dead, no cenotaph will conceal their corpses, and only those that survive countless games, cheating death again and again, those that kill even the *bestiarii* and remain alone in the arena at the end earn themselves a posthumous reputation and a name: the she-bear Innocentia and the lion Cero II, who in the end was savaged by a nameless tiger before a clamoring crowd.

The tigress shakes herself free, rolls to one side. The lion lashes at her with his right paw, catches her on the head, rips a flap of skin from her scalp. He scents blood, he scents the injured kid bleating for its mother that once lured him into the trap in the wastelands of the Atlas mountains, he scents victory and defeat. He hurls himself onto her back with all his might, his hind legs on the ground, buries his claws in her neck, tugs her head backwards. The tigress yelps, hisses, bares her fearful teeth. Again the lion moves to attack, drives the tigress back until her tail is brushing the walls of the arena, pursues her, pounces at her once more, aims for her throat and sinks his teeth into her neck with full force. The battle seems already decided. A soft moan escapes the tigress, like a sigh. A bloody triangular wound gapes beneath her left ear. She ducks, writhes, finally frees herself from his clutches, leaps onto the back of her adversary, buries her paws in his neck, drags him to the ground, digs her claws into his fur, springs apart from him again and lands a distance of two rods away in the swirling dust. Cheers go up, applause resounds, a fanfare plays.

The lion, looking dazed, gasps for air, turns his heavy head and surveys his wounds, two red gashes running across his back. Then he shakes his mane, reverts to combat stance, charges at the tigress, groaning, snorting—with a bellow of pain. She lunges out, aims for his forelegs. The two of them rear up and lash out at each other. Red, yellow, and black fur goes flying. The crowd yells, erupts into chanting, shouts wild encouragement for the fight it has contrived. They call it a hunt, but there is no undergrowth, and every way out is blocked by the barricade, the high walls resembling occupied battlements.

They are watching a cross between an execution and a theatrical performance. A crude throng with refined tastes, accustomed to the magnitude, the sheer numbers, the monstrosity.

To everything the mind can imagine. Every boundary only there
to be overstepped. Their delight is laced with disgust, and their
disgust with delight born purely of curiosity, the urge to act on
every thought. For they, though they pride themselves on having
a choice, are similarly only following their instincts, like children
who throw stones at frogs just for fun.

Curiosity also spawns the question of who would win if all
the animals from the menageries were brought here to test their
powers and penned in together in this sandy abyss. A drama that
simultaneously quells every fear it unleashes. A spectacle, bigger
than the games staged by Augustus to honor his prematurely
deceased heir. What, then, would represent the pinnacle of all
ferocity? A trained tiger that tears apart a tame lion? A lion that
chases rabbits around the arena, scoops them up and carries them
around in its jaws like its own flesh and blood, toys with them
then releases them, only to catch them again? Hecatombs of big
cats being paraded and slaughtered in the arena in a single day
until women faint and the ground is littered with bodies that can
no longer be called bodies, lacerated, torn to pieces, drenched in
blood, the heads twitching, the carcasses half-eaten, the limbs
cold and rigid?

The Circus will be reincarnated. For once a thought comes
into the world, it lives on in another. Big cats crouching on ped-
estals, piled into pyramids, posing in quadrille formation. They
will ride on horses, glide on wheels, rock on seesaws, balance
on ropes, jump through flaming hoops—use dressed-up dogs
as hurdles until the crack of the whip, which is the signal to lick
the sandals of the animal trainer dressed in a gladiator tunic and
tow him around the ring in the chariot: lion and tigress—the
social animal of the steppes, the loner of the damp forests—side
by side, an unequal pair yoked together as if pulling Bacchus's
chariot as depicted in the mosaics found at ancient sites: Africa
versus Asia, control versus passion. What use to them their heroic past, their honorable titles on a par with those of the Cae-

sars? The lion has become the pet of emperors and saints. While he is fulfilling martyrs' deepest desires, others are pillaging his realm. One privilege is gained, another lost. Cities, countries, kings demand his image on their crests. And in assuming this new role, he forgets his origins, the broad plains, the strength of the sun, hunting as a pride. And what use is it now to the tiger that it remained forgotten in Europe for a thousand years? True, its rarity did save it from becoming a frozen emblem. A strange creature classified in Latin bestiaries as either a serpent or a bird, judged by a foreign concept of virtue. They cursed it as cowardly when they should have called it clever. It evaded humans for as long as it could.

Look far into the future, see their sorry fate: their house will fall like that of the Julii, their lineage snuffed out, their last descendants stuffed like bird carcasses. Forever trapped in dioramas with the dusty steppe or broken reeds in the background, hissing, with glassy eyes, mouth open wide, their mighty eyeteeth bared menacingly—or beseechingly, as at the moment of their death. A life in nature reserves and in the custody of humans, behind glass and ditches, among artificial rocks, in tiled rooms and barless enclosures, their days sacrificed to inactivity, flies swarming around their heads, an existence marked only by eating and digesting, in the air the smell of mutton, horsemeat, beef, and of warmed-up blood.

The audience rages. The fight ceases abruptly. The animals release their grip on each other, pause, breathing heavily. Blood trickles down their flanks. The tigress drags herself away, leans her broken body against the barricade, struggles for air. The lion stays put, muscles twitching, chaps drenched in blood, mouth brimming with foam. His gaze is dull and empty, his eyes bottomless. His ribcage rises and falls, breathing the dust. A shadow falls across the stage, a cloud obscures the sun, just for a moment.

Then all of a sudden the arena brightens; unfamiliar light illuminates the scene. An opportunity appears, like a miracle, an unimagined glimpse into the future, a way out, a departure from the preordained path, something new and different that banishes any thought of approaching death. Yet it is also the need, the urge to survive that drives the two animals inevitably towards one another in that vision. A force connected not with the end, but with a beginning. Their ritual obeys a powerful age-old rule: safeguard your clan, preserve your species before its line dies out. And when coming into heat, know no choice. If one instinct fails, let another take its place. Whoever lives must eat. Whoever eats must procreate. Whoever procreates will not perish. The signals may encourage hostility, but the message is clear, the musk in their urine an invitation to a game with consequences: menacing gesture is followed by a hint of timidity, proximity by flight, and resistance by sudden, fleeting submission.

They rub up against each other, nuzzle their heads together. They swipe at one another, hesitate, their paws raised, their eyes locked on each other, they fend off the inevitable, flee their beloved foe, stir the embers, feel their fervor build to the point of no return, rapt and mesmerized.

Eventually the orange-and-black cat slumps down, prone, and the lion steps over her, lowers his fawn body, sinks down on her, and while, for all their kinship, a vestige of unfamiliarity remains, the process is well known: he sinks his teeth into her neck with a roar until she lashes out at him, hissing, and—be it with a blind or seeing eye—they mate, driven to it only by their unnatural proximity. Nothing on earth can prevent what is now happening. Who decides what is contrary to nature and what is part of it? What are those cats doing if not heeding the call to be fruitful and multiply? Traitors to their species yet also its preservers. That their nuptials were enforced need not trouble their descendants.

And after a hundred days, what began as a dream reappears like an illusion, a creature resembling a chimera, in which the parents' nature is both doubled and halved: the tail black, but without a tassel, the belly pale, the mane short and the coat light as sand, a reddish ocher dappled with patches that gleam like stripes, the father's stature, the mother's profile, their unmatched silhouettes, the straight back of the lion, the roach back of the tiger. Monstrous in size, its being intrinsically divided, quick-tempered like a tiger, stoical and tenacious like a lion—a social animal condemned to solitude, a swimmer that shuns water, a popular attraction, a spellbinding sight—bastard, lion-tiger, liger.

They're everywhere, aren't they? In the color copperplate of the three cubs from the traveling menagerie of an English performer, which were taken from their tiger mother and given to a terrier bitch to nurse, and all perished in their first year of life. In the naively rendered, colorful painting of a hybrid feline family in their enclosure, their trainer in their midst like their own child. In the footage of the sandy-colored liger beside a lady in a silver bathing costume, a colossal animal, the world's largest cat, a male of keen instinct and lost potency.

A cry resounds around the upper tiers, people wince, momentarily avert their gaze then turn their faces back to the arena. The dream ends abruptly; the offspring remain unborn. And as if to dispel the thought, the spectacle gathers pace. The entire globe and its myriad worlds dwindle to this semicircle, this inhospitable place, the bare enclosure composed of sand, spectators, and stone, where flies buzz and some in the crowd fan cool air on themselves with a restless hand.

The tigress picks herself up and circles her adversary again. The embattled lion fends her off, but his blows miss their target. The orange cat draws back and launches into a leap, shoots through the air like a bullet, lands on the lion's back. The huge bodies, now streaked with blood and brown with dust, roll across the arena. The lion gives a hoarse roar, shakes the tigress off, pants, stumbles, sinks to his knees. He has two gaping wounds running across his back; blood streams from deep tooth marks. Immediately the tigress leaps onto his shoulders once more, sinks her fangs into his throat. Only his mane saves him from certain suffocation. The tigress loosens her bite, gasps for air herself, great mouthfuls of lion hair catching in her teeth. At this the lion lunges out, hits her hard. The tigress sways but recovers herself, surges forward anew. They go in for another attack. The tigress throws herself on the lion, sinks her teeth into his flesh. He rears up, shakes her off, opens his mouth wide, collapses on the sand with a fading moan. And lies there, motionless.

The tigress surveys her work, sinks down and, trembling, licks her wounds. The stripes in her fur are barely visible for blood.

Emperor Claudius laughs his loud, depraved laugh. There is spittle clinging to the corners of his mouth. He stands, takes a step forward and starts to speak, keen to praise the mother whose memory today's games are intended to honor.

He stutters, though, and the words disintegrate in his mouth. Mute, he slumps back into his seat, hearing in his head the abominable name his mother once called him: a monster. The vile word echoes inside him, a curse that has haunted him for as long as he can remember. Who could blame her? What then brought him to power? The mere fact that he was alive, the only member of the imperial family, the last of his line. Nobody had ever taken him seriously, him, the monster.

So it was pure chance that bequeathed him the office that was never meant for him: benefactor to the masses, ruler over life and death. He sees the marble seats of the senators, the narrow purple hem of the knights' togas, the quizzical looks. Were it not for the fear, it would be easy to rule. Sweat trickles down his temples.

A bell rings. A gate opens. The crowd yells. A man enters the arena. A *bestiarius*, wearing nothing more than a tunic, no armor nor shield, bandages around his legs, in his left hand a bridle, in his right a spear which he keeps raising aloft, directing the masses. The tigress sees the half-naked figure, stalks him, prepares to pounce—but in that split second the lance pierces her chest. The tigress writhes, staggering blindly, trying to shake off the spear. Her head hangs, her eyes search, incredulous, her gaze moves over the fighter, the spectators, who are in a raging frenzy—and the animal slumps down. Her eyes fade, her gaze freezes. Bright blood flows from her nostrils; red froth streams from her open mouth. Already the *bestiarius* is performing his lap of honor, taking in the applause, the chants, the dancing pennants, the wild behavior. Duty has been done, order restored, chaos defeated for a moment.

Gradually the grandstand empties. Quiet descends. Men come and drag the carcasses out of the arena, down into the catacombs to join those of the other animals piled there in their hundreds. The odor of decay hangs in the air. In the afternoon comes the main event, the gladiator games.

Valais Alps
GUERICKE'S UNICORN

* The physicist Otto von Guericke, who was known principally for his vacuum experiments, is also credited with being the first person to have recreated an animal skeleton from individual finds. In actual fact, Guericke, who in 1672 in his New Magdeburg Experiments *mentioned the discovery of the "skeleton of a unicorn" in 1663 in the gypsum quarries of the Sewecken hills near Quedlinburg, could not have discovered those bones, let alone have reassembled them. Indeed two copperplate engravings dating from 1704 and 1749 suggest they originated from a number of ice-age mammals including the mammoth and the woolly rhinoceros.*

† The bones in question were initially kept in Quedlinburg Castle, but were later handed out piecemeal to anyone interested.

A more than three-meter-tall plastic replica of the unicorn skeleton, on permanent loan from the local municipal savings bank, can be seen today in the Museum of Natural History in Madgeburg.

Years ago I spent some time in the mountains. Tired out from a lengthy endeavor, I decided to spend a few weeks staying in a deserted Alpine hamlet in a chalet that an acquaintance had invited me to use. I was toying with the idea, which I had thought original at the time, of writing a guide to monsters, those beasts that, despite having sprung mostly from human imagination, still, as I had once blithely asserted when pitching this book project, in spite of all denials of their existence, populated the world just as surely as all the varieties of real-life fauna, meaning that, as I suggested to the group of potential financial backers, it was possible not only to research but also to categorize their nature, their physical features, their ancestral habitats and individual behavior. Dragons should not be slain but dissected, I added rather pathetically, and without giving any great thought to my target group, or the size or format of my book, I signed a contract and caught the next night train heading south.

I arrived around midday at the railway station of a little medieval town. It was mid-April, the air still chilly, the sun feeble, the connecting bus journey seemingly interminable, and the footpath from the last bus stop up to the hamlet stony and steep, just as I had imagined the walk to a retreat would be. I remember, as I followed the twists and turns of the bridle path across a rugged expanse of scree, being amused by the thought that I, who as a child had been rather anxious and afraid, especially, of horror films and of being alone, now, in self-imposed isolation, wanted to concern myself with, of all things, the often terrifying monsters born of human imagination. That my climb was so slow and arduous was mainly due, however, to the huge number of books I had packed.

It was not until darkness was beginning to fall that the black and white houses scattered over the mountainside came into view behind a rocky slope. All around was silence. Only the power lines carried by the pylons buzzed above me. I found the key in the agreed hiding place, entered the modest but spacious upstairs living room with its broad larchwood paneling, fetched firewood from the side of the chalet, stacked it next to the stove, lit the fire, brewed myself some tea, and made up my bed. It was not long before darkness descended over the mountainside and over my new home, and my sleep on that first night—if my memory serves me well—was deep and dreamless.

When I awoke the next morning, the sky through the roof light looked like a pallid pulp, and it took me a moment to remember where on earth I was. Outside, rising above the shaded, densely wooded valley were jagged, snowcapped summits which, not for lack of trying, I was unable to match up with the names on a map I had found lying ready on the kitchen table. Perhaps it was due to having grown up by the sea, which knows neither elevations nor depressions and remains shapeless even during stormy weather, I thought, as an area of dark hatching indicating a trench projecting laterally into the broad valley basin caught my eye.

I put on my parka, stepped into my walking boots and went out, straight into the wood. Bluetits chirruped, a ring ouzel whistled, lingering patches of snow glistened in hollows, and the trunks of quite a few of the trees were enveloped in a neon-green fluorescent weave of tiny spiky armlike branches, which further corroborated my observation that even completely artificial-looking organisms occur in nature. It came away easily from the bark and felt like moss in my coat pocket. After half an hour I came to a ravine gaping like a jagged wound in the mountainside. A narrow wooden footbridge of barely a hand's breadth spanned the damp shadowy abyss.

I made an about turn, and the sun had just risen over the eastern ridge when I arrived back at the hamlet. The air was still chilly. I could see my breath, which, along with the smoke from my chalet chimney, was the only sign of human life far and wide. The two dozen houses stood there mute, their living quarters of dark timber set on stone bases, their roof ridges facing the valley, with blank windows and closed shutters, and the door of the chapel on the edge of the village would not open either. In front of it stood a water trough hewn from a boulder. The water was ice-cold.

The first week passed without notable incident: I got up at eight o'clock each day, went for a long walk to the ravine and back before breakfast, and on my return, as if I had done it every day of my life, I threw two or three logs on the fire, brewed coffee, boiled myself an egg, sat down at the round kitchen table, and read. I had the place to myself and had stocked up with supplies in the first few days to spare myself the walk to the grocery store in the village lower down the valley for a time. I had plenty of wood, as well as books and a document folder full of photo-copied psychoanalytical, medical history, cryptozoological and other fantastical research literature, and it pleased me to think that, in the event of the kind of disaster that I fantasized about in recurring daydreams, at least there would be enough combus-tible fuel to last me a while.

And so I immersed myself in my studies and quickly filled a whole notebook with details of the diverse features of the mon-sters and mythical beasts, as well as the legends surrounding them and the functions each of these creatures performed in the teeming cosmos of fear. I admit I was a little disappointed. The similarities were all too obvious: each new story soon turned out to be an amalgamation of old familiar set pieces, and each figure an unsurprising hybrid of the imaginary and the true to life. In short, there was not exactly an abundance of species, in-deed real life was considerably more eccentric than fiction. So all the stories of monstrous beings testified to little more than the dogged persistence of repeated narrative patterns and motifs: the phoenix that is consumed by flames every five hundred years only to rise from its own ashes, the self-important sphinx with its riddles, the deadly gaze of Medusa, of the catoblepas, of the basilisk. All the varieties of dragon, which are always slain in the end, their membranous wings, their breath that befouls the air, their hunger for gold, the inevitable bloodbath. Even fabulous creatures from foreign cultures failed to deliver the variety I had hoped for. It always basically boiled down to the same: a wom-an's innocence had to be protected or sacrificed, a man's bravery proved, the wild tamed, the unfamiliar conquered, and the past overcome. What I particularly disliked about these accounts were the hints at deeper meaning, the grandiose air of the incredi-ble, their inevitable allusion to some calamity either impending or having occurred in the dim and distant past. More wearying still were the conclusions drawn by researchers eager to see these beasts as nothing but a misunderstood reality. For them there was no mystery whatsoever. The dogheaded people, the cynocephalics, were merely a group of marauding baboons, the phoenix a flamingo blurred by the dazzle of the morning sun, the bishop fish of the historical pamphlets simply stray monk seals, and the unicorn a misinterpreted rhinoceros or an oryx antelope in profile. But, to my disappointment, I was nowhere able to find a convincing answer to the most obvious question of why dragons bore such a striking resemblance to dinosaurs.

Nevertheless, I persisted with my plan and attempted an initial categorization of the monsters, only to come rapidly to the conclusion that my provisional system was no more useful or curious than, say, the classification of Swiss dragons drawn up by a Zurich naturalist in the early eighteenth century. And so I learned that the griffin originated from Hyperborea or India and the enormous roc from Arabia, that Chinese dragons possessed five, Korean four, and Japanese three toes, that basilisks liked to live in damp well shafts, and that the thorny tentacles of the South American flesh-eating plant, the Ya-te-veo, caused fatal ulcers, and I agonized over whether the scarlet Mongolian death worm, olgoi-khorkhoi, belonged with the cryptids, a group in any case only loosely defined, or alternatively with the snakelike beings, yet was unable to register any noticeable advance in my understanding or gain any sense of satisfaction whatsoever.

No wonder, then, that one day I decided to invent some better monsters of my own, possibly a whole world complete with its own cosmology, a veritable Olympus, and, as so often when I find I am getting nowhere with my writing, I turned to painting. However, the very first creature that I sketched one afternoon using a handful of watercolors I had brought with me looked more cute than terrifying, despite its scaly, bilious-green skin, the leathery webbing of its clawed feet, and its runny, bloodshot eyes. Seldom have I felt so incapable, so empty and dull-headed. There was no denying that evolution was vastly more inventive than the human mind. What were the monstrous octopuses of seafaring legend compared to the giant squid's quest for a female—which was so interminable that, as he roamed the lightless ocean depths, he would unceremoniously squirt his seed under the skin of every fellow member of his species he encountered without first checking its gender? What were the crooked claws of the harpies of Greek antiquity compared to the hideous faces of the hook-nosed birds of prey of the same name, the agonizing death of the nine-headed hydra decapitated by Heracles compared to the potential immortality of the freshwater Hydra polyp, or the dragon of myths and fairy tales hysterically guarding its treasure compared to the sublime indifference of the giant lizards dozing on the rocks of the Galapagos Islands?

I interrupted my reading more and more frequently, stared into the embers, fingered the little nest of lichen with its sulfurous glow, painted my name in various scripts on the back of the photocopied articles on monstrosities, which I had put to one side soon after I had arrived. From time to time I would read snippets from an anthology of legends of Upper Valais I had found in a drawer of the bedside cabinet so that the wandering souls of godless servants and child murderers described therein would distract me from the monsters, I would cut my fingernails or comb my hair until the strong dark hairs lay like bookmarks in the folds of the books, look at the screen of my mobile telephone, even though there was virtually never any reception, and out of the window at the opposite side of the valley, just as if I were expecting someone or something.

Then, on the twelfth or thirteenth night, I dreamed of a bathtub full of snakes with short stout bodies that actually reminded me more of monitor lizards with their legs amputated. The strangest thing about them was that each one had a girl's head with a youthful, rosy face and blonde hair braided into long plaits. I tried speaking to them but they remained mute, and instead took off into the air and flew around the room. Their facial expressions were the only sign that they had feelings like me. When I woke up, I found myself thinking of Baku, a Japanese monster with an elephant's head, a bull's tail, and the paws of a tiger that fed mostly on human nightmares, and wondered whether it would have liked the taste of mine.

I decided to take a day's break from my research and spend some time among people. The sky was overcast, and the clouds hung above the forest in loose gray plumes. The colors were pale, but for that very reason everything seemed surreally clear: the stretch of paved road, the cracks in the asphalt, and a bright red mark at the edge of the road surface which might equally well have represented a serpent or a question mark gone wrong. I knew that a double-headed snake was not in itself a sign. Only the walker who encountered it turned it into one. The steeper the terrain, the shorter and quicker my steps became in an effort to compensate for the downward gradient. In the distance, a few sheep clung to the mountainside. Animals evidently coped better than humans with steep inclines and could simply live their lives on sloping ground. A temporary state that was as normal for them as level ground was for me. The slope was littered with jutting boulders looking as if they had been scattered over the landscape in deliberately random fashion, their windward side covered in moss. Hard to believe that all this had simply come about rather than having been carefully designed. Had come into being unaided and then been tamed. Although the unpredictability remained. Nature deserved credit for much more than God. All the same, I was touched by the notion that He had actually hidden the fossils of animals that had never existed in the Earth's crust just to fool us. What a lot of work for such a crude joke. For a moment I wished it were true.

As time went by I started to sweat, though it was not warm enough to be out and about in just a jumper. The hardest part was finding a rhythm for the descent, converting gravity into momentum. Behind a hill, the mist was clearing. Below me the steppe-like slopes and lower still, laid out before me and suddenly remarkably close, the light-green valley plain, the floor of what was once a sea. The realms of possibility were a fertile breeding ground, even if it was fairly unlikely that there were vertebrates thousands of years old living in labyrinthine caves inside the Earth in fear or even hope of being discovered. Might dragons in fact be faded reflections of past experiences, vestiges of ancient times? Why shouldn't memories push for their own survival, preservation, and propagation in the same way that organisms do? After all, virtually nothing was more formidable, probably, than the power of images, of the once seen. I was reminded of the incredible tales of fair-skinned women who bore black-skinned or shaggy-haired children after looking at images of St. Maurice or John the Baptist at the time of conception. But if that were the way of things, what kind of creatures would populate the world? How far back could memories be traced? Beyond a certain point, everything disappeared into the fog. The ouroboros, the world serpent, bit its own tail.

The customary yellow signpost stood at the place where the paths forked. I was impressed by its presence, its minutely detailed information, its single-mindedness. Some things were indeed perfectly clear, perfectly unambiguous. My head was full of phrases and sayings. What was that lovely one again? A path is made by walking on it. Just let go. How many times had I heard that and immediately tensed up? You could think all you liked, but it didn't alter how you felt. Your whole body a fist that could only be prised open with brute force. Everything in hand, yet not that elusive heartbeat. The old you-just-have-to-believe-it. Painted slips of paper under the Christmas tree. Ultimately, the demystification of the world was the biggest fairy tale of all. A child's magical thinking more powerful than any statistic, any empirical value. A counting rhyme suddenly came true, a crack in the pavement held unspeakable horrors, and anyone who stepped on it was irretrievably lost. Against myth you could only lose.

True, miracles weren't out of the question, but they couldn't be taken for granted. Cause and effect were easily confused. What was desire, what was will, what merely a bodily function? Let go or hold tight? Become a vessel. Give up calculating, acknowledge something bigger than existence. Something like mercy. Something like humility. One long humiliation.

Finally, the terrain began to level out. The path now led past terraced fields and a meadow. In it stood a single cow with prominent horns, its nostrils pink and damp, a shaggy coat, not an eye to be seen, nothing but reddish-brown matted hair. The hum of electricity. A few cherry trees, the scabby bark shimmering like verdigris. And then a sense of surprise, after all, when from behind the barn I caught the glint of the gray-blue roofs of the village, a settlement perched midway between valley floor and mountaintop, where the air was thin and the pasture green. The footpath joined a road. The pavement glistened as if after rain. The place looked abandoned. There was not even a cat to be seen. The buildings were huddled so closely together that you could have jumped from roof to roof. Dwellings alternated with barns, stables, and garages. In between them narrow alleys and flights of stone steps barely wider than the length of a forearm, and as dark as if they were leading straight into the bowels of the mountains, into the deeper layers of time.

From somewhere I became aware of a kind of rasping, then a dull thud, a clatter, followed by a sudden groan. It seemed to have come from the lower ground floor of a chalet. The wood of the door was old and silvery gray. A crack at knee height, just large enough to look through. I peered in. Pitch black inside. It was a while before I could make anything out. A shapeless lump in the straw, its surface slimy, a whitish, festering film streaked with blood. Whatever it was, it was still alive. Its pulse irregular, in its final throes, the beginning of the end. A growth: whether benign or malignant you only find out after the procedure. The doctor's words unequivocal: physiologically everything's tiptop.

Physiologically. The body was always right. The lump of flesh in front of me twitched like an organ exposed in an operation. I thought of the faded, often indefinable organic matter on show in museum display cases. Preserved in formaldehyde, classified, a jumble in which the abnormal was hard to distinguish from the typical. What mattered was that it was eye-catching. The music and lighting had to be right. The rest was down to the imagination. The eye alone was stupid. The lump convulsed again, moved or was moved. A bubble appeared, full of blood. It wobbled, slid to the ground. The bundle began to wriggle, as if tied up. A battle scene. A wounded animal. All of a sudden a black mouth that descended, small pointed yellow teeth, an outstretched tongue that licked off the slime in rhythmic movements and swallowed it. A hoof that nudged the lump until it moved again, took shape, a body, individual limbs stretched out—thin, spindly black and white legs pointing crookedly upwards, a short tail, a head, the back of it flat, the face completely black. A single eye. Only now did I notice the foul smell. The odor of dirty wool, of sheep droppings, of congealed blood. I felt sick. I drew my head back. Felt a stabbing pain in my knee that only eased after a few steps. Down the deserted main street to the whitewashed church, its tall pointed spire like a screwdriver bit. The square in front with its bus stop, the mailbox, a red hydrant, it all looked as innocuous as a fresh crime scene in the newspaper, on the page with all the bad news, the one headed "Miscellaneous," "Panorama," or "From Around the World." Crimes that suddenly had a two-fold presence in the world—as deed and thought. One person's desire, the other's fear. Every boundary only there to be overstepped.

A little bell rang with a bright, busy sound as I entered the shop. Not a soul to be seen. The shelves were chock-full all the way up nearly to the ceiling, the colorful wares neatly arranged. A maze whose few, narrow aisles in fact only ever led to the till and back to the exit. I was not hungry or thirsty, nor did I have any desire to choose something. Perhaps I already had everything I could wish for; at any rate my basket remained empty. The bell tinkled again. A man came rushing in. He was wearing an old uniform with shiny buttons and looked at me as if he wanted me to speak to him. Passing the till, I saw a woman, the shop assistant, standing there, having seemingly appeared out of nowhere. Her gaze was as empty as if she had spent her entire life in this place, weary and simultaneously expectant. I had not noticed her before. Instinctively I grabbed a newspaper, rummaged around for some loose change. The shopkeeper called out something to the man. I did not understand a single word. And no matter how hard I tried, I would never understand any of it. She sat down, her hands dropped into her lap, and it was then that I saw it, a tattoo on the inside of her right wrist, a white horse's head with a pale blue spiral horn on its forehead, surrounded by pink clouds. My coins jangled in the little bowl. A question from the shopkeeper, a hurried shake of the head from me, and again the shame that, whenever anyone here addressed me, I could never understand a word. A cluster of gold bangles slid over the tattoo and back again. Hand and unicorn drifted up to the shopkeeper's face, she fiddled with her dyed blonde hair, patted a few strands into place. For a brief moment it was right up close, looking at me. A bright spot shone in its big blue comic-book eye. Its gaze was friendly, harmless, and penetrating all at once. Then the creature was gone again, searching in the open drawer for change.

Nonetheless a sign, an unmistakable pointer. There was no ignoring it. I tried to close my eyes and ears to it, rushed out, the irritating tinkle sounded once more, then I was back in the square and turned into the main street, with rapid steps, almost light-footed, not rushing, uphill, back or away, it didn't matter. My heart suddenly loud, like on a hunt or on the run. It was easily startled, its pounding went right up into my neck. It did me good simply to walk on, to abandon myself to gravity. Step by step, away from the horn. Dragons may be vanquished, dead and buried, their fossilized bones assembled into skeletons and exhibited in museums with the aid of steel stays, but the unicorn, that vulgar, ridiculous, transparent thing, was immortal, indestructible, ubiquitous—be it on the wrist of a cashier or in the Cabinet of Curiosities in Basel's Totengässlein. Smooth and lustrous, it had stood there, hard, the size of it breathtaking. A specimen of itself. The largest monster of all. "Do not touch," it said. As if I might have been wanting to stroke the ivory, calcium phosphate turned on nature's lathe. An antidote to any poison. A miracle remedy. But I was not ill. I was tiptop. And not so desperate that I would fall for a horn. After all, I was no longer a virgin. Although in its eyes perhaps I was. What would it do with me, then, in the middle of the forest? Nestle its head against my breast or lay its horn in my lap? Really it all amounted to the same thing. The joys of virginity? Where there's a horn there's a hole. The hymen, too, was merely an enemy to be speared. An apple needing picking. If only it were that simple.

The road curved around, and beyond it, on a plateau, a small village appeared, its blackish-brown houses huddled around the church, surrounded by grazing land, perched above a steep rocky drop, barely a hundred meters away but separated from me by a ravine. Not far from the precipice, two brown horses were grazing in a paddock. They stood facing in opposite directions, with not their heads but their tails turned towards each other, mirror images, as if wearing an invisible harness and awaiting their orders. That scene looked familiar. But from where? Two horses, rear to rear. From school, an illustration in a history book, a drawing in shades of sepia. A picture showing horses straining in opposite directions, their necks thrusting forward beneath the whip, the huge effort, their bits covered in foam. Lines of sweat under their harnesses. Two six-horse or even eight-horse teams, their heads turned away. And between them an orb with everything sucked out of it: a vacuum, an unimaginable void, a dead space. Behind it the panorama of a hilly landscape, and above it, floating in the sky, two hemispheres, a pair of divine, blind eyeballs. Nothing was more terrible than empty space. And every single monster there solely to fill it, to obscure the blind spot of fear, making it doubly invisible. A feeling in my stomach, lifeless and heavy. No boulder in sight, nowhere to sit down. I stopped walking, dropped into a squat. My insides a clenched fist. Is this what emptiness felt like? How heavy was emptiness? The realms of possibility were a fertile breeding ground. The realms of impossibility too. A white delivery van thundered past me. I crossed the road, discovered on the other side a dark opening in the undergrowth, a sunken path, a channel that dug itself ever deeper into the forest, the brushwood like a wall on each side. Bare deciduous trees, then before long the shade of fir trees. The ground was spongy and strewn with copper-colored needles. A hollow knocking was audible from somewhere. Otherwise it was completely quiet. My footsteps deadened, almost soundless. The path meandering aimlessly. It descended along a gorge for a time, then carried on close to the rock face, until eventually it fizzled out altogether on a shady knoll. The terrain now became more open, affording a view of the broad western basin. The mountain flanks protruded into the lowlands like pieces of stage scenery. Glinting in the haze was the river from which the valley took its name. Now I also saw, not that far off, a bare patch in the forest where the trees were lying higgledy-piggledy like fallen matches. Alpine choughs screeched high above, let themselves fall and then climbed their way back up beyond the tree line. Behind them, a semiderelict barn clung to the slope, unreachable, like a painting—framed by the white of the snow, as remote as summer. Incredible that there could actually be a track leading to it. Where were the signposts when you needed them? On an embankment, a handful of stones between two lumps of rock, piled in layers, almost a flight of steps, a marker, the hint of a path. Pains in my knees, in my groin, in my lower back. Why couldn't my body just work the way it said in the textbook? What had I done to it that it was reluctant to obey? That it did whatever it wanted. And not what I wanted. The path was getting ever steeper now, more like a chamois track. It was better on all fours anyway. At least that way I made some headway. I felt my way up, crawled through loose shale and scree until there was more vegetation again, a sparse covering of grass, almost a meadow. Then a house, then another, a whole group scattered over a mountainside. A settlement, a little village. And then the white chapel, the water trough. It was the hamlet, my hamlet! The same place I had set out from hours ago. As if I had known the answer to a riddle all along. All my ramblings for nothing. I couldn't even get lost properly. Was I relieved, or was I disappointed? Probably both. A thin plume of smoke rose from one of the chimneys, and there was a red car in the small parking lot. I was no longer alone.

The living room was cold, the stove giving out no warmth. The logs simply wouldn't light. In the end, I helped things along with a stack of photocopies, until the flames finally sent some sparks flying. Even after supper there was no letup in the pain. It felt as if something was drilling into my innards. My legs leaden. Then, on the toilet during the night, the blackish-brown blood in my pants. A sign, as unmistakable as the dull ache in my lower abdomen and the pain in my breasts. The newspaper lay on the tiles, on its front page the photograph of a forest after a fire, a hazy landscape with charred tree trunks and spindly green pine trees. By the time I finally fell asleep, it was already getting light outside. A few hours later I woke up. Everything was bathed in a gray haze, which initially I took for fog until I realized that it was clouds that had drifted down from higher altitudes. I put wood on the fire, went back to bed and browsed a guide to Alpine wildlife until my eyes went woozy and I nodded off. When I awoke again, the clouds had grown denser. It was so silent that the thought briefly crossed my mind that mankind had perished. The thought did not frighten me; on the contrary, it was comforting. I cleared the books off the table, washed my laundry in the sink, hung it up over the stove and cooked myself a few shriveled potatoes. In the evening I opened a bottle of red wine I had found under the sink. Then I decided to paint a self-portrait, but the only mirror was on the wall of the unheated bathroom and I couldn't manage to release it from its brackets.

A few days later, as I was heading home from a walk, a man came towards me. He was small and his skin smooth as leather. Apparently pleased to see me, he immediately started chattering away to me in animated fashion, and unusually fast for that dialect. It seemed to be about something important. I told him that I couldn't understand what he was saying. He repeated his litany, just as rapidly as before, until I shook my head again. He had blackish-brown, deep-set eyes protected by bushy brows. He looked at me, then at my boots and walked on without any gesture of regret or apology.

That night there was a thunderstorm with persistent sheet lightning. The storm tore at the shutters. As I was unable to sleep, I took a look at the photographs in the wildlife guide, and spotted among them the neon-green weave that was now gracing my kitchen table. It was the wolf lichen, which is highly toxic to the nervous systems of carnivorous vertebrates. I took the dry, green bundle and a shovel and buried it behind the house in the rain. Then I spent a long time washing my hands, arms and face with dish soap. Finally, I fell into a deep, exhausted sleep.

When I woke up in the morning, a cuckoo was calling. I heeded its call and went out. A warm fall wind was blowing. The jagged outline of the mountain ridge against the pale-blue sky looked like a paper cutout. It was hard to tell whether the sky had pushed in front of the mountains, or the mountains in front of the clouds. Dew lay on the grass. The white patches in the forest had melted to dots. The rushing sound was audible even from a distance. The ravine now had water flowing through it which plunged, gurgling, into the depths. The thaw had begun. I went back, packed my things, vacuumed, hid the key behind the firewood stacked against the wall and set off downhill towards the valley.

Valle Inferno
VILLA SACCHETTI
also known as *Villa al Pigneto del Marchese Sacchetti*

* *Commissioned by brothers Giulio and Marcello Sacchetti and built between 1628 and 1648, Villa Sacchetti is regarded as the most important early work of master builder Pietro da Cortona.*
† *Towards the end of the seventeenth century the mansion is already starting to deteriorate. In the mid-eighteenth century both wings of the building collapse. The last remnants of the ruins are taken away after 1861.*

Like every ruler, this city has two bodies. Its mortal one lies there like a defiled corpse; a quarry whose marble burns to lime in the furnaces. The pale stone harbors no fossils, yet is itself an imprint of a prehistoric age, a raw block of memory. But its immortal body rises out of the spoil heap in the imagination of strangers daydreaming before the ruins, who pause, frozen in awe, as a whole army of noble and distinguished sons, led by painters, copper engravers, and literary figures, marches into the city and besieges the inns around the Spanish Square. Year in, year out, artists from northern latitudes step down from dusty stagecoaches, a letter of recommendation from some house of high standing, an allowance from a patron or an academy grant in their leather bag—and undoubtedly the address of some fellow countryman who came here many years ago for one winter and has stayed ever since.

They revere the ruins like relics, hoping for their resurrection, insatiably enraptured by lost splendor. Something is always missing. The eye sees, the mind completes: fragments become buildings, the deeds of the dead spring to life, more glorious and perfect than ever. It was here, in the Holy City, the capital of history, that the preservation of monuments was first invented and an entire people proclaimed as heirs, when the Roman Senate decided to protect the more than thousand-year-old Doric column erected in honor of Trajan and his victories, in order that it might remain whole and unscathed for as long as the world exists, and to impose the highest punishment on anyone who so much as attempted to cause it harm. Rome has not fallen; the past is not over; it is just that the future has already begun. This place is stuck between ages, between all the architectural styles vying, in this global arena, for the favor of the public who have always flocked here: Romanesque basilicas with triumphal arches sunk in sand, medieval gables with the facades of Baroque churches, pale Renaissance villas with sooty pyramids—an enormous, tangled organism composed of dead and living matter, governed by chance and necessity and the law of the sun.

No barrier separates the ruins from the miserable working lives of their occupants, who do not stand in awe, but live as they would anywhere else: half-naked beggars loitering in arcades; fishmongers hawking their perishable wares in the shade of a bricked-up portico; women washing their linen in ancient thermal baths; shepherds cramming their sheep into dank temples, where the one-time sacrificial animals graze at the foot of pagan altars; day laborers salvaging blocks of porous, yellowish-white travertine from the catacombs of the Flavian Amphitheater, where the bones of wild animals and unshakable Christians lie. Anything serviceable is used for construction or shipped. Trade in spolia is flourishing. The ruins are pure capital: not treasures to be recovered, but semiprecious minerals to be extracted, just like copper from the Alban Hills.

Few are concerned about the preservation of the Roman ruins, certainly no one as passionate and combative as Giovanni Battista Piranesi, originally of Venice, who falls out with anyone who offers him encouragement or affection. So it almost verges on the miraculous that this man, who prefers the company of stones to that of human beings, in his thirty-third year finds a wife who tolerates him and bears him five children, even though he invests the whole of her not inconsiderable dowry in a massive hoard of copper plates. Besides his tendency to be quarrelsome and irascible, the tall man with the smoldering dark eyes is also given to single-minded devotion and self-sacrifice, and the person who claimed that even a quarter of an hour in his company would make you ill has missed what it is that truly ails the choleric type with the clouded brow: the ruins speak to him as if in a fever, rob him of his peace and sleep, constantly evoke images, visions, which he thinks he has to capture in order to prove wrong any future generations and ignoramuses who dare to claim that ancient Greek art was superior to Roman. Besotted like a man in love, he blames the vacuousness of the present, whose pitiful naivety, as he declares in pamphlet after pamphlet, is enough to drive anyone familiar with the immense grandeur of the past to despair. And Piranesi is familiar with it, has beheld it, for the ancients have populated his dreams ever since, as a child, he read about it in the annals of a Roman historian, in the living room—bathed as it was in the shimmering light of the lagoon—of his uncle, an engineer, whose job it was to maintain the defenses designed to keep the intrusive Adriatic Sea at bay.

And since the present, coral-like, always colonizes that which is sinking, his not old but already ponderous body is magnetically drawn into the depths, into the bowels of the Earth, into the underground vaults and catacombs, out to the sunken burial sites by the main thoroughfares beyond the city gates, whence the ancient Romans had banished their dead, since there was nothing on Earth they feared more than Pluto's underworld. There they had erected necropolises for them, which now held only the ashes of the deceased, ever since countless wars had taught them that cremation alone prevents the corpses from being defiled by the enemy.

So Piranesi hacks his way, with ax and flaming torch, through the undergrowth and darkness, lights fires to ward off snakes and scorpions, wrapped in a black cloak, bathed in moonlight like a figure from some nineteenth-century novel. With pickax and spade he digs his way into the earth, uncovers plinths and sarcophagi, measures the fortifications of old defensive structures and the buttresses and piers of weather-beaten bridges, examines masonry bonds and the order of columns, studies facades and foundations, deciphers the inscriptions on ancient sepulchers, copies the fluting on columns and the moldings on arches, sketches the ground plans and elevations of buried predator cages and theater arenas, the cross sections and longitudinal sections of forts and theological colleges choked with vegetation— and draws with a restless hand the levers and beams, the hooks and chains, the pivots and brackets that were needed to construct those formidable structures. For him no stone is so mute, no masonry so brittle, no truncated column so damaged that he would not recognize in them the limbs and muscles that once formed the strapping body of this city, and the blood vessels and organs that once supplied it: bridges and arterial roads, aqueducts and water reservoirs, and in particular the many-branching channels of the labyrinthine *Cloaca Maxima*, which, although or indeed because it served the basest of needs, he names as the pinnacle of all architecture, whose glory, in his judgment, surpasses even the Seven Wonders of the World. And just as the anatomist Vesalius a century earlier dismembered the still warm corpses of condemned murderers on the dissecting table, so he does with the dilapidated buildings, remnants of a past empire which, to his mind, was not to blame for its demise.

From the eloquent ruins, the architect, who his whole life long will never build a single house, sketches the ground plan of an imagined past and simultaneously the vision of an entirely new creation which, in his copperplate etchings, captivates more people than any building anchored to solid ground. His gaze effortlessly penetrates sediment and other material as, in his workshop, he bends over the cold, smooth-polished metal and copies the impermanent red chalk sketches onto the etching ground, an infinite number of dashes, dots and flicks, patchy shapes and vibrating lines that seldom intersect, even though they change direction with every detail as if setting out on a new course. He immerses the plate in the bath and, with each repetition, covers some areas and gives others a drizzling, so that the acid still eats into the slightest hollow and captures forever what he does not want to forget, what he cannot forget.

When the rollers release the large sheets, the sun shines mercilessly on the etchings, the shading is velvety and black as oblivion, the architectural sight lines almost endless, the visual angles fantastic and the crumbling buildings colossal even from a bird's-eye view. The monuments stand up boldly against an inflamed sky, below them an army of tiny figures, gawky Harlequins with flailing arms. This city must have been built by giants, Roman Cyclopes at the zenith of their creative powers.

Piranesi's etchings are soon all the rage as anatomical records of ancient life, even though most of the plates tell only of death. They show interior views of burial chambers, ground plans of mausoleums, sarcophagi enthroned on marble plinths, or a cross section through the cobblestones of a gateway leading to a crematorium. Piranesi becomes the high priest of a death cult that grips the entire continent and every week spurs new disciples to make a pilgrimage to the master's house on the far side of Monte Cavallo, where he has retreated in search of peace; his old workshop on the magnificent Corso was plagued by hordes of visitors. When the beardless folk ask to be admitted, he calls out "Piranesi is not at home" until they give up without having caught a glimpse of their idol.

Only once, on one particularly hot and humid afternoon in early summer, the knocking simply does not cease. When Piranesi throws open the door with the usual cursing, on the threshold stands an elegantly dressed young man with shoulder-length, curly hair carefully combed and held together in a ribbon at the nape of his neck, smooth facial features and small round eyes that sparkle, and from his well-formed mouth, accompanied by an old-fashioned sweeping bow, come the words, spoken with a fine French accent, that he has been murmuring to himself for days, trying to strike the right tone: "Sir, if I may. My name is Hubert Robert. I love the ruins as you do. Take me with you anywhere you please."

Two years later, on the morning of a misty autumn day in the year 1760, Hubert Robert walks out of the Porta Angelica, follows the winding course of a small, partially dried-up stream into a valley at the shady far end of which, he was told, there stands a crumbling mansion. Beneath the cloud-covered sky the colors appear washed out. He breathes in the damp air, wants to shake off his tiredness, a leaden weariness which has been bothering him for some time, and which is fundamentally alien to his being.

He is young, twenty-seven years of age, a scholar of the Académie de France, the son of a Parisian valet in the service of a diplomat at the court of Versailles. He arrived in Rome, via Basel, St. Gotthard and Milan, six years ago as a member of the entourage of the diplomat's son, in order, as one gifted man among many, to draw all the monuments and buildings that, rather than concealing the signs of the times, display them almost proudly. Only this spring he traveled to Naples and visited the new excavations on the Gulf, saw Pozzuoli and Paestum, and in Tivoli drew the gnarled olive trees reaching with their parched branches towards a copper-colored sky in the derelict interior of a Temple of the Sibyl. He had not wanted to spend another summer in the feverish heat of Rome, which a year earlier had almost cost him his life. Since his return, he is somehow changed. Beset by a strange weariness that has suddenly spoiled his enjoyment of all the ancient remains, he is seized by an urge to visit some ruins from his own era, namely those of the villa of the Sacchettis, which, after another bend in the path, now appears behind the branches of the cypresses at the end of a sandy avenue.

He leaves the bridle path behind, makes his way towards the grounds, sits down on the hard, brown grass and looks. Then he starts drawing the tumbledown premises, quickly and accurately, just as, during the long evenings of his first Roman winter, he drew the muscles of a wiry Italian in the high-ceilinged painting room of the academy on the Corso. He guides his graphite pencil purposefully over the paper, rarely looks up, capturing the scene with only an occasional glance: the way the straggly garden extends up over the slope in three tiers, the way the crumbling building, a pavilion with a protruding facade and two curved wings, sits enthroned on an embankment as if on a pedestal, at its center the tall semicircular apse, a water feature on each of the three terraces: a fountain, a fishpond and a shady nymphaeum with Doric pilasters behind a colonnade. But the flights of steps are bare except for the crumbling stonework. The roof structure is disintegrating, the balustrades are falling down, the coffered half dome of the apse is cracked, the fountain without water, and the seashell-shaped basin guarded by a pair of Tritons is bone-dry right down to its stone floor. Even the lintel above the entrance has slipped lower as if after an earthquake.

Robert draws all of this, allowing himself to add the familiar figures of the household staff to the abandoned scene: on the sheet of paper a girl balances a jug on her head, a woman holds an infant to her breast, another leads a child up the steps, a dog follows an invisible scent, a cow and a sheep stand by the fountain, and a donkey lowers his head to the basin, which is filled to the brim with water.

Hubert Robert casts an eye over his drawing, rolls up the sheet of paper, crosses the overgrown track that was once the drive, ascends the cracked steps, past the mortar remnants scattered at the foot of the wall. The entrance is littered with rubble. He climbs inside through a window aperture, a cool room of not particularly large dimensions, which must once have been the drawing room. A musty odor hangs in the air. Broken roof tiles and rotten beams lie in a heap on the ground; barely an arch of the vault is intact. And in the middle of the coffered ceiling is a gaping hole like a giant wound with the whitish-gray bank of clouds shining through. Only around the edges, under the crumbling plaster, is it still possible to make out the remains, rimmed black with mold, of a ceiling painting, faded scenes populated with shadowy figures, the only distinguishable one depicting an impaled head with wide-staring eyes—a grisly vision that reminds Robert of a line from Virgil's *Aeneid*: "Unum pro multis dabitur caput." One head will be sacrificed for many.

He stares at the gruesome head until a thought strikes him: the present is merely the past of the future. A shudder comes over him, he clambers over the rubble and steps back, strangely elated, into the open, but then a foul smell hits him, bringing back memories of the previous summer, of the intolerable stench which, in August, after the heavy rains, when the Tiber was swollen and as so often had burst its banks, had settled like a bell jar over the entire city and dissipated only briefly during the twilight hours when he, like everyone else, took the opportunity to go for a stroll to recuperate from the heat of the day. Later he was told by the doctor, a thoughtful and experienced man who trusted above all in the salutary effect of bloodletting, that during those eerily fresh evening hours he must have been infected with the swamp fever, which few survive. Nobody—neither his landlady nor his friends—had still believed Robert would recover, so far advanced was his physical deterioration and accompanying mental breakdown. After the tenth bloodletting in the space of eight days, he too, coming round after fainting from lack of blood, was himself so resigned to his own irrevocable end that, even as the symptoms were already receding, he was still expecting to die and is surprised to this day to have survived the illness.

He turns around once more, surveys the house, which now seems to him transformed. Greenery sprouts from the walls, moss covers the marble gods, stonecrop springs from the cracks, ivy clings to the stone with its sturdy roots, Virginia creeper adorns the parapet, its many-branching tendrils twining themselves around the fragile cartouche which identifies the builder and still bears the royal coat of arms of the Sacchetti family, three black stripes on a white background.

When Giulio Sacchetti was appointed a cardinal over one hundred years ago, he had commissioned this villa with its high apse, proud and imposing like that of the Belvedere—a summer house in Valle Inferno, a sandy depression between Monte Mario and the Vatican, a dusty wooded hollow near the papal state, full of tall pines and slender cypresses. He is a rich man, Rome's wealthiest cardinal—with a glittering future in prospect. From the bedrooms of his summer residence he can see the dome of St. Peter's Basilica. Twice he hopes to be elected Pontifex Maximus, and at the conclave in 1655 he is not far short. But others become pope.

One year later he stands at the window of his country house for the last time and gazes again at the object of his failed dreams, in his bony hand a perfumed sachet containing herbs, bitter orange and lemon peel, which he keeps pressing to his nose. The plague is raging in the city—yet again, but with more devastating effect than in a long time. The streets are populated with figures enveloped in clouds of smoke, wearing beaked masks in an attempt to ward off the disease with aromatic vapors of myrrh, camphor, and wild calla—and carrying a stick to keep the sick at bay, those poor devils who are carried off so quickly that he, Giulio Sacchetti, papal adviser on disease control, can come up with nothing better than having the wretched dead buried outside the city walls—as swiftly as possible and without any manner of religious ritual—before decomposition can set in and the corpses emit their reputedly highly infectious effluvia. This secluded valley is particularly prone to miasmas, those damp mists that fester in the shallow margins and spongy banks of bodies of still water, hang low above the earth—and exude a stench so repulsive that it is inevitably perceived as toxic and sinister. Giulio Sacchetti knows what is written in every treatise on the plague: a piece of land, once contaminated, is lost forever. From now on he receives his guests in his city palazzo again. Only a few decades after its construction, Villa Sacchetti is abandoned.

First the tiled roof sags, then the rotten beams warp under the colossal weight of the vault. Soon water trickles through the cracked tiles, seeps into the timbers and walls, and the disintegration begins. The house's outlines, which a young master builder once traced on the drawing board with a ruler, are gradually losing their shape, crumbling and unraveling. The stone, once cut and layered to make walls, becomes weak and vulnerable, defenseless in the face of weeds and weather, to the point that there is no distinguishing what is tuff, what is slate, what is marble, and what is rock. Only the thick, sturdy outer walls of the pavilion will stand firm for a while longer against the water that, in the summer months, cascades down the hillside after every downpour as if the end of the world were nigh.

Meanwhile in Paris, Europe's other capital, the stench of bodily excretions reigns longer than the House of Bourbon—a vile odor of urine and feces. At night, especially, it engulfs whole districts, when the sewer emptiers climb back out of the cesspits and, to spare themselves the trip to the waste dump, tip the excrement into the gutter, a viscous sauce that, as dawn breaks, runs down the streets towards the Seine, on the banks of which the water carriers later fill their jugs, oblivious.

Early infirmity will deliver them. There is a bed ready for each one of them in the Hôtel-Dieu, the ancient hospital in the labyrinthine old town, a bed they must share with four others. There the insane and the elderly lie alongside orphans, women who have just given birth and postoperative patients one floor up from the corpses, the sick among the dying. The walls are damp, the corridors poorly ventilated, and even on summer days, a perpetual twilight filters through the window openings. The children smell sour, the women sickly sweet, the men of cold sweat, and hanging over everything is the fetid odor of decay which—as surely as the incessant fumbling with the bedclothes—heralds the approach of death, as on the night of December 30 of the year 1772, when a fire accidentally started during candle-dipping jumps across to the timberwork and spreads to the entire warren-like compound. For two weeks of winter the hospital is in flames. As the inferno takes hold, destroying an ever-expanding tract of the old heart of the city, spectators revel in the spectacle that is bathing the cityscape in a red glow.

What is left is a hollowed-out shell against a black sky, which Hubert Robert captures in several drawings and paintings. He has been back in Paris for eight years, and has earned himself the nickname "Robert des Ruines." Ruins are in demand. Anyone who cannot wait for time to do its work has them built or painted. The collapse of a building attracts almost as many onlookers as an execution. So Robert paints monks preaching in ancient temples and washerwomen on the quaysides of underground rivers, the demolition of houses on the Pont Notre-Dame and Pont au Change; he paints the horse carts taking the rubble from the ruins and men loading whatever is left behind onto barges, the day laborers hunting for reusable materials on the battlefields of urban regeneration and piling them up for sale, to keep the eternal cycle in motion. And so ruins turn into building sites, the one indistinguishable from the other in Robert's paintings. On his canvas even the ditch for the foundations of the school of surgery resembles an archaeological excavation. He paints the blaze at the opera house as an erupting volcano, the sea of flames, the pillar of fire and the clouds of smoke against a June night sky, the sooty pall of the morning after, as well as the leveling of the Château of Meudon, the demolition of the Church of the Feuillants and the storming of the Bastille, the black bulwark before it was razed to the ground—a compelling, eloquent image: the falling lumps of stone pile up in the moat like ancient spolia, clouds of smoke billowing all around them. The new, says this picture, demands the ruthless destruction of the old. From now on, monuments disappear every day; every week a cavalcade of statues is dispatched to the furnace. Paris is the new city of ruins. Palaces are stormed, fortresses torn down, churches laid waste, and skeletons of kings and queens, abbots and cardinals, princes of the noblest blood dragged from their graves, their lead and copper coffins melted down to make shotgun pellets in purpose-built foundries and the bones consigned to hastily dug pits and sprinkled with the kind of unslaked lime that suppresses the stench of corpses and hastens their decomposition. Robert paints his panorama of purposeful and purposeless destruction with the stoical equanimity of a chronicler. Anyone at the time who asks him which side he is on receives the answer: "On the side of art."

In his picture, the desecration of the centuries-old tombs becomes an everyday exercise and it is impossible to tell whether something is being destroyed or preserved here. Before the canvas is even dry, he is arrested. Like so many other protégés of the aristocracy, he ends up in Saint-Lazare, the prison that was once a leper colony. There, too, he paints: the distribution of milk, the ball games in the prison yard, the suburbs of Clichy and La Chapelle glinting in the distance through the barred window, and the fields lying fallow around Montmartre, which rises up on the horizon—on earthenware and door timbers at first, until he is given permission to acquire canvases and paper. Every afternoon he practices gymnastics in the inner yard, not far from an enormous wooden cross, at the foot of which a marquise cloaked in black begs heaven for mercy—and the restoration of the old order, when "a lord was still a lord, and a servant still a servant."

One March evening in 1794 laughter issues from the third-floor corridor. Not unusually, there is a feast in progress, pike and trout are served, fruit and wine. A little monkey roams from cell to cell and Émile, the five-year-old son of a prisoner, takes a rabbit for a walk on a lead, to general amusement. Two female inmates play the harpsichord and harp, oblivious of everyone around them, then once the instruments have fallen silent, Robert starts telling the story of how, as a young man, he had scaled the Colosseum and almost fallen, and how he had plucked up the courage to call on Piranesi. How he was mentored by him and allowed to draw the subterranean burial sites with him. He makes no mention of the gruesome picture in Villa Sacchetti. As always he wears a knee-length purple robe, beneath which his bodily proportions can only be guessed at. He has two deep wrinkles etched into his high forehead, and a few pockmarks dotting his otherwise rosy, smooth face. His black, bushy eyebrows are now as gray as his sparse hair. In spite of his age and his corpulence, he nearly always wins the games of catch in the prison yard. And his small eyes are as cheerful as ever. When he laughs, his fleshy lower lip trembles, and two dimples appear on his chin. He raises his wine glass and proclaims contentedly that he is the least unhappy inmate in Saint-Lazare. He does not, though, speak of the reason for his unshakable gaiety: that absolute certainty that he, like everyone here, will die by the guillotine. "Stat sua cuique dies," he says, quoting Virgil, as he so often does, and laughs his infectious laugh that would have you believe that misfortune had never befallen him. Yet his four children are all dead, borne away by illness. He is fully prepared. He has already done a painting of his own grave and built himself a miniature guillotine out of scraps of firewood to familiarize himself with the workings of the apparatus that before long, when his turn comes, will nice and neatly sever his head from his body. Every few days, the drumroll announcing the arrival of the dark horse carts that come to fetch the prisoners and take them before the court echoes through his cell.

A few weeks later, on a cold, clear sunny morning in May 1794, he is standing among the prisoners gathered in the inner yard when his name is called out. He realizes that his final hour has come and is about to step forward when another man makes himself known, someone on whom fate has bestowed the same surname, who will now face the blade in his place. Hubert Robert is released. Only many years later does he eventually die of a stroke in his studio in rue Neuve de Luxembourg. He drops dead on the floor, his palette in his hand.

One year after Robert's death, in July 1809, two architects accompanied by a doctor take a drive into the deserted, muggy valley near Rome. Since the horses start to take fright before they have reached their destination, and even the whip cannot persuade them to pull the carriage all the way to the end of the almost impassable avenue, the men have no choice but to finish their journey on foot, until they are standing in front of Villa Sacchetti with Monte Mario behind it, the hill on which all Rome's occupiers set up camp, including Napoleon's staff officer in February 1797, when he issued the order to seize all works of art deemed worthy of being transported back to the French Republic, the self-proclaimed land of freedom, to Paris, school for all the world, whereupon the officers fanned out across the city and plundered the pope's treasure chambers, cut up Raphael's tapestries, sawed frescos and paintings to pieces, hacked the limbs off statues.

While their fathers had come here to marvel, they came to steal what they had marveled at. All the metal, all the marble in the churches was prised free and sold, the tombs of the saints ransacked, gold reliquaries, monstrances, and tabernacles auctioned off, high altars smashed that even the Goths had spared, and all the insignia of the nobility wiped from the face of the city: the oak tree of the della Rovere family, the bull of the Borgias, the balls of the Medicis, the lilies of the Farneses, the bees of the Barberinis and the three black stripes of the Sacchettis, which survived the frenzy only out here in the Valle Inferno.

The gentlemen ascend the dilapidated steps. They are looking for a place for the dead, a cemetery for all. The two architects want to turn the ruins into a chapel and the grounds into an airy, expansive necropolis shaded by high walls, because all the burial grounds inside the Aurelian Walls were closed soon after the pope was taken prisoner and carted off to France like some particularly precious find. Rome's treasures have gone, Apollo, Laocoön, even the Belvedere Torso, paraded as trophies on ox-drawn chariots decked out with laurel, from the Jardin des Plantes, past the Panthéon to the Champ-de-Mars, together with African camels, lions, and a bear from Bern, a two-day-long triumphal procession under a leaden sky, which cleared towards the evening of the first day, prompting self-important reporters to comment that the sun had prevailed over the clouds as had the forces of freedom over those of tyranny.

Only the weighty Trajan's Column still stands where it has always stood. Rome has lost nearly a third of its population; it now has more dwellings than residents. Palaces and monasteries are crumbling ruins, and from the crypts of churches comes the familiar, sickly sweet smell of decay, even though doctors warn in notices and lectures of the dangers emanating from the decomposing corpses, and urgently recommend that the dead be buried outside the city gates. From now on, the law of hygiene must apply, superseding traditional ritual. Yet the Romans refuse, do not want to bury their dead out in the bare soil of the Valle Inferno, but to inter them in boxes of stone, in mausoleums and crypts, near the bones of the saints, as they always have done.

The cemetery is never inaugurated. Brambles grow in the Colosseum. There is digging in the Forum. Sand begins to submerge the villa in its valley; sheep graze on the avenue. Pines and cypresses exude their delicately aromatic scent, and for a long time painters keep coming, until the very last of the surviving remains have sunk into the ground as well.

Manhattan
THE BOY IN BLUE
or *Emerald of Death*

* *Friedrich Wilhelm Murnau's first film was shot in spring 1919 at the moated castle of Vischering in the Münster region, and in the countryside around Berlin. The plot revolved around a painting based on Thomas Gainsborough's "The Blue Boy," with the face replaced by that of Murnau's protagonist Thomas van Weerth, played by silent movie star Ernst Hofmann. There are various accounts of the film's plot, but in all of them the principal character, the last of the family line, is living an impoverished, lonely life in the castle of his forefathers with only an old servant for company. He often contemplates the portrait of one of his ancestors, with whom he feels a mysterious affinity, not merely because of their strong physical resemblance. Is he the reincarnation of this young man in blue, who wears on his breast the notorious Emerald of Death, which has only ever brought bad luck to his family? To keep the curse at bay, one of his ancestors has hidden the emerald. One night Thomas has a dream in which the "Boy in Blue" climbs out of the painting and leads him to the hiding place. When Thomas wakes up, he does in fact find the emerald in the place indicated, and ignores his old servant's pleas to throw the jewel away. Meanwhile a band of minstrels turns up at the castle. They steal the emerald, burn down the castle and destroy the portrait, leaving him with nothing. Thomas falls ill, but survives thanks to the true love and selfless devotion of a pretty actress.*

† *No record of the premiere of the silent movie has been found to date. It was probably never screened as a main feature, for it is not mentioned by any of the contemporary critics. It is considered lost. The Deutsche Kinemathek in Berlin holds in its nitrate film collection thirty-five short fragments of the film in five different tints.*

She must've caught a cold. Her nose was running. Had she even been blocked up? Not that she could remember. Which made her suspicious. After all, she did her best to look after her health. Where were those damn Kleenex? The pack was right here a moment ago. What a nuisance. There was no way she was going anywhere without tissues. Ah, there they were, under the mirror! Right, in the purse they go, hat on, sunglasses on, close the door and let's roll. What the hell was that strange whiff in the hall? Ah, that's it. It was soft-soap Monday. Every week the cleaning crew from Queens would turn up at some unearthly hour and scrub the marble like a gang of crazed monkeys, and she found herself rudely awakened at the crack of dawn. No one else in the entire building got up as early as she did. The stink left by the charwomen was bound to hang around until Wednesday at least. She would have to think about moving yet again. Was there no end to it? It was enough to make you weep. Luckily the elevator arrived quickly. The boy could've been a bit more polite, though. Had no one told him who he was dealing with? Pretending not to recognize her. Hadn't anyone told him how to greet her? Barely out of diapers and already gone to the dogs. Probably getting ideas in his head. After all, there was no one else in the elevator. That's all she needed. It seemed to be taking forever. But then it *was* seventeen floors. Finally they made it. At least the doorman did things the proper way, came out of his lodge and opened the door for her. You're welcome. Heaven! The coast was clear. No vultures in sight. No one noticed her. Probably because of the new sunglasses. O.K. then. She wasn't choosy, so she just went for the first guy to come along, a man in a gray flannel suit. He wasn't that elegant, to be honest. But a good choice all the same. He walked fast towards the East Side, piloted her through the crowd, gave her a direction, a rhythm. That in itself was a good thing. Sometimes he disappeared in the crowd, but she soon caught up with him again. After all, she was a seasoned pedestrian. It was the only field she'd become remotely expert in. Basically it was her only pleasure, her religion. If need be she could get by without her calisthenics, but definitely not without her walks. Her outings to browse the store windows, her wanderings, her random detours. At least one hour a day, preferably two. Usually down to Washington Square Park and back, sometimes up to 77th Street. It was good to follow close on someone's heels to start with. She'd have an aimless wander later. After all you couldn't get lost. One advantage of islands.

It was colder than she thought. Too cold for April at any rate. Even by East Coast standards. It was always either freezing cold or boiling hot in this city. God knows why she even lived here, in this unpardonable, drafty climate where you catch a cold at the drop of a hat. She should've gone to California back in March. Just as she normally did. March would've been right, March rather than later. O.K., it was deadly boring there when you had nothing to do. But all the same, the climate was perfect: fresh air, plenty of sunshine. You could run around butt naked all day. Well in theory anyway. Too bad Schleesky hated it. It meant she had to sort everything out herself: a flight, a driver and even someplace to stay now that the house was sold and Mabery Road was no longer an option either. As if she didn't already have enough on her plate. For weeks she'd been hunting for the right sweater. It had to be cashmere. In dusty pink, her favorite color. She loved colors: salmon, mauve, hot pink. But none as much as dusty pink. She also had appointments, stupid meetings. She canceled most of them, but it was tiring all the same. Cecil had been at it again. He obviously imagined he could simply suggest any time, any place or, worse still, ask her to suggest something. How was she supposed to know whether she would be hungry or thirsty or wanting to see him tomorrow or in three days' time? Not to mention her poorly state. Her health had never been the best. Even though she took good care of herself, always dressed warmly enough and never, ever sat down on the toilet seat. That was just how it was: a puff of wind and she was laid low with some damn wretched cold. The last time was when she had tea with Mercedes. She'd only leaned against the open window briefly. But by that evening her throat was sore as hell, and even though she'd gone to bed wearing two sweaters and woolen tights as always, she'd woken up the next morning feeling at death's door. It was weeks before she was anywhere near back on form. In fact, it was simpler to say when she *hadn't* been ill. And on top of that the goddamn hot flashes out of the blue. What a pain in the ass. She urgently needed new panties. She'd even seen those light-blue knee-length ones in London last fall. Cecil had said in his letter that Lillywhites only stocked them in royal blue, bright scarlet, and canary yellow. He should've looked in Harrods then. After all, he had promised to track some down for her. To think she was having to deal with that now as well. Perhaps she ought to meet with him after all, if only on account of the panties.

Hey, what had gotten into the gray suit? He'd just veered off-course, drifted over to the right and approached the bank of windows. What the heck! Surely he wasn't going to . . . or maybe he was. No! No way! He made a beeline for it. And disappeared through the revolving doors of the Plaza, of all places! Just as she'd gotten used to him. It could at least have been the Waldorf Astoria! Wild horses couldn't drag her into the Plaza. It had the scruffiest rear entrance in the city. That such a swanky hotel could have such a foul-smelling backyard. She knew a bit about rear entrances. Yes, if only she knew as much about everything else as she did about rear entrances! About garbage cans and those hampers full of stinking dirty linen and the service elevators reeking of leftover food. Just her luck! Not even ten o'clock and already she'd had her first disappointment, not counting the elevator boy. She should just stop having anything to do with other people.

Now there she stood with a runny nose, snot trickling down. And no one to stop it. What a nightmare! No one was there to take care of her. To pay attention to her, acknowledge her, help her. Everyone just hurried on past. Past her. A woman rummaging in her purse with gloved fingers. Those damn Kleenex, vanished into thin air. The fountain on Grand Army Plaza wasn't even on. But to abandon her walk after not even two blocks just for that? Alright then, just keep sniffing back the snot, cross the street on the next Walk signal, and then no more experiments, down Fifth Avenue for a little way and across to Madison. The gray suit had been a mistake. One more mistake, that's all. Yet another. No great surprise. She was forever making mistakes. Nightmare. It hadn't always been that way. It used to be different. She never used to keep screwing up all the time. Always knew exactly what she wanted and how much. Had the knack. Without having to think about it. Thinking had never done her much good anyway. Thinking had never helped her come to any kind of decision. The whole bloody mulling over of things—all it did was give you wrinkles. She'd never thought anything over in her life. Couldn't see the point of it. The fact was she was an intellectual write-off. She simply didn't know a thing. Completely uneducated. She'd never read anything in her life. So what *had* she learned? The different ways of holding your head and what they meant: bowing the head indicated submission, tilting it back the opposite, a slight inclination of the head showed empathy, while a head held high suggested calm and resilience. Amazing that she'd remembered that. Normally she never remembered a thing. Not a clue about anything, but her intuition was spot-on! It was something she used to be able to rely on. Ever since she was a little boy, she'd known what she wanted. In the past, at least. And now it was gone, her darned intuition. Evaporated into thin air. Where the hell was it, her famous intuition, when she forced herself into that monstrosity of a bathing suit? Rushed knowingly towards her downfall, as the camera rolled. Utter suicide. The air was thin at the summit. You only had to look down and you were done for. It was then that the goddamn fear took hold. And then there was nothing left.

Did a runny nose come before or after a blocked nose? What was the normal order of a cold for god's sake? She would call Jane later and ask her. Jane knew stuff like that. Or at least she pretended to, which amounted to the same thing. Although last night she hadn't known what to suggest either. Surely it's O.K. to call a good friend during the night if you're in distress! She'd been in a really bad way. Dumbass thoughts the whole time, crazy dreams. Unbearable. Now it was clear what had been going on: a cold on the way, but last night it could just as easily have been a stroke or rheumatism or cancer. Did nose cancer actually exist? It probably had a different name. But a cold might well lead to sinusitis, judging by the amount of snot. And she hadn't even washed her hair yesterday evening. Why the hell not? Oh, that was it, Cecil, the old charmer, had telephoned yet again and gone on and on. To think she'd even had the call put through! Give him the slightest bit of attention and you soon live to regret it. The old whining sissy was even worse than Mercedes. Nothing but reproaches and declarations of love. No wonder she'd gotten a migraine afterwards. If only she hadn't answered the telephone and had washed her hair instead. Then that would at least be out of the way. Her nose again. It was all so god-awful. And now a red light. What the devil was it? A camera, over there, pointing at her. There you go. I thought so. Behind it a woman, a young thing, of the thrusty-busty variety. Which made a change. Oh no, did she just . . . ? Would you believe it! Now she's been snapped blowing her nose. In broad daylight. The cheek of it! Could it get any worse? The photographer was already gone. The street teeming. One helluva crowd. Salvation Army ladies with leaflets and an accordion, the poor soul with his hot-dog cart, the newspaper man behind his pile of nickels and bundles of paper. Everyone had something to do. Everyone except her. She didn't even read the newspaper. It never had anything in it. Well now, who was that honey on the cover of *Life* magazine? Boy, who'd've thought it! Little Monroe, eyelids at half mast, platinum blonde, shoulders bared—half minx, half deluxe doll, but not without style. She definitely had talent in that department. The "Talk of Hollywood," was she? You don't say. So word had finally got around that the fluffy bunny had what it takes. She'd seen it coming years ago. A hotshot. No, a bombshell. And the perfect choice to play the girl who turns Dorian Gray's head. Heavenly! That would've been it! Monroe as Sybil and she herself as Dorian. Yes, that would've been it, the perfect comeback role. And at some point in the movie, Monroe naked as a jaybird! May as well go the whole hog; anything less would be a waste. That would've been it! The great Garbo, ruined by the little Monroe. A triumph of acting! Goddammit, that would've been it. And she'd known it. Just known it. Only they didn't get it. But they never got anything, those schmucks. Always coming up with those bloody female roles. Dying of true love or some such pathetic nonsense. A corpse from the Seine carving out a career as a death mask with a moronic grin. If you're going for a mask, you may as well do it properly. She'd wanted to play a clown, a male clown who, beneath the makeup and silk pants, is actually a woman. And all his female admirers don't get why he won't reply. But Billy hadn't got it either. A traitor just like all the rest. All the nauseous memories were bubbling back up in her like yesterday's dinner. To think he'd dared to mention her in the same breath as all those old silent-movie has-beens. As if she were already written off, as if she'd already snuffed it! Just despicable. The truth is there was only one director she would've trusted blind, and he was dead as a doornail. For him she would've happily played a ghost, even a lamppost! He could've done anything he liked with her. Anything! But he didn't want to. He'd liked her, though, that time at Berger's place. And she'd liked him, all suntanned as he was. Just back from the South Pacific, tall and lean as ever. Stony broke, but staying at the Miramar with his German shepherd. Wonderfully arrogant and fantastically authoritarian. You never knew quite what he meant by something. The way he'd told her that his family had emigrated from Sweden centuries ago. And stood there all stiff as if that proved something. Simply adorable. But then later, on the pool table, he went all soft. Not surprising, considering how sloshed they both were. His sharp brown eyes, his red hair, his twitchy mouth, that voice rolling on. Her kinda squeeze. But it wasn't to be. Again that was just the beginning of the end. Five weeks later he was dead. Like all the people who'd really meant something to her: Alva, Moje, and then Murr too. They would've been good together. He hadn't been against the idea, at any rate. The fact he was into boys wasn't an obstacle. On the contrary: she'd never been a girl. How Cecil had mocked her about that. "Come on, you were never a boy." But then he'd dug out a photograph of her and seen something, a moment that didn't yet contain all the others that came after. Her gloomy childhood. The goddamn poverty, the ash-gray life on Söder. Father in one corner of the room bent over a newspaper, mother in another, mending clothes. Always a bad atmosphere. Then she did want Cecil to touch her after all. And above all not to let go until she cried *Nicht machen!* Schleesky never touched her. Even though his hands were as big as toilet lids. It was a damn shame.

The window displays of the fashion houses weren't as tasteful as they used to be. Where the devil could she get hold of a mauve carpet? And where was it again that she'd seen that painted furniture? But what's the point? Her apartment would still be boring as hell even with that in it. A shithole with a view of Central Park. There was nothing in it she liked. God, what a nightmare. She would have to move again. A vagabond existence, a life on the run, on the fringes. Always lonely, all on her ownsome. Going to bed with the chickens. Theater hardly ever, the movies only when there was no line. There was nothing for her to do. Virgos are said to be good at mending things. But the only thing she was good at was moving apartments. *C'est la vie.* No, it wasn't life. It was her. Cecil was right. She was wasting her best years. If only someone else could live for her, nourish her with their blood.

But who could it be? Even Jane's patience had run out last night. Then of all times! And to have the nerve to tally up in front of her the number of times she'd already called! Ten times? So what if she had! First Cecil's grotesque accusations, then the realization that she didn't have an ounce of energy left to wash her hair today. And then Jane's coldness towards her. Cecil, meanwhile, had gotten so clingy, it was just pathetic. Nearly as bad as Mercedes. Except that the old crow brought her bad luck to boot. That chiropractor she'd recommended. Dr. Wolf—his very name was a bad omen! She'd only actually had a problem with her wrist. But then he'd gone and started crunching away at her back and her hips as well. He'd pushed her whole bone structure out of place! Once he'd finished, not only were her hips out of joint, her mouth was lopsided as well. He'd almost done her in.

Should she get a coffee? But where? She was already too far downtown. Ah, dammit. Shame she hadn't thought of it sooner! Oh, and she had to go to the health food store! She was meant to go last week to pick up her nettle tea. How could she have forgotten something so important! Typical. So she did have something to do, a destination, after all. The health food store on the corner of Lexington Avenue and 57th Street. She *was* sick, after all. Maybe the funny-looking little brunette would be there. Not exactly a beauty, but so nice and trusting. Everything would be fine. What a marvelous idea. She could let her have some more Kleenex as well, and possibly mix her up a vitamin cocktail. After that she would call Jane and summon her to lunch at Colony's. Give her another chance. Or simply go to the Three Crowns on her own and eat smorgasbord. No deadly dull steamed vegetables, no grilled chicken for once. Afterwards treat herself to a nice whiskey at the Peacock Gallery and smoke her way through a pack of Kent Gold. She could go to the tailor's and have some new pants made to measure. Yes, she could even call Cecil and ask him to track down a sweater in dusty pink. He would probably manage it too. He was so vivacious and so tremendously capable and so terribly interested—in things and in people. So why the devil he wanted to spend time with her was a mystery. She knew better than anyone how unbelievably boring she was. After all, she was the one who had to put up with it the whole time. Couldn't just hang up when it got too much for her. Couldn't get away from herself. Sadly that wasn't an option. Ah, how she'd love to have a break from herself. Be someone else. That was the good thing about all the damn filming. It was handy when there was a script. Schleesky wasn't a particularly gifted writer, of course. But better a bad master than none at all. And there had been a fair few men. Into double digits, certainly. The women didn't count. They were on a different page. Perhaps Cecil was too. She liked him, at any rate. Who else could she say that of? A crime that he hadn't simply grabbed her by the scruff of the neck and led her up the aisle. Instead the fool had waited for a yes. That he hadn't realized she had to be forced into happiness. That all she needed was a kick up the ass! That she'd simply forgotten how to say yes. Of course she wanted to make movies. But she was entitled to wait for decent offers. She owed herself that, after that disaster with the bathing costume. It's just it wasn't that easy to judge what was a decent offer. Madame Chichi in "The Magic Mountain"? Marie Curie and her X-rays? Her intuition had deserted her. Just like that. And that devoted creep Schleesky, sure, he was good at getting her a car and a bottle of vodka in the middle of the night, but where roles were concerned he was anything but helpful. He was a bloody tyrant, obviously. That was the glorious thing about him. For a small man he had very big hands. He could order everyone around with them. Without even raising his voice. And everyone was shit-scared of him. A Cerberos or Cerberus, or whatever its name was. But someone who at least knew what he wanted. The way he looked at her sometimes. With cold fish eyes, as if she wasn't even there.

There it was now, next to the automat. Her destination, her lighthouse, her beloved health food store. And she was in luck.

The little brunette was there. And she already had the tea in her hand. You could count on her. The white coat really suited her as she leaned forward. But why the strange expression on her face? "My goodness, Miss Garbo, you don't look at all well." What the hell? "What? Have I changed that much?" A look of horror. "No, no, not at all." Now she was playing it down, trying to erase what had been said. But she knew what she'd heard. Oh God, she had to get out of here right away. Take the tea. It was already paid for anyway. And out. What a nightmare. Shit. She obviously looked a wreck. Worse than usual anyhow. She had to see for herself. Where, though? A mirror in the store window. Shit. What a sight! It was true, she looked hideous, just awful. Red eyes, red nose, wrinkles, more of them than ever before. Her neck all saggy. Lines everywhere that would be wrinkles in no time. Furrows, more like, deep crevices around her mouth from the goddamn smoking. Ones that no mask-maker could disguise. The marble was crumbling. The firm contours she still had would soften and be gradually lost. The role of the death mask would've suited her well. If you died young you at least had that consolation. She'd actually kept Murr's mask.

The lengths she'd gone to for this face. Had her hair-line straightened, her teeth fixed, her hairstyle and hair color changed. No wonder the bastards imagined it belonged to them. She only need blink an eye and the whole world was interpreting it. Her smile, mysterious. Her eyes, prophetic. Her cheekbones, divine. What complete bullshit. Adoration always spelled the beginning of the end. After that you just became an effigy or a martyr. Christ. So much for goddess. A tarted-up ass, that's what she'd been all these years. Somebody'd missed a good man in her. Nice and tall with broad shoulders, huge hands and feet. But they didn't want that body. In fact they'd taken to their heels when they'd seen it half-naked. An oversized pedestal, a support system for this goddamn face of hers! That was her true enemy. So much for marble. Nothing but a mask, an empty vessel. They were so hell-bent on finding out what was behind it. Nothing was behind it. Nothing!

But now it occurred to her: it wasn't the bathing suit! That hadn't been the problem, as she'd always thought. It wasn't the bathing suit but the damn bathing cap! That blasted strap under her chin which left an imprint on her skin. Her flesh was already soft there, a little bit slack. Aging started early. Basically at birth. It was all too late now anyway. To hell with it! Who cares. A cigarette would be good now. Bring them on, those little sticks of death! Father always used to say tomorrow will be better. And then he'd died. The last ten years had been difficult enough. The next ten would just be horrendous. She was so tired of everything. Even tired of being tired. Others had husbands, children, or memories. She had nothing besides her accursed fame and her lousy money that condemned her to not having to go to work on a Monday in April, to some office downtown, to some dusty studio in Culver City, to anywhere. The truth was her life was over. So much for a woman with a past. A woman without a future, that's what she was. A rudderless ship, always alone. Poor little Garbo! A hopeless case. Once a crowd puller, now a stray dog roaming the streets of Manhattan day in, day out, that cesspool of a city that reeked of trash even in April. But where the hell was she meant to go? Her face was known the world over. She could hide under a fishing hat or wrap herself in a full-length seal-fur coat, it made no difference; sooner or later she was discovered. There were vultures everywhere. It was only ever a matter of time. No, she was glad it was over. That it had been her decision. The time comes when you have more to lose than to gain. She'd worked hard. Never used to have any time. Well she had plenty now, just not the foggiest fart what to do with it. The East River was too filthy for anyone to want to drown themselves in it. A lot of women lost their mind. Not her, unfortunately. She just got sick. Or perhaps she'd been crazy for ages and simply hadn't noticed. Or dead even? Who knows, maybe for years now. Had she ever even been young? She couldn't remember. She could never remember anything. Except the sense of having already seen and experienced everything: the mountains of mail, the hum of the spotlights, the flash guns, the whole damn circus. Los Angeles was one long nightmare. There was no place on earth more boring. A godforsaken city without sidewalks. For crying out loud! How often had she had her chauffeur drive her the five hours up to Santa Barbara, just to have a bit of a stroll around, only to realize that she couldn't stop for a cup of tea anywhere there either. That there too the hounds were lying in wait everywhere. All she wanted was to be left in peace. But how come she had no one to take care of her? How come she didn't have a husband and children? All the people she loved died. And the ones who still admired her were old. As old as she was. She should've done like Murr. Sold everything and disappeared for good. It didn't necessarily need to be the South Pacific. It was coming back that spelled the end for him. A truck coming in the opposite direction, an embankment. All the others were uninjured, the chauffeur and the little Filipino who'd been at the wheel. The German shepherd had just run off. It was probably still roaming the valley to this day. The back of Murr's lovely head completely crushed. There was no sign of that, though, when he lay there in the funeral parlor, in his gray suit, his proud, noble face plastered with gaudy makeup like some old Berlin faggot. A stick-thin, dolled-up corpse surrounded by wreaths and crosses crafted from gardenias. Here, even the dead were made up as if for Technicolor. And all around, masses of empty garden chairs with those waxy, brightly patterned chintz cushions, which no one wanted to sit on. Only a handful of old fools turned up anyway. The last of the faithful. Fire or earth, that was the question. She hadn't even made up her mind on that. Ah, what she would give to be able to turn back the clock! And rather than missing the boat, to get married or even make another movie! She'd wanted to, after all! She'd even done screen tests. She'd recited her lines nicely in La Brea, the wind in her hair from the machine. Weren't they all delighted? And hadn't James said to her, "Miss Garbo, you're still the world's most beautiful woman?" And he really meant it. That wasn't even all that long ago. Two or three years. So close. What was it again? A duchess who was unlucky in love and became a nun. Whatever. She was living the life of a nun now anyway. Although it had been nice with Cecil. Queers were simply better lovers. The way he'd grabbed her by the hair and pulled until it hurt. Sometimes he just knew what she needed. She'd come so close. She'd have played any old nonsense. She'd worked her ass off, even done upper-arm workouts. But no, whenever she thought it was about to happen, something got in the way. It was like she was jinxed! Schleesky was always saying she was like Duse. She'd hidden herself away for eleven whole years too, and then returned to the stage. Notched up triumphs like never before. What year were they now again? 1952, dammit. So her eleven years were up. It was eleven lousy years since all the world had seen her in the pool and laughed at her. And now, what was she now? A woman with nothing to wear. An out-of-work actress. A living fossil. A ghost who wandered around midtown in broad daylight on the lookout for dusty-pink cashmere sweaters and some kind of meaning! A zombie, buried alive in these ravines, these dreary straight streets of towering red-brick buildings. To think of all the things she'd tried! Astrology, theosophy, even psychoanalysis—with Dr. Gräsberg, the only Swedish psychoanalyst in the whole of West Hollywood. How he told her after a few weeks that she was suffering from narcissistic personality disorder. Genius! And as she walked out, there was that poster of her plastered above the highway, larger than life. With that, how could you *not* have a disorder? She'd never gone back. In any case she didn't like to see her soul laid bare. In fact, Cecil doubted she even had one. He was probably right. She was probably really just a bad person. Yes, that's what she was: a bad person with bad manners. She wouldn't change now. Had he ever really believed she could play his wife? An offer of a part, all the same. Her last one. Now it was too late for anything. How long had she been old, though? It couldn't be that long. When had it started, this blasted aging? When she started getting excited about the spring. In the past it had always left her cold. She only used to miss the winter. That single withered dead tree in the backyard of her apartment on San Vicente Boulevard, her winter tree. How often had she imagined that the cold had made it leafless, and that soon there would be snow on its branches. But of course it never came. How could it? In friggin' California! Instead what you got was the rain after Christmas, when it pissed down until the canyon overflowed. You could leave everything behind: your parents, your language, your nationality, just not the climate of your childhood. But then: roses blooming in April, the sweet scent of orange blossom. The damp, foggy days in Mabery Road, mornings on the beach, the only place you could go for a walk. In the end, all her attempts to get away were defeated by the climate. And where had she wound up? In this crummy city that stank of formaldehyde, sweat, and garbage. When she came here for the first time she'd been a youngster, still wet behind the ears. It was summer, so scorching hot that you couldn't go out. She thought she would die. At night she didn't get a wink of sleep because of the noise of the garbage being crushed in the yard. Just lay there listening to the vile chomping of the infernal machine, the sirens of the fire trucks, the honking of the cars, that nerve-shattering din. She could've happily drowned herself in the bath, only the room didn't have one. And now? Now this hole of a city was the only home she still had. She wasn't dead. The dead didn't catch colds, as far as she knew. No, she was alive. She was still alive.

And that was the problem. California then? Or Europe after all? Staying here wasn't an option. Perhaps start small. One step at a time. First go home, make tea, call Jane, wash her hair. Then maybe California. With a detour to Palm Springs. Then in summer over to Europe. Nice is supposed to be such a lovely island.

Lesbos

THE LOVE SONGS OF SAPPHO

* *The songs of Sappho were composed during Greece's Archaic period in around 600 B.C. on the island of Lesbos in the eastern Aegean.*

† *Although Sappho's songs were probably written down immediately after her death on Lesbos in such a way that they could be performed again, nothing remains of the notation of the musical accompaniment. It may already have been lost long before Alexandrian scholars in the third and second centuries before Christ published her known work, which at the time was split between various Athenian editions and anthologies, in complete editions with critical commentaries. A comment by Philodemus of Gadara from the first century suggests that, in his day, hetaerae would sing Sappho's songs at banquets and during love play.*

Her poetry is presumed to have been lost at some point during the Byzantine era—by an effective combination of sheer neglect and willful destruction. The philosopher Michael Italicus, writing in the first half of the twelfth century, refers to Sappho in a way that implies he was familiar with her work. Yet the scholar John Tzetzes, writing around the same time, mentions that her poems are lost. Some believe they were burned in the year 1073 under Pope Gregory VII or obliterated in the sack of Constantinople in the Fourth Crusade in 1204; others speculate that her texts were destroyed on the orders of Bishop Gregory of Nazianzus back at the end of the fourth century, while still others hold that it must have been even earlier, as her poems were not quoted by any of the later grammarians.

Studies of numerous albeit fragmentary papyri have uncovered a considerable number of additional texts in recent years.

As Nebuchadnezzar II is plundering Jerusalem, Solon ruling Athens, Phoenician seafarers circumnavigating the African continent for the first time and Anaximander postulating that an indefinite primal matter is the origin of all things and that the soul is air-like in nature, Sappho writes:

> He seems to me equal to the gods that man
> whoever he is who opposite you
> sits and listens close
>   to your sweet speaking
>
> and lovely laughing—oh it
> puts the heart in my chest on wings
> for when I look at you, even a moment, no speaking
>   is left in me
>
> no: tongue breaks and thin
> fire is racing under skin
> and in eyes no sight and drumming
>   fills ears
>
> and cold sweat holds me and shaking
> grips me all, greener than grass
> I am and dead—or almost
>   I seem to me.
>
> But all is to be dared, because even a person of poverty ...

Buddha and Confucius are not yet born, the idea of democracy and the word "philosophy" not yet conceived, but Eros—Aphrodite's servant—already rules with an unyielding hand: as a god, one of the oldest and most powerful, but also as an illness with unclear symptoms that assails you out of the blue, a force of nature that descends on you, a storm that whips up the sea and uproots even oak trees, a wild, uncontrollable beast that suddenly pounces on you, unleashes unbridled pleasure and causes unspeakable agonies—bittersweet, consuming passion.

There are not many surviving literary works older than the songs of Sappho: the down-to-earth Epic of Gilgamesh, the first ethereal hymns of the Rig Veda, the inexhaustible epic poems of Homer and the many-stranded myths of Hesiod, in which it is written that the Muses know everything. "They know all that has been, is, and will be." Their father is Zeus, their mother Mnemosyne, a Titaness, the goddess of memory.

We know nothing. Not much, at any rate. Not even whether Homer really existed, or the identity of that author whom we for the sake of convenience have dubbed "Pseudo-Longinus," who quotes Sappho's verses on the power of Eros in the surviving fragments of his work on the sublime, thereby preserving her lines for future generations, namely us.

We know that Sappho came from Lesbos, an island in the eastern Aegean situated so close to the mainland of Asia Minor that, on a clear day, you might think you could swim across—to the coast of the immeasurably rich Lydia of those days, and from there, in what is now Turkey, to that of the immeasurably rich Europe of today.

Somewhere there, in the lost kingdom of the Hittites, must lie the origins of her unusual name, which either means "numinous," "clean," or "pure source," or—if you trace its history back by a different route—is a corruption of the ancient Greek word for sapphire and lapis lazuli.

She is said to have been born in Eresus, or perhaps in Mytilene, in about the year 617 before our calendar began, or possibly thirteen years earlier or five years later. Her father was called Scamander or Scamandronymus, or otherwise possibly Simon, Eumenus, Eerigyius, Ecrytus, Semus, Camon, or Etarchus, according to the Suda, a highly eloquent but not very reliable Byzantine encyclopedia from the tenth century.

We know she had two brothers named Charaxus and Larichus, and perhaps a third named Eurygius, and that she was of noble birth, since her youngest brother Larichus was a cupbearer in the Prytaneion in Mytilene, a post reserved only for the sons of aristocratic families.

We believe her mother was called Cleïs and that Sappho had a daughter of the same name, even though the word, which she uses when addressing the beloved girl in a poem, can also mean slave.

Nowhere does Sappho refer to a husband. The name "Kerkylas of Andros Island" mentioned in this connection in the Suda has to be a smutty joke by the Attic comic poets, who undoubtedly took pleasure in ascribing to her, of all women, a husband with a name sometimes rendered as "Dick Allcock from the Isle of Man." The legend of her unhappy, even self-destructive love for a young ferryman named Phaeon, later embellished by Ovid in his *Letters of Heroines*, must date from the same time.

We know from an inscribed chronicle dating from the third century before Christ that at some point—when exactly is not recorded on the Parian marble tablet—she fled by ship to Syracuse. We can conclude from another source that it was in around 596 B.C., when Lesbos' fortunes were in the hands of the Cleanactidai clan.

Seven or eight years later, when the island was under the rule of the tyrant Pittacus, she must have returned from exile and founded a women's circle in Mytilene, which may have been a cultish community set up to honor Aphrodite, a symposium of fellow females bearing an erotic attachment to one another, or a marriage preparation school for daughters of noble birth: no one knows for sure.

No other woman from early antiquity has been so talked about, and in such conflicting terms. The sources are as sparse as the legends are manifold, and any attempt to distinguish between the two virtually hopeless.

Every age has created its own Sappho. Some even invented a second in order to sidestep the contradictions of the stories: she was variously described as a priestess in the service of Aphrodite or the Muses, a hetaera, a man-crazed woman, a love-crazed virago, a kindly teacher, a gallant lady; by turns shameless and corrupt, or prim and pure.

Her fellow countryman and contemporary Alcaeus described her as "violet-haired, pure, honey-smiling," Socrates as "beautiful," Plato as "wise," Philodemus of Gadara as "the tenth Muse," Strabo as "a marvelous phenomenon," and Horace as "masculine," but there is now no way of knowing what exactly he meant by that.

A papyrus from the late second or early third century for its part claims that Sappho was "ugly, being dark in complexion and of very small stature," "contemptible," and "a woman-lover."

At one time bronze statues of her were common; even today, silver coins still bear her laurel-crowned profile, a water jug from the school of Polygnotos portrays her as a slim figure reading a scroll, and a gleaming black vase from the fifth century before Christ shows her as tall in stature, holding an eight-stringed lyre in her hand as if she had just finished playing or were just about to start.

We do not know how Sappho's verses sounded in Aeolic—the most archaic and tricky of the extinct ancient Greek dialects, in which the initial aspiration was omitted from words—when they were sung at a wedding ceremony, at a banquet or in the women's circle, accompanied by a stringed instrument: the hushed sound of a plucked phorminx or the festive ring of the cithara, the deep tones of the barbitos or the harp-like strains of the pectis, the high tones of a magadis or the dull resonance of a tortoiseshell lyre.

All we know is that the word "lyric" derives from one of these instruments, the lyre, and was coined by Alexandrian scholars some three hundred years after Sappho's death. It was they who dedicated to her an entire edition in eight or nine books, many thousands of lines on several rolls of papyrus, arranged according to meter, several hundred poems, of which only a single one has come to us intact, because the rhetorician Dionysius of Halicarnassus, who lived in Rome during the reign of Augustus, quotes it in full in his treatise *On Literary Composition* as an example worthy of admiration. Other than that, four consecutive stanzas were recorded by the scholar known as Pseudo-Longinus; five stanzas of another poem were successfully reassembled from three different papyrus fragments; four stanzas of another were discovered in 1937 carelessly scrawled on a palm-sized potsherd by an Egyptian schoolboy in the second century before Christ; fragments of a fifth and a sixth poem were preserved on a tattered early medieval parchment, and large portions of a seventh and eighth were recently discovered on strips of papyrus forming part of the cartonnages used for the preservation of Egyptian mummies or as book covers, although the deciphering of one of the two poems still divides the throng of experts to this day.

A handful of words or isolated lines cited by grammarians like Athenaeus and Apollonius Dyscolus, the philosopher Chrysip-

pus of Soli or the lexicographer Julius Pollux to illustrate a certain style, a particular item of vocabulary or the meter named
after her, were provided by the large-format codices of medieval
scribes—the rest is nothing more than scraps: a scattering of
stanzas one or two lines long, fragmentary verses, words plucked
from their context, single syllables and letters, the beginning or
end of a word, or a line, nowhere near a sentence, let alone a
meaning.

> ....
> and I go ...
> ...
> ... immediately ...
> ......
> ... for ...
> ... of harmony ...
> ... the chorus, ...
> ... clear-sounding
> ...
> ... to all ...
> ...

It is as if, in the places where the singing has faded away and the
words are missing, where the papyrus scrolls are rotten and torn,
dots had appeared, first singly, then in pairs, and soon in the vague
pattern of a rhythmic triad—the notation of a silent lament.

These songs have fallen silent, turned to writing, Greek characters borrowed from the Phoenician: dark majuscules, carved into
clayey earthenware in a clumsy schoolboy hand or copied onto
the pith of the woody wetland grass by a diligent professional using a reed pen; and delicate minuscules, written on the pumice-
smoothed, chalk-bleached skins of young sheep and stillborn
goats: papyrus and parchment, organic materials which, once
exposed to the elements, eventually decompose like any cadaver.

...
... nor ...
... desire ...
... but all at once ...
... blossom ...
... desire ...
... took delight ...

Like forms to be filled in, these mutilated poems demand to be completed—by interpretation and imagination, or by the deciphering of more of the loose papyrus remnants from the garbage dumps of Oxyrhynchus, that sunken town in central Egypt where a meter-thick layer of dry sand preserved these rock-hard, worm-eaten fragments—fragile, creased, and tattered from being rolled and unrolled—for nearly one thousand years.

We know that people wrote on papyrus scrolls in tightly packed columns without spaces between words, punctuation, or guidelines, making even well-preserved items hard to decipher. *Divinatio*, in the ancient art of the oracle, was the gift of prophesying the future by observing bird migrations and interpreting dreams. Nowadays, in papyrology, it refers to the ability to read a line where all that is visible are faded fragments of ancient Greek letters.

The fragment, we know, is the infinite promise of Romanticism, the enduringly potent ideal of the modern age, and poetry, more than any other literary form, has come to be associated with the pregnant void, the blank space that breeds conjecture. The dots, like phantom limbs, seem intertwined with the words, testify to a lost whole. Intact, Sappho's poems would be as alien to us as the once gaudily painted classical sculptures.

In total, all the poems and fragments that have reached us, as brief, mutilated, and devoid of context as they are, add up to no more than six hundred lines. It has been calculated that around 7 percent of Sappho's work has survived.

It has also been calculated that around 7 percent of all women feel attracted solely or predominantly to women, but no calculation will ever be able to establish whether there is any correlation here.

The history of symbols contains a number of markers of the unknown and indeterminate, of the absent and lost, of the void and the blank: the zero on the corn lists of the ancient Babylonians, the letter x in an algebraic equation, the dash used when someone's words are abruptly interrupted.

> ...   .
> goatherd   longing   sweat
> ...   .
> ... roses ...
> ...

Aposiopesis—the technique of suddenly breaking off midsentence—we know is a rhetorical device which Pseudo-Longinus, too, will certainly have written about in that part of his treatise *On the Sublime* that has been lost owing to the carelessness of librarians and bookbinders. If someone stops speaking, starts stuttering and stammering or even falls silent, it suggests he is overcome by feelings of such magnitude that inevitably words fail him. Ellipses open up any text to that vast obscure realm of sentiments that cannot be verbalized or that capitulate in the face of the words available.

> ... my darling one ...

We know that the letters Emily Dickinson wrote to her friend and future sister-in-law Susan Gilbert had a series of passionate passages deleted from them, prior to publication, by her niece

Martha, Gilbert's daughter, who omitted to indicate these deletions. One of these censored sentences from June 11, 1852 reads: "If you were here—and Oh that you were here, my Susie, we need not talk at all, our eyes would whisper for us, and your hand fast in mine, we would not ask for language."

Wordless, blind understanding is as much a firm topos of love poetry as is the wordy evocation of unfathomable feeling.

Sappho's words, where decipherable, are as unambiguous and clear as words possibly can be. At once sober and passionate, they tell, in an extinct language which has to be resurrected with each translation, of a heavenly power that, twenty-six centuries on, has lost none of its might: the sudden transformation, as wondrous as it is merciless, of a person into an object of desire, rendering you defenseless and causing you to leave your parents, spouse, and even children.

> Eros the melter of limbs (now again) stirs me—
> sweetbitter unmanageable creature who steals in

We know that the categorization of desire according to whether its protagonists were of the same or different genders was a concept foreign to the ancient Greeks. Rather, what mattered to them was that, in sexual relations, the role of each of the persons involved mirrored their social one, with adult men taking an active sexual role, while youths, slaves, and women remained passive. The dividing line in this act of control and submission ran not between the sexes, but between those who penetrate and possess, and those who are penetrated and possessed.

Men are not mentioned by name in the surviving poetry of Sappho, whereas many women are: Abanthis, Agallis, Anagora, Anactoria, Archeanassa, Arignota, Atthis, Cleïs, Cleanthis, Dica,

Doricha, Eirana, Euneica, Gongyla, Gorgo, Gyrinna, Megara, Mica, Mnasis, Mnasidica, Pleistodica, Telesippa. It is they whom Sappho sings about, with tender devotion or flaming desire, with burning jealousy or icy contempt.

> Someone will remember us
> I say
>   even in another time

We think we know that Sappho was a teacher, even though the first source to refer to her as such is a papyrus fragment dating from the second century A.D., which reports, seven hundred years after her death, that she had taught girls from the best families in Ionia and Lydia.

There is nothing in any of Sappho's surviving poetry to suggest an educational setting, although the fragments contain descriptions of a world in which women come and go, and there is often mention of farewells. The place seems to be one of transition, which led some to interpret it as hosting the female equivalent of the more widely attested Greek practice of pederasty. This reading also conveniently enabled the undeniable presence of female eroticism in poetry to be accounted for as a form of preparation for the main focus, the undisputed culmination of that teaching, namely marriage.

We do not know the exact nature of the relationship between Hannah Wright and Anne Gaskill, whose marriage was recorded without comment in the Register of Marriages of the parish of Taxal in northern England on September 4, 1707, though we do know that the expression "Where you go I will go" commonly used in Christian marriage ceremonies is borrowed from the words spoken by the widowed Ruth to her mother-in-law Naomi in the Old Testament.

We also know that in 1819, in the court case involving the two headmistresses of a Scottish girls' boarding school who—a pupil had alleged—had engaged in improper and criminal acts on one another, Lucian's *Dialogues of the Hetaerae* was quoted to show that sex between women was actually possible. In it the hetaera Clonarion asks the cithara player Leaina about her sexual experience with "a rich woman from Lesbos" and in particular presses her to reveal what exactly she had done with her and "using what method." But Leaina counters: "Don't question me too closely about these things, they're shameful; so, by Aphrodite, I won't tell you!"

The chapter ends at this point, the question goes unanswered, and so what women do with one another remains both unuttered and unutterable. At any rate the two teachers were acquitted of the charge, as the judge came to the conclusion that the transgression of which they were accused was not actually possible: Where there is no instrument there can be no act, where there is no weapon there can be no crime.

For a long time, what women do with one another could only be regarded as sex and therefore an offence if it mimicked sexual intercourse between a man and a woman. The phallus marked the sexual act, and where it was absent there was nothing but an unmarked blank, a blind spot, a gap, a hole to be filled like the female sexual organ.

For a long time, this empty place was occupied by the concept of the "tribade," that specter that haunts the writings of men, namely a masculine-acting woman who had sex with other women with the help of a monstrously enlarged clitoris or a phallic aid. As far as we know, no woman has ever described herself as a tribade.

We know that words and symbols change their meaning. For a long time, three dots in a row along the writing baseline designated something lost and unknown, then at some point also something unuttered and unutterable; no longer only something omitted or left out, but also something left open. Hence the three dots became a symbol that invites one to think the allusion to its conclusion, imagine that which is missing, a proxy for the inexpressible and the hushed-up, for the offensive and obscene, for the incriminating and speculative, for a particular version of the omitted: the truth.

We also know that in ancient times the symbol for omissions was the asterisk—the little star that only in medieval times took on the task of linking a place in a text to its associated margin note. As Isidore of Seville writes in the seventh century in his *Etymologies*: "The asterisk is placed next to omissions, so that things which appear to be missing may be clarified through this mark." Nowadays the asterisk is sometimes used as a means of including as many people as possible and their sexual identities. The omission becomes an inclusion, the absence a presence, and the empty place a profusion of meaning.

And we know that in ancient times the verb *lesbiazein*, "to do it like women from Lesbos," was used to mean "to violate or corrupt somebody" and to refer to the sexual practice of fellatio, which was assumed to have been invented by the women of the island of Lesbos. Even Erasmus of Rotterdam, in his collection of ancient sayings and expressions, renders the Greek word as the Latin *fellare*, meaning "to suck," and concludes the entry with the comment: "The term remains, but I think the practice has been eliminated."

Not long after that, at the end of the sixteenth century, Pierre de Bourdeille, seigneur de Brantôme, comments in his pornographic novel *The Lives of the Gallant Ladies*: "'Tis said how that Sappho the Lesbian was a very high mistress in this art, and that in after times the Lesbian dames have copied her therein, and continued the practice to the present day." From then on the empty space had not only a geographical but also a linguistic home, although the term *amour lesbien* remained in common use until the modern age as a term describing the unrequited love of a woman for a younger man.

We know that the two young poetesses Natalie Clifford Barney and Renée Vivien were disappointed when, in late summer 1904, they fulfilled a long-cherished dream and visited the isle of Lesbos together. When they finally reached the port of Mytilene, French chansons were blaring from a phonograph, and both the visual appearance of the island's female inhabitants and the crudeness of their idiom were at odds with the poetesses' noble imaginings of this place so frequently evoked in their own poems. Nevertheless, they rented two neighboring villas in an olive grove, went for long moonlit and sunlit walks, rekindled their love that had grown cold some years earlier, and talked about setting up a school of lesbian poetry and love on the island.

The idyll ended when a third woman—a jealous and possessive baroness with whom Vivien was in a liaison—announced she was on her way, and a telegram had to be sent to stop her. Barney and Vivien separated. Back in Paris, their mutual Ancient Greek teacher served from then on as the bearer of their secret letters.

We know that, in 2008, two female residents and one male resident of the island of Lesbos unsuccessfully attempted to introduce a ban on women not originally from the island naming themselves after it or being named after it by others: "We object to the arbitrary use of the name of our homeland by persons of sexual deviation." The presiding judge rejected the application and ordered the three Lesbians to bear the court costs.

Who, these days, is still familiar with the "Lesbian rule" alluded to by Aristotle in his *Nicomachean Ethics*, used in cases where general laws cannot be applied to concrete situations, following the example of the master builders of Lesbos, who used a leaden rule that "can be bent to the shape of the stone," since it was better, in a concrete situation, to have a crooked but functioning rule than to follow an ideal which is smooth and straight but useless.

And who, these days, is still familiar with the Sapphic stanza, that four-line verse form comprising three hendecasyllabic lines of matching structure, consisting of trochees with a dactyl inserted in third place, and an adonic as the fourth line, in which each line starts directly with a stressed syllable, every line ending is feminine, and the solemn dignity so characteristic of this meter yields at the end to a sense of reassurance or even serenity.

For a long time terms like "tribadism," "Sapphism," and "lesbianism" were used more or less synonymously in the treatises of theologians, jurists, and physicians, though in some instances they denoted a perverse sexual practice or shameless custom, and in others a monstrous anomaly or mental illness.

We do not know exactly why the term "lesbian love" has endured for some time now, only that this expression and its associations will fade in the same way as all its predecessors.

L is an apical consonant, *E* the vowel expelled most directly, *S* is a hissing, warning sound, *B* an explosive sound that blasts the lips apart ...

In German dictionaries, "lesbisch" ("lesbian") comes immediately after "lesbar" ("legible").

Behrenhoff

THE VON BEHR PALACE

* *From the fourteenth century, the Gützkow branch of the old von Behr family, also known as the "Swans' Necks" in reference to the motif on their coat of arms, owned a large amount of land in the area in Pomerania known as Busdorf, near Greifswald.*

In 1804, with the approval of the Swedish-Pomeranian government in Stralsund, the place was renamed "Behrenhoff," and cavalry captain Johann Carl Ulrich von Behr turned the farm estate into an entail in favor of his grandson Carl Felix Georg, with the stipulation that primogeniture should always apply in event of its inheritance.

The latter had a new, two-story mansion built behind the old farmhouse in the late classical style based on plans by Friedrich Hitzig, a pupil of Schinkel, which was completed in 1838. In 1896 the building was extended by Carl Felix Woldemar, who had been elevated to the Prussian rank of count in 1877, and the two single-story verandas enlarged, with another story added on top.

From 1936 to 1939, Countess Mechthild von Behr, widow of the last count, the Imperial District Administrator and longstanding member of parliament Carl Friedrich Felix von Behr, who died in 1933, placed the mansion at the disposal of the Confessing Church as a lecture venue. The theologian Dietrich Bonhoeffer is said to have been a guest there on several occasions.

† *On May 8, 1945 the mansion went up in flames. The burned-out ruins were used by the local residents as a source of building materials for new farmhouses.*

The nine-hectare landscaped park designed by Peter Joseph Lenné and laid out between 1840 and 1860 today has protected status.

I remember the open window. It is night, and the air is cool. An open window on a summer's night. No moon in the sky. Only the diffuse light of the street lamp. It smells of earth. Perhaps it has rained. I cannot remember.

It was July 31, says my mother. She is quite certain, because July 31 is Tante Kerstin's birthday, and that evening she was having a celebration in one of the old estate workers' cottages opposite. It definitely didn't rain, she adds. It was a fine day. Sunny the whole day. As you'd expect in July.

The weather records also show that it was a hot day, indeed that the whole summer was warm and exceptionally dry.

Summer 1984. It is my earliest memory: this I know, I think, I claim. I could telephone Tante Kerstin. She is still alive. As are my mother and both my fathers. The one who conceived me, and the one who, later that night, would cool my legs with ice and wrap them in gauze bandages.

I play in the cemetery between the mounds overrun with greenery. I hide behind the graves and headstones, I crouch between plants with tiny blue and white flowers. An elderly woman, shrunken from stooping, throws wilted blooms and dried-out wreaths onto the compost. She holds a tin watering can under the rusty water tap then disappears behind the box hedges.

I duck down, run my fingers over the smooth stone, feel the rough indentations of the chiseled letters and wait for the improbable. I wait to be found. I want to be found. I'm afraid of it.

Throughout my childhood we lived in villages, in rural localities that gave little hint of their more glamorous past. Then, too, we were living in a village, just a few steps from its one and only bus stop, on the first floor of the old verger's house next door to the towerless church with its high stone chancel. Our backyard was directly adjacent to the cemetery. Not even a fence separated the two compost heaps. In my memory, I was almost always alone. Alone in the graveyard, alone in the orchard surrounded by high red walls, alone on the heap of stones which, according to my mother, I kept jumping from on that day.

But no one came; the miracle, as always, failed to materialize. Instead I picked a few flowers from the little flower beds, plucked pansies out of the ground and extracted single tulips from their pointy plastic vases stuck in the earth.

I had some kind of inkling, but I did not know. Not, at least, that the flowers belonged to the absent, to the dead rotting in wooden boxes beneath the earth. When I took the posy home, my mother was cross and did not explain why.

I had no knowledge of death as yet. That people die, that I myself would one day die, lay beyond my imagination. When, some time later, my cousin let me in on this secret, I did not believe him. I was certain he had overheard something and misunderstood it, as he often did. He grinned. He was sure of himself.

I felt dizzy. I raced through the new-build apartment that was our home at the time, into the kitchen and asked my mother whether it was true that people really died, whether we would all die one day, in other words, me included. She nodded, said yes, and shrugged her shoulders. I looked at the trash can and, for some reason, imagined that the dead ended up in this container, as shriveled beings, to be carted off by the garbagemen. I clamped my hands over my ears, even though no one was speaking now, and ran into the hallway. Yellow light was shining through the ridged glass of the window onto the dusty green plants in the stairwell.

I keep my eyes closed on the ghost train at the funfair in a neighboring village. My parents let me go on it. Two of their pupils sit to the left and right of me, a boy and a girl.

As we plunge into the darkness, I cross my arms in front of my face. A cool draft brushes my skin. I hear a clattering, the jolting and rolling of the car, a scream. I feel the skin of my eyelids, squeeze my eyes even more tightly shut, hold my breath for a moment, hum and wait. An eternity goes by.

At some point someone taps me on the shoulder. My mother's voice says: It's over. I open my eyes. We are back outside. I kept my eyes closed the whole time, I say proudly. I cheated it. I cheated fear. What a waste of money, says my mother and lifts me out of the car.

I play in the garden among the apple trees. I pick masses of buttercups and stain my fingers with dandelion juice. By the compost heap I discover a spiky ball. It is breathing. It is alive.

When my mother sets a saucer of milk in front of the ball, it transforms into a wondrous creature. We crouch down. Black button eyes look at me. I feel my mother's hand on my head. A pointy nose sniffs out the milk. A tiny pink tongue darts out. The animal grunts and slurps. Its prickles bob up and down.

I enjoyed life. I was expecting nothing. My mother was expecting a baby. But I have no memory of a rounded belly or a man's hand stroking its curves. She must have been pregnant, the dates tell me. She was pregnant, the photographs show. One month after that July night which cannot have been cool, my brother would be born and my grandmother, having taken the telephone call from the hospital, would stand in the bedroom doorway in her midnight-blue dressing gown and speak his name for the first time.

I sat there in my grandparents' bed, heard the name, which meant nothing to me, and turned back to the lipsticks, an astonishing collection of small shiny cylinders which my grandmother kept in a case above the bed.

The bedroom window is open, but the door of the apartment is closed and locked, and the key is not hanging on the key holder or lying on the kitchen table. I have woken up and climbed out of my cot. I have opened the bedroom door and searched the whole apartment. All the rooms are dark, all the other windows closed: the semicircular dormer window in the living room, the skylight in the kitchen and the jet-black hole of the windowless box room which my father has turned into a small workshop.

There were no other rooms. The bathroom was downstairs on the ground floor. We shared it with Tante Viola from the top-floor apartment. We shared the bathroom, the roaring boiler, the four-footed bathtub and the raffia mat in front of it. Tante Viola worked in the school canteen in the old stables at the north end of the grounds, a yellow brick building with a stone horse's head looking down from either side of the entrance gate. Where once horses ate their hay, we now had our midday meal. We stood in long lines, the kindergarten children, the school pupils, the teachers, half the village. Tante Viola had bleached blonde hair, purple eye makeup, and a truck driver for a husband, who came home on Saturdays and left again on Sundays, a large faceless figure. The school was behind the grounds, two new buildings with long rows of windows. My parents and also Tante Kerstin taught there. The grounds were large and belonged to the palace that no longer existed. Neither Tante Kerstin nor Tante Viola was a real aunt. We just called them that.

The palace was not a real palace either. It was a mansion, an elongated two-story building, the center of the estate, with, next to it, a stable block, a sheep shed, a cattle shed as well as an outbuilding and two barns. An avenue of lime trees led directly to it from the Bear Gate on the village high street, through the northern part of the grounds, which was out of bounds for villagers.

My kindergarten stood on what would once have been the generous front drive, a grass-centered circle in front of an open portal that also served as a porch, surmounted by a balcony supported by eight pillars, with triangular gables over the windows, and Virginia creeper growing up the facade.

The window is open; the door of the apartment is locked and bolted. My arm stretches up, reaches for the door handle, grips it, pulls it downwards—but the door stays closed.

I remember the big wall cabinet in the living room, the toys lying around by the stove, the rocking chair in suspended motion, an oversized, tidy dolls' house. Only the bedroom window is open and the air outside cool.

The church was in the middle of the village, but everyone just walked on by. Nobody looked over the red brick wall, nobody glanced at the graves and crosses. Only a few stooped old women ever ventured through the creaking gate into the graveyard. We lived right next to the church. But none of it meant anything. Not the huge edifice of hewn granite and rough stone, not the vicarage diagonally opposite, not the wooden bell cage down at ground level, not the bell ringing on Sundays, not the lopsided rusty crosses in the churchyard, not the weathered burial chamber of the counts behind the wrought-iron gate, the crosses in amongst the ferns, the stone angels in half relief above a crumbling bench no one ever sat on, nor the plaque bearing the motto I did not understand, even that time when my mother read it out to me: "Love never fails." They were remnants of a past that, so it seemed, had been overcome once and for all.

It was an old, aristocratic family that had given the village its name, vassals of the counts of Gützkow and the dukes of Pomerania—"brave, beloved, and trusty knights," according to an old deed of enfeoffment.

They are words from a fairy tale. They appear in columns of dense writing in which the branches of the family trees go off in many directions. The von Behrs were squires and stewards, chamberlains and counts, provosts and professors, district and town councilors, curators and commanders, court tutors and cavalry captains, *valets de chambre* and young nobles in court service, soldiers, marshals, majors and captains, lieutenants— in the Polish war, in the Swedish household guard, in Danish or French service. A canoness and a prioress, a captain's wife, even a poetess. But most importantly they were the owners of this place, including their fief, their possessions, seeds, chattels, and livestock. A feudal estate which, for lack of an heir, passed back to the old ancestral line in which, since time immemorial, the firstborn had counted for more than those born later, and the daughters for virtually nothing. They had goods which they sold and exchanged, retained and acquired, collecting inter-est on them or pledging their shares in them. Sometimes they signed deeds of enfeoffment, affixed their seal to thick paper, a sticky mass, as red as ox blood: a dancing bear with a swan on either side.

My mother's ancestors were farmers, livestock and timber trad-ers, carters and master butchers, a forester, a pointsman, a sailor. My father's ancestors, my biological father, that is, were millers and master tailors, cartwrights and carpenters, a musketeer, a few doctors, a seamstress of fine fabrics, a fisherman, a railway guard, a chemist, an architect, a factory owner, an armaments manufac-turer, who after the war became a cemetery gardener.

We only lived in that village a year, but it is the first year I can re-member. It was not the cemetery but the grounds of the mansion that our yard backed on to, my mother says. And there were also the remains of a tumbledown wall, she adds.

Some said the mansion was demolished after the end of the war, others that it had burned down before the end of the war, along with its entire inventory: the magnificent chandeliers in the entrance hall, the leaded glass of the doors to the two drawing rooms, the dark furniture, the books, the silverware and the china, the gilt mirrors, the old maps and the gallery of ancestors with its massive portraits of serious-looking gentlemen on large horses.

We do not own any old things, any heirlooms. Only the house we live in is old. At night you can hear the marten in the attic. My parents are waiting for an apartment in the prefabricated building behind the swan lake. Three rooms, central heating and a bathroom with hot running water. They are on the waiting list. Time is short. The baby is due soon.

It was not uncommon for the old buildings to be in such a dilapidated state that they collapsed in the night, like the cooperative store the previous autumn. The roof had simply caved in. In the morning the door could only be opened with brute force. I remember the cluster of people gathered in front of it, shop assistants and customers, women in flowery house dresses carrying limp string bags, men who came and pulled tin cans out of the rubble. They loaded the dusty goods into wheelbarrows and piled the tinned food, bags of flour, and bottles that the milkman delivered in a dark, musty room on the ground floor of our building. An emergency sale got under way. The light was on all day. The ringing of the till could be heard all the way up to our apartment.

I was wearing sleeveless batiste pajamas with a pattern of tiny orange flowers. They had an elasticated waist. I remember the open window, the mild air, because it wasn't cool, it couldn't have been cool, and not so much as a breath of fresh air entered the room, for it was July, and Tante Kerstin's birthday, and why Tante Viola had not come to check on me I do not know. I was three and a half years old, nearly four. Four fingers stuck up straight, nearly a whole hand.

I have no memory of a pile of bricks, of a heap of stones in the yard which, that day, I apparently climbed on, higher and higher, and kept jumping down from. I see only the open window. The windowsill is level with my chest. I try to hoist myself up, but it is too high. I take a few steps back, think: Judith, you are not stupid, and say: Judith, you are not stupid. I keep repeating these words, first quietly to myself, then out loud. The words lead me into the kitchen. I take hold of the kitchen chair and slide it across the tiled floor. It makes a loud scraping noise. I drag it over the threshold, I haul and heave it over the orange living-room carpet, over the threshold into the bedroom, past my parents' big bed to the window, which is standing open. I think of little Häwelmann in the fairy tale, but my nightshirt is not a sail, nor is my cot on wheels. It stays put next to the heater all night. I peer through the bars. I stand at the rail. I am Häwelmann, but the moon, which, speaking in my mother's voice, asks, "Surely that's enough?" has disappeared behind a cloud. Its edges glow. No one can stop me. I clamber onto the chair, my feet in their slippers. Dark-blue corduroy ones. I climb onto the windowsill and crouch there. The toes of my slippers are pointing out into the open air. I don't wait. I don't wait for anything. I don't look at the lamp. I don't look at the branches of the apple trees. Only down. The pavement. The patch of greenery below me.

My mother leaves the hospital without a baby, takes the train to the new village, which has not only a bus stop but also a railway station. She walks past the church, on top of which there are storks feeding their young, past the co-op, a new building with bicycle racks on the concreted area in front. But the gossips in house dresses are already there. They look in her direction and whisper: a teacher from Behrenhoff who's just moved into the new block. They beckon her over and ask if the baby was stillborn. They ask in standard German and in dialect: Were 'e stillborn?

An old woman finds me. She leans on her walking stick, bends over me and says: A right pickle you've got yerself into, duck!

My mother comes home without a baby. She does not even come home, because while I am at my grandparents' for a week, my parents move to a newly built apartment in a neighboring village seven kilometers away, endlessly far away. Kilometers, that's the largest unit, as inconceivable as years. I am three and a half years old, nearly four, but this I only know because it is shortly before my fourth birthday that my brother has his first glimpse of daylight—or rather the strip lights in Greifswald women's hospital—and soon afterwards the light of the phototherapy lamp on his jaundiced skin. The apartment has a bathroom but no central heating. In the cellar there is some coal left over from the previous tenants. It is enough.

Like a snake, the umbilical cord had twined itself around the baby's neck and first delayed his entry into this world, then complicated it and ultimately so jeopardized it that the live birth of the infant, whose hands and lips had already turned blue, bordered on miraculous.

I remember a nightmare in which I am underwater, sinking ever deeper, a layer of ice above me. I remember a cartoon on the television where a woman dives into an empty swimming pool and, like a doll, shatters into pieces. Even today that image still sparks a nameless terror in me.

I do not know what it feels like to be dead. I ask the teacher in my new kindergarten, a tall woman with a shock of curls.

She shakes her head. I don't know, she says. I've never been dead.

I want to know what happens to the dead and buried. They rot. I do not understand the word.

Like a wrinkly apple which, as time goes by, gets infested and eaten up by worms and maggots, she explains.

I find myself thinking of the trash can in our kitchen, then she adds: You don't notice anything though. Because you're dead, of course.

Evil is the skin on heated-up milk, the thin layer of ice on the frozen village pond, the dozen shiny-black slugs in the yard. Death is an old woman in a flowery house dress. Goddesses of destiny wear a headscarf, walk with a stick and speak in dialect. They talk about stillborn babies, about a right pickle, and rake the graves of their prematurely deceased husbands.

The von Behrs were once brave, beloved, and trusty knights. Their palace burned down, say some. It was demolished, say others. The villagers looted it themselves and set it alight when the Russians came and the old countess had fled, says one elderly lady, who ought to know. They took whatever could be taken: the magnificent chandeliers in the entrance hall, the leaded glass of the doors to the two drawing rooms, the dark furniture, the books, the silverware and the china, the gilt mirrors, the old maps and the gallery of ancestors with its massive portraits of serious-looking men on large horses, the silver cigarette case bearing the count's crest: a black bear rampant on a gray escutcheon, its front paws raised as if in greeting, surmounted by a helmet topped by two swans facing away from one another with curved necks.

I land in a patch of stinging nettles. My slippers still on my feet, an ache in my legs. A numb feeling. The stinging of the nettles. The silhouette of a hunched old woman in the light of the street lamp. The asphalt shines. It has rained.

I read recently that stinging nettles grow wherever people settle, by walls and among debris. Like most prickly and thorny plants, they have traditionally been ascribed antidemonic properties. Pliny writes that the root of the stinging nettle can cure three-day fever if, as you dig it up, you utter the name of the sufferer, and whose child they are.

I did not know whose child I was.

I see the dazzling bedroom light, the cupboard with its woodgrain pattern beneath its smooth varnished surface. I lie on my back with my legs in the air like a beetle. I see my parents, larger than life. They do not look at me, only at my legs, which they wrap in gauze bandages. My legs hurt, my feet are numb. Their faces are bright patches with hairdos.

Nothing was broken. The X-ray images left no doubt about it. Nobody spoke of a miracle. Neither my mother nor the doctor in the nearby town. The nurse wrapped my sprained ankle in a zinc-paste bandage. My vaccination card, which she stamped, had three strips of plaster stuck on the first page. On them were written in block capitals my name and my new address in the village by the railway line, in my mother's handwriting, a clearly legible teacher's hand.

Nothing was broken, but I was unable to walk properly for many weeks. I hopped and hobbled, I held my arms out. My mother picked me up. Legs wide, I cling to her hips, inside her belly the unborn child.

Later on, my parents often talked about all the troubles my leap had caused them. But not about happiness or about the miracle, because miracles did not happen at that time, in that country.

I knew no god and no angels. The first time I saw one, in a colorful framed painting above the curiously short bed of an old woman, I was already going to school. The picture was a relic from a bygone age as dark as all the rooms in the estate workers' houses with their rough stone gables and masonry, as remote as a world in which children are led away over a wooden bridge by the light of the moon by a long-haired man, colorfully attired, with large wings, glowing cheeks, blonde curls, and shining eyes.

At supper I looked at my mother for a long time. Was she really my mother? Was it not possible that she was only pretending to have given birth to me, after days of pain, as she mentioned repeatedly? Was it not just as feasible that she had simply found me somewhere and kept me, or had taken me from my actual real mother, who was waiting for me somewhere, inconsolable, as in the song of Little Hans?

I watched her butter my bread, cut it into small pieces and put it on my board. I studied her brown eyes, her mouth that was hiding something. I ran into the bathroom and positioned myself between the two mirrors, stared at the image repeated ad infinitum and looked for similarities.

It was a riddle, but I did not even understand the question, the task before me. The question was an open window. The answer was an open window. A jump from a height of four meters.

Years later I am lying ill in bed at my grandparents'. It is the holidays. The guest room is unheated. I am in pain and running a fever. They call the doctor. A tall man, who lays his pale hand on my neck and studies me with a long, hard look. He has a soft voice. His eyes are so deep-set they look as though someone had pushed them back in their sockets, from where they now peer out all the more urgently, strangely enlarged by the glass of his spectacles. It is a look that is trying to tell me something. His hand slides a photograph out of his wallet. It shows a child with sturdy calves in white socks, a huge umbrella in her hand. I nod and am none the wiser. It is a riddle, but I do not even understand the question, the task before me. The child in the photograph is me. The doctor is my father, and is not my father.

More than thirty years later, one cold spring day, I hold a measuring stick up to the facade of the refurbished verger's house and am amazed that it is four meters exactly, to the last centimeter. The first-floor window has been widened. The old vicarage diagonally opposite is for sale. From its veranda you have an uninterrupted view of the open country, a flat landscape, meadows, fields with sandy, clayey topsoil. A man comes and points through the milky windowpanes. Saltpeter, he says. It sounds like a death sentence. Only now do I notice a white encrusted scum on the walls. It looks like an infectious disease.

For the first time I go into the church. On the north wall of the chancel is a painting of the jaws of hell. Frogs, snakes, and people are tumbling in, condemned souls who are devoured by the flames. And sitting in splendor in front of all this is a pigfaced prince of hell complete with scepter and lightning bolt.

Is the jump out of the window my earliest memory? I ask my mother about the hedgehog. The hedgehog appeared the year before, sometime in the autumn, says my mother. But I do remember the hedgehog, which has to mean that my earliest memory is of that curious creature, and not of that night in July.

The stone bears still stand supreme on their rendered pillars at the entrance to the grounds, their paws clutching the weathered escutcheons, the crest of the last counts. An avenue of lime trees leads into the grounds. The cobbles have almost sunk into the earth. A landscape full of rhododendrons, sweet chestnut trees and magnolias, with two copper beeches, even a red oak and a tulip tree. Spreading over the ground is a white carpet of flowering spring snowflakes, snowdrops, and anemones.

At the edge of the sports field I discover the moss-covered stones of a hip-height wall. It must be the remains of the palace. It must be the remains of the mansion, which only became a palace when the only part of it left standing was the cellar vault. In the southern part of the grounds, a pair of swans sit in front of two artificial islands, as if painted.

Babylonia

THE SEVEN BOOKS OF MANI

* *Mani was born in the year 216 in Babylonia, near Seleucia-Ctesiphon on the banks of the Tigris, to Persian parents, and was raised by his father in a Jewish-Christian baptism sect on the lower Euphrates. From his earliest youth he received revelations. At the age of twenty-four he left the Elcesaite religious community and started preaching, gained followers and made enemies. He proselytized throughout Babylonia, in Media, Ganzak, and Persia, in the land of the Indians and Parthians and on the fringes of the Roman Empire. Mani was patronized by the Sasanian ruler Shapur I and his son Hormizd I, before being imprisoned by their successor Bahram I at the behest of Zoroastrian priests in the year 276 or 277. He died on the twenty-sixth day of his incarceration. His corpse was mutilated and his severed head left to rot above the main gate of the city of Gundeshapur.*

Manichaeism spread beyond Mesopotamia to the whole of the Mediterranean region including Spain and North Africa, as well as into Asia Minor and central Asia and along the Silk Road, reaching as far as the Indian and Chinese empires.

Its syncretic teachings incorporated elements of Zoroastrianism in Persia, Gnostic Christianity in the west and Buddhism in the east. In late antiquity, Manichaeism was a global religion with followers on three continents.

† *There are barely any sources describing the demise of Manichaeism, as practically all its writings were destroyed during ancient times and the Middle Ages, the practice of the faith was suppressed everywhere, and its followers persecuted. From the year 382 onwards, in the western Roman Empire, any avowal of Manichaeistic faith was punishable by death. In the Chinese Empire, the religion was not banned until 843, and it persisted in some parts of East Turkistan until the thirteenth century, and in South China even into the sixteenth century.*

Although all Mani's books written in Eastern Aramaic once existed in translation in mission languages like Greek, Latin, Coptic, Arabic, Parthian, Middle Persian, Sogdian, Uygur, and Chinese, virtually nothing has survived of these texts. All that remains is the beginning of the Living Gospel, *portions of the* Fundamental Epistle, *some fragments of the* Book of Giants *and a few snippets of the sacred book written in Middle Persian, the* Shabuhragan. *So for a long time efforts to piece together Mani's teachings were dependent on the testimonies of the persecutors and on Arab encyclopedists of later times.*

It was not until 1902 that some poorly preserved fragments of original Manichaean manuscripts were recovered in the central Asian oasis of Turfan. Large parts of a Manichaean-Coptic library, found in 1929 near the Egyptian oasis of Faiyum, ended up in collections in Berlin and elsewhere. Some of these manuscripts that had not yet been analyzed, including the volume containing Mani's letters, were lost yet again in the process of shipment to the Soviet Union after the Second World War.

And if holy things really are only revealed to holy people, then it would be here—in the shimmering noon glare of a high desert sun, beneath the ragged date palms lining the banks of a sinuous tributary of the mighty many-branching Euphrates, which in late spring swells with the snowmelt from the northern mountains into a torrential river prone to burst its banks and dams, pumps vast masses of water into the impressive channels of the finer and finer branching irrigation system, which reaches into remote, indeed the remotest rain-deprived and rainless lowlands, fills diked basins, soaks fallow ground, makes bucket wheels turn and seeds sprout and flourish—and guarantees the two annual harvests that are the reason for this land's fame and riches: the corn, the mountains of pomegranates, figs, and dates that float downstream on countless hundreds of rafts, until the water course, reaching the marshy delta, is united with its twin river and flows, swollen, towards the sea.

Here is the land of the beginning, the alluvial land of civilization, to which our remote ancestor with his heavy skull and freed-up hands was once drawn, in the process driving his wide-jawed cousin with the nostril-like flared nasal orifices and the melancholy bulges above his primate's eyes ever further north, where he hid himself away in caves—armed with stone tools and bones gnawed bare—to die the unlamented death of his species. And out of the zigzag movements of the nomadic tribes there evolved a vague order: tribes became peoples who lined up their settlements along the meandering rivers like beads on a long, finespun thread, each town a kingdom in itself, a community of commoners who began to share the work and wages, the harvest, the yield—and, in the absence of stone, wood, and ore, built themselves a world of clay: mortar-rendered reed huts and simple round buildings for the shoeless peasants, square palaces for curly-bearded kings, wind-buffeted citadels and dust-swept ziggurats, avenues of blue-glazed bricks guarded by bull men and winged lions, gently raised reliefs of priests in long robes with crossed arms, densely inscribed clay tablets covered in dainty symbols like bird tracks in wet sand.

While those Adamitic tribes are still feeling the fleece of the wild sheep to test the woolen undercoat, snapping the ears of einkorn wheat off the stalks, collecting the husks of emmer wheat in brightly painted ceramic bowls and breaking up the earth with a crooked pickax prior to each new sowing, things, too, became more settled, supplies are accumulated and claimed as possessions, cattle are fenced in, wild horses tamed, land surveyed for the first time, and harvests eked out to supply the coming years. Tribal community is followed by tribal economy. Honey flows. Souls wander. The stone age is drawing to a close. Bronze shimmers, iron gleams, the age turns first golden, then gray. And the more settled those peoples become, the more restless grows their quest, their desire for truth and meaning, an inner agitation which is as novel as the sight of the never-changing horizon that swallows up the sun each evening. They gaze into the darkness and see no land, only the flickering patterns on the insides of their eyelids and the bottomless blackness punctuated by glowing specks that engulfs anything that dares approach it. The world is day and night, heat and cold, hunger, thirst, and repletion, a valiantly turning potter's wheel, a wooden cartwheel, the tip of a cane that works the wet clay as the ox plows the field.

In the beginning—only this much is certain—was work, the circling of the great perpetuum mobile, which, once in motion, preserves energy, causes the rivers to swell and flow into the sea and the water to rise up to the sky, feeds into the great cycle, the changing of the seasons, the return of the conceptual pairs that have been stepping up, two by two, since the dawn of history, to play heaven and earth, mother and father, brother and sister, a pair of deities, two monsters that hate each other's guts. The desolate emptiness of prehistory seems richer than the tedious law of opposites, which henceforward weighs like a curse on mankind, which from now on has to decide between gathering and hunting, plowing the field and tending the flock, stoking the fire and going to the well. No one can say what is awaiting understanding, there in the depths, at the very root of being. Whether, in the beginning, a storm of chaos reigned, or a gaping void, or both or neither, whether creation happened randomly or for a purpose, the result of a contest between different generations of gods, a battle between Old and Young.

The cosmologies that spring from here are as countless as they are contradictory. What unites them is the concept of the imperfection of this world. There is a rift, undeniably large, a painfully deep gulf between the gods and the people cast into this world, between the eternal, unblemished soul and corruptible and hence corrupted flesh. The questions, old though they may be, are more pressing than ever before: what man is, where he comes from, where he is going, when and why this world has heaped guilt upon itself.

For its guilt is proved by the drought that knows no end. The

days when the seeds yielded a twenty- to thirtyfold crop and
every spring rain transformed the steppe into a sea of flowers
are past. Water accumulates in the flooded fields, the harvest is
spoiled, while the unremitting current flushes more and more
sand onto the southern bank of the river, and the sea gradually
recedes, leaving behind nothing but scurfy marshland. Sometimes rain falls, sometimes not. When the water levels rise, even
just a cubit higher than usual, the floodwaters arrive too early, in-
undate the lowland, wash away the dikes and destroy the harvest,
then the currents breed nothing but hunger and agony—and the
memory of that great flood, on whose fatal waves a pitch-sealed
wooden box carrying a select few drifted towards a new era, an
age in which one of the gods conquered the others and, like a
king, issued laws: no alliance without conditions, no trust without a contract.

And yet the moods of that god are as fickle as the currents
of this river, and as contradictory as the auguries of the seers
who read the future in the twitching of lambs' livers and the
twinkling of the stars. For here, on this sweeping plain with its
drafty steppes and fertile river valleys where the pictures once
crystallized into writing, everything is full of signs that need deciphering and interpreting. They are tidings of fate, messages
from the sky, that truly endless sky above the steppe, from which
a voice now begins to speak: call it spirit, call it wind or breath!
When an angel speaks, one must listen. And so, in a palm grove
on the lower Euphrates, a child, barely any older than the boy
Jesus among the temple elders, cranes his neck and hears what
the voice has to tell him: "You are the apostle of the light, the
last prophet, the successor to Seth, Noah, Enos, Enoch, Sem,
Abraham, Zoroaster, Buddha, Jesus, Paul, and Elkesai—and the
one who will complete all their teachings." The revelation is like
a boast. This angel is bragging. And what is the child doing?
He is afraid and requests proof. So the angel does what angels
do. He comforts the boy, sends signs and miracles, makes palm

trees speak in the manner of men and vegetables cry like infants, and reveals to him one of those secrets which had hitherto been hidden from the world: that the fundamental drama of the universe was a battle between light and darkness, and this existence nothing but a transition between two eras.

Whoever wants to will understand. And the boy Mani wants to. He wants to take up the place assigned to him, to become the glorious culmination—to be the last in a line of great prophets. But since no one ever believed a child, he has to wait. What does a Chosen One do, whose time has not yet come? He prepares himself. He studies the teachings handed down from his predecessors. Great men, all of them, ascetics, prophets, semideities. They had all accomplished much, yet must have failed, since he was now appointed to finish their works.

Anyone can practice asceticism, renounce the world and resist the devil. Many have heard God's word and more than a few have proclaimed it. Yet even those angelic tidings are blown away by the wind. Who is supposed to gather them up and one day proclaim their wisdom if time disperses them? Words become verbiage, and a vision becomes a mirage. That which shall become truth must be written down, says the angel. That which shall remain truth must be written down, thinks Mani. Only the written word will be proved right and will endure, will weigh as heavy as the material on which it is captured, a chunk of black basalt, a terracotta tablet, the flattened fibers of the papyrus plant or the stiff leaf of a palm.

Years pass. Understanding forges a path for itself, a veil is lifted, content reaches for form, craftsmanship for art, the verbal for the written. A remarkably clear shape crystallizes in Mani's mind, a circle, as round as a compass drawing, as complete as his teachings, which reconcile the beginning with the end, cyclical thinking with linear.

Autumn is already well advanced when Mani's time finally

comes. The Euphrates lies there as ever in its winter bed, a feeble rivulet trickling along a groove in the wide, sandy river bed, making it easy to forget that it was its water that once supplied the seven terraces of the Hanging Gardens with the aid of endlessly rotating screw pumps.

And Mani sets off in a northerly direction, towards the town of his birth on the left bank of the Tigris, passes through the gate guarded by winged creatures of stone, mingles with the crowds streaming by, raises his voice and speaks the words that prophets have spoken since time immemorial: "You are the salt of the earth. The light of the world. He who follows me shall not walk in darkness, but shall have the light of life."

People stop. The reason is unclear. Perhaps it is the heat that prompts them to seek a moment's rest, or the strangely lopsided figure of Mani, so appealing and yet repellent that, even in passing, one cannot help noticing him and his stunted leg. But perhaps it is also his message, in the light of which all colors disappear and everything turns black or white: the soul good yet lost, the material world evil and corrupt—and man a ligature combining both, who yearns for salvation and purification. It is a contrast that creates clarity and promises purity, that darkens the world such as it is and at the same time presents the bright prospect of a remote but safe future which claims to be nothing other than the recreation of a lost, perfect prehistoric age. It is the good news in a country full of good news, the gospel at a time of gospels aplenty, the answer to many questions. Mani can read these questions in the faces, now, as the sun reaches its zenith and siesta time approaches. And since he knows that in this land, you are only heard if you are able to talk about the beginning, he starts to relate how everything began: in the beginning, before the world came into being, everything was good. A wind blew, gentle and fragrant, light radiated in every color, peace and contentment reigned. And the god who ruled over that realm was an eternal god, a good god, the father of greatness, the lord of light. For an eternity, peace prevailed in this paradise, and nobody was bothered by the smaller, tumultuous land of darkness in the south, where the princes of the individual provinces had waged war on each other for as long as anyone could remember. Indeed, the two powers lived side by side; the light shone for itself, the darkness raged against itself; the one fulfilled its own purpose, and the other likewise. Until one day—no one can say when exactly—the darkness attacked the light and both were drawn into the battle, the soul versus the material world, unlike versus unlike, and the second, middle era began, the great universal drama, the Today, Here and Now in which mankind is trapped.

Mani speaks the softly undulating Aramaic of the east, but his words are incisive and brook no contradiction: everything in this world, he repeats, is an amalgamation of good and bad, of light and darkness, of soul and matter, of two natures that are intrinsically separate, as life is from death. Therefore one must not feel at home in this world, nor even build a house, and must neither conceive children nor consume meat nor yield to carnal desire. All activity should be limited to what is strictly necessary, to keep contact with the material world to a minimum. For the plowing of the earth, the cutting of vegetables, the picking of fruit, yes even the crushing of a blade of grass underfoot damages the sparks of light they contain.

He pauses and listens to the effect of his words. A good speaker knows when to stop talking.

And so, before long, he withdraws to one of those caves in the semidesert that are the dwelling place of prophets, sits down on his left leg and puts his right leg, which refuses to obey him when walking and which he has had to drag behind him since he was little, out in front of him as a prop. On it he places a codex, unties the strings, opens the book, touches the reed pen to the blank sheet, and begins to write on the unlined page—a few lines of that immaculate script that he invented: it is dainty and delicate, and even a thousand years later what is left of it, though barely visible to the naked eye, will be razor-sharp and legible under the magnifying glass.

Mani turns the page, he applies the brush to the papyrus, he paints the teeming creatures of darkness and the creation of the world: the way the Lord of Light peels the skins off the slain demons and uses them to line the firmament, the way he forms the mountains from their fragile bones, the earth from their limp flesh, and the sun and moon from the sparks of light released in the battle, and he also paints the divine messenger who set this cosmos in motion and each heavenly body on its orbit. And then Mani turns over a new page and sketches the panorama of a disturbing truth: it was the Lord of Darkness who created the first human couple, modeled on the image of the divine messenger, from the pitiful remnants of the light—and implanted in them the deplorable urge to conjoin and multiply. The first human beings cling tightly to one another, two naked pale figures who conceive child after child, thereby dispersing the light into ever tinier particles and pushing the day of their homecoming to the kingdom of heaven ever further into the future.

Mani cuts the gold leaf into minute pieces, sticks them to the papyrus and keeps on applying opaque pigment until the page shines brightly. Morning comes. Evening comes. Days and weeks go by. Mani does not cease painting: the vast revolving, never-flagging wheel of the cosmos which little by little drives all light from the world, the virtuously waxing and waning moon—a golden ceramic bowl in a night sky of lustrous lapis lazuli—in which the light is collected and cleansed of any traces of earthly grime before returning home on brightly shimmering ferries via the Milky Way, having escaped the cycle of birth, a light-bearing soul that is allowed to cease existing.

Finally, he reaches for the squirrel-hair brush and goes over the folds of the messenger's robe one more time, the eyebrows of the Mother of Life, the contours of the gold-gleaming armor of Primeval Man, the goaty grimaces of the demons. Even the beard hair of the Lord of Darkness and the claws of his scaly feet he paints with the diligence of an artist who loves all his variously shaped creatures equally and even forgets that evil was never good, was neither related to good nor its offspring, was not some fallen angel or rogue Titan, and that there was no accounting for its wickedness. In Mani's miniature it is a self-savaging monster with a dragon's body, a lion's head, an eagle's wings, and a whale's tail, which since the dawn of time has been ravaging its own kingdom—a battlefield obscured by clouds of ashes, poisoned by the foul stench of carrion, full of dead tree stumps and seething scarlet abysses with chrome-yellow smoke rising out of their depths. Mani's doctrines may be black and white, but his books dazzle with color. Whoever possesses such books has no need of temples or churches. They are themselves places of contemplation, of wisdom, of worship: magnificent codices, the weighty tomes bound in unsplit leather, the counterspaces delicately inlaid with thin slivers of tortoiseshell and ivory, in convenient duodecimo format, their covers clad in gold leaf and trimmed with precious stones, but also books as tiny as a charm that can be hidden within a closed fist. The ink made from pomegranate and lampblack has a uniform raven sheen to it on the chalk-whitened papyrus, on pale silk, soft leather, or gleaming parchment. Only the titles are decorated to the point of illegibility, twined around with flamboyant floral rosettes and edged with dots of crimson, the color of redemption and destruction, the color of the world conflagration. Scarlet glows the fire which has blazed for one thousand four hundred and sixty-eight years, which has set the cosmos alight and will not cease burning until its heat has freed the last particle of light and consumed the entire universe. And the glorious images of the future shine brightly, a heavenly world of light in opaque white and gold leaf, in which good and evil are separated again, all parts of the darkness submerged, conquered and engulfed, a lump buried alive, and all parts of the light raised up, purified in the moon, cleansed by the rotation of the stars. Whoever wants to may believe it. Many want to.

Zoroaster had numerous pupils, Buddha five companions, Jesus twelve disciples—but Mani had seven books which carry his teachings out into the world in many tongues, uniting what was split apart by the building of the Tower, and dividing like no man before him: into those who follow him and those who curse him. They call him Mana, vessel of good or vessel of evil, and they call him Manna, bread of heaven or opium of villains; they call him Mani, the winged savior, or Manes, the monster with the lame leg, Mani, the enlightened one, who set out to redeem the world, or Manie, the insane one, who set out to corrupt that same world—Mani, the balm, Mani, the plague.

And as the time of his martyrdom draws near, Mani speaks to his people: "Heed my books! And write down the words of wisdom I have spoken from time to time so that they are not lost to you."

They are ablaze. Pure gold flows from the fire that devours them. Yet it is not a world conflagration, not a flaming cosmos that consumes the sacred writings of the Manichaeans, but the pyres of their enemies. No objection is tolerated, and every doubt punished. For with the believers come the godless, with the pious come the heretics, and with any true teaching comes the swiftly inflamed zeal of those true believers who separate right from wrong as strictly as Mani separated light from darkness. The fire is not choosy, even though they say that the flames consume only what is untrue.

What else burns along with the holy scripts of the Manichaeans? Calculations of the end of the world and innumerable books of magic, evocations of the devil and countless conflicting philosophies of being, thousands of copies of the Talmud, the collected works of Ovid, treatises on the Holy Trinity and the mortality of the soul, on the infinitude of space and the true magnitude of the universe, on the shape of the Earth and its position in the configuration of the stars. The interrogations last for days, the pyres burn for centuries. The fire warms the hearts of the omniscient, it heats the baths of Alexandria, Constantinople, and Rome, until the eye can no longer deceive the mind, and books start to be informed by nature. How immense does the truth have to be for its light to outshine the darkness of all the errors surrounding it? Every time a new telescope is invented which brings the far-off ominously close, the boundary has to be moved, horizons enlarged: celestial spheres turn into orbits, circles into ellipses, patches of fog into globular clusters, spiral nebulae and galaxies, six planets into seven, eight, nine—and then eight again, and mysteries into forms of matter whose genesis is no less eccentric than Mani's cosmology—suns that maintain planets on their orbits, black holes that rend and swallow up stars, fogs that radiate light that in the distant future will be received by no one. No matter how many numbers and formulas describe the cosmos, no matter what knowledge illuminates its nature: as long as time still exists—and who could doubt it?— then every explanation remains no more than storytelling, the familiar tale of attraction and repulsion, of beginning and ending, of coming into being and passing away, of chance and necessity. The universe is growing, expanding, forcing the galaxies apart; it is almost as if it were fleeing from the theories that attempt to capture it. And the notion of this flight, of this rampant growth into the anchorless void seems more terrible than that of a shrinking, a contraction back to the ancient raw point where it all began, where all power and mass, all time and all space fused, coalesced, a dot at first, then a lump, buried alive: an explosion, a dilating space, a hot, pressurized state, expanding, cooling, until atoms are formed, light and matter separate and create the visible world—as improbable as that may be: suns, clouds of molecules, dust, cosmic worms. Asking about the beginning is asking about the end. Whether everything will expand and accelerate, or will one day go into reverse and contract back into itself, caught up in loops that know neither birth nor decay. After all, what do we know! Only this much is as good as certain: there will be an end to the world, possibly a temporary one, but still the most appalling thing imaginable: the sun will swell to gigantic proportions, swallowing up Mercury and Venus, and the whole of Earth's sky will be nothing but sun. And its immense heat will evaporate all the water of the oceans, melt the rock, rupture the Earth's crust, turn its insides out, until cold descends, the end of time.

But for now the sun hangs large as a ball in the glorious deep-blue sky above a land with a history going back many millennia, one that considers itself as old as humanity itself and knows only a pair of opposites: the murderous desert of sand or stone and the life-giving water of the River Nile, which, every summer, used to flood its valley for a hundred days, transform its alluvial land into a huge lake and leave behind it that greasy, earthy-black sludge that rendered the soil so fertile. But since its floodwaters have been dammed up behind massive walls and forced into a labyrinth of thousands upon thousands of channels contained by dikes and dams and leveled out by weirs to provide year-round irrigation for the fields that are expanding ever further into the desert and wring two harvests out of even the sandiest soil, the beneficial Nile flooding no longer occurs. And the ancient Fellahin people native to the area, who since ancient times have worked the earth with strong-boned oxen and wooden plows, have no choice now but to send the children into the desert, to the dumps of abandoned settlements, to hunt for sebakh, the nitrogen-rich fertilizer produced by the decomposition of the sunbaked mud bricks that formed the walls of ancient towns.

It is a particularly hot day in 1929 when three teenagers roaming around the sanded-up, semisubmerged ruins not far from Medinet Madi discover in a vault a rotten wooden box that, on exposure to sunlight, immediately falls apart revealing a number of disintegrating bundles of papyri. Water has permeated the sheets to the extent that, despite having resisted countless generations of worms and populations of ants, they have been eaten away not by living creatures but by the finest salt crystals, so that the men who, not long after, hold the codices in their hands in the room of an antique dealer initially hesitate to pay good money for these black-edged, stuck-together book blocks. Even the restorer who eventually examines one of the musty packages doubts whether its age-old secrets can ever be coaxed out of it.

Only after months of work does he succeed, with the aid of an inclined plane and tiny tweezers, in unsticking individual sheets, which are so wafer-thin and fragile that a sneeze would be enough to reduce them immediately to dust. Call it chance or destiny! While in Berlin manuscript experts hunch with their mirrors and magnifying glasses over the silky-sheened remnants of an evidently sacred scripture pressed flat under panes of glass, in a Californian observatory on a mountaintop not far from Los Angeles, the physicist Fritz Zwicky points a 200-inch reflecting telescope at an area of sky within the Coma Berenices constellation. And as he observes the movements of the blurry fog patches, which reveal themselves to be separate galaxies, and compares them with his calculations, he is hit by a realization.

Never could visible matter be sufficient to hold these clusters of galaxies together. There must be invisible matter in the universe whose presence is indicated only by the gravity it exerts. It was this that began to coalesce a fraction earlier than other matter, its gravity laying a trail that everything else had to follow. A mysterious force, a new celestial power, which Zwicky, on account of its unknown nature, names "dark matter."

Meanwhile the manuscript experts in Berlin have arranged the scraps under the protective glass in order and are starting to decipher the skillful writing. The fragments prophesy the downfall of Mani's community, and describe the atrocities committed against its members. But they also proclaim:

A thousand books will be preserved. They will come into the hands of the just and the faithful: the *Gospel* and the *Treasury of Life*, the *Pragmateia* and the *Book of Mysteries*, the *Book of Giants* and the *Epistles*, the *Psalms* and the *Prayers* of my Lord, his *Icon* and his *Revelations*, his *Parables* and his *Mysteries*—not one will be lost. How many will be lost? How many will be destroyed? A thousand lost, another thousand recovered; for they will find them at the end. They will kiss them and say: "O Wisdom of Greatness! O Armor of the Apostle of Light! When you were lost, where did they find you? I rejoice that the book came into their hand." And you shall find them reading them aloud, uttering the name of each book among them, the name of its lord; and the name of those who gave all for it to be written and the name of the scribe who wrote it and of the one who punctuated it.

Rycktal
GREIFSWALD HARBOR

* Between 1810 and 1820, Caspar David Friedrich painted the harbor of his native city of Greifswald crowded with the masts of sailing ships, among them galleasses, brigantines, and yachts. The old Hanseatic city was con- nected with all the major commercial centers via the navigable estuary of the river Ryck, which flows into the Baltic Sea, and even though the channel of the river Ryck was much broader then, it frequently threatened to silt up. † The 94-centimeter-high, 74-centimeter-wide oil painting had been in the possession of the Hamburger Kunsthalle since 1909, and in 1931 went on show at Munich's Glass Palace as part of the exhibition Works by German Romantics from Caspar David Friedrich to Moritz von Schwind. *On June 6 a fire broke out there that destroyed more than three thousand paintings, including all the works in the special exhibition.*

The problem is not locating the source but making it out. I am standing by a meadow with a map in my hand that is no help to me. In front of me is a ditch, the water not deep, the channel at most half a meter wide, the water's surface covered with a holey carpet of yellowish-green duckweed. Sedge grows along the bank, yellow and pale as straw. The place where the water appar- ently rises to the surface from the depths of the earth has been colonized by thick green moss. What did I expect? A bubbling spring? An information board? I refer to the map once more, look for the slack blue line that starts in the eggshell-colored open terrain below the green-shaded woodland area. It may well be that the true source is more likely to be found up there, in the forest stretching out behind the handful of houses which turn this spot into an actual place with a name that I was able to tell the taxi driver. No doubt he was wondering what I was planning to do here, especially on an Easter Saturday, but in this part of the country, curiosity alone has never tempted anyone into speaking. The people here are serious and indifferent—as if submerged in a nameless sorrow—and, like this landscape, get by perfectly well without words.

This wholly inconspicuous rivulet probably is, in fact, what I am looking for: the source of the Ryck, formerly the river Hilda, which supplies the port of Greifswald many kilometers seawards of here, before flowing, broad and almost majestic, into an inlet of the bay, the Danish Wieck. I see the fissured, graying timber of the fence posts to my left, the two lines of rusty barbed wire, behind them the grassland dotted with countless mounds of freshly dug earth, the work of industrious moles, and, as was my intention, start to follow the upper course of the river in a southwesterly direction.

The great blanket of cloud spread out across the sky hangs low and heavy over me. Only in the distance are there breaks in the cloud, giving a glimpse of a streak of pale powder pink. A few broad-shouldered oak trees stand overlooking the paddock, remnants of a wood pasture long since cleared. Their branches are reflected in the hollows brimming with rain and meltwater, big as lakes. Grass grows up like rushes out of the pale-blue pools. A wagtail runs through the water, dips its tail feathers in a curtsy, and takes off on its springy flight.

Encrusted patches of March snow, barely three days old, glisten from the shaded grassy corners, from the indented tractor tracks, and from the white plastic wrappings covering the round bales, in which the hay ferments into silage. An overturned trough is rusting on the riverbank. Spreading above it are bare branches of hawthorn, its bark enveloped in sulfur-yellow lichen. The trumpet call of the crane rings out, triumphal and indignant. Beyond the ditch, two lead-gray birds raise their oversized wings and propel themselves into the air, only to wheel around ready to land again not long afterwards—in perfect unison, their legs reaching out towards the ground—and with three breathless beats of their wings come to a standstill. Their call resonates for a while longer, until it is finally swallowed by the east wind. It hisses in from the sea, a piercing wind that sweeps moth-gray oak leaves before it. The arable soil feels soapy underfoot. Blackish brown lumps of clay lie bare and sodden on the surface. In the furrows, rape is sprouting, its leaf edges already stained peroxide blonde by pesticides. The colors are pale, the light feeble, as if dusk might descend at any moment.

In the lee of a swampy depression, a herd of deer browses. As I draw closer, they gallop down to the wood, their white flags flashing. On the edge of the kettle hole a scrap of camouflage material flutters on the frame of a raised hide. Not far off some mossy concrete roof slabs are piled up in front of leafless hedges of bramble, elder, and blackthorn. Rusty loops of low-grade steel poke out of the reinforcement holes, now exposed and at the mercy of the weather. Moss as black as algae has taken over the porous blocks. Behind this, sheltered by the sparse undergrowth, a streaky green pond lies quietly in its ice-age hole, a spawning place for frogs and toads, which wait, out of sight, for the signal to procreate. The withered grass has dried to a waxy yellow, bleached by the winter. Only the leaves of the buttercup burst in abundance, spinach green, from the damp black earth.

I go back to the ditch, follow it until the water disappears underground in a concrete pipe. On the horizon, the bright blades of the wind turbines go round, living machines. I think of the black horsehead pumps I saw as a child, and their sinister stoical thrusting into the depths of the earth. It was the last ice age that formed this region, the lowlands of the Ryck valley, a tongue-shaped basin in a gently undulating moraine landscape, its fields and kettle holes edged with massive boulders worn smooth by sandy debris and glacial water. The deeper layers hold rich resources of crude oil and salt.

A few hundred meters further southwest, gray-barked birches mark out the onward path of the stream. I cut across country until I reach its now slightly broader bed. The narrow unplowed strip meanders between the field and the ditch, barely two meters wide. The carpet of greenery is ripped open in places. The peaty earth shimmers damply, churned up by wild boar. A skylark ascends, warbling, into the sky and its breathless song announces the spring, though it seems far off, inconceivable even. For the first time the water is audible now too. It flows, gurgling softly, towards a patch of woodland and disappears beneath some hazel bushes. I plunge into the intimate stillness of the wood. Here, sheltered from the penetrating east wind, the ground is still thick with the withered, ash-colored fallen leaves from the previous year. The undergrowth is earthy and gray, all except for the heath pearlwort, green as parsley. And the winter aconites on the point of blossoming into egg-yolk yellow stand erect with their leaves fanned out. As the wood begins to thin, I discover—among brushwood, pine cones, and deer scat with its blue-black sheen—the shed antlers of a stag. The dark brown bony structure weighs heavy. I run my hand over the pleasantly chapped, leathery hard surface with its knobbly protrusions, and over the smooth tips of the tines. At the bulging ring that was once attached to the pedicle on the stag's skull there are still tufts of hair from the animal, which must have discarded its headgear only recently. The alabaster-white, scabbily rough bone tissue at the rupture point feels sharp as coral. It must have taken some strength to cast off the antlers. The bark of the nearby spruces is streaked with score marks. Milky resin hangs from the wounds like frozen blood. Some trunks have been gnawed bare by the hungry deer.

A gust of wind rustles the treetops, the sky brightens, and for a moment the pale disc of the sun glows through the wall of cloud. It casts no shadows, but immediately there is a buzz of activity in the air, and the birds grow louder: the mechanical chatter of the magpies, the unflagging song of the chaffinches, the tuneful warble of the blackbirds and the melancholy sing-song of the robins.

As I emerge from the wood, a carrion crow takes flight, sails, cawing, over the field speckled green with winter barley, swoops down time and again without interrupting its hoarse call. The landscape looks different, peaceful, tidy. A perfectly straight clay footpath lined with leafless willows follows the ditch as far as the next hamlet. Schnapps bottles from obsolete brands lie in the water. Arching out left of the footpath from the withered undergrowth are reddish-gray bramble stems. Birds' nests are perched in the bare hedges. And beneath a hawthorn bush lie dozens of chalky-pale, shattered snails' shells and the stones where blackbirds and thrushes have smashed the armor-plating to extract the soft flesh. The mud churned up by tractor tires and softened by rain and meltwater yields underfoot with every step I take. The puddles have taken on the color of their surroundings. It is the umber of wet clay and the murky swamp, a uniform waxy hue with little in the way of contrast, save for the spring-green-tinged branches of pussy willow quivering with silvery young catkins in the frosty air. Their silky fur has only just unpeeled itself from the sticky buds.

At the edge of the city the watercourse forks. I follow the most inconspicuous of its branches, the stream hidden deep in the scruffy field margin and lined with crack willow. The trees rise up out of the karstic brushwood like bulky beings moored upside down to the undercut riverbank, their crowns pollarded, their branches stunted, hollowed out by wind and weather. Rotting wood bulges from their burst insides.

Soon the footpath crosses a water channel which, on the map, now bears the name of the river of my quest. Uncurving, it heads east, breaks loose from its surroundings, a natural boundary between two paddocks, hemmed in by willow fences. Lying on the meager soil of the riverbank are blades of sedge beaten flat by the rain. Silently the water follows the course designed for it, fed by more and more drainage ditches branching off to the north and south. The open countryside lies there frigid. Everything is remote, the land occupied, cultivated, providing pasture for cattle still crowded in their sheds. Only the wind rages, whipping my breath away, stormily impeding my steps. The sky is clustered with bulging clouds. The hum of traffic is audible from somewhere near or far.

It is a while before anything catches the eye again. Dogwood and blackthorn bushes enclose the fields and provide shelter from the harsh northeasterly. A flock of grayish-brown, blackbird-sized birds swoops over the fields, repeatedly touching down en masse to rest, and taking to the air again at the slightest disturbance. They are fieldfares, the gray-speckled thrushes that feature in the cookbooks of bygone days, which overwinter in the Mediterranean. Yellowhammers, too, soon appear as dabs of broom yellow in the gusty air. Imperceptibly the ditch grows fuller, the water level rises, the channel broadens out, the rippling water flowing through the open shutter of a mechanical weir.

When, after a time, a road approaches and crosses the ditch, the smooth, tin-gray asphalt is alien to me. Cars zoom past. To the north, shiny concrete-gray barns, bilious-green silos and a grayish-white pyramid of plastic-wrapped bales of straw are visible through a row of poplars. From somewhere comes the drone of farm machinery. Solitary flakes of snow dance noiselessly above the boggy ground of the yellowed pastureland.

In the grass of the riverbank I find a brown-grained river mussel, as large as a chicken's egg. Its inner surface shimmers in shades of mother-of-pearl. Not far off, some mallard ducks are dabbling in the water. They fly away with an irritable whining and flapping as I approach, more easily startled than their town-dwelling cousins, and gather on the nearby fallow field. Their webbed feet show up in shades of orange and the heads of the drakes shimmer peacock blue against the gray expanse of the field. After the monochromy of the last few hours, the birds' bright coloring appears almost exotic.

Then I arrive at the place I had picked as the end point of my first leg. The little village of Wüst Eldena consists of not much more than a restored manor house and a row of brick-brown farmworkers' cottages. Apart from a dilapidated fire station and a few tumbledown barns, all the buildings look lived in: there are curtains hanging in the windows, cars standing on the driveways, and chickens strutting along by the fence surrounding their run. Neglect pervades the place. Its name is an empty claim. It refers to the Cistercian monastery at the mouth of the Ryck, Greifswald's ancient founding building, which has been languishing in a state of ruin since the Thirty Years' War.

My mobile phone has reception again. I dial the number, and just as the taxi appears at the end of the lane, snow begins to fall steadily from the sky in big thick flakes.

Three weeks later, the world is divided into a *Not Anymore*, an *Already*, and a *Not Yet*. It is the end of April. Everywhere else spring is well advanced. From the train I saw green-stippled hedges and the white blossom of the blackthorn bushes. But here in the far northeast the lingering chill is still delaying the appearance of the new spring shoots. The sun is shining, but with a pallid light. It has no warmth as yet. As always, the four-lobed flower heads of forsythia are the first to appear, though it is not yet a blaze of sulfurous yellow. A milky haze lies over the village, which, with its gardens and sheds, soon gives way, beyond a hedge of fast-growing poplars, to pale-green pastureland. The rigidity is unlocked, the frozen ground thawed, the land peaceful, innocent, almost shy. Crack willows and birches still stand bare, though the outlines of their branches are enveloped in a soft bloom. The briar hedges are only just coming into leaf. Blackthorn leaves are unfurling in yellowish rosettes. A few withered berries from last summer still hang in the branches. Their gentle shade is home to creeping ivy and delicate, pale-downy stinging nettles. A young chestnut tree displays its crinkly leaves freshly emerged from their glossy buds. The farm track, two graveled sandy ruts carved in the turf by cars and farm vehicles, hugs the line of the ditch. In the hedges of dogwood and blackthorn, sparrows fluff up their plumage. Blackbirds chirp, a blackcap warbles, and a chaffinch recites his never-changing tune. At some point the fences have all vanished. Broken reeds surrounded by the remains of rotting leaves poke up out of the flat water that lies virtually unclouded in its rusty-brown bed. And the layers of rushes felled by the autumn winds, when they were dry and brittle, glow like straw on the pale-green grass of the bank.

Feathery cirrus clouds veil the upper skies, crisscrossed by dissolving aircraft vapor trails. Gray-green woods border the eastern horizon. To the south, the countryside unravels into scattered settlements, individual trees, and kettle holes. To the north, clouds of dust billow in the wake of a plowing tractor. A bluish cereal crop is emerging out of the ground in the nearby field. The smell of slurry pervades the air.

The field margin is awash with the chrome-yellow of lesser celandines, dandelions, and marsh marigolds with their waxy, heart-shaped leaves. A small tawny-colored tortoiseshell butterfly flutters past. A bumblebee buzzes in search of food. Dead-nettles stand tall on their lofty stems, their purple-lipped petals protruding beyond the stamens.

To the left, beyond some weather-beaten pine trees and a bank of mossy boulders, a copse stands entrenched on a slight elevation. Sprouting in front of this is a colony of brown spore-bearing spikes resembling the capped stems of black morels. It is young horsetail, a vestige of ancient times, the farmer's enemy. And flourishing in the middle of the footpath is a crop of tiny marsh gentian in all its pale violet glory. High in the sky, which is now clear, kites circle, rise and fall, bank and swoop daringly on the lookout for prey. The landscape is tinged by an ash-blond light. The earth seems to breathe in long gentle breaths. Below the mirrored surface of the water, many-stranded pondweed sways with the soundless current. All at once a heron takes off from the water, rising into the air on outstretched slate-gray fans, water droplets fizzing from its wings. It labors skywards in a wide arc and flies seawards, its head flat and tucked in. Then Sunday quiet is restored. The path mimics the bends of the ditch, the water flowing at a leisurely pace along its imperceptible descent. At one point the water is dammed up in the reservoir of a pumping station. Motionless, the sinister greenish brew stagnates beneath a scum of semirotten reeds and duckweed in front of the lowered wooden sluices. Signs warn that it is forbidden to swim or to enter the enclosure. A narrow iron bridge leads across to the other bank of the clear waterway, now broad as a river, where, beyond open fields and embankments flecked with linden green, further patches of woodland come into view.

A common toad sits in the sap-green grass. The tiny thumb of its right hand is resting on a stalk. Beneath heavy, half-closed lids its copper-red eyes stare at nothing in particular, the only movement the pulsating of its wrinkled, agate-brown body. It is covered with warts and grains of sand.

People appear as if out of nowhere. A boy speeds across the clearing on a quad bike. A spaniel follows him, barking. A group of adults walk by with a young child in tow and disappear behind the pumping station without a word of greeting. I stand still and try to locate the confused landscape on the map. The air is fresh and clear, and for a moment I even imagine I can taste spring. The map shows neither a riverside path nor any entry point into the forest. All the marked footpaths start out from the inside of the wood.

I want to follow the watercourse into the willow marsh, but after a bend in the ditch I come upon a festering black bog. The squelching sodden soil impedes my every step. The ground grows ever softer, and I sink ever deeper in the miry, bare earth.

Water holes of fathomless black shimmer from the bottom of the hollow. I realize that I can go no further this way and must turn back. So I pick my way through the pale-green dappled woods of the water meadow, bending young branches aside with my arms until, some way further south, the ground, now concealed by undergrowth, hardens. From beneath the faded carpet of leaves, light-craving anemones raise their heads, showing as flecks of white on the cool forest floor. A woodpecker raps a tattoo in the treetops. Filtered light falls on the slender shoots of hazel, the young beeches and slim birches. Before long tall spruces cast deep shade on the ground, which is springy now, and strewn with scaly pine cones and yellowed needles, then, as I pass under oaks and beeches, it grows lighter again.

There are signs everywhere of animal activity: the reddish loose detritus churned up by wild boar, the dark entrance to a fox's earth or badger sett under a root, the hieroglyphic drawings of bark beetle larvae on a bare stick, and the high-pitched voice of the bullfinch. Several times I reply to its cheerful single-syllable call. And when I lie down on the soft grass of a small knoll in the dappled semishade of some pine trees, the bird ventures out from his cover and perches in the boughs directly above me. Its breast is a radiant vermilion. I answer it again, and so we go on, taking turns for a while, until all of a sudden it launches into a rousing, completely different tune in five verses, which I am unable to imitate.

I close my eyes, and the tangle of branches reappears, imprinted on the blazing red of my eyelids. The shrill cries of birds of prey can be heard in the distance.

When I set off again, the sun is high in the sky, and its light, for a moment entirely undimmed in the dusty clearing, gives a foretaste of the shimmering, scorched sand-flavored heat of the summer, the sound of the sea. From time to time, the rhythmic loop of the bullfinch's song rings out again. I amble through plantations of young and more mature trees. The ghostly shadows of the kites circle over the washed-out sandy soil, which glistens with the burst, honey-scented pods from which hornbeam leaves have unfurled.

I reemerge into the open, and a hare darts out from the young rye only a few meters from me, doubles back on the farm track, and disappears into a tilled field. To the east, a flock of rooks passes above some drooping power cables, cawing hoarsely. A stork sails over them with outstretched wings to its nest overlooking the gables of all the houses in a nearby village, and in the shady margin of the wood another ditch peters out, bordered by an ash-colored belt of strawy sludge. It must have been washed up by floodwater, along with the succulent finger-leaved yellow irises, and masses of pale-violet mollusks, which resemble fossils on the dried mud.

The Ryck itself runs further to the north. I want to take a shortcut, so I clamber under electric fences and cut across country, directly through grazing land. But soon every step I take is hindered by the wet, and wherever I tread, the waterlogged ground yields beneath my feet. Further north, the Ryck is eventually joined by the abundant waters of the river Riene, before flowing, contained by slightly concave dikes, towards a village. A prefabricated high-rise is already visible from far off. When I finally reach the riverbank, the first seagull appears in the sky without a sound, black-headed, ready for the breeding season. For a moment the air tastes salty. The village street leads across a level bridge. A siren wails. And above the wooded horizon, the deep-blue sky is turning a misty white.

When I cross this same bridge three weeks later, the riverbank is lined with knee-high grass. The sky is leaden. Heavy, bulging clouds cast a gloom over the land, all except for the western seam of the horizon, behind me, which glows with a streak of ivory light.

I follow the watercourse eastwards past tousled clumps of withered reeds. A Haflinger mare and her foal graze in a lush green paddock. Warblers babble from hedgerows newly in leaf behind drifts of gangling stinging nettles. From a farm building comes the whine of a chainsaw. Its rising and falling din accompanies me for a long while along the small dike streaked lavender gray with vernal grass, and mingles with the call of the cuckoo, clear as a bell, from the green-tinged white willows on the south bank. When I return its echo-like call, it hisses like a cat and flies from tree to tree in search of its rival. Above it, in the higher reaches, three gray herons drift solemnly, with angled, unmoving wings towards the bay. House martins zigzag busily back and forth over the rippled surface of the water, on which the occasional lily pad floats. Lupins hold their pale-blue flower spikes majestically aloft. Herbaceous speedwell with its little bluish-violet flowers and the tiny feathery shoots of yarrow appear dainty and fragile by contrast. Rotting amongst the fibrous broadleaf plantain is the scaly-blue gleaming rear end of a half-eaten perch, which must have been left behind by an osprey. Lanky bittercress dots the hay meadows birch white. Caramel-breasted whinchats flit, chirping, from stalk to stalk. From the quivering reeds comes the vehement call of the reed warbler, followed soon after by the melodious piping of the golden oriole from a nearby wood.

I try in vain to locate it. Instead, way out to the east, I spot a black and white creature rising up out of the water and spreading its boardlike wings wide. The sheer size of it alone makes it seem strange, almost unearthly. I stop walking and take up my binoculars. An osprey? No, it must actually be a sea eagle, which has now found itself a lookout point some distance away, ready for the next stage of its hunt. Not far from it, beyond fields of buttercups, the oilseed rape is a blaze of brilliant yellow. Standing tall again in the distance are the wind turbines with their gray propellers. All but one are motionless. Further eastwards, a crop sprayer makes its way across a field of barley, sprinkling as it goes.

Because all this is happening on the other side of the river, it seems far away, as does the group of people, even though we are separated only by the river channel. They stand, arms folded, next to a tractor with a large water tank. A Saint Bernard pads around, brushing past their legs, examines the submerged red pipe, walks to the small blue-and-white-painted pumping station, and barks across. Are they collecting water? Or pouring something into the Ryck? For decades, newly dug ditches have been draining ground water from the marshes to transform the poor grassland into arable land. Indeed, I soon stumble across an offshoot which disappears into the thorny scrubland bordering an adjacent wood. Bubbly black mud oozes in the undergrowth. Tired light filters through the tree canopy. Silence reigns now; there is not a bird to be heard. It is not long, though, before I am back in bright light again, because a swathe of the wood has been chopped down to make way for overhead power lines. Japanese knotweed has run riot here, growing several meters tall, with large oval leaves and flailing bamboo-like canes. I walk on and take the first turning leading out into the open.

On the edge of the wood, a profusion of hawthorn flowers forms a luxuriant froth abuzz with insects—while the middle of the white clover-dotted meadow is home to swallowwort and western marsh orchids with purple, helmetlike flower spikes and broad leaves marked with reddish-brown spots. And for a moment Greifswald cathedral and directly in front of it the brick-red pyramid of the tower of St. Jacobi's appear between the riverside copse and a far-off embankment.

A barely distinguishable path leads alongside the waterway, now framed by dikes on both sides. Behind the strawy palisades, graceful, clean-limbed birch trees stand tall, their fresh leaves fluttering like bunting. Swaying in front of these are the frayed pennants of the reeds. Yellowhammers repeat their uninflected tune, a chaffinch chip-chips. Soon another, smaller pumping station comes into view on the far bank, its facade daubed with graffiti. An angler casts out her fishing line in front of it. Two large brown dogs are lying next to her. Soon afterwards, in the middle of my path, I come across a thick bronze-colored bone sticking up out of the dried earth of a molehill. It appears to be a cow's femur. A thicket of eared willow is lush with bristly yellowy-green flower spikes. The Ryck, entirely overgrown with buckthorn and reeds, is no longer visible. The reeds rustle. Azure damselflies flit among the branches or sit on stalks of meadow-grass, the hint of a horseshoe mark on their iridescent abdomens.

A sound now reaches my ears that I cannot place, a dull metallic clicking, which is repeated soon afterwards. And then, behind a bank, the freshly mown green of a golf course opens up before me, its artificial hillocks continuing right up to the bypass embankment. People in brightly colored peaked caps hit balls into the air, while from the dense hedgerow next to me a thrush nightingale pipes up, more strident than a nightingale but just as brilliant.

The hedges that hemmed me in a moment ago have given way to a carpet of butterbur. Snails have munched holes in its rhubarb-sized leaves. A trail leads through a boggy willow grove and under the road bridge, then up again to a pedestrian bridge. I rest my hands on the railing and look at the peaceful, brownish, roughly three- or four-meter-wide watercourse, which only officially counts as the Ryck from this point, the outer limit of the city. Lily pads float at its edges.

All at once the sky clears, and I feel the sun burning my neck. I take the sandy farm track along the top of the small dike on the south bank. I pass a meadow of buttercups, before coming upon the municipal cemetery. On the far bank is a row of detached houses. This group of dwellings is not shown on the map. It must have been built only recently. In the branches of a hawthorn bush choked with knotweed glows a spot of rusty red. It is a common linnet, and a hand's breadth away from him, larger and less colorful, is the female. But before I can get a closer look at them, they both swoop down and disappear. Soon the Ryck is hidden by the reeds again, and only the blue railway bridge in the distance reveals which way it flows from here.

My path takes me further south past a firefighting pond ringed by barbed wire and pink-blossomed apple trees. The trunk of a willow has been colonized by ocher-yellow slime mold. It looks like construction foam. Tall poplars line a cracked asphalt road leading into town. Horses graze in a paddock, and soon after, beyond a small stream, are some apartment buildings. There are plastic slides and trampolines in the gardens. On the other side of the street is a huge derelict storage depot behind a holey wire fence. Soon I reach Grimmer Strasse with its narrow, pastel-colored old buildings. I walk past a farmyard and across a supermarket parking lot park. In a paved yard in front of a stonemason's premises, two Rottweilers growl behind high fences. They have rubber chewing rings in their mouths, drool hanging from their chops. The Ryck is a long way off. It is only when, walking along the earth rampart, I turn into the park surrounding the zoo that am I able to spot its reed-fringed bed again behind a disused railway line. I follow the pavement downhill, past the old hospital building where I was born. After the bridge on Stralsunder Strasse, the river opens out and flows into a trapezoidal basin some seventy or eighty meters wide and several hundred meters long—Greifswald harbor. Two floating restaurants are moored to the paved northern quay, and several tall-masted sailing boats to the southern quay. Behind them, the prefabricated buildings cast long shadows.

I sit down on the south bank. On the other side is a line of low buildings and wooden sheds, boatyards and a rowing club where, as a youngster, I trained one spring. Somewhere behind it, in the Rosental valley between the Ryck and the Baberow, is where the salt flats must have been that—together with the river—were the

reason why woodland was cleared here and a market town established on swampy ground. A dead bream floats in the brackish
water. Swifts dart low over the rippled surface with shrill cries.
Three swallows are perched on the taffrail of a schooner, their
fox-red breasts aglow in the evening sun.

Valle Onsernone

ENCYCLOPEDIA IN THE WOOD

* *At the age of fifty, Armand Schulthess, a clerical assistant in the commercial section of the Swiss Federal Department of Economics in Bern, decided to start a new life from scratch in Ticino. Schulthess, who in his younger days had run a ladies-wear company, Maison Schulthess, with branches in Geneva and Zurich, gave up his office job in 1951 and moved to Valle Onsernone, having already purchased several plots of land there, eighteen hectares in total, in the 1940s. From that point on, his life revolved around a grove of chestnut trees, which he gradually transformed into an encyclopedia in the wood, organizing human knowledge by subject area and inscribing it on more than a thousand metal plates. The often multilingual inscriptions included summary descriptions of different fields of knowledge, lists, tables, and bibliographic information, as well as suggested leisure activities, interspersed with invitations to get in touch, though any actual attempts were always emphatically rebuffed. Schulthess lived the rest of his life in seclusion. He died on the night of September 29, 1972, in his garden, from exhaustion and hypothermia following a fall.*

† *In July 1973, his legal heirs had his house cleared, which had been crammed wall-to-wall with books, papers, and household items, and burned or disposed of virtually its entire contents. During the clear-out, which took two days, a library of around seventy handmade books, probably collage, on the theme of sexuality was incinerated. The outdoor collection was completely destroyed. Only a handful of the metal plates and nine of the handmade books were salvaged; three of these books ended up in the Collection de l'Art Brut in Lausanne, while the rest are now in private ownership. Today the house's name is the only reminder of its former owner: Casa Armando.*

Testing, testing, one, two, three, four, five. You're listening to
Radio Monte Carlo. Testing, testing, six, seven, eight, nine.
Good. Let's get going with our evening program. So, we have
now arrived in the village in the Onsernone valley. The village
is about two hours from Locarno. You take the train and get off
in Auressio. It's a bit of a walk to the house. You take the little footpath downhill. You'll come in May as the weather's nice
then. You'll find the house easily enough, and the sign outside
that invites you to knock on the door as the bell isn't working
anymore. You'll encounter Gorgo at the front door and brave
her stare. You'll see the garden, all the metal plates. You'll read
them, understand them. It's a large site, a nice piece of land:
sloping, rocky, covered in dense chestnut woods. It falls away
steeply towards the south. From the fence at the bottom you
can hear the burble of the river Isorno. The old main road runs
right through the site. Nowadays it's a public footpath, so I have
strangers walking across my plot of land, domain number one. I
also own domain number two in Alp Campo to the south of the
mountain pass into the Maggia valley, and domain number three
in Sotto Cratolo.

The people who come here read the plates, but they don't
read properly. They don't know how to read; they only read to
stimulate their minds, to stimulate their feelings. But you have
to read to organize. And whatever's being organized has to be
written down first. That's the only way to create order. My system is based on putting like with like: the "Miraculous" section
groups the phenomena associated with the cult of St. Thérèse of
Lisieux and the tears of blood and stigmata of Therese Neumann
of Konnersreuth together with the astonishing invulnerability of
Mirin Dajo, who allowed his body to be pierced with swords,
and, right next to it, the world's greatest maritime disasters. The
Nobel prizes go with the encyclopedias, Linné with the plants
and animals, the butterflies with philosophy, fertilizer with a
diet table, radiesthesia and radiation with gambling odds, the

moon landing with UFOs, UFOs and fakirs with parapsychology and the mysteries of mankind. The table of sunspots with the barbecue, the secrets of Tibet right behind the psychoanalysis tree and the plate about ant colonies directly above the anthill. The written word must connect with the real-life experience. An encyclopedia in the wood. Human knowledge is assembled here. It hangs in the trees. It is not complete, of course. It cannot possibly be complete. What a job that was, writing all those plates! You must always do something useful in life. Collect something if you're out and about, pick up an apple, a chestnut, a tin can. Everything has a use. You mustn't throw anything away, not even a scrap of paper. You can do accurate work even with pencil stubs. Tin cans can be turned into signs, if you flatten them out. There is always work to be done: weeds to be got rid of, rusty signs to be repaired, chestnuts to be peeled. They swell right up and take on the taste of whatever you put them in. In syrup they turn really sweet. And in a broth they become savory. They have a high nutritional value. It is important to know the nutritional value. Especially when you don't have any teeth left. I can't eat almonds anymore. I'm a good cook. For lunch all I need is a pint of milk and a bread roll. There's nothing one really needs. One doesn't need anything really. At most a woman. She should be interested, keen to learn, young. Someone who knows nothing yet. Someone I could teach about everything. Ideally a young girl between eighteen and twenty-five who I could marry or adopt, an orphan or a young heiress.

You won't break things, unlike the children who sometimes visit, who don't answer when you speak to them. Not even when you ask what language they speak. I speak German, French, Italian, Dutch, and English. But the people who come here only want to collect chestnuts and make fun of me. They haven't got a clue. Take no notice of them. He's a weirdo, they say, a nutcase, a lunatic. Just because I sometimes play the gramophone at night. The fact is, the acoustics are best in the open air and at nighttime.

It doesn't disturb the birds as they're asleep. Sometimes I like to sing. As long as no one hears. I used to sleepwalk as a child. But then I grew out of it. Enrico Caruso was the greatest tenor of all time. I've got a lot of records by him, and a hundred and fifty records in total: operas, operettas, classical music, dance hits, the most famous of the Viennese waltzes. It's all there. You love music.

There are plenty of lovely places to sit and relax all over the site. Above the cold buffet there's a water feature, a little gully made using the traditional drystone wall method. Two grottoes that supply the site with water all year round, an open-air cinema, a fire pit, and a bathing spot. I went to great trouble to set it all up. I layered hundreds of stones on top of each other, dragged tree trunks and branches uphill to make it a nice place, a place of beauty. Because beauty is important. Everything—life, progress—depends on beauty. Those who make light of beauty don't realize how much our lives depend on it. When I met my first wife, I was wearing a coat from Paris, a beautiful piece. That's why she married me. She was already pregnant at that point. Misshapen by the bulge on her front. First the money dried up, then so did our relationship. We had a child. But before long it was dead.

The niche in the wall there might make a nice little spot in the summer. There are still some fireclay plates in decent condition at the dump. I'd just need to bring them over here, and they'd make a good cooking spot in the culinary arts department. You'll learn how to barbecue food. There's a griddle pan with a lid you can use. Or you can wrap the food in tin foil to cook it. At a Mexican barbecue they actually roast a whole animal that way. There's a large library of books on a culinary theme, including the popular titles *Second Only to Love* and *What Men Like to Eat*, lots of barbecue recipes and marinades, as well as books on cultivating a community or kitchen garden and a volume on the language of flowers in French. When you come, it'll be summer. You'll enjoy the cool shade. You'll hold on to the old iron bars, climb down the rock face on the little ladder, balance across the narrow bridge over the ravine and arrive at Casa Virginie, a single-room building with a flat roof and no terrace, measuring four meters by four. I built it myself, a year before I embarked on my second life, my actual life, the dream of self-sufficiency. That was in 1950. You can see the plans for it on a board at the house. If you live like me, it's free. I don't rent it out. You have to earn the right to stay there. It's called the Cottage or else Casa Virginie, after the state in the Wild West, after a female person, after a physiological state. That's also why the front door is bricked up. There's a bell at Casa Virginie that rings through to the bedroom in the main house. Everything's there: nice wallpaper, nice curtains, a lamp-shade, even benches to sit on, and brackets for window boxes of geraniums. You can live in it if the separate little room gets too small for you. It'll only take a night to unbrick the door. By the light of the moon is best. It's light enough then. And nearby you've got the big windmill I designed myself, along with its generator, and the components for the water pump, which is nearly ready. Power generation is a problem in itself when you want to be self-sufficient. Chickens would be good. They lay eggs. They're very useful. It would be easy enough to build a henhouse out of windshields. The chickens need a ladder, a hi-erarchy, a system. The whole plot is on sloping ground. So the gradient's already there. I had goats once. But they were stupid. I put down a mattress for them in Casa Virginie, got them settled on it for the night and even covered them with blankets. But they kept getting up again and went and slept on the floor. Three or four goats, it was. Later I tied them to the trees with a rope. They went round and round and kept on walking in circles until they got all tangled up. Then one day they were dead. They were nice animals, a nice breed, sadly just very stupid.

If you carry on along the footpath, you'll arrive back at the house and see the big celestial disc on the east gable showing all the constellations of the zodiac. The skies interest me, human destinies, blind chance and the connection between all things, the mechanics of life-threatening events, events that cause premature death. You'd really need to collect specific case histories with dates of birth and dates of ill fate, analyze them and work out rules from them. The more cases you studied, the more accurate the results. You'd need to write up the horoscopes for certain days: the day Swedenborg was born, the day of the break-in at the house of Erich Maria Remarque, the day the pop singer Alexandra died in a car accident. About twenty cases of people dying out of the blue like that. You're bound to find something in common. But, alas, almost nobody knows their exact time of birth. Goethe said: As the clock struck twelve, I came into the world. That gives you something to work with, at least. The timing of one's birth isn't random. Not many of those born on the same day as Mussolini survived. You see, every day of one's life corresponds to a year of one's life, and if a crisis occurs in early infancy, which is indicated if the planets Mars, Saturn, Uranus, and Pluto are positioned at zero, ninety, and one hundred and eighty degrees to one another, it is repeated in the corresponding year of one's life and signals death. You can find all the calculations for this in the astrological folders at the house. And there are plenty of examples available of skies associated with birth deformities. My calculations are precise. The biological recurrences form an obvious pattern: certain events occur on these nodes, giving rise to highs and lows. Longevity and length of life are age-old preoccupations. But everyone has to die. That's a fact. That's a comfort.

The best thing in school was giving a talk. You could pick a topic and find out everything about it. Because it's important to know what's what, to be well informed, whether from a historical, geographic or fashion perspective. You can deliberate over the way things are and will be. One school of philosophy after another has done just that, and each of them has come to some conclusion. In the East, you reap what you sow. That's what is meant by karma. You'll find plenty about that in the books of theosophy. Questions concerning the soul are all addressed in the theology books. Our impulses, perceptions, inhibitions, memories and so on are dealt with in the psychology books. You see, the Ego, the innermost core of our being, shouldn't necessarily be regarded as merely a reflection of our body. You can find out more about that in the books of anthroposophy. A lot stays in our subconscious. It can cause inhibitions and neuroses. Psychoanalysis brings it out into the open and provides release. Infants' perceptions are still completely undifferentiated. Then, very slowly, they become polarized. Sigmund Freud discovered that many of the errors we make stem from the repression of our sexual drive. Someone else demonstrated how the desire for superiority is all-determining. And individual psychology is the result. Professor Jung is the one who discovered the archetypes—the universal, inborn patterns that reside in our collective unconscious. Coué of the Nancy School demonstrated the power of suggestion. Parapsychology examines phenomena that cannot be explained by our everyday senses, while astrology collects past evidence and considers whether the celestial configuration on the day of one's birth has a bearing on what follows. Darwin demonstrated the evolution of and relationship between all living beings, whereas Genesis describes how the spirit breathed life into matter. Some say spiritual beings exist on as yet inhospitable planets. The problem with spiritualists' professed contacts with the dead is that nothing positive ever emerges. One mustn't forget, though, that the fourth dimension is outside of space and time. Perhaps everything really will grind to a halt. There are still quite a few unanswered questions: the problem of divining rods, of death rays, and of whether Eusepia Palladino's séances were a matter of pure trickery or only occasional trickery.

I used to arrange everything very precisely by field. Physics here, bones there, and parapsychology over there. Today, though, it's all a big mess. Knowledge proliferates. The trees just get bigger, they spread out, they reach up towards the sky until the writing peels, the wires come undone and the plates drop off. At first I used to repair them, but then it happened to more and more of them. It's not possible to work in the wood when it's dark or raining. That just leaves the house. It's old and, like most houses in Ticino, has granite walls. It has a stone roof and a lot of rooms, just no heating. You don't really need it anyway. In winter you can cover the floor with cork tiles, newspapers, and linoleum and insulate the walls with jute and battens. Plastic bottles work too. When it's cold, you can put them in sacks and use them as a quilt. The Valvoline engine oil canisters work best. Those should never be thrown away. But people are forever throwing stuff away without a second thought. Especially the visitors. The dumps are real treasure troves. The things that end up there! Dolls, magazines, stilettos. There's a use for all of it. Once there was a radio lying there which still worked. In the evenings, after work, I listen to Radio Monte Carlo between 9:00 p.m. and 2:30 a.m. We'll be able to listen together. There's not just one radio, but three, as well as three bathtubs, two boilers, two refrigerators, seven electric mixers, but one doesn't need anything really, not even a toilet. One doesn't even need other people. At most a wife. A dog would be good. I've got a dog harness, and a brochure on breeding dogs.

Sometimes the front door won't open. It's because of the folding grille, which often gets jammed, and all the chestnuts blocking the entrance. There are newspapers, slips of paper, and photographs everywhere. I always used to copy out the newspaper articles and file them in their correct place. Now there are so many of them I no longer even find time to read them. But I make lists of keywords, which I keep. For later, when I happen to have time, or in case people come looking for something.

My guiding principles are: read everything that can be read. Put like with like, and keep everything you've read. Only write down facts, knowledge that can be verified. Wherever possible, keep phenomena separate from established rules and always start with the general and work towards the individual. Because what's on the outside always points to what's on the inside. You can deduce more about my essence from my room than from my lung or my heart. That's because the external and the internal go together, just as the external sexual organs of the man and the internal ones of the woman are two variants of the same thing. And just as the garden is my domain, so the house will become yours. You'll see that sometimes the interior and exterior are out of balance. But in summer the shade of the chestnut trees and the findings of science can help with the heat, while in winter philosophy can help with the cold. Sometimes in winter I have to go outdoors to warm myself in the snow. A hot-water bottle can be a lifesaver. If you put it on the stove it saves you having to add hot water. I used to have a flat, curved metal water bottle to put by my feet. Nowadays I use a proper bottle and hold it to the sensitive place between my legs, as that's the best way to get the heat circulating.

There is a lot of equipment. Each item is inventoried: AS1, AS2, AS3 and so on. I have the AS6, the film projector, the AS2, a video camera—a massive drum duplicator, a Rajah photographic enlarger, a beaded screen that makes the projection appear brighter and more lustrous, a reducer that allows you to make images so small they fit on a tiny bead, a low-frequency amplifier, a Thorens wax-disc cutter, the AS7, as well as books describing the physical processes involved in engraving your own 33- or 78-rpm gramophone records. I used the AS7 to record a serenade by Enrico Toselli on the clarinet, which I'm going to play you by way of welcome. Now, too, the buttons are pressed, the stylus is cutting, the turntable is turning constantly, recording everything I say. The microphone is older. For very short-distance experiments there is also a minitransmitter and a shortwave adapter, plus a crank telephone and a device used to produce stereo images. I wanted to try it out once. But the female just ran away. You really have to keep an eye on women.

I have the *Encyclopaedia Britannica*. I have numerous books about problems to do with love and marriage. I have books on the problems of existence and books about death. If you copy out keywords that interest you from your Brockhaus encyclopedia and bring them with you, then I can copy out the same ones for you from my *Encyclopédie Larousse*. They complement each other, you see. The largest flower is the corpse lily from the Philippines, the largest den that of the grizzly bear, and the largest bird is unable to fly. Milk stays in one's stomach for two to three hours. The navel divides the human body roughly according to the golden ratio. One's arm span is roughly the same as one's body length. All living tissue is made of carbon compounds. The male is an accident: the female would have sufficed, writes Gourmont. She always has the principal role. This is evident if only from the fact that, in civilized humanity, more females are born the closer civilization comes to a state of plenitude. The egg, recent research has shown, is by no means passive: it actively sends out a crude extension in the direction of the approaching sperm cell. Something grows on the ovary, something resembling a wart. When it bursts and drops off you get a rise in body temperature. It's called ovulation. And that's when you need to take care! I once had a girlfriend in Paris; she was from Mexico. And we had sexual intercourse. One time Aunt Flo didn't come. So we went to the pharmacy and the pharmacist gave her something to take, I think it was called Algos. And then the blood came, and in amongst all the blood was a tiny something. I've never seen anything like it. On holiday in the Tyrol I once had intercourse with the chambermaid. But I was still afraid after the last time. So we drove straight to Innsbruck to see a doctor, to check if anything had happened. But he just laughed.

The first on the right is my bedroom. It's always dark in there. The light bulbs have blown, and the window is insulated with books. Only in the morning does a little bit of light filter through the gaps. It's like an alarm clock, a reminder to get up. And there are the women gazing out from the Lux soap advertisement and the magazines. They look straight at you. You can walk around the room, but they're everywhere, looking at you. Never averting their gaze. One of them is hanging on a coat hanger looking out from the top of a jacket. I dressed her in it. But her face is still naked. So much skin. Even when I'm lying in bed she sees me, looks down on me from above. Watches everything I do. Sometimes lust gets the better of one. Then one needs to find an outlet, especially if one's sex drive is very strong. Apart from masturbatory release, there are only three forms of sexual activity, the context and acceptability of which depend on the prevailing social climate at the time: there is prostitution; there is the free bond of love; and there is the officially governed and recognized contractual sexual relationship of civil marriage based on Article 4 of the Civil Code, section 1, paragraph 1353. In biological terms all three involve the same thing. I've been married twice. Both marriages ended in divorce. We weren't a good fit. Not even in the place where we should have fitted. Plenty of people have written about it. It's in all the books. There is, says La Rochefoucauld, only one kind of love, but there are a thousand imitations. One has to question one's own inclinations. Do they stem from an inner urge, or from the lure of the forbidden? Perverse sexual inclinations mostly develop at an age when the sex drive has not yet erupted. The person may well have a certain innate predisposition, but in the vast majority of cases, these preferences develop when one is experiencing the heights of ecstasy for the first time. The actor can portray nothing that is not already latent within him in some albeit rudimentary form: king, beggar, patriarch. As for the urge to dress up, there is a distinction to be drawn between transvestites, who like new clothes that don't come with memories attached, and fetishists, who like clothing that carries the hint of another person, in other words who love worn items.

You know what's cruel? Rousing a man into a passion with kisses, with all kinds of exposures and disclosures, touches, looks, by the way you read to him, talk to him, unreservedly inflaming his desire, but then, contrary to all the promises made, not being willing to go all the way—apparently solely in order to heighten his agony and allow you to revel in the sight of this suffering.

There is no denying the superiority of female beauty. Its source, its secret lies entirely in the unity of the female figure. What makes the woman more beautiful is that her genitalia are out of sight. The male sexual organ, which offers no advantage whatsoever except when it comes to answering the call of nature, is a constant burden and badge of shame. Our upright posture, especially, makes it the most vulnerable place in combat and an eyesore to behold since it is a bump in a flat surface, a blip in a smooth line.

The harmony of the female form is far more complete, if only in terms of geometry, particularly if you think of man and woman in the heat of desire, at the moment when they are engaging in the most intense, most natural manifestation of life there is. The woman, whose stirrings all occur internally and are expressed only in the undulating motions of her body, preserves her full aesthetic value, whereas the man sinks, as it were, to the lowest animallike state, appears humiliated, forfeits all beauty the moment he exposes his genitals. In terms of technical ability to achieve coitus, too, the woman is superior to the man since she does not, for example, need an erect member to accomplish the act. As far as the mechanical process is concerned, a woman is capable of uninterrupted intercourse.

The size of the clitoris can vary greatly. However, a relatively undeveloped clitoris can, as indeed can the entire genital apparatus, grow in size over the years if the woman engages in plenty of sexual activity. No one has yet studied the effects of practice and experience. In most cases, the larger labia are close together in women who have not given birth. They need to become engorged and the clitoris must start to become erect prior to any act if the woman is not to be left unsatisfied. Most married women submit passively to sexual activities and thereby miss out on the chance to ease and enhance the experience by getting involved themselves and controlling the relevant muscles.

You take the ladder to the first floor. You climb up it, rung by rung. It's still dark, but you'll be able to feel with your hands that you're going the right way. There's a ring dangling from the ceiling. You can grab hold of it in an emergency, if you're in danger. After all, there's not a lot of space up there. And there's even less as you go on. But you'll fit through. At the back you've got the balcony with two sun loungers, though the balcony door is blocked up with books. Books make an excellent insulating material, you know. Not many people know that. There's a lot that people don't know. Then it'll get a little lighter, because on the left is your space, your domain, the separate little room. Sometimes the door won't open. And you'll be coming in au-tumn. Everywhere will be full of sweet chestnuts. The whole val-ley, the garden, the house. They fall down. They fall on you. They could strike you dead. The largest of the three fruits tastes the best. The nuts are glossy, their shells prickly. The tip of the nut is hairy, a sweet down. Like burrs, the chestnuts collect everywhere. The only clear space is in the separate little room. The chestnuts don't get in there. They don't belong there. Because that space is yours. Everything is there, close to hand, in the place where it belongs: the window behind the books, the dressing table next to the mirror, on the window ledge a little washbasin, a watering can, a fire pump, and the little hollow among the piles of paper, that's it—the sleeping space I've made especially for you, the female. Everything is ready: the mattress on its wooden frame, a nice bed, the fabulous clothes and furs. All of them the lat-est fashion. You can try them on. Hanging on a coat hanger is a yellow-and-green-patterned ladies' swimsuit. The other coat hangers are spare. You can hang your own clothes on them.

You'll look around, see the two nude photographs above the bed, and right opposite them the black and white nude photo of a young woman lolling on a sheet, the romantic images of couples kissing, the classical relief of a pair of lovers. You will look at your reflection in the mirror on the dressing table, and find everything you need there: nail varnish, beauty magazines, and brochures, books on hat fashions and hair care, along with the book *Female Attractiveness and Beauty. What a Girl Needs to Know*, studies on pregnancy, fertilization, and the menopause, menstruation pills, an ashtray, a pair of scissors, a powder compact, toilet paper. Everything is catered for. An alarm clock, lots of hot-water bottles, a washbasin and water jug, a radio, and a vibrating device.

Once some girls turned up and walked along the winding footpath. Unfortunately they were stupid, though they could read. Not that this means anything. Nowadays everyone can read. They were two sisters. Or so they told me. They came into the garden. They read and looked and were even pretty. Young, at any rate. They said they were hitchhiking. Not many cars stop here though. After all, the valley doesn't go much further. It doesn't lead anywhere. Only into the grotto. It's nice there. Damp even in summer. I nearly thought one of them was you. I showed them the house. They laughed when they saw the newspapers and the chestnuts. And again when I showed them their sleeping place and when I gave them ravioli from a tin. They kept laughing. Even though that's a perfectly decent meal. Yet when I knocked on their door they just screamed and ran away. I was only going to tuck them in. Tuck myself in with them. Show them everything, teach them everything. I was glad when they were gone. They ate too much anyway. The stupid nanny goats.

There's an illustration in the book about the female organs of sexual arousal containing a view of the vulva. It shows the external pubic area of a deflowered woman, those instruments of the sublime orchestra that has so many different names, and is symbolized by the peach or the seashell. You can see the mound of Venus and the pubic arch, the large and small labia, the urethral, anal, and vaginal openings, the perineum, the vestibular glands, the vestibular bulbs, and the hymen. The pubis is a well. It is damp, fathomless and smells of moths and moss. A precise opening, a hollow, an abyss, a blind chasm. Desire is boundless and hard to pin down. There are so many questions. The term psychosexual perversion should be used with care. Every abnormality is rooted in the normal. And every normal state contains a grain of abnormality. Every pervert retains a tiny remnant of normal perception. How do you define perverse, anyway? A man actually looks much more elegant in women's stockings than in socks and suspenders. The sexual practices of male and female homosexuals are no different from those of people of normal sexual orientation.

There is a remarkable photograph in the book *Abnormal Traits*. It's obscene. It's beautiful. You won't want to look at it. You won't be able to take your eyes off it. An emotionally charged scene: first you see a man and a woman, the woman's buttocks, the act of coitus. But then you'll notice that they're both wearing black silk stockings, and realize that the phallus is not a real member, but is fastened around the woman's buttocks with two transparent straps, the kind that are popular these days. Like must go with like. It's the only way to achieve order. A friend sent me the photograph a long time ago. Nowadays I no longer open any post. I haven't known anyone for years, so that's that. The postman used to come once a week to check if I was still alive. Now he doesn't come anymore. I don't open letters either. After all, you never know what they might say. It might be you writing to say that you don't want to come anymore. How am I meant to reply to that? Anyway, at some point I would work out for myself that you weren't coming. I couldn't send you anything either. And who knows whether the postage stamp I have is still valid? Who knows whether the letter would arrive? Who knows

whether you would read it? So it's better to keep it. To keep everything. There's nothing one really needs. Just a pint of milk, a
bread roll, and a radio that plays through the night.

East Germany
PALACE OF THE REPUBLIC

* *Designed by a collective of architects led by Heinz Graffunder at the East German Building Academy, the symbolic government building was erected on the derelict land known as Marx-Engels-Platz on the former site of Berlin's City Palace, which had been demolished in 1950. It took thirty-two months to construct, and was inaugurated on April 23, 1976 as the People's Palace.*

The most conspicuous feature of the elongated, five-story, flat-roofed edifice was its facade of bronze-mirrored windows framed by white marble. The building housed not only the plenary chamber of the East German parliament or Volkskammer, an auditorium accommodating nearly eight hundred and another holding up to five thousand people, but also several conference and meeting rooms, thirteen restaurants, eight bowling lanes, a theater, and a discotheque.

It was the social hub of the party and state leadership, the home of the party conferences of the Socialist Unity Party (S.E.D.) and the seat of the Volkskammer, a venue for major national and international conferences as well as a cultural and entertainment center. The "Glass Flower" in the forty-meter-wide, eighty-meter-long double-height main foyer was a popular meeting place. Its walls displayed a collection of sixteen large-format pictures by well-known East German artists entitled "May communists dream?"

† *To enable the building to withstand the pressure of the groundwater in the glacial valley of Berlin, a concrete slab one hundred and eighty meters long, eighty-six meters wide and eleven meters deep was cast as the foundation. A skeleton of steel girders was constructed around eight concrete cores, before being encased in asbestos cement. A special legal provision permitted the use of sprayed asbestos, even though this technique had been outlawed in East Germany in 1969.*

On August 23, 1990 the parliament in the palace voted in favor of reunifica-
tion with the Federal Republic. One month later, on September 19, the same
body took the decision to close the palace with immediate effect because of
the asbestos contamination. In 1992 the German Bundestag declared itself in
favor of its demolition. Between 1998 and 2003, specialist companies cleared
the approximately five thousand tons of sprayed asbestos from the building,
doing so in a way that would allow the building to be either demolished or
renovated afterwards. With the carcinogenic material removed, the palace
was reduced to a shell.

After several architectural competitions to determine the future of the square
which, in 1991, reverted to its original name of "Schlossplatz," the Bundestag
decided in 2003 to have the palace demolished. Between spring 2004 and
the end of 2005 the gutted palace was temporarily reopened to the public for
cultural events.

In the end, the demolition of the building had to be postponed several
times—in part due to heated protests. Work on dismantling the building
finally began in February 2006. The Swedish steel in the basic structure was
melted down; some was sold to Dubai for use in the construction of the Burj
Khalifa, and some bought by the automotive industry and recycled into
engines. Work on the reconstruction of the historic Berlin City Palace began
in March 2013.

She lifted the bundle out of the string bag, unwrapped the cloth
around the asparagus, and laid the spears on the kitchen table.
Then she fetched a couple of handfuls of potatoes from the box
in its dark corner next to the refrigerator. Several of them already
had green patches on them, and some had even sprouted short,
knobbly shoots. Evidently the box was not dark enough after all.
The best way, of course, would be to store them in the cellar, but
then they always tasted a bit of coal. She fetched one of the gray
tea towels and laid it over the box as if it was a tablecloth.

The hot wash in the washing machine was on its second rinse.
With luck it would be dry by the end of the day, as the sun had

actually come out at lunchtime. All morning it had been overcast as if it was about to rain any minute.

She peeled the potatoes, slicing off a bit more where the green patches and shoots were, washed and halved them and placed them in a bowl by the cooker. She wanted to have everything prepared in advance as much as possible. At lunchtime she had only made herself some sandwiches, even though it was Sunday. She had never liked cooking just for herself. It simply wasn't worth it.

She had just started rinsing the sand off the asparagus spears when the doorbell rang. She quickly reached for the towel, went out into the hall and opened the door.

"Ah, Marlene, have you got a moment?"

It was Lippe. He lived downstairs across the landing on the first floor.

"Sure. Come in. I just need to finish off in the kitchen quickly."

Lippe had a worn-out look about him. He was a nice, easygoing guy. Sometimes they would all sit together of an evening and have a drink, although not so much lately.

"Holger not back yet?"

He glanced in the living room.

She shook her head. Lippe was studying military medicine, like Holger, but his specialism was stomatology.

He hovered in the doorway.

"Really, Lippe, you could have kept your shoes on, you know."

"Oh well, never mind."

He shrugged his shoulders.

"And the kid's having a nap?" He motioned with his head in the direction of the bedroom. He looked really tired. Perhaps there was something up with Carmen.

"Yes, she's dead to the world. She was exhausted. The fresh air. We had quite a long walk."

Straight after lunch she had drawn the curtains and put the child down in her cot. She had babbled for a bit, but soon all was quiet. She had actually been meaning to prepare some lessons, but it had completely slipped her mind in the morning.

"Mmm." He tucked his hands in his trouser pockets. "Jule's asleep too. It's no bad thing, a bit of peace and quiet on a Sunday."

She laid the asparagus spears one after the other on a dry tea towel.

"Queued up for asparagus, too, did you?" He took his hands out of his pockets, folded his arms and grinned broadly.

She couldn't help laughing. She was not the only one pinching asparagus from the field behind the allotments. Green asparagus. She had never once seen it on sale in the shop. Rumor had it that it all went straight to Berlin, to the Palace of the Republic.

"Yes, I hope no one rats on us." She dried her hands on the towel and took off her apron.

"Like a drink?"

He was still standing barefoot in the doorway. Lippe was quite a bit shorter than Holger. He had a thick, dark mustache and a receding hairline. His skin was sallow, almost waxy.

"No, no. I won't," he replied. "I'm going to go down to the garden again in a minute."

The Lipperts, like themselves and a few other families from their block, had been allocated a plot in the field behind the new buildings and had cultivated it over the spring months. The soil was very sandy. They had had to cut away the turf with a spade and shake it out before a thin layer of topsoil appeared, and had then planted potatoes to keep the weeds at bay. Lippe had even got hold of some fertilizer from the agricultural cooperative and set up some cold frames, to improve the yield. They had reaped a fairly meager harvest. But she was glad of whatever she did get. Peppers, radishes, carrots, beans, parsley. They had even managed some strawberries. A small bowlful, but still worth it.

"Come on, let's go in the living room."

He let her past into the hall, she pulled the bedroom door to and went ahead.

The sun now cast a shaft of bright light onto the aquariums, which stood on a homemade shelf unit to the left of the door. They were Holger's fish tanks. Guppies, black mollies, neon tetras and a single catfish that stayed hidden away in its hollow most of the time. To start with they had only had one, but then Holger had kept producing more wooden spindles and sawing more planks, and created space for a second, smaller aquarium above the first, and eventually even a third one, smaller still, right on top. Like a pyramid. The playpen stood in front of the aquariums.

Lippe sat down on the settee. His checked shirt was a bit tight across his stomach. His sleeves were rolled up. His forearms were covered in a dark fur.

"Marlene, we ..."

He took a deep breath.

Then he sat forward and folded his hands in his lap.

"We deliberated for a long time whether we should tell you."

Strange that he referred to "we," even though he was sitting there on his own in front of her.

He hesitated.

"Well ...," he started again, "you know we were in Berlin yesterday. Carmen had a lecture, and I had gone along with Jule. A long old trek, but it was worth it." His right hand was wavering in midair.

"Oh yes." She had completely forgotten.

"And afterwards, we thought we'd give ourselves a treat."

He looked over at the window. The cactuses looked really dusty against the light. They could do with watering.

"So we went into the Palace of the Republic, something a bit special, you know."

There was something indecent about his bare feet with their hairy toes on her carpet. She looked at the carved legs of the coffee table. Holger had discovered it a while ago in a derelict house in a neighboring village. A shabby old thing. You could clearly see the woodworm holes. They would be there for good. The two of them had managed to transport it home by bicycle along the sandy paths through the wood.

"You see, Marlene . . . ," he resumed, straightening his back.

"We saw Holger there. With another woman."

He looked at her now.

"In a compromising situation." He tilted his chin up a fraction, passed his hand over his face and slumped down slightly again.

"We just wanted you to know." It sounded like an apology.

"At first Carmen said it was none of our business." He ran his tongue over his teeth.

"But this morning I said to her: How would you feel if Marlene spotted me somewhere with another woman and didn't say anything?"

A compromising situation? A compromising situation. Poor Lippe. Such a nice guy. Much nicer than Carmen, with her severe plait and her beauty spot, just above her mouth on the left-hand side, which looked as if it had been drawn on.

"I don't know what I'd do either."

His right foot bobbed up and down. "Perhaps you'd like to have a chat with Carmen? You know, woman to woman?"

Carmen was a pharmacist. She had never really felt comfortable in her company.

"I don't think he noticed us," he added.

The table was green. They had painted it themselves. They thought it would be kind of nice.

"Thank you," she said, without knowing why.

Lippe stood up. "I'll get going." He wiped his hands on his trouser legs.

She heard him slip his shoes on in the hall, close the door of the apartment, and go down the stairs. The dust danced in the light. Actually, the table looked vile.

He twisted round, took his briefcase from the rear seat, laid it on his lap and undid the catch. In amongst his clothes was a water-filled sphere, a present for his daughter. He picked it up.

"Nice," said Achim. "She'll like that."

The greenish water sloshed back and forth. The duck smiled. Holger returned the ball to the briefcase and got out his sandwiches.

"Would you like one?"

He took them out of their greaseproof paper.

Achim turned towards him briefly and shook his head.

"Nah, it's all right." He looked back at the road. There wasn't much traffic.

"I don't want to spoil my appetite."

Holger bit into the sandwich. Spam. The bread tasted old. He had made the sandwiches yesterday morning, while Marlene and the little one were still asleep. To avoid waking them, he had not put his shoes on until he was out in the stairwell, then he had taken the stairs two at a time in his usual way and walked the kilometer to the main road. But an eternity had passed since then. He put the sandwich down and wrapped it up again in the paper.

"Hankering for something proper, are you?"

Achim indicated, stepped on the accelerator and overtook a moped.

Holger wiped his hands on his knees. Only now did he notice how tired he was. His head was hammering. He seldom drank. It just wasn't compatible with the early-morning starts and training. He still had his sports shorts on. Achim had been anxious to get away on time. He probably couldn't wait to see his wife again. After the presentation ceremony he had not even had time to say goodbye to Birgit properly. To be honest, that had suited him.

"Can you just pull over somewhere? I need a piss."

He did not like farewells. He never knew what to say and was glad when it was over.

"Man, you've got the bladder of a girl."

Achim was all right, a bear of a man. Not the fastest, but in long-range hand-grenade throwing he beat the lot of them. From a standing start, and with an action that looked like slow motion. His on-target rate was over 50 percent.

Achim glanced in the rearview mirror, let a car overtake, downshifted, signaled, and drove a little way along a rough farm track. Then he switched off the engine, took his hands off the steering wheel and turned to face him.

"There you go. All yours!"

Holger got out and went and stood facing the bank. He directed his stream at a patch of stinging nettles. The green hedges were choked with knotweed. Unripe blackberries hung in thorny hedges. Beyond the boundary strip, power lines led directly across the field to a single brick-built farmhouse with a wooden barn and, next to it, a flagpole without a flag. The corn was still green and swayed in the wind. It all looked so peaceful. The combine harvesters would be along at some point though. He felt the sun on the back of his neck.

He found himself thinking about how happy he had been when he had finished school and immediately received permission to embark on a degree. That feeling that now nothing could go wrong. And then his name on the roll of honor. In gothic lettering as on the certificate. His record was still unbroken.

And now? A couple of midges danced around him. He batted them away. If all went to plan, in three years' time he would be a doctor. At least that was something tangible.

"Get a move on, mate."

Of course, Birgit had asked once more when they would see each other again. He hadn't known what to say to that.

He yawned. He pulled up his trousers by the waistband and walked back to the car.

Achim started the engine and set off again. Holger took his tracksuit jacket from the back seat, stuffed it between the seat back and the window frame, and laid his head on it. He looked at Achim. There were little beads of sweat on his forehead. Achim always knew exactly what he wanted. But you didn't have to chat with him the whole time.

Holger turned to the window. Everything looked completely different from the car. He had only ever seen the route from the train.

They drove through a small village with cobbled streets. He looked at the people outdoors. An elderly lady in a house dress standing in her garden, with arms akimbo. A young couple with a pushchair crossing the road. Two boys on bicycles, weaving their way hands-free along the pavement.

Then he closed his eyes. The car vibrated. He tried to relax. He had been in the palace once before, with his parents. Soon after his swearing-in. In a suit even. But he couldn't remember much about it now. Although everyone had talked about it. About the flags, the mirrored glass, the marble, the lines of people.

He didn't know whether it had been his idea or Birgit's. It was just how it worked out. They hadn't had to wait in line for long either. And then, in the wine bar, they'd even got a table with a view over the Spree. On a Saturday evening too. It had all been so easy. He'd pulled out the chair for her and she'd sat down, as if it were all perfectly normal. Neither of them was appropriately dressed, but they didn't care. Birgit thought they had something to celebrate. Although they hadn't even won. She was the only girl he knew who shaved her armpits.

He opened his eyes and stared at the squashed insects on the windshield. The assault course was actually the toughest. Once you'd got that over and done with, the worst was out of the way.

The water jump and the cross-country run were a walk in the park by comparison.

He straightened up again, rolled down the window, and leaned his elbow out. The air rushing by felt nice.

Outside, fields and woods went by, telephone poles, a huge tumbledown engine shed, an avenue of lime trees that seemed to go on and on. He was a doctor, though, wasn't he. Or halfway there at least.

He crossed his arms behind his head.

The child stood in the cot with eyes wide open. One hand gripped the bars with fat fingers, the other was reaching over the top rail and flailing in her direction. Her little teeth flashed white in her laughing mouth.

She lifted the little girl up, laid her down on the chest of drawers next to the double bed, peeled off the onesie, the plastic pants, and the sodden cloth diaper.

The child babbled away, punched the air with choppy movements of her little fists, and kept kicking Marlene's arms and breasts with her bare feet. The padded changing mat was printed all over with yellow teddy bears: one holding a bunch of balloons, one seesawing in an umbrella, and another riding on a pony. The sequence continually repeating.

She took the toddler, sat her on the potty, went into the kitchen and put the kettle on the stove. Then she opened the wall cupboard, took out the tin of coffee and measured a spoonful of powder into a mug.

When she came back into the bedroom the child was chewing on a corner of the quilt, which had slipped off the double bed. She carefully extracted the saliva-drenched bit of fabric from her mouth, pressed the crocheted toadstool into the child's hand, hoisted the quilt back onto the bed, and smoothed it out with a couple of sweeps of her hand. Then she lifted the little one back onto the mat and wiped her bottom with a damp flannel.

She was just passing the diaper, folded into a triangle, through the child's legs when the kettle started whistling in the kitchen. The toadstool fell to the floor. With a few rapid movements she fastened the diaper and pulled the plastic pants on over it, picked up the little girl in her arms, and hurried into the kitchen.

She turned off the gas stove and poured boiling water onto the coffee powder. The child clung to her blouse and pressed her head to her neck. She felt the clenched little hands on her breast. She carried her over to the playpen in the living room and tried to extricate herself from her grasp.

"It's all right," she said. "It's all right," and managed to disentangle herself.

Then she went back into the bedroom, carried the potty to the bathroom, emptied it into the toilet, flushed, lowered the lid and sat down.

The window was tilted open. Outside, children were kicking a ball back and forth. Their shouts echoed around the new apartment blocks. She stood up, pushed the curtain aside, and looked out. A small boy was dangling upside down from the climbing frame. His hair hung like streaks in the air. A blonde girl wearing glasses, whom she had never seen before, sat alone on the seesaw. She held the handle firmly, stood up, pulled the plank up, let herself fall and crashed down onto a bit of car tire sticking out of the sand. Then she immediately stood up again, went on tiptoes and let herself drop down again, over and over. Marlene quickly closed the curtain again. The wash ought to be long finished by now.

She opened the drum, hauled the wet things out and stuffed them in the spin dryer over the bath. She used her right hand to hold the lid on firmly, and her left to slide the control knob downwards. The spinner started up. Water sloshed into the bathtub in several surges, first a big gush, then less each time, a thin, slowly dwindling stream. Once it was producing no more than droplets she let the machine come to a halt.

The rubber ring had slipped out again. She pushed it back, opened the lid and began lifting the laundry out of the spinner one item at a time and hanging it on the clothesline strung across the bathroom. It was mostly cloth diapers, underwear, and hand-kerchiefs. There was no way they would be dry by tomorrow. Only last week she had had to strip the sheets in the morning because Holger had wet the bed. Unbelievable.

She closed the lid of the spin dryer.

She was about to carry the potty back to the bedroom when her gaze alighted on the medals hanging from the oval mirror in the hall. Athletics, decathlon, military multisports. Metal dan-gling on colorful ribbons. But she was still so young. She was so young.

She grabbed the medals and yanked them down. They fell to the floor with a clatter. The mirror wobbled but stayed on the wall.

She set the potty down in front of the cot, tilted the window open, went back into the hall, and picked up her coffee from the kitchen. Then she carried the mug into the living room, put it down on the green table, and flopped down on the settee.

The child was sitting in the playpen with legs wide apart, crying. Her face was flushed. A string of saliva hung from her mouth. In one of the yellow-lit aquariums, a shoal of iridescent blue neon tetras chased back and forth. Little air bubbles floated up. The guppies had disappeared. The pump hummed steadily. The black-and-white marbled catfish was feeding on the algae on the glass walls with its big suction mouth. Its white-rimmed eyes looked dead. The bedroom door slammed shut.

Her gaze drifted over the rose-patterned wallpaper and the ocher-colored heater, then along the wall cabinet with the tele-vision set and the atlas, the two-volume encyclopedia and the illustrated books on socialist realism and the Olympic Games, passing over the snake plant and the cactuses on the windowsill and the cushion covers with flower motifs that she had embroidered during her pregnancy. Two small framed prints of sailing boats hung above the sofa. On the table was the fruit bowl Holger had turned on the lathe.

The mug was still full of coffee. She hadn't touched it.

She got up and went to the playpen.

They could see the red light flashing even from afar. It was the crossroads by the Moeckow-Berg radio tower. Then they entered the wood that he knew so well. It immediately turned cool. Holger wound the window up. Achim indicated and pulled over on the right at the bus stop outside the old tollkeeper's house.

"See you tomorrow then."

His fingers skimmed the steering wheel. It had a silvery-shimmering fur cover.

"Thanks, Achim."

Holger reached for his briefcase, opened the door, got out, and swung the passenger door shut.

The dark-blue Lada signaled and rejoined the road. Holger watched it go. He tried to remember the numbers and letters of the license plate, but he couldn't. Eventually the car rounded a bend and disappeared into the wood.

He turned around and took the narrow, paved footpath on the left-hand side of the road. A single streetlight stood halfway along the route into the village. It was already lit, even though it was only just beginning to get dark. The old street cobbles shone in its glow.

The row of detached and semidetached houses began even before the village sign. Roses and delphiniums bloomed in the front gardens. Above the door to a stable turned garage, an old horse's harness dangled from a rusty horseshoe. At the filthy bus shelter by the roundabout, a bunch of teenagers were hanging around with their bikes, smoking. Two of them glanced up briefly, gave him an almost imperceptible nod and went back into their huddle. At least they greeted him, even though he lived in one of the army blocks. He crossed the street. He could hear the stream burbling softly behind the hedge. A river helped you get your bearings at least. It was something tangible. Everything was easier when the requirements were clear.

After the bridge his route took him uphill. He turned onto the path behind the church. There was a ladies' black bicycle with a crocheted spoke guard parked in front of the cooperative store. It wasn't even locked. Behind it loomed the outline of the school building. In the left-hand window of the mayor's yellow-painted bungalow, a curtain was pushed slightly to one side. Now you could see the three new apartment blocks too, all staggered. Some of the windows were lit up. This was where the tarmac ended and the sandy footpath began. It had grown cool all of a sudden. He stopped for a moment, took his tracksuit top off his shoulder and put it on.

Lying in between the play apparatus in the playground was a dirty, dented volleyball. The paint had already flaked off the lower bars of the climbing frame, even though it was still quite new, not even two years old. He looked up at the apartment. The light was on in the kitchen. The bathroom was dark. What had he expected? He didn't know.

He opened the door and ascended the two flights of stairs, a step at a time. The television was on in Lippe's apartment. His footsteps echoed. Outside the Splettstössers' door there was a smell of pea stew.

Her gardening shoes stood next to the doormat. Earth stuck to them, and they were covered with a fine layer of dust. The doormat was askew. He shoved it straight with his feet. The nameplate on the door bore his name, her name, engraved in brass. He was so tired.

He rang the bell, even though he knew his key was in the front pocket of his briefcase. Inside the apartment, he heard the sound of the refrigerator door closing. It was an age before the door opened.

She already had her nightie on. She let him hug her, then turned away. He let go of her, put his briefcase down under the coat rack, crouched down and took off his shoes.

"Is the kid asleep?"

He looked up at her.

Marlene nodded briefly and disappeared into the kitchen. Everywhere was in darkness. Only the lamp above the kitchen table cast a circle of bright light on the tablecloth.

He slid his feet into his slippers and opened the bedroom door. The child was lying peacefully in her bed, both arms stretched out next to her head. She was breathing in long, regular breaths. He placed his index finger in the little half-open hand. How incredibly contented she looked. Then he pulled the covers up a little, left the room and quietly shut the door. His briefcase was still there at the foot of the coat rack. He picked it up.

When he went to take out the packet containing the sandwiches, he discovered the ball with the duck inside. He took it with him into the kitchen.

Marlene was sitting at the kitchen table with her head tilted back.

"We didn't win, but I've got a present for the littl'un." He placed the ball in front of her on the table. Then he went to the refrigerator, opened the door, looked inside for a moment and closed it again. Next to the sink were some peeled potatoes and green asparagus. He would have liked to make himself a chamomile tea, but he didn't dare use the kettle.

He went over to the table, pulled out the chair, sat down, touched her fleetingly on the arm, but then didn't know what to do next and took his hand away again.

Only now did she look at him. He drew his shoulders back and breathed deeply, in and out. Her eyes were almost black.

Lacus Luxuriae
KINAU'S SELENOGRAPHS

* *Gottfried Adolf Kinau, a priest and amateur astronomer from Suhl in Thuringia, dedicated more than thirty years of his life to selenography. His topographical drawings of the moon were much admired by the contemporary lunar research community for their meticulousness.*

† *Only a few of the documents containing Kinau's observations have survived to this day, including his essay "Lunar Rilles," dating from 1848. Of his selenographs, only two had been published in* Sirius, *a journal of popular astronomy, and they are presumed to have been lost to fire, as part of its image collection, during the Second World War.*

In 1932, the International Astronomical Union gave the name "Kinau" to a crater in the southern highlands on the nearside of the moon, as originally proposed by astronomer Edmund Neison in 1876. Who's Who in the Moon, *a handbook of lunar nomenclature published in 1938 by the British Astronomical Association, contains the following entry:* C. A. Kinau (?–1850). Botanist and selenographer. He had an official post on the estate of the Prince of Schwarzenberg in southern Bohemia, and published in 1842 two works on Poisonous Plants and Fungi. *Despite a worldwide search, no botanist by the name of Kinau could be found. In 2007, he was replaced in the U.S. survey authority's records by the priest Gottfried Adolf Kinau as the man who gave his name to the crater. To this day, no trace has ever been found of C. A. Kinau.*

Knowing when and under which constellations I was born does little to illuminate the subject of our investigation. Suffice it to mention that my entry into the earthly world fell on one of those annually recurring nights in which the Leonids reveal themselves, in one of the most impressive celestial light spectacles visible to the naked eye, at least back in the days when the blackness of the night had not yet been diluted to a perpetual twilight by the glare of gas lamps and their inglorious successors. One year, as a young student, I was treated to a blazing shower of shooting stars around the time of my birthday, a festive rain of fire which soon filled the entire firmament with innumerable flaring meteors and planted in me that invisible seed which would eventually germinate some decades hence and bring forth the most passionate blossom: my love of the starlit night, of the planets and their satellites, which is what ultimately led me to that certainly higher, yet also undeniably remote sphere which I am now obliged to call my home.

At first, though, I was seized—a natural consequence of my rural upbringing—by a penchant for botany, and there awakened in me a fervent desire, on completion of my studies in Advanced Forestry, to acquire a permanent paid position with a broad scope that would enable me to advance my research.

I found it in my local vicinity as an administrator for the southern estates of His Highness Prince Johann Adolf zu Schwarzenberg, the second to bear this name, and as such my role was initially to oversee the leasehold farm of Bzy, then the Forbes estate, two tracts of land particularly exposed to the adverse effects of their unprotected location on the right bank of the Moldau, until the reform instituted by the supreme authorities dispatched me to the central seat of princely power, namely the large castle perched on a steep rock above the Moldau in the town of Krumau. I grew fond of this region, despite its harsh, damp climate with its early and late frosts, for which the fertile but weather-beaten soil barely compensated, especially since agricultural conditions became increasingly difficult the closer the lands of this sprawling territory were to the Bohemian Wood—a vast forest whose quasiprimeval interior was inhabited by wild bears.

In addition to that activity, which I performed with the single-minded zeal characteristic of young provincial officials of the pre-1848 period, I dedicated my few free hours deliberately not to the fodder plants and crops that dominated the agricultural cycle, but to the wayward phenomena of toxic flora, having since my young days felt a particular attraction to those plants which bring no benefit to mankind, but rather tend to cause harm to people and their livestock. What captivated me most of all about them was the mysterious way in which they worked, seemingly according to a wholly obscure system that manifested no firm features whatsoever by which one might have distinguished these often life-threatening plants from benign ones, for one and the same family frequently included both nontoxic species—even edible vegetables—and ones that induced breathing difficulties and vomiting. In those days, fungi formed an important part of the diet of the rural Bohemian community; mothers used to place bunches of *Solanum nigrum* in their babies' cradles to help them sleep or, rather, forcibly send them off to sleep; herbalists everywhere carried on their deadly trade in sacred *Anemone pul-satilla*; and every now and again some simpleton lured by their beauty into partaking of the glossy black fruits of the *Atropa bel-ladonna* would find himself struck down by raving madness.

So I collected and examined the plants that grew in abundance along footpaths and streams, on heaths and in meadows, studied the burned entrails of livestock that had come to grief following a fateful indulgence, and filled my observation journals, all with the worthy aim of publishing a compendium of the poisonous plants of Bohemia and a paper on the fungi found in this part of the country—some of them eminently edible, but many more of them toxic. The study of cryptogamia, long-neglected at the time and admirably revived by Krombholz only a short time previously, was an activity that would prepare me like no other for my subsequent field of endeavor: the unseen work of legacy preservation.

The results of my research were favorably received, notwith-standing the fact that no general underlying principles could be deduced from my observations. An amiable scientific dialogue ensued, and as a newly elected member of several learned societies I soon came to regard myself as one of the select circle of those who have added to our knowledge of the world, even in a discipline as lowly as botanical classification. They were good times. I botanized, oversaw the accounts of the princely estate, excelled both as a strict supervisor and an eager subject, and took a fancy to a woman who reciprocated my affection to a sufficient degree that I was not deterred from making my proposal. The years went by; grain harvest was followed by corn threshing, hop picking by fruit harvest, green fodder distribution by beet sowing, and meanwhile the numerous measures I had taken to maximize the amount of arable land available proved as effective as intended: woods were cleared, heathland cultivated, moors drained and ponds emptied down to their peaty bottom. With my attention so focused on the future and on practical considerations, my research gradually ground to a halt during this time, and the more closely I scrutinised the natural world through my magnifying glass, the more it seemed to me in every one of its countless metamorphoses to embody unbridled chaos untamable by any governing hand—a phenomenon familiar to anyone seeking to unite theory and practice. One goes to great lengths to organize and configure this chaos in one's mind, only to confuse the scientific picture just when one believes oneself to be enriching it.

And so the glorious vision of an all-encompassing system became bound up in my heart with an unspeakable feeling of worthlessness, bitterly fueled by a series of flagrant offenses against forest laws. Every mangled trunk was a thorn in my side, the flesh around it festering with a sense of injured pride—the poison of weakness, which I endeavored to dispel on lengthy forays into the forest, which gradually became my habit in place of attending church. Indeed it was on a Sunday, as I roamed the impenetrable undergrowth of the Bohemian Wood as was my wont, making my way into its dark heart of nothing but spruces, where all the tree debris blown down by the wind had caused bare patches littered with dead trunks, which lent the wood an almost wounded appearance, that, visited by a peculiar fear that I am inclined in hindsight to call prophetic, I pulled from the ground the frond of an especially magnificent fern, and on closer examination it became apparent that the roots of the regal plant presented the shape of a waning crescent moon, no less. This moment, which has since haunted me like a vision, was embedded in a solemn silence uninterrupted by any song, call, or indeed the slightest sound from any bird. And as if this unmistakable sign, which I was immediately willing to acknowledge as the mark of a higher power, did not already weigh heavily enough on my soul, only a few days later—in the early hours of July 8, 1842—the big circle of the moon cast its gray-blue shadow over me, although my place of abode at the time was not granted the pleasure of a total eclipse of the sun, something that one would have been able to witness a mere hundred miles further south. When, on that day, the fireball narrowed to a thin sliver and its now deathly pale light transfigured the courtyard, the poultry fell silent again and fled to their coop, while all my blood rushed vertiginously to my heart, and all at once it struck me with glittering clarity that anyone wishing to scale the sturdy botanical branch of the tree of science all the way to its outermost fork must reach up towards the mighty phenomena of the all-overarching sky. No sooner had I embarked on my new studies than the logicality of turning from plants sprouting in obscurity to the secret order of the stars became for me a fortifying certainty. After all, throughout the ages, the vast majority of alchemists had been botanists first and foremost, and the most prominent alchemists had simultaneously been astrologers and astronomers, like the architect of that compelling theory which posits that every plant has its own heavenly twin in the form of a star. The degree to which the study of poisons and the study of the heavens are intertwined is manifest not least in that verse from the Book of

Revelation, unfathomable at that time, which had predicted the fatal impact of the comet Wormwood, known to have wiped out a third of the Earth's population as well as the DNA quartz glass archives designed to last forever, consequently rendering our work here all the more urgent, although our activities have very wisely always been confined to those goods generally classified as analog, and not those belonging to that ephemeral, electrical device-dependent state between zero and one. In those days the human race, fooled by its confidence in the infallibility of its supreme ingenuity, experienced once again the most appalling consequences of its lack of knowledge. The Earth was not a safe place and never would be.

Within the space of a year not only was I wholly familiar with celestial phenomena, I had also discovered my special liking for the closest of all the heavenly bodies, deriving unprecedented pleasure from studying its scarred form in detail and devoting myself nightly to the gradual discovery and detailed drawing of its peculiarly damaged yet chastely shimmering surface, which I learned to examine through a five-inch refractor with a focal length of three feet that I had purchased in Budweis, in the same way as I had once examined spores concealed in tender membranes. For that which is near is far off—and the higher truth is revealed in the most inconspicuous of creatures and the most remote—both under the microscope and through the telescope. Given that my previous labor of love had been concerned with outlying phenomena, it is not surprising that, with my new subject too, it was primarily its outermost edges that fascinated me, in other words those regions which, due to the slightly swaying proper motion of the moon in accordance with some complex law, may be glimpsed only in certain phases. The cratered landscape of Tycho with the incomparable shadows it casts at sunset, Plato, the circular mountain range, in the early dawn hours, Gassendi, the banked plateau close to the light limit, and the evenly shaped bowl of Linné were to me what Cicero, Seneca, and Virgil were to Petrarch: faithful friends and mute recipients of my nightly monologues. Not that they ever answered me. The moon is notoriously silent by nature. Yet it was a gracious silence, which, unlike that of the prince's smug attendants, did not punish me with contempt, but seemed to reward each one of my rapt looks with benevolence and kindness.

Henceforward I lived each day only for the night, longed for its blackness which obliterated the earthly realm and caressed the starlight, and for the dark time of year, when the early sunset would allow me to neglect my worldly duties and silently devote that time to my new master.

Very few are prepared to go as far as I went, for it takes not audacity but humility to exchange people's memory of you and the secure career of a civil servant for the vague prospect of attaining some higher truth or greater glory. To disappear, as long as one person remembers you, demands considerable skill, all the more so if you hold a highly responsible position on an estate like Krumau which, even after the fateful year when the authorities had to suffer the loss not only of serf labor but also of some of their best goods, still ranked as one of the most preeminent in the realm. The prince was known for visiting his estates year in, year out, watching them thrive like a father watching over his children, hence he followed my activities, too, with fond suspicion, since I was fatherless and only a few years younger and could have been his brother, or perhaps actually was, as my mother hinted to me on her death bed. Her funeral would be followed by other, more painful ones, until I elected never again to have to embark on this most harrowing of all processions and, of my own accord, chose the fate that overtakes us all one day, since it was now of no consequence whether my name were to fade to illegibility forthwith or only in four or forty-four generations' time. Circumstances favored my undertaking more than they hindered it: the lands under my administration were now considerably smaller in area, and the two children who would have been able to carry tidings of me to future generations lay in the graveyard, borne off by plagues that my wife, laboring under an ineradicable misconception, ascribed, along with the catastrophic failed harvests of those years, to the sinister influence of the moon, and I was unable either to disabuse her or to ease her pain, which bore a silent reproach. She in turn could not abide my moon addiction—and possessed neither parents nor siblings who could have mourned or been suspicious of her abrupt passing. In any case, it was not possible, under the prevailing laws of nature, for me to take her with me; each one of us must leave everything behind, as if he were crossing the final threshold.

I landed, like all those before and after me, in the Mare Imbrium, the sunless lake, naked and freezing, fighting for breath, as befits a birth. As soon as the decreed quarantine period had elapsed, I was appointed as an assistant, and hence the lowest member of what seemed to me to be a completely and utterly perfect institution. Inspired by the irresistible regularity of its routines, I took care faithfully to perform all tasks entrusted to me, the most lofty of these duties consisting in the preliminary sorting of all incoming goods.

As everyone knows, Ariosto, in his *Orlando Furioso*, once set abroad a rumor that everything that is lost on Earth ends up here with us on the moon, an idea he had copied almost word for word from Alberti, who had previously overheard it from a muddleheaded washerwoman in Padua. Truly all three were overindulging their imagination if they thought to find in this fabled place everything they themselves secretly missed: bygone days and fallen empires, long-lost loves and unanswered prayers.

The truth is that the centrifugal forces act in the opposite direction, just as it is not the Earth that keeps the moon in its orbit, but the moon that keeps the terrestrial body in *its*, which is why the moon essentially merits the title of mother planet, or at the very least that of the Archimedean point from which the world may be lifted off its axis. For the Earth is nothing, and the moon in its appalling feigned dependence, that mute, calcified mirror, is everything, especially since it is in any case only a matter of time before the cosmic page turns and Earth's satellite finally assumes the dominant role in this fragile configuration, a role it has covertly played since its very origin. For it is invariably the servant who places an obligation on the master—and not the reverse, as my experience as a mediator between the domestic staff and the prince taught me on multiple occasions.

My relocation happened to coincide with the first crude experiments by the physiologist Mayer, which suggested that movement and warmth are merely different manifestations of one and the same force, and that consequently any loss of energy is a near-impossibility. This basic principle of energy conservation—which here on the moon had been known since time immemorial as the law of loss avoidance—governs the extensive interactions between the two stars and implies that anything that arrives here on the moon disappears on Earth, having been selected by an independent Moon/Earth Council on the basis of a fair yet ultimately impenetrable principle, before finding its way into this world and hence crossing into that weightless intermediate realm of the archive, which eludes the traditional assignment to either the living or the dead.

Only for a brief, yet glorious period now in the distant past were all incoming items kept without exception. If one believes the myriad stories passed down by word of mouth despite the prohibitions, these included the stones of the Olmecs; a clay model of the Cretan labyrinth from the workshop of the historical figure Daedalus; a vase depicting the feast of Hybristica held in Argos in honor of the Muses' servant Telesilla, at which the women would wear men's clothes and the men women's clothes; the magnificent nose of the Sphinx of Giza; the second Arabic translation of the *Almagest*, inscribed in gold lettering on a 220-foot-long dragon gut, as well as Euripides's play *Polyidus* with its line that shines out across the darkness of oblivion: "Who

knows whether life is death and death is life?"—a line that seems
to me to express most admirably that to which we are elected or
condemned here; also half a dozen atomic bombs preserved in
Greenland's ice; a neat crucifix made out of the cross-bone of
a frog's head; several complete, but entirely different sounding
transcripts of the *Secretum Secretorum*; Simone Martini's elaborate
portrait of Petrarch's beloved Laura de Noves, which apparently
served only to prove how conceited the much vaunted beauty
was in reality; the grotesque codices of the Maya, which could
be read only by their priests and by no one else, along with a
remarkable number of works by women, whose titles alas I can
no longer recall.

That era was followed by a time of transition in which the task
of selection and safekeeping was entrusted to an army of chosen
ones, which included some of the greatest experts in the art of
memory, who had been unable to escape the call to our sphere,
until they were replaced by some equally great experts in the art
of forgetting, since it had gradually dawned on those in charge
that the latter were more adept at managing the flow of incoming
goods.

It was much like on Earth: each generation reorganized the
goods, every new regime, for its own edification, invented a
whole new approach, and if practical activity declined under one
ruler, theory, by contrast, blazed all the more brightly. Periods of
deliberate neglect were followed by spells of excessive concern,
and the oft-raised objection that, while much was achieved in
both, even more was omitted, fails to take into account the immense challenge posed by the general space problem that hangs
over every archive from the hour of its birth, which no system yet
invented is able to solve, particularly considering that space here
is limited to an area not much larger than the Russian Empire at
its most extensive.

On one occasion the order was issued to adopt the model of
a permanent but limited library as the basis for goods storage,

while another time the originals were replaced with improved, scaled-down copies, until it emerged that the material selected did not possess all the specific qualities advisable for an undertaking of this magnitude, and soon some of the most wonderful photocopies became unusable and were disposed of as expertly as their fragile originals before them.

The council's directives frequently met with astonishment on the part of the lunar population, which was not, in fact, composed of the most worthy representatives of the human race, but rather resembled an arbitrarily thrown-together community of disparate people with nothing in common save for the tender bonds they had once forged with Earth's satellite, which from a distance presented itself in an entirely different light in each of their respective cultures. Indeed the moon, which, in accordance with both my native languages, I have only ever been able to conceive of as masculine, had charmed more than a few of the administrators here as the seductive Madame Luna; it even appeared to the Manchu as a divine rabbit holding a mortar, and alas occasionally it also—in keeping with the English expression—tempted lunatics and somnambulists into staying here. The madmen showed themselves to have a particular fondness for the wanton custom of reciting in seemingly never-ending songs the names of those monuments that had already fallen victim to the malignant action of the solar wind, an incantatory practice that continued through the long lunar nights, something that some, and not solely the most depraved of our colleagues, would pay for with the abrupt end of their eternal life, if one is disposed to refer to what we have here in those terms. A complete absence of history is the highest virtue in this life; not the feeblest remnant of earthly melancholy is tolerated here on high, and anyone who nonetheless falls prey to it forfeits his existence here, since the lunar archivist, more even than any terrestrial curator, is required to treat each object equally and, in the interests of all, must not become emotionally attached to any of the goods, particularly as the greedy ravages of time in any case allow only a fraction of the material to maintain its original form for a certain period.

Needless to say, the allocations from the council were never-ending, and soon forever relegated any efforts to preserve all goods—including the creation of an indelible memory containing everything that ever has been and will be—to the realm of impossibility, along with any prospect of a return to Earth, which turned serenely like a white-clouded marble before our eyes, having not the slightest inkling of our labors. I was not alone in finding this sight increasingly hard to bear. And so, when my long-awaited promotion finally came to pass, I was able, without encountering any appreciable resistance, to implement my plan to relocate the archive initially to the side facing away from the planet, and eventually to move it entirely underground. Demoralized and spurred on in equal measure by the failure of my predecessors, I created there, in the lightless depths of the Lacus Luxuriae, a system whose supposedly illustrious centerpiece consisted in the directive henceforward only to retain goods that made reference to the moon, this seeming to me the most worthy approach, if only for the reason that in the works destined for Earth's satellite, the story of the self-absorbed planet forever turning on its own axis is replicated like the product of a dream. For, as Aristotle once suggested, the dream and the cesspit are inseparably bound to one another, and the moon, like the bowel from which dreams emerge, is the true seat of the soul, nurtured by the longings of our lunar confraternity, like a cheerful, diverse population of simpleminded, insatiable bacteria.

It was an indescribable blessing to be rid of all those goods we had been keeping which had committed the unforgivable error of not mentioning our homeland, the moon, at least once—if only in the improper, metaphorical sense of the Romantics or their numerous successor movements. Those items that had measured up to my strict selection criteria and survived the tumult of long-established regulations were admitted to the Lunarium. The centerpieces of the innermost department were a Babylonian canon of eclipses, an album of Japanese ink drawings of pink protuberances, a strange silent film called *The First Men in the Moon*, a mechanical musical box containing a Selene riding on a gilded centaur, and the print template of Galileo's *The Starry Messenger*, in which he likens the shape of a moon crater to that of my homeland Bohemia, along with vast quantities of lunar rock recovered in response to repatriation requests, to which some notable improvements were made in the course of my negotiations. In short, this seemed like a splendid arrangement, until the time came when I ruled, in my professed wisdom, that it was no longer sufficient just to mention the moon; rather it was necessary for it to be referred to in its true sense, since, after all, even the most brilliant lunar theories had always suffered from the flaw that, in the moon, they were only really looking for the Earth, only wanted to see in it their own inadequate self, a small, stunted twin, the remnant of that prehistoric cataclysm when the fledgling Earth collided with a nameless planet—the event that sparked life itself—and a piece was violently ripped from it which, as a satellite, settled into its own orbit, a late-born, wayward copy, a blind mirror, a star gone cold.

Oh, if only I had moderated my mania! For when I examined the stores of items again, between the Nebra sky disc and an early wax relief of the lunar mountains crafted by Wilhelmine Witte, wife of Court Councilor Witte, I happened upon a bundle of selenographs which, to my silent horror, were signed with my own name in an unknown hand. Kepler must have felt similar emotions when he came face to face with his demon in a dream. In me, likewise, all manner of sensations were awakened which I thought I had left behind on Earth, since in those drawings, which betokened more diligence than talent, I encountered again the mountain formations I had long idolized, the sight of which had shaken me less when in their immediate vicinity than when

I used to observe them from afar, an activity to which I had devoted the best of my years on Earth. And so, from behind the veil of oblivion, a memory reemerged of that blessed afternoon on which an unusually favorable opportunity had arisen, on account of the secondary earthshine, to observe the night side of my present place of work and to record it in drawings: Aristarchus shone brightly, the Mare Humorum stood out with dark clarity, Grimaldi appeared grayish-black, and, as I savored the aftertaste of the memory jogged from its slumber, I was again overcome by that long-dormant urge that had once brought me to this remote place, to this labyrinth of lightless caverns with its interlocking villous aisles, a place where—it now irrefutably dawned on me—the object of my highest admiration had become for me one of daily chores, and the radiant future had faded away into an inaccessible past. Only the present, the tender blossom of the moment, had always contrived to hide itself from me.

There I was, at the pinnacle of my life's work, in the supposedly legitimate possession of supremely precious goods, from which the ghosts of my past joys and most recent sufferings drifted up to me, sensitive as an exposed nerve. The body in which I had, not long ago, considered myself as safe as in my mother's womb, had suddenly turned cold, my high-mindedness had vanished and I felt a strong antipathy towards the prospect of uselessly repeating over and over like Sisyphus the task already performed countless times, since none of the future methods would be able to banish the thought that only now was ripening in me to a sad certainty: that the moon, like every archive, was not a place of safekeeping, but one of total destruction, Earth's own knacker's yard, and the only practicable way of saving my foolish work, the Lunarium, from the inevitable—its certain replacement by infinitely stricter and better conceived systems—was for me to preempt the downfall that awaited it myself.

To understand the moon means to understand oneself, and

today, at the very limit of my wretched existence, I can make so bold as to say that I have succeeded in this to some small degree, though that realization did not, like the vast majority of truths, also serve to alleviate the pain it engendered but, on the contrary, the sheer size of the dose turned the medicine to poison. This insight gained too late tastes as bitter as the semiripe fruits of the nightshade. The moon has stayed the same, and the universe with its constantly twinkling lights of long-extinguished stars is the eternally old, historic place. I was a person like any other for whom the moon, like an ever-painful phantom limb, was merely a reminder of a now-lost state of perfection, of the immeasurable trauma of birth, whose raw violence inherently presents more of a riddle than ineluctable death itself. But because remembering can be learned, whereas forgetting cannot, I am denied the possibility of returning home, or of finding sanctuary in a belief in Linné's classification or in Jesus on the cross, which is what saved my doppelgänger from my fate. So I am departing a life that is no longer deserving of its name, and perhaps never was, and an occupation which, strictly speaking, was no more pointless than any other. The terrible thing, I now know, has already happened and any terror to come is only the inevitable consequence of the beginning of all time, including the hour, so near and yet so far, when the central luminary—the sun—will burn up and all the celestial bodies associated with it will be vaporized. How I wish the remains of my mortal shell would go the same way as that tall spruce in Tusset wood, which was felled by lumberjacks while still healthy and in its 125th year, but whose trunk they were unable either to cut up or to process as no saw could be found that was large enough to span the width of the shaft, so that they were left with no choice but to leave the colossal trunk to rot where it lay. For whereas on Earth the rotten body of every toppled trunk is soon colonized by the richest flora of mosses and fungi, and decay fuels the cycle of life with a constant ardor, in the lunar disposal craters no rebirth awaits, but merely a disintegration into fine gray electrically charged dust—an irreversible process uniquely aided by the extremely thin, vacuum-like atmosphere of this place.

INDEX OF PERSONS

INDEX OF IMAGES AND SOURCES

JUDITH SCHALANSKY was born in Greifswald in former East Germany in 1980 and studied art history and communication design. Her international best seller, *Atlas of Remote Islands*, won the Stiftung Buchkunst (the Art Book Award) for "the most beautifully designed book of the year," while her novel *The Giraffe's Neck* in an English translation by Shaun Whiteside won a special commendation of the Schlegel-Tieck Prize for the best translation from German in 2015. Both books have been translated into more than twenty languages. Schalansky works as a freelance writer and book designer in Berlin, where she is also publisher of a prestigious natural history list at Matthes und Seitz.

JACKIE SMITH studied German and French at Selwyn College, Cambridge, and then undertook a postgraduate diploma in translation and interpreting at the University of Bradford. In 2015 she was selected for the *New Books in German* Emerging Translators Programme and in 2017 won the Austrian Cultural Forum London Translation Prize. *An Inventory of Losses* is her first literary translation.

The Will

BY HARVEY SWADOS

THE WORLD PUBLISHING COMPANY

CLEVELAND AND NEW YORK

Published by The World Publishing Company
2231 West 110th Street, Cleveland 2, Ohio
Published simultaneously in Canada by
Nelson, Foster & Scott Ltd.
Library of Congress Catalog Card Number: 63-20240
FIRST EDITION

HC963

TO

Henry Allen Moe

AND THE

Guggenheim Foundation,

WITH GRATITUDE

FOR THE TIME

AND TRANQUILLITY

GRANTED TO ME.

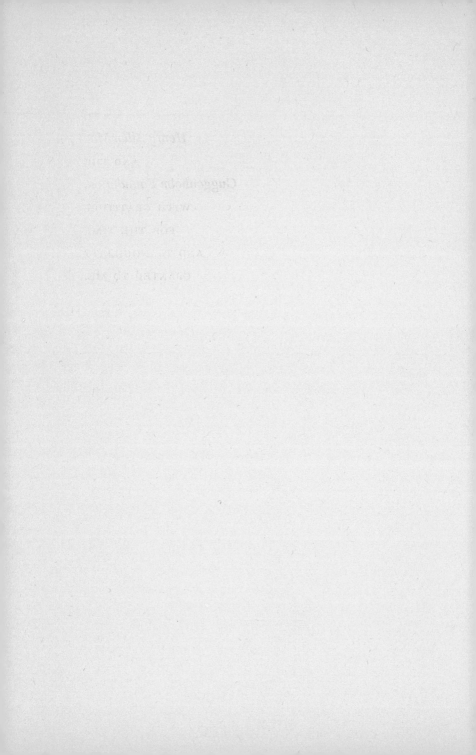

The Will

1: DR. STARK

WHEN YOU WERE YOUNG and a friend died, Solomon Stark reflected as he steered absently through the slush on the road to the municipal airport, you wept; but when you were past seventy, the tears did not come so easily, even though the loss was correspondingly greater. Instead you felt the shuddering wind that was building up to gale force to blow you down too, in your turn; and, driven onward by the wind, a swirling flood of reminiscence. At least the memories were less chilling than the frosty intimations of mortality, and if you had been lucky there was a certain sweetness about them, as if flowers had been uprooted and were borne past you on the crest of the flood.

Leo Land, that strange man, his friend of forty years' standing, had died the day before, on New Year's Eve. Now Leo's son Ralph, having been away ten years and more, was flying out from New York to bury him and to find out what he— and his older brother Max, carried off by a malignancy only the week before—had left behind. Ralph would find out a lot more than that before he was through.

If not for me, Dr. Stark thought, in all likelihood there would have been no Land sons; but at this point he was uncertain whether it would be worth while to take credit for the consequences of his single exercise in matchmaking. When he had first met Leo, shortly after World War One, the druggist had been a shy young man, still a greenhorn, content to let Max do the pulling and hauling, both in their pharmacy and in their personal affairs. Left to his own, and to the domination of a brother aggressively confirmed in bachelorhood, he would surely never have married. But Solomon Stark had intervened at last, after ten years, by introducing the timid schoolteacher daughter of some patients to his friend, who at thirty-nine was fifteen years her senior. With luck and a shove, he had married them off over the opposition of Max, already cracked and more excited by hoarding than by women.

The years before Leo's marriage had been the best ones of their friendship, the doctor thought as he rolled through suburbs still silently sleeping off the New Year's celebration. Not that they hadn't remained close thereafter, through the Depression, the war, and the rest, until the moment yesterday when he had leaned over the hospital bed and lowered Leo's blue-veined lids over his faded lifeless eyes. But it was Leo's bachelor years—less careworn for them both, not yet marked by their mutual retreat to personal concerns, and punctuated with leisurely encounters and the exchange of intimacies that neither had ever been able to discuss with others—that had welded the bonds between them. The friendship would have continued, by occasional correspondence, even if one or both had moved away; and perhaps, the doctor thought wryly, that would have been easier on them both.

Certainly he himself would not now be stuck with the multitude of miserable problems that refused to follow either Max or Leo Land to their graves. Nor would he have had to watch, over the years, the slow dying of the glow in Leo's beautiful eyes, as he cringed in the dusty depths of the store, shrinking from his brother's growing mania for the collecting of everything from bottle tops to broken scooters.

Installed behind the brothers' pharmacy in their dank and airless rooms, Jenny Kadin Land had done her best to make a home, and within two years had presented Leo with two sons. All that she had succeeded in doing, however, was in confusing two men who had been committed bachelors, making their common life impossibly crowded, and squeezing out her brother-in-law to satisfy his eccentric cravings by pawing over garbage. As the boys grew, Jenny came to feel that she was losing them, to admiration of the wrong traits in their uncle, and worse, to hatred and disgust for their whole mean existence. In a last desperate effort to have something that would be all her own, she gave birth during the Second World War to her last son—and drove out Max for good, to the rambling relic of Victorian eccentricity that he had picked up for tax arrears.

As for Leo, pinched in a vise between younger brotherhood and fatherhood, he had shrunk almost visibly, frightened by what was happening to his sons. In the process he had lost whatever connection he and his wife had, however shyly, established between them. Almost inevitably, it seemed when you looked back on it, Jenny had given up the struggle and died apologetically, of a myocardial infarction, leaving Leo to do what you might have known he would: take his motherless remaining boy to that nutty house of the brother who had wished for nothing else than a resumption of their interrupted bachelors' menage.

But before all that, good God, what a charming and sympathetic man Leo had been! And how few people had known or understood this! Max had been quick and clever, and occasionally even admirable (at least in the youthful immigrant's doggedness with which he had whipped the two of them through pharmacy school, helped by no one, and into their own drugstore just in time for the flu epidemic). But if Max himself had not recognized the rare virtues of a brother to whom he was devoted only because he wished to dominate him, how could anyone else? At his best, not yet haunted by a sense of failure and dissolution, Leo had been full of whimsy. Imagine, whimsy, in a town like this! Dr. Stark was rather proud that he had spotted Leo's special qualities, for the druggist had been a man who withdrew tortoiselike into himself if you didn't extend yourself to him.

In the Land brothers' drugstore—with Max ostensibly at the wholesaler's or delivering prescriptions, but usually roaming the streets for other people's leavings or searching for bargains that no one else would want—Leo had always been hospitable with a glass of beer rushed from the saloon next door, always eager to discuss scraps of news and gossip he had picked up on odd subjects: symbiosis, parthenogenesis, photosynthesis, words which despite his mispronunciation he breathed with a lover's fervor. Half the time he wasn't wholly serious, with his schemes for preserving sperm, abolishing eyeglasses in favor of his own eyeball exercises, rearranging the menstrual cycle for women athletes. When you proved to him that he was all wet, he'd even giggle.

He was willing to listen. That was rare enough to make anyone endearing and, with Leo, what made it more so was that he understood you. You could talk about Strindberg, Tolstoy, D. H. Lawrence, to say nothing of Stekel or Stack Sullivan, without his calling you evil-minded—an expression which had actually been used on the doctor by a local matron.

So, weary from climbing long flights of stairs, satchel in hand, to attend young women with fibroids, middle-aged women with imaginary ailments, and old women with varicose veins, he had refreshed his spirits from time to time with Leo, in his clutter of powders, salves, unguents, and tinctures, surrounded also by the incredible junk that Max was sneaking in through the back door.

For years the back of that store had been Dr. Stark's haven, in a city that had no membership bars or private sporting houses where a man like him might cock a leg, down a beer, and discuss matters that no ambitious clubwoman or gossipy shrew would want to, or even ought to, comprehend. Leo had been the only man in whom he had ever been able to confide his unrealized aspiration . . .

Well, all that was over. Aside from any sentiment aroused by the finality of death, the truth was that their connection hadn't suddenly been ruptured yesterday, or even the week before, when Max had died, but had perished slowly and for a long time, over the years. All that time, though, it had flickered; during the young manhood of his own son Marty, Dr. Stark had been glad to drop in on Leo while Marty had taught fiddle to the snot-nosed kids at the Settlement House down the block from the pharmacy. Among those kids had been Ralph Land, a good ten years younger than Marty, but white-faced and withdrawn even then.

Ralph had grown up and gotten out, as so many of them did. He had never come back, not until now, when the old man was laid out waiting for the boys to bury him next to his wife and his brother, and to dig out the dirt that had surrounded them.

What a mess Ralph would be walking into! No, it was no time for tears. Remembering what Ralph had been like before he went off, the doctor rather doubted that he would cry today. Not he, a man who had been all too glad to leave the city and the other Lands, and must now be around thirty, with his own life and hopes elsewhere.

He swung his car into the airport interchange and coasted slowly to a stop in a two-hour parking zone. Ten minutes early, just as he had calculated. He locked the car carefully, checking all four doors (it was his satchel, and the drugs in it, that tempted certain kinds of strangers), and picked his way through hummocks of crusted dirty snow into the waiting room. A few flakes of confetti, bright but forlorn, still speckled the glossy tile just inside the glass doors; either they had escaped the washer-waxer or they had since fallen from the clothing of flying travelers, molting after New Year's Eve. As if somewhere people were still celebrating, a hidden melliferous loud-speaker emitted, barely audibly, "Auld Lang Syne." But nobody was celebrating here, neither the yawning ticket clerks leaning, half awake, on the counter tops, nor the bored kids pawing fretfully over comic books. The lounge— who the hell would want to lounge in it?

Nevertheless, Dr. Stark adored airplane travel. The saving of time on his semiannual vacations was considerable, but that was just an excuse. It was fun to float above the clouds and sip coffee poured for you by a well-corseted Big Sister whose seams were always straight. He admired too the impersonal architecture, airport-modern, with its airy escalators, floating mobiles, endless baggage-delivery belts. They made moving about seem easier, they directed you toward the future rather than the past, they made you feel younger.

More important, though, he had associated travel for the greater part of his life with the city's drafty, vaulted railroad station. Its moth-eaten bison, defeated, killed in fact, without ever knowing what had hit it, stuffed and mounted on a pedestal near the Information Booth, had always been for him a symbol of the city and of all his years in it, the whole kit and caboodle. Depression and war, those were what came to mind when he entered the overblown terminal and stood beneath the bison, gazing at dwarfed travelers hurrying to or from misery (a job lost, a funeral, a draft call), stumbling lopsided under the burden of sagging suitcases strapped with rotten leather belts. Mothers weeping as they turned away from their boys; white-faced children shipped off like parcels, tags tied to their buttonholes; sailors blustering to conceal their loneliness. The arrivals passed under the bison without a glance, huddling outside on the raw and wind-whipped mall, waiting numbly for a bus to jerk them away.

With the airlines, you came or went in a limousine, by God, you didn't stagger along with monstrous heavy valises (if only because you couldn't afford the overweight), and you didn't have to carry baloney sandwiches to eat on the way, either.

The music, melting like a pat of butter on a pancake, disappeared. A sexually indeterminate announcer proclaimed the arrival of Flight 181 from New York City at Gate Three. Obediently, Dr. Stark made his way to Gate Three and, gloved hands deep in his pockets, surveyed the disembarking passengers. They did not seem pleased with the advantages of air travel. Bilious and weary, looking as though they had stayed up all night to celebrate their soon-to-be-severed connection with the greatest city in the world, they might have been all but shanghaied aboard, to be conveyed for whatever depressing reasons to this provincial city on the frozen margin of the lake. Well, never mind. Which of them was Ralph Land?

There he was, no doubt of it. Resisting the impulse to hurry up to him, the doctor hung back to observe his friend's son for a moment. Ralph was a head taller than his father had been, but the years since he had left home had not fleshed out his angular form. His stern and essentially humorless face, with its narrow upper lip and high-bridged nose, was pallid, almost garishly so, in the morning light: razor nicks, with their bright dried beads of blood along his stubborn chin, bespoke a hasty careless shave and threw his city pastiness into relief. He did not appear grief-stricken, though, as he proceeded swiftly, storm coat swinging, to retrieve his bags. Rather he looked, the doctor thought, angry and—despite the quick abruptness of his walk—uncertain. He had a lot to be uncertain about; if he were to know how much, maybe he would never have come.

Dr. Stark strode up to him from behind and gripped him by his thin but wiry upper arm.

"Welcome home, my boy."

Ralph whirled about tensely. If his recognition was unsmiling, it was nevertheless unhesitating. Yet it seemed to

Dr. Stark that it was his own voice more than his features which had at once resonated in the young man's mind. Weren't people supposed to remember more readily what they had seen than what they had heard? But then of course they had spoken only yesterday, when he had phoned Ralph long distance to inform him of the second Land death in a week.

As Ralph was saying nothing, he went on doggedly, "I only wish that we could be meeting under happier circumstances. Still, it is good to see you after all these years. You look very well."

"I never thought . . ." Ralph started to speak in his rather reedy voice, revealing that he had acquired a New York accent—neva for never—which to one who had known him forever was funny, like a mustache on a growing boy. He stopped abruptly and started again: "I just couldn't get away last week for Uncle Max's funeral. But Papa's death . . ." He stopped again, his Adam's apple working.

Yesterday, on the phone, he had said Father. Now he said Papa. Did it mean anything? For ten years, practically ever since his departure for Korea, he had rarely troubled to write home.

"We'll talk about that in a little while," the doctor said in his most businesslike fashion. "Are these your bags?" He took Ralph's claim checks from him and bent over the belt line. "I'll take one."

"Please, you mustn't."

"Nonsense. You shouldn't consider me as feeble just yet." He inclined his head toward Ralph's shoes, which, like most New Yorkers', were not even encased in rubbers. "And the going is treacherous outside. Come, follow me."

He led Ralph Land out into the frosty air, saying, "You've managed to keep from putting on weight, but then none of you ever were good eaters. Care to stop on the way for a cup of coffee?"

"I had some on the plane. It was kind of you to meet me. I'm sure you're busy."

The doctor waved this away with his free hand and pressed on to his car, a big newish model with flaring fins and many lights fore and aft, like a small yacht. It was splattered with dried salt crystals and bore frozen crusts of drifted snow along its window edges, but inside it was still warm and close. Dr. Stark tossed his satchel into the back seat alongside Ralph's valises, then quickly started up the motor. Almost at once, the hot air began to circulate about their legs.

Ralph cleared his throat. "I didn't know how much to bring along, because I wasn't sure—"

"Yes of course. A rotten way to start off the new year, I'm afraid. I'd say you're going to have to stay on quite a while. You might as well face it, Ralph: things are a mess."

Ralph did not even blink. "They've been a mess ever since I can remember. Certainly ever since my mother's death. So I'm not surprised. I don't suppose you approved my staying away, but I've never regretted it."

"Approved? You've got the wrong guy." The doctor grunted as he swung the car out of the lot and headed back for the city. "Listen, I've put a lot of effort in trying to dope out why people's bodies, to say nothing of their minds, behave the way they do. That's a hard enough job. As for passing judgment, I leave that to the priests and the novelists. And whoever else gets ego gratification from it."

"I would have stifled if I'd stayed here."

"Or died of shame, right?"

Ralph did not respond to this. He remained sitting quite stiffly upright as the doctor stole a glance at him. His thin lips were pressed firmly together.

"Well anyway," Dr. Stark said casually, "I think I understand why you pulled out. But I think I understand too— although that's a little more complicated—why your uncle and your father lived the way they did. And died the way they did too, for that matter." He felt compelled to add, "As for your kid brother, that's another question."

That jerked Ralph around. Nervously he undid the buttons of his storm coat and loosened his scarf. "What about him?"

The doctor considered for a while before replying. This was a poser, harder by far than picking up the telephone to tell Ralph that his father of seventy-one had been laid low by a doughnut truck. At last he began, "Raymond took both deaths very hard. Just the same, he didn't go to Max's funeral, even though he was right here in town."

Ralph turned to face him. The doctor could feel his stare, hard and full. "Why not?"

"Because he hasn't left Max's house in three years." Dr. Stark looked sidewise at his passenger. "Didn't know that, did you?"

"Is he sick?"

"He's perfectly fit. He simply doesn't want to go out."

"But . . ." Ralph pulled off a glove and bit at a thumbnail. "My father never wrote me about this."

"Didn't want you to worry, no doubt. Anyway, he was embarrassed and scared, and he wanted to protect the kid. Max couldn't have cared less— I bet he was pleased. It gave him another dependent, made him more the master of the house, you know? But except for me and, I think, your mother's cousins, nobody realizes that he is still in that damned house. Nobody. The few who remember him from school, or the neighborhood, believe that he's gone off. Like you, and . . ." The doctor let his voice trail off, then picked up decisively. "Raymond is going to be your number-one problem."

Ralph pushed the wind wing closed and shrank into his coat, as though he had received a sudden chill to the marrow. "My problem?"

"Who else's?" Annoyed, the doctor decided to stop horsing around. "I'm sorry, Ralph. I like Raymond very much, and I think he likes me, but by the average man's standards he's lost his marbles. Ever know any monks? He lives more or

less like one. He has no desire to see the outside world, not
a movie, not even a mailbox. With Max and Leo gone, someone is going to have to look after him."

"Why me? I'm not trying to duck out, I'm only being practical. Ray was ten years old when I left for Korea. I hardly
know him. After Korea, when I was finishing college in New
York, I wrote and told him, Get out as soon as you can. No reaction. I pleaded with him. It was useless. Whatever he's like
now, I don't think he'll listen to me. I got the feeling from
his last letter that he was smiling at me, as though I was the
one to be pitied, not he."

"Exactly. Then you understand him already, at least to that
extent. He feels as though the whole world ought to be pitied.
I think he does see, after a fashion, that the world doesn't
want to be pitied, which is probably why he's locked himself
in."

"He's going to have to get out of that dump. If he wants
me to help him, I will, but he's got to get out."

How simple things looked and sounded when you were
young! Although he found Ralph to be the least appealing of
all the Lands, Dr. Stark had no wish to be cruel to him; still,
he was going to have to shock him into comprehension, even
though he had already been shocked—you couldn't tell how
severely—by the deaths.

"I've told Raymond you're on your way," he said. "He's
counting on you. I don't mean to get sticky, but all you have
left in the world is each other." He counted to three and
added, "That is, each other and Mel."

"Never mind that. I appreciate your help, but never mind
that. I'll do whatever has to be done for Ray, but the kid is
going to have to co-operate with me."

At least now I know his attitude toward Mel, the doctor
thought; as for Raymond, Ralph would see with his own eyes
in a matter of minutes. Still he felt an obligation, having gone
this far, to set Ralph straight.

"Remember, he hasn't been out in three years. Not only

that—he stays in the attic. I don't think he could just walk out. It would be like letting Rip Van Winkle loose in Times Square. And he's very idealistic."

"You mean he thinks he's better than anyone else, is that it?"

"Is that your definition of idealism?" Dr. Stark raised his hand from the steering wheel to forestall any more of this. "I meant that he thinks the world is bad. It doesn't follow that he thinks he's good. Quite the contrary."

"My father wrote me very little, Raymond wrote me practically nothing. If you don't tell me what's wrong, who will?"

"I wish I could. Raymond discovered suddenly that he was physically very powerful. But since this happened during his adolescence, it was very confusing to him. He became fearful that he might hurt someone, even accidentally. So he decided to take himself out of circulation, instead of adding to the confusion, until such time as the world was ready to handle him, or vice versa."

"But that's crazy."

"Ah, you too. Is it any crazier than those zealots who walk halfway around the world, or swim under the hulls of atomic submarines, because they're afraid of the bomb?"

"I didn't say—"

"For that matter, who's to say that he—or they—are any crazier than the presidents and prime ministers, and the way *they* behave? Isn't Raymond, hiding behind his muscles, doing exactly what they all want us to?"

"I'm not saying that I'm not my brother's keeper, but supposing he won't listen? Supposing he looks down his nose at me?"

The doctor reached inside his overcoat for a handkerchief, shook it out, and blew his nose with a firm honk. "There's another reason why you boys are going to have to come to terms. I don't suppose you've given it any thought, but there is a substantial fortune involved."

Ralph yawned suddenly, or at least opened his jaws. No, he was not bored; he must have experienced a sudden pressure on his ears, as though at these last words the automobile had taken an unexpected leap into the air. Dr. Stark asked pleasantly, "I guess this time I surprised you, hey?"

"It's very confusing." Ralph ran his hand over his face. "All I can think of is my uncle's bicycle pumps and Ann Sheridan pictures. And my father's correspondence with the Patent Office."

"And real estate? How come you don't think of real estate?"

The doctor observed that Ralph Land was cracking his hairy knuckles, quite unaware of what he was doing. "Uncle Max's house? It may have a million rooms, but it's in the middle of nowhere."

"Not any more it's not. You'll see very soon. But besides, you must recall the houses where your Uncle Max used to go knocking on every door to collect his rents."

"Those dumps? They were nothing but slums."

"Times change. It's funny how young people resist such simple truths. It's the younger ones who are always saying, My God, the war seems like only yesterday, or some such rubbish. That's when I feel almost complacent about growing old. It makes for realism, and recognition of change."

Ralph was growing restless beside him. The doctor gestured ahead, at the street beyond the long massive hood of his automobile. "I've been taking the liberty of driving you considerably out of the way before we head for Max's house, and your brother. For one thing, it gave me the opportunity to prepare you a little for Raymond. For another, I do think that before we head out to the other end of town, you ought to take a look at the old neighborhood, where I first met your father so many years ago, and where you grew up. After all, that's where most of Max's property is, in the Thirteenth Ward, not far from the Land Brothers' Pharmacy—the slums, as you call them so aptly."

"And my father . . ."

"Your father's body is at the funeral parlor." Presumably that was what Ralph had been going to ask about. "There'll be a brief service there before the interment. Just as was done with Max. There was simply no place to lay either of them out in the house. It's an unimaginable mess. I can tell you I dreaded this day for more reasons than one."

Ralph did not come back to the estate, or the money, although surely he was itching to ask about it? Instead he remarked somberly, "You said on the phone that my father didn't suffer before he died."

"Fortunately. He suffered a good deal from your uncle's illness and death, yes, and maybe he felt that there was no compelling reason to step out of the way of the doughnut truck. But that's neither here nor there. Leo didn't last more than forty minutes after being hit. They notified me from the emergency room, but by the time I reached the hospital he was gone. They assured me, and of course I determined for myself when I got there, that he was unconscious from the second his head hit the fender, which was merciful. In actual fact, Ralph, it was your Uncle Max who really suffered before his death. No one ever knew how much, how painful it must have been. He kept it strictly to himself."

"Why?" Ralph seemed more polite than concerned. "What good did it do him?"

"Your brother Raymond says Max's silence was a form of penance for the sin of avarice. Myself, I think of his silent suffering—and boy, I'd hate to have what he had, I'd blow my brains out—as an expression of his old penury. Both of them were anal-erotic in origin, the way I look at it; I don't have to tell you how stingy the old boy was. He figured, I suppose, why should he call me in, or any other doctor, he'd been misreading our prescriptions for forty years and more, those few of us who still sent patients to him. We'd only have prescribed expensive medication and insisted on hospitalization. So he dosed himself, first with salts, then with a mess of stale patent medicines that nobody else has even heard of for twenty years, anything he could find rotting on the shelves of the Land Brothers' Pharmacy. Toward the end he knew perfectly well what was gnawing at his insides—Max was cuckoo, yes, but he was no fool—and if he didn't want anybody with a license, like me, to tell him what he had, it wasn't that he was afraid to hear. He just wanted to keep it to himself as long as possible, like his old bicycle pumps, his real estate . . . and his family too, your father, your brother . . ."

The doctor paused, and wound up briskly, "He was in the hospital less than two weeks, and then he died."

Ralph was staring out the window at the familiar streets, weirdly quiet on the holiday morning as though the great graying heaps of snow at the curbs had silently buried the city's inhabitants. His jaw resting on his fist, he said, without turning away from the window, "And my father knew all along. I mean about Uncle Max."

"Oh, I think so. The pain got too bad for Max to hide, and your father was too intelligent to deceive himself. The last time I saw Leo alive, at Max's funeral last week, he told me that the two of them had more or less settled things between them. If we only knew what they settled, your job would be a lot easier."

"I've had no experience in handling estates. And especially with my family . . ."

"I know. Don't worry, though, we'll see it through. The first thing you ought to get clear on is what's been happening to this town since you left. That's why I thought we'd head for the old haunts first. The value of Max's property will be more evident after you get a sense of the city. We've all changed in the years you've been gone, the city itself perhaps more than any individual. You remember how the lakefront was, flophouses, saloons, tattoo parlors. Now it's being renewed, the planners' word. And out at the east end of the city, where there were only truck farms when you were a kid, suburbs are popping up like rows of cabbages."

Deliberately, the doctor allowed himself the luxury of a digression, at the cost of being thought a long-winded old bastard. "Even though I've delivered my share, I'm flabber-gasted at all the thousands of kids in the new developments. Where the hell do they come from? Sometimes it seems to me that the whole damn United States must be thirty-three years old, with two point five kids between the ages of one and six. You know what that makes me? A fossil, a freak that hasn't got sense enough to exile himself with the rest of the senile has-beens to St. Petersburg or Santa Barbara."

Dr. Stark stopped, not because he had wearied of the topic—actually, he could have gone on at length along the same lines—but because it was clear that Ralph Land, who was not even married yet, much less a suburban father, had absolutely no interest in what he was saying.

Besides, the area through which they were driving had nothing directly to do with the new suburban generation. As Ralph Land stared out at the streets on which he had played as a friendless kid, the corners of his mouth drew down with disgust and horror. No wonder he didn't want to listen to complaints about the insipidities of the suburbs. Despite his guide's little lecture, it must have seemed to him that his native city was hideously unchanged, the more they pene-trated into its grimy and crumbling core. The very names fading on the cracked walls of the Victorian red-brick fac-tories were the same: PREITZ BEER BREWED WITH PRIDE—PIETRO-SELLI FOR PEPPERS AND SPICES—FINE'S TANNERY, FINE HIDES. Characterless and rotten, the seedy metropolis rose up on both sides, still mournfully proclaiming NEHI and KIRKMAN'S VAL-UABLE PREMIUMS, reinforcing Ralph Land's conviction that he had indeed been right in fleeing from it . . . and never return-ing until this moment, when at last it might be ready to present him with the means of final escape. Not simply the physi-cal escape which he had in a measure already achieved, but freedom to enter a world which, Dr. Stark strongly suspected, Ralph Land had been unable to conquer in the decade since he had left home.

The doctor's cumbersome but comfortable automobile

lurched silently over the frozen humps of ice that had resisted the snow plows. Spreading his gloved fingers over the
narrow steering wheel, he went on, "I've been rambling, I
know. But there's a connection. Those new suburbanites are
going to have to be able to reach the waterfront easily, because that's what's being redeveloped and that's where they'll
earn their livings. So an elevated speedway will be built
across town, across all this old crap, to connect lakefront and
highway, industry and suburb. Most of those old dumps that
your uncle bought around here lie smack on the right of
way. D'you follow me?"

His passenger nodded mutely. Was he dazed by the news?
He was gazing out the steamy window at the frozen buildings
that teetered lifelessly on either side of the ice-patched street,
staring at them hard, his brow so contracted that his heavy
eyebrows met to form one thick black accent mark, as if he
were trying to assimilate the notion that these were to be
the means of his deliverance, these less than worthless structures that had surely been the shameful bane of his childhood—and, probably, the backdrop to the secret nightmares of
his manhood.

Cut-rate funeral parlors, curtained taverns lingering half
alive from the era when they had been saloons, basement
poolrooms with bleached and peeling orange arrows pointing
the way downward into their corroded depths, empty ice-
cream parlors behind whose unwashed windows stood discolored glass jars packed with long-stale stuck-together
candies, wholesale cleaning plants closed today so that at
least their rank hiss of hot steam did not escape into the
sunless street, secondhand clothing stores with rusted racks of
five- and seven-dollar suits, bicycle repair shops which had
surely done no business since the days of the Model T—anyone who had grown up here must know them all by heart,
these decaying excrescences of a decaying city.

The Lands' drugstore had been one more such, Ralph's
prison and his springboard. How well Dr. Stark remembered

the relief with which this boy, a college junior he must have been, had greeted the opportunity of the Korean War: he had fled in horror, appalled that other thousands remained, unwilling to seize the opportunity to escape the collapsing city before its cracking mortar and splitting, rotten-hearted beams should have crushed the marrow out of their bones. And yet—this was what puzzled and intrigued the doctor—had Ralph really been so pleased with himself for escaping that he had not even once suspected how, concealed in these ruins, there lay the substance which would free him once and for all?

Ralph turned to him at last, his eyes veiled. "Dr. Stark," he asked in a neutral tone, "did my father leave a will?"

"I'm honestly not sure. The fact that one hasn't been found means nothing—there must be tons of papers in the house. I'm inclined to think he did, because he talked to my son Marty once about the mechanics of it, and not long ago I witnessed some document for him with my signature. He didn't tell me what it was, though, and I didn't ask. I suppose I should have."

"And my uncle?"

Took you long enough to get around to it, the doctor wanted to reply, for somebody who must like money at least as much as the rest of us.

"Why yes," he said instead. "Your uncle left a will. They found it at his bedside when he died."

Ralph Land's fingers paused in midair on their way to the heater knob, then rather too casually went on to turn down the heat just a bit. But he remained stubbornly silent, refusing to ask the imperiously necessary question. Pride, maybe.

"He left everything to your father."

The only sign that Ralph had heard was a tightening of his frame, as if something were happening inside his chest that he did not want the doctor's trained ear to detect. Dr. Stark coasted slowly alongside an abandoned cheese factory and stopped, then cut the motor.

"Here's your old block," he murmured. "Familiar?"

It was indeed the Lands' old street. Tattered green shades hung limply behind the sooty bay windows of off-center clapboard houses sinking slantwise into their foundations; rows of rumpled garbage cans lined the narrow alleyways, stained with dogs' urine and girdled by circlets of orange peel and eggshells frozen fast in the ice. Coffee grounds blacker than poison lay sprinkled like rotted seed on the crusted curbside snow. There was no visible life, not even on the leafless trees which had been allotted one to every fourth house, as if no more could be spared.

"It's practically all colored now," the doctor said. "Yours was about the last white family on the block. How long ago was it that the Lands left?"

"It was in 1952, after I went to Korea, that Papa and Ray closed up the flat and moved in with Uncle Max. It was too lonesome for them to stay here, just the two of them," Ralph replied, and began to cry.

"I'm sorry," the doctor said, after he had recovered from his own surprise. "I suppose you think it was insensitive of me to bring you here. But I meant well. Sooner or later—"

"It's all right," Ralph muttered, his hand still to his face. "I was thinking of my mother."

Then he peered out, as the doctor had known he would have to, at the boarded-up drugstore across the street, catercorner from the closed-down cheese factory. The second-story sign, LAND BROS. PHARMACY, raised gold letters on black in the style of another day, hung askew on its rusting iron crosspiece, bird droppings streaking its face. Below the sign the grilled window revealed a hopeless clutter: an absent cat's pallet, a cracked and fallen mortar and pestle, the cardboard BEFORE display of a proprietary drug (an expressionless man in steel-rimmed glasses, his nose and cheeks mottled with swollen to bursting red pustules), a spider-webbed cardboard rack of children's sunglasses, most of them broken or dangling. Tacked to the door was a scrawled notice, unreadable at this distance. Did it announce, to anyone at all interested, or even curious, Max Land's death? Or Leo's? Or the fact that there were no longer any such Lands to scurry like rodents through the musty shelving in search of an occasional Bromo, enema bag, or tin of condoms?

So it's his mother he's weeping for, the doctor thought. Well, maybe so, who knows? He sighed.

"Look here," he said, "you can't imagine what a load of responsibilities a man accumulates as he goes through life. The irony is that half the time he isn't even aware of the moral cargo he's taking on. Do you think, when I introduced Leo Land to Jenny Kadin, that I gave any serious thought to how tough it might be for her, living in this neighborhood with two eccentric brothers? I assure you, it never even occurred to me then that in a sense I'd be responsible for the appearance of you boys in this world."

"Once I'm here, I'm here." Ralph blew his nose. "But I've never understood how you could have encouraged my mother to get lost in this rathole. She was your friend, or your patient. If she couldn't see what she was getting into, certainly you must have."

"It's true, she couldn't see. But what makes you think I could? Here's one thing you may not know: I was never inside the flat behind the drugstore until after Leo's marriage. Your father and I were good friends, but for ten years or so we met only in the drugstore. And half of the time—no, more —your Uncle Max wasn't even there. I knew he was odd, and I suspected how much he dominated his brother, but I didn't really see the junk he was storing up in the flat until after the marriage that he resented so much."

"Still—"

"Still what? Your father was shy, but even if he let Max walk all over him, he was serious-minded and he had charm. Jenny responded to those qualities. It's very possible that your mother stayed in love with your father until her dying day, despite all this ugliness that he surrounded her with.

We have no way of knowing for sure that she didn't, do we?"

Ralph was cold and self-possessed again. He said simply, "I'd doubt it."

Stung, the doctor violated his own injunction to calmness. "If you would," he retorted, "it would be because you'd want to, not because of any evidence to the contrary. So I'll just take advantage of my years to assert my opinion. And whether or not it was love, you boys were the fruit of that connection."

"Just as Uncle Max's junk was the fruit of his bachelorhood. But even with us boys my mother was disappointed. She had married two bachelors, that's what it came down to, and she wanted one of her children to be a girl."

"She actually said that?" the doctor inquired sharply.

"I could tell."

"Well, in any case, here is the crop: you boys, Max's junk over there in the store, in the flat behind it, and in his house, and"—he swung his arm about in a sweeping arc in the warm closed space between them—"Max's tenements, scattered through this whole miserable neighborhood. There'll be no need, though, for you boys to go around collecting Max's rents, with his dog at your heels. Once the condemnation proceedings go through and the wreckers get cracking, there won't be any more tenants. But since I do have a certain responsibility, which as you say goes back before your birth, I'll do my best to help you see it through."

Ralph remained silent.

The doctor swore to himself. He said aloud, "Ready for your brother?"

"Let's get out of here."

Dr. Stark backed his car around and drove off, heading across the city now at a faster clip.

Ralph wrenched about and turned his back on the streets. Leaning against the door, he said, as if the hour had struck for polite conversation, "You haven't told me yet about your own family, Doctor."

"Maybe you remember, my wife suffered for many years from multiple sclerosis. Her death was a release for her, if not for me. I've been in a little bachelor apartment for three, four years now. Marty wanted me to move in with him, but I said no to that."

"He's married, isn't he?"

"And how! He's got a wife, a mother-in-law, and three daughters—five women, that's more than I could ever manage. Oh, Marty's doing famously, he was just recently made full professor at the Law School."

"I'd like to see him again."

"You will. He'll be at the funeral this afternoon."

The doctor could not tell whether it was the definiteness of his reply or the reference to Leo's burial that took Ralph aback; in any case, he was momentarily silenced. Then he asked, obviously uninterested, "I suppose Martin still plays the fiddle."

"He certainly does, even though it's been many years since he taught it to the likes of you at the Settlement School. We're just around the corner from it, in case you want me to make a detour for sentimental reasons."

"I don't care if I never see that place again."

"Understandable. But do you still play?"

"I've given it up. Too busy with other things."

"Your father told me only recently that you've been making your way in the movies."

"Making a living, and not much more. I haven't been doing as well as I'd hoped when I went into the picture business."

"I used to think movies were made in Hollywood."

"Not the specialized ones. I've been working as a kind of glorified salesman, persuading business firms that we ought to make their films. It isn't glamorous, it isn't even particularly interesting, after the first half-dozen trips to cities like Utica and Toledo. The Uticas and Toledos in Greece and Spain must be better."

"Perhaps they are, but life can be disappointing if you don't enjoy your daily work."

"I used to have ideas about producing on my own. Or even going into feature films. New York has pretty much knocked all that out of me." To the doctor's surprise, Ralph's voice roughened as he blurted, "But there's one thing I do believe with all my heart. That is that I have the ability to control my future by planning it. And that I can take advantage of opportunities in order to achieve a decent life style. Ray will never be able to do that, because he's committed to irrationality. He's ten years younger than I am, but from what you yourself say, he's acting like a little old man. I'll never settle for that."

Taken unawares, the doctor did not immediately reply. On the one hand he was pleased to be addressed frankly at last, with youthful impetuous honesty. It was much more agreeable than Ralph's earlier cold and withdrawn manner (and certainly more tolerable than his strange brief moment of tears). On the other hand, what was that stuff about a life style? Did he just mean that if he fell into money, he'd know how to spend it? What an unoriginal illusion!

The doctor said tentatively, "You need a wife, I think, for the kind of thing you're talking about."

"I do have a girl. And I think she'd marry me if I asked her. But I'm holding off. Don't misunderstand me, Doctor. It isn't just bachelor fear of being trapped. I dislike living alone as much as anyone, but I don't want to become a statistic. You know those suburban couples you were talking about, with the two point five kids? I can't take the chance, the prospect is too awful."

"Yes, it comes back to me," the doctor remarked ruminatively. He fingered the pouch of flesh under his left eye as he waited for a red light to change. "You were always the conservative one in the family."

Now why did I say that? he asked himself. Even if it was true, it was uncalled for. Ralph had offered a confidence; after this rebuff he would have to withdraw, if only to protect himself against more such jibes. Still, he was being stuffy even when he turned to intimacies. It was this which impelled the doctor willfully to needle Ralph even more sharply.

"Hasn't your girl friend got money? Traditionally that's the best solution for a poor but ambitious young man."

Ralph Land flashed him a glance of purest hatred. It was the kind of hatred, with the nostrils of his narrow sharply bridged nose flaring wide, that grew from shame at having so lately attempted to confide in the kind of man who not only rejects but mocks your confidences. He said coldly, "Kitty hasn't got a dime. She went to Syracuse University. Her parents have got a mill-end store there. She does research in my office. They pay her a fast ninety-five bucks a week."

"You don't say," Dr. Stark murmured noncommittally. So he's really an idealist, he thought. Like all good Americans he's outraged at the suggestion that a poor boy ought to take up with a rich girl. Just the same he wants "style." He means he wants dough, already he's hungry to sink his teeth into the Land estate. That was always a dangerous combination, an idealist who yearned for money.

The sleeping city, which they had been traversing diagonally, now came slowly to life, or at least thawed ever so little under the pale disk of the new sun. As they proceeded northeast they passed areas which had been uninhabited swamp twenty years earlier, even ten—"Remember?" he demanded of Ralph. Here and there had been a bankrupt machine shop or tire retreading plant among the scatter of grubby subsistence farms on whose rutted side roads high-school couples parked to neck. The echelons of bulldozers had obliterated even the memory of all this more effectively than the lava that had submerged Pompeii. The side roads had become streets, the subsistence farms and potato fields had become housing developments, the swamp itself a business block. The avenue down which they drove was a jungle of garden tool supply stores whose frozen snakes of hose lay greenly looped among snow shovels and rock salt; floor- and wall-covering depots ablaze with spatter, Saran, and Sanitas; patio and swimming-pool builders hooked back to back against the huts of used-car dealers whose lots were filled with machines standing stiffly to attention beneath flags which flapped, not to lead them into battle, but solely to catch your distracted eye. And real-estate wolves, hiding in fake log cabins.

Max Land's house, which Ralph must surely remember from childhood visits as his uncle's prize of prizes, his private white elephant, had for sixty years stood all alone in the middle of noplace, sticking, solitary, out of field and swamp like a great discolored tooth jutting up from an otherwise empty lower jaw. Now that field and swamp had been overwhelmed by suburban midden, it loomed up before them, more crazily out of place than ever. You could not see it from any distance, so it was always shocking to come upon it, bulking on its block-wide lot, its countless bays, dormers, barge-boards, and fluted porch posts grimacing wildly at what had sprung up before it: A shopping center climaxed with Early American A & P, servicing endless cubes of three-bedroom, one-and-a-half-bathroom tract homes, a veritable and literal Happy Valley complete with the doctor's earlier evocation: kids on tricycles and daddies washing Chevys.

"My God," Ralph muttered.

"A little different from when you were a kid, isn't it?"

The doctor could not keep the complacency of the professional guide from his voice as he brought the car into a carriage drive deep with unspotted snow, just far enough to get its tail clear of the street. "No point in commenting on either Happy Valley or Gargoyle Acres. But you should know that a man is already interested in buying up this property. He wants to pull down the house and put up a taxpayer—isn't that what they call it?—with professional offices."

"In other words, Ray is going to have to—"

"Exactly. There's one other thing." Dr. Stark paused, his

fingers on the door handle. With his free hand he reached out and touched Ralph on the arm. "Ever since Max's death, people have been guessing as to what he left here. It's only natural that you should be the number-one target for the local reporters. They don't know about Raymond's still being up in the attic, but they want to find out about the haunted house. The Liberty Bonds, the Czarist jewels, all that crap. You follow me?"

Ralph's thick brows were coming together again over his long narrow nose. "I'm going to have to cover for Ray? But for how long? Supposing he won't want me to? Supposing I can't?"

Now he was beginning to get the pitch.

"Supposing we go inside and see," the doctor said, smiling. "It's cold out here."

They left the car together, the doctor pausing to lock the door with his habitual caution, and proceeded up the unswept walk, through freshly drifted snow marked only by a dog's paw prints. The porch steps creaked thinly, like a kitten crying, as they mounted them.

Dr. Stark had the feeling that they were being watched, that they had been watched ever since they had pulled into the drive. He glanced at Ralph. The young man was paler than ever, not in the least flushed from the fresh air or the expectation of what lay within; his face was expressionless. The doctor looked past him. Was that an eye peering at them from behind the porch window, through the slats of the wooden blind?

He rapped smartly at the door with his gloved knuckles, ignoring the old bellpull. Once, pause, then twice rapidly. "Our signal," he explained to Ralph, looking not at him but at the knob before them. Finally it turned, slowly, and a bolt groaned as it was withdrawn.

The hallway into which they could barely squeeze, the doctor urging Ralph ahead with his hand, was so dark and crowded that for a moment it was possible to discern only an

Alps of dimly looming white mounds. Slowly they took shape as old newspapers, stacked head-high and more, teetering in great piles to within inches of the tall ceiling, from which a cloudy festoon of spider webs descended to attach itself to the peaks.

Between two of these moldering mountains shrank a stoop-shouldered but powerful figure. He wore a khaki army sweater, formal trousers with a satin stripe down the side of each leg, and plaid carpet slippers through which his little toes protruded. His untrimmed tangle of beard disappeared into the V neck of the sweater, and his eyes, extraordinarily blue even in this dimness, glinted with wariness and fear. At last he spoke.

"Hello, Ralph," he said. "Welcome home."

2: RALPH

UNABLE TO TEAR HIS EYES away from those of the stranger who held himself in shadow like some wary woodland creature, Ralph did not realize until Dr. Stark had murmured his few words and departed that the old man must have had an additional motive in escorting him here. Besides preparing him for this apparition, the doctor had perhaps feared that Raymond would not recognize his brother, and would therefore not have unbarred the door had Ralph arrived alone.

"Tell me something," he said to Ray. "Did you recognize me just now?"

"Of course. My own brother?"

"Yes, but you were expecting me. Supposing I'd come unannounced?"

"Wouldn't have made any difference. I've got pictures of you. Anyway, you haven't changed so much since you were going to college, Ralph. I wasn't a baby when you left, I was in fifth grade. The real question is, do you recognize me?"

The boy sounded no more crazy than Ralph's boss, a man

given to choleric mutterings and, when hung over, to unreasonable Monday morning rages. "I'd be a liar if I said yes. You weren't shaving in fifth grade. Not that you are now." Partly because of his relief, Ralph could not keep the irritation from creeping into his voice. "Why don't you? That beard makes you look like one of those phony poets."

"Don't worry, I'm no poet. If anything, I'm more the scientific temperament than the poetic. Still, I don't trust the scientists, do you? I mean, look what they let the politicians do with their work. That's why I don't trust myself either. I'm as much of a coward as any of them, with all my strength. So I'm protecting other people, as well as myself, by staying upstairs." He laughed a high unnatural laugh that filled Ralph with alarm, even more than had his words. Almost immediately, however, he reverted to matter-of-factness. "And if I don't go out, why should I get dressed up, or shave? I never see anyone, no one ever sees me."

"Isn't there someplace where we can sit down and talk?"

"I'm sorry, I didn't think. Would you like to come up to the attic, where I stay?" Ray added eagerly, "It's the only comfortable spot in the house."

Ralph hesitated. Crawling up to the hide-out could only lead them away from what they really had to talk about, the funeral, the estate, the will. "No," he said, "let's put that off. We've got some important matters to settle first."

"Only one thing is important," Raymond replied, with the precise dogmatism of a schoolteacher. "That's for the strong not to misuse their strength. I haven't yet figured out how that can be done. So until I do, I think I ought to stay right here. You know what I mean? Take the bomb, for example."

For a moment Ralph thought he might have misunderstood. The palm? The balm? But Raymond was already pressing on, leaving no room for doubt.

"Do you think we should have dropped it, Ralph?"

"How do I know? I assume they had good reason."

"Not they. We. Did we abuse our strength?"

So this was what Dr. Stark had been trying to explain. If you talked about practical matters, Ray came back at you with abstractions. But why? And how could you get him off his cloud?

"I'll be glad to discuss all that with you by the hour," Ralph said reasonably. "You can take one side and I'll take the other. But first I need your help with this mess we've inherited. One thing at a time, all right?"

He had been leaning against a sooty player piano. As he stepped forward persuasively, anxious for his brother to behave and to be helpful, his arm brushed against a pile of perforated piano rolls. They crashed to the floor like so many logs, raising a cloud of dust and sending a train of barely visible specks (maybe dead insects?) scattering across the dismal floor.

Ray stood quite still. But in the dim wintry light, filtered and colored by an incongruous stained-glass window on the landing behind him, a tear stood out with perfect clarity in the inner corner of each eye. "Poor Papa," he said.

Ralph stared at him wordlessly, uneasily.

"The rolls were Uncle Max's idea, but Papa was crazy about them. Don't you remember? I must have been in kindergarten or first grade, and Uncle Max made me ask all the kids in school if they had any player-piano rolls at home. He tried to get you into it too, only you were more interested in Henry Wallace. The funny part is that those rolls did become valuable again, just as Uncle Max predicted. At least, a man called about them only a few weeks ago, but poor Papa was so upset about Uncle Max's condition that he put him off."

"I doubt that any of the rest of this junk is worth anything."

"Still, there are the rolls." Ray nudged one with his carpet slipper. "So you see, you never can tell. And there I go, talking just like Uncle Max and Papa!"

"It's no wonder."

"But I haven't been close to them, not really, not for years. People thought they were strange. What did that mean? Only that they wouldn't disguise their weaknesses. When they were dirty and disorderly you could see it and smell it. And when they were featherheaded they let you know about it, whether it was Papa with his inventions or Uncle Max with Ann Sheridan. That's why it was hard on me, the filth, the useless things piled up, the miserliness—everything about them reminded me of my own weaknesses. The only way I could protect myself was not to become involved in their daily existence, and to build my own instead."

"I cleared out, why didn't you?" Even as he threw out the challenge, Ralph knew that it was ludicrously insufficient for a man who, he now began to see, was as frighteningly complicated as the timer for an engine of destruction. Nevertheless he could think of no other way to proceed, so he persisted. "I wrote you more than once to get out."

"And I have. It's only that you and I took different paths. You went out"—Ray's teeth gleamed in the tangle of dark hair as he gestured sacerdotally with raised index finger—"I went up. And that was a matter of compromise as well as of convenience."

"You make everything sound reasonable, but it proves nothing. Compromise with what?"

"With my conscience. It was convenient for me to have them look after me, get me my books and groceries. But they needed me too." Innocently—but how innocent was he?—he stared at Ralph, and wound up almost pleadingly, "They needed the feeling, Papa especially, that there was somebody who needed them, who wouldn't laugh at them, or die. Or walk out on them."

Ralph was enraged. The gall of the kid, to pass judgment on him, and worse, to lump him together with Mel.

Then Raymond, as if completely unaware that he had said anything out of the way, extended his arm in a comradely fashion and declared, in another of his sudden turnabouts, "But I know you want to talk about practical matters. Let's go see if we can find a place to sit down."

He led Ralph, who had suddenly been deprived of anything to protest about, through a four-pillared hallway,
forested between the pillars with narrow dowels spooled at
intervals with varnished wooden balls like those of an abacus.
They had been stylish, if just as pointless, forty or fifty years
earlier; now they supported moldering ranks of rusted umbrellas and fishing rods. Ralph could not remember the layout
of the house, but in any case there was no longer any visible
differentiation between foyer and living room, dining room
and kitchen. All had become one teetering warehouse for this
garbage museum of discarded artifacts appropriated and
reinvested with significance by Max Land. Ralph followed his
brother through the mossy, greening forest of poles, canes, and
rods, but tripped over an unforeseen heap of what appeared
to be the feed bags of dray horses: at least, an odor like oats
came up to his nostrils as he drew back his foot gingerly
from the pile of rotting burlap and leather.

"There were some school desks around that Uncle Max
picked up one day." Ray peered about. "They might do."

"Isn't that a couch under all those aprons?"

"Those are kids' Halloween costumes. Remember the
cockeyed man, Evil Eye, that ran the candy store? He went
out of business and Uncle Max bought up his stock. Say,
here's a couple of church pews. Give me a hand with these
folders, will you, Ralphie?"

Stung by the diminutive which no one had used in a decade
or more, Ralph hastened to help his brother clear a place on
the pews. Still in his bulky storm coat and gloves, he managed
to pick up only one accordion-pleated folder while Ray was
energetically brushing others to the floor. That one, however,
was relatively new and unsoiled.

"Wait!" he ordered. "Don't throw those around."

Ray's smile was amiable but devastating. "So you really
are another Land."

Ralph replied stiffly, "They look recent, they might have
Papa's papers in them."

"So?"

Ralph seated himself next to his brother on the scarred pew, took off his gloves, and opened his coat. "Don't you care?"

"It's Papa I miss, not his papers."

"A nice sentiment, but not very practical." Ralph checked himself, and began again, in what he hoped was a more friendly tone. "Ray, you're going to have to get fixed up a little for Papa's funeral."

"Why?"

"You can't expect to go like that."

Ray's shoulders humped forward, his hands hanging loosely between his thighs. He replied simply, "I'm not going at all."

Ralph bit his lower lip until he tasted blood. Angry accusations crowded forward, but he swallowed them with the blood. What was most maddening was the air of sanctimoniousness that his brother exuded, from his tangle of beard to the holes in his slippers. Who in God's name did he think he was, to play the saint when he didn't even have the decency to bury his father properly?

"I thought one reason you stayed on in this house," Ralph said, with as much reasonableness as he could summon, "was that you loved Papa."

"There were so many reasons. It's hard to talk about even one without sounding like a crank. I did love Papa—but I don't see what that's got to do with going to his funeral."

"A simple mark of respect, that's what."

Ray smiled slyly. "Did you respect Papa?"

Ralph leaped to his feet. A grease-stained faience vase, decorated with blue shepherdesses in bell skirts, toppled to the floor from the lid of a hand-winding Brunswick phonograph. "You know damn well I didn't. Why should I have? Look at the life he gave Mama. Look at the way we all grew up. Look at yourself now, for Christ's sake."

"Then why did you come home for the funeral?"

"Somebody had to. I suspected I couldn't count on you. How would it look, to leave everything to Dr. Stark?"

"I don't care how things look. I care how they are. Dr. Stark doesn't mind making the arrangements. I would."

"There are times when you have to do things whether you want to or not. That's life, and it's damn well time you found out about it."

"But I'm afraid, Ralphie. Instead of getting more beautiful, life grows more ugly and dangerous every day. And me along with it. Can't you understand that I'm afraid not just of the world, but of myself too? Haven't you ever been afraid of yourself? If you had, you'd sympathize."

"I find this very funny," Ralph said bitterly. "Here I stand in this junk shop, this filth heap, pleading with you to grow up and assume your responsibilities. In return you intimate that I'm unreasonable. If you're the reasonable one, tell me something: what am I supposed to say this afternoon when everybody asks where you are?"

"Nobody knows that I'm still here except Mama's cousins. People won't ask where I've gone, not at the funeral. You don't even have to be afraid that they'll ask after Mel."

That was exactly what he did fear, and he hadn't even been able to broach it to Dr. Stark, who might only have sneered, or gone into one of his self-indulgent long-winded analyses. How could Ray have known? And how did he manage to turn it so easily to his advantage, dealing himself the upper hand even while he pleaded for an extension on his eviction notice?

Ralph sat down next to him once again. "Supposing I do cover up for you this afternoon. Let's face it, sooner or later you've got to come down out of the attic."

"Why do I have to face such things? Why?" His voice rose. "Why? Why?"

It occurred to Ralph that maybe he had been seeking to delude himself about his brother's sanity through some simple mechanism that Dr. Stark would be happy to explain; maybe Ray really was as crazy as a loon, despite his recurring and receding reasonableness. But how did you handle someone who was crazy like that? He could think of nothing better at the moment than countering with more reasonableness.

"First of all," he said, "both Uncle Max and Papa are gone now. You're alone, in an oversize pigsty."

"If I want to stay for a while, it's partly because I really did love them both. They thought I was kind of crazy too, imagine! But they didn't mind, they wanted this to be my home and they were willing to leave me alone. Does that sound funny, to love someone because he leaves you alone, so you can think and wonder?" Ray put his fists to his cheeks, like a small boy, and then rubbed his knuckles into his eyes.

"That must be why a lot of people marry. To be taken care of, and at the same time to be left alone. That's probably the ideal existence for some, I imagine. But now the old boys are gone and you've got a pressing problem in this place. And you're my responsibility."

"I'm so happy to hear you say that!" Ray cried, and clutched Ralph by the arm.

Even though he had already heard about it, Ralph was astonished at the strength of his little brother. He could feel the powerful grip of the boy's fingers through the gabardine of his storm coat, through its wool liner, through his tweed suit, through his shirt sleeve. Dismayed, he almost tried to yank his arm free, but desisted. He knew he would be physically unable to, and then how much more ludicrous he would look! Or was that what Ray wanted? How could you know, with someone who was practically a stranger, in a sense reborn for you, whether he was truly ingenuous or whether this desperate clutching was in reality a considered sacrifice, a preliminary gambit in a prolonged maneuver?

Ray was saying, "You don't know how I've been hoping that you'd say that to me. There's no reason why you can't stay on here for a while, is there? You said you had to go through all Uncle Max's and Papa's papers." With his free hand he indicated the accordion-pleated folders at their feet. "I'm sure you'll be occupied settling up the estate with Martin Stark, and that'll take some doing."

"With Martin?"

"He's more or less the family lawyer." Ray laughed unsteadily and released him. "Except that nothing seems to be exactly legal in this household."

Ralph sat silent. He had come expecting he knew not exactly what, but prepared if necessary to bully or bluff or even father the kid in order to do what had to be done so he could get out as soon as possible. He felt now instead that it was Ray who was preparing to define the terms of their connection. For even though he had proposed that Ralph take up where Papa had left off, he was not simply asking to be fathered; he was suggesting that Ralph become his accomplice, indefinitely, in this unnatural clandestine existence.

"It wouldn't be too bad, Ralphie. You'd be comfortable here, and undisturbed, while you do what you have to."

"Would you help me do what I have to?"

Again Ray gave him that clear yet guarded glance, simple yet inordinately sophisticated. "I wouldn't get in your way." He gestured upward with his thumb. "I'd be up there."

"Don't you want to see the estate settled?"

"What difference does it make?"

"If you looked out the window—"

"Oh, I do!" Ray laughed. In that moment he sounded like a beardless boy. "I do every day, from my little attic window. You'd be amazed how much I see."

"Then you must see that this house is doomed."

"Doomed?"

"It's going to have to come down."

"Then I'll come down with it. Sooner that than profit from it."

"Haven't you been profiting from it for years?"

"Yes, I have, I have, it's true." Ray's face shone with sudden sweat. "But I couldn't help it. Is that so awful, just because it's not logical?"

What was galling was that Ray didn't have to be logical. All he had to do to queer things was to sit there, stubbornly, on the slab-sided wobbly pew.

"Regardless of how you feel about it, matters are going to have to be brought to a conclusion."

"To a conclusion, yes." Ray peered into Ralph's eyes, his neck thrust oddly forward. "But not regardless of how I feel about it. You don't mean that, do you, Ralphie?"

Reluctantly Ralph shook his head—and was embarrassed to be rewarded with a spontaneous, powerful, and woolly embrace.

"Please, let me take your coat. It's not cold in here." Ray helped him out of his overcoat and asked pleadingly, "Can we forget, for a little while, why you came?"

There was nothing to be gained, Ralph thought, and maybe a good deal to be lost, by antagonizing the boy, who was all mixed up between strong bombs and weak relatives, and so inside out about money that even the discovery that there was a sizable estate might impel him to do something foolish, or even destructive.

So he said, "You're right, Ray." His brother struck him suddenly, not as frightening, but as pathetic in his eagerness to be pals, his paws clutching the storm coat, his mop of black hair, wiry like their mother's, standing every which way on his head, his threadbare bridegroom's trousers glinting as their satin stripes caught the light. "Let's get to know each other. We have to try, we can't count on anyone else."

After that, things went better. Ray led the way into the kitchen, threading through stacks of sheet music, bound sets of *Popular Mechanics*, and boxes marked "Lotto" and "Parcheesi," and insisted on preparing sandwiches and coffee, as well as tomato soup, which he made with milk and stirred carefully as he talked, taking care that it should not be lumpy.

Despite all the hair and the moth-eaten clothes, he was meticulous.

The kitchen was not like the rest of the house. The ceiling had been painted white not too long ago, even the tiles had been washed. Everything was old—the refrigerator's round guts were coiled away atop the box, the stove's flue slanted across the room and out the window to the courtyard, the kitchen table top on which he leaned was not plastic but baked enamel—but everything was clean.

"So you've been in charge of the kitchen." Ralph blew at his steaming soupspoon.

"No, this was Papa's domain. He wouldn't let Uncle Max store anything here. This was their center, just like the kitchen used to be when I was little and we lived behind the drugstore, remember? The main difference was, Mama wasn't here, or you . . . or Mel. So Uncle Max never brought his junk in here, just groceries, newspapers, and accounts. Late in the evening, after supper, when the store was closed, they'd sit here like we are, and go over the books before doing the dishes. And when Papa's eyes began to go bad—I think he never saw that truck—Uncle Max would read to him. Walter Lippmann, or David Lawrence, over a glass of tea. And sometimes your letters. When they came."

"They should have put a fan in here." Ralph's eyes were smarting. "But at least they had your company."

"No, they didn't. I couldn't eat what they did. Papa and Uncle Max had to have their soup meat just about every night. You remember? But I've become a vegetarian."

Ralph took a bite of the cheese sandwich, which Ray had prepared carefully with lettuce and sharp mustard, and glanced across the table at his younger brother, who was turning a cup of soup around in his fingers with evident embarrassment. "A vegetarian? What brought that on?"

"Well, all the killing," Ray replied hesitantly. "I read that more human beings and more animals have been destroyed in this century than in all human history. And I thought, what right do I have to add to it? I don't need the flesh of killed animals. I'm strong enough without it. Too strong."

Ralph shrugged. "I suppose it doesn't do you any harm. But you certainly are missing things." He surveyed his brother and could not refrain from adding, "Boy, are you missing things!"

Ray's cheeks flushed above the curly beard. "I don't think so. Really." He was speaking fast. "It's amazing, after you clear away the nonessentials, like shaving, and ironing shirts, and cooking stews, how much more time you have."

"Time for what?" Ralph was amused and, despite himself, touched in a way that he could not exactly identify. Everybody wanted more time; when you asked them why, they stammered or fell silent.

Not Ray. "For reading, radio, exercise. For watching what goes on in the neighborhood. You know something, Ralphie? The houses in that new development across the way were not built well. They're not worth the price."

"What is, nowadays?"

"Neither would the building be that they want to put up here."

Aha, Ralph said to himself, I am not the only campaigner in the house. How bold of the boy, to move over to the offensive! And how subtle. Who knows, Ralph thought, maybe he thinks that I am the crazy one, as paranoiacs believe that a crazy world is leagued against them, and he is planning a slow program of attrition against my worldly ambitions and vanities. Remembering his resolve, Ralph refused to be drawn into a premature discussion of the estate's disposition.

So he asked coolly, "What's this about radio?"

"I wrote you about my ham station. I must have."

"I forget."

"It's mostly Hallicrafter, but I hooked it up myself from parts that Uncle Max dragged home. I put a pretty good rig together, and I got my FCC license, and I'm in touch with people who think more or less like me, all over the globe. You'd be amazed."

"I am."

"When you come up, you'll see. The world keeps up with me, even if I don't keep up with it. And I hear music."

Ralph felt as uncertain and shaken now as he had yesterday when the phone had rung and he had heard the hoarse voice of Dr. Stark, thin and disembodied like that of an oracle. It wasn't just that Ray was unmanageable; it was more that he was indefinable, as if he were not a brother, but someone exotic, beyond the boundaries of ordinary experience.

"You don't sound like a hermit," Ralph said rather lamely. "Not when you talk like that."

"But I never think of myself as being one. I was never thwarted in love, I never did anything to make me hide from the police, or even from the draft. And I haven't lost interest in the world."

"Then I don't get it."

"It's more that I've got *too* much interest in the world. It frightens me. What can I do about all the horrible things that are happening? People making terror weapons and holes to hide in? I'm frightened for myself, as I am for everybody. Because here I am, strong as an ox, and what can I do?"

"You make a good cup of coffee."

"No, Ralph, I don't understand myself, I don't deny it. I try to study science, but it seems to me as though the more scientists learn, the less they can tell us about ourselves. And where else can I find out about myself? To say nothing of the world, which may not even be here one of these days."

"You could find out more about yourself by living your own life, instead of hiding from it."

"I hear that on the radio all the time." Ray glanced at him shrewdly. "Has it helped you? If it hasn't done anything for other people, why should it for me?"

But then an alien noise intruded from outside, and in an instant Ray's face crumpled with fear. The sound, at first like an old pig rooting and squealing, was in reality the heavy squeak and crunch of rubber packing into snow, releasing it, flinging it away. Ralph was almost pleased to see his younger brother's eyes go wide, humbled and supplicant.

"Don't worry, Ray," he said. "It's just a car."

Ray put down his coffee quickly. "Of course. It must be Dr. Stark again. It's nearly time." He tagged after Ralph to the front hall, where Ralph put down his coffee cup and picked up his coat from the tied bundles of newspapers on which Ray had draped it. "I'm sorry about your having to be the only one to represent us. At least if Mel were here . . ."

"I'll make out somehow. I just worry about one thing. If no one knows you're still here but the Starks and Mama's cousins, then people must think this house is empty, now that Uncle Max and Papa are gone. With you up in the attic, what's to prevent prowlers or neighborhood kids from trying to break in?"

"We've never once had a burglar, in all the years that the junk has been piling up here. Who wants it? Anyway, you've forgotten Sasha."

The name penetrated Ralph's being as if borne by some strange arrow released many years earlier, from a sprung bow that no longer even existed, but had once served to send this cisely to pierce him with its wounding reminder of the vivid humanity, the coarse and comic vitality of Sasha's owner, Max Land. If before he had thought that he could wipe his uncle from his mind as though the man had never existed, he now knew that effort to be vain.

Sasha! It was as if Ray had suddenly, gratuitously, uttered the forgotten name of the girl whom Ralph had kissed, trembling, under a damp lilac bush, at the age of fourteen, and from whom he had learned the dazzling possibilities of adult pleasure; she too would remain with him and in him until he drew his last breath; only by suicide could he deny her.

And then, more shocking still, the sounding of the two soft syllables had caused Sasha to materialize from that dark nameless realm where he had lain concealed these ten years and more. As Ralph stared, his uncle's ancient police dog, gone gray about the muzzle, his once glittering coat turned stiff and patchy, tottered silently from the gloomiest fastnesses of the dining room (now crammed with dental equipment and porch furniture, spiders' webs sparkling delicately between rusting dental drills and cracked, motionless gliders) to come to rest, a string of drool dangling from his chops, at the satin pants leg of the final resident.

Ralph fell to his knees before the dog. "Sasha," he whispered, and met the mucid gaze of the old hound. One eye was thickly filmed with the silver-gray cataract that was already forming over the other. His breath had gone bad. But it was the same beast, Uncle Max's pet and companion of a thousand rent-collecting expeditions through the slums, his protector against those who would make an attempt on the solitary fortress and its priceless collection of refuse. The old dog muttered, and bent its silvered head humbly to receive Ralph's brief caress.

"You see," Ray murmured. "I wasn't the only one to recognize you. Believe me, he still barks at strangers. And they fear him. They don't know that he spends all day sleeping on a porch rocker in the dining room."

Ralph arose and dusted off his knees. Fighting to regain his composure, he calculated aloud, "Sasha must be almost fifteen."

"Do you remember how Uncle Max trained him to heel, when he was just a pup? And how Mel used to tease him and say that he was raising an obedient Nazi hound?" Then, reversing his field, Ray said soberly, "But I won't keep you any longer. If you don't go out now, the doctor will come in, and it's hard for an old man like him to get through the snow."

Quickly, Ray closed the door behind him. Thus evicted by the brother he had thought only moments earlier would cling to him, weeping, refusing to permit him to leave, Ralph stumbled in confusion through his own reversed footsteps back to the old doctor and the waiting automobile.

If the funeral services were not unceremoniously swift, they were certainly businesslike. The man of God, a young intellectual obviously hired for the occasion, had not known Leo Land. He made that plain, protesting, though, that the pharmacist had been—if "a man of retiring ways"—of good repute and of refined intelligence, beloved by those few who had been privileged to know him. Thirteen people (Ralph counted carefully), including the hired hands and two strangers whose attendance had surely not been motivated by grief, listened politely as the hard-working young man concluded by calling attention to the sad coincidence of the two brothers' proximate deaths, "a coincidence that may have been, like many events so labeled, inspired by divine kindness."

When the youthful orator had retired to enwrap himself in scarf, burberry, and galoshes for the cortege to the cemetery, everyone was invited tacitly to queue up for a final lingering farewell to the dummy who lay rigidly wrapped in satin and plastic, waiting only for the lid to be screwed into place.

Ralph declined the invitation to view him proffered by a whispering usher, unctuous in gloves and striped trousers not unlike those of his brother. There were murmurs, but he turned firmly from them to Dr. Stark, who had been kindly trying to distract him in his own peculiar way with a meandering account of exotic burial rites, from the burning Ghats to Southern California.

"Now what?" he asked of the old man. "Does everyone go out to the cemetery?"

"Not me." The doctor shook his head and blew his long nose, which was quite red at the wings, either from the weather or from a grief which he attempted to master with jocularity. "Duty calls elsewhere. I had planned on going on to say good-by to Leo, but there's a primipara with a breech delivery, tricky business, which calls me to the hospital. That was one of the few matters on which your father and I were agreed: birth must have priority over death. I'm sure you agree too."

Startled by the unexpected desertion, Ralph could only nod.

"I knew you when you were a little boy," a withered woman with a trembling head and a terrible strawberry mark suddenly said to Ralph, with no provocation. She had him by the arm and was tugging at it gently, as if testing it to find out whether it was real. "I haven't seen you in a long time, you're working downtown or what?"

"I don't live here any more," Ralph said, freeing his arm from her grip. "Thank you for coming."

"It's my pleasure," she replied at once, and was about to say more when the doctor interposed himself. With the conversation ruptured, she turned her attention to the casket.

"I've often said to Marty," Dr. Stark went on imperturbably, as if the branded old lady had done no more than to ask Ralph for the time, "that if he doesn't have me cremated I'll never forgive him. Marty finds that corny, coming from an old atheist, but he gets the point. Now as for your own arrangements, I should like you to take my car to the cemetery."

Ralph started to protest, but the doctor persisted. "It will be more simple for me to take a cab to the hospital from here. There are several out front. And I've already spoken to Marty on the phone. His home isn't too far from the cemetery, so he'll meet you there, he simply couldn't come in for the services. Then he'll drive you back in my car."

"I couldn't think of it."

"But you must. You see, you forgot your bags. They're still in the back seat of my car."

Ralph felt himself growing red. Chattily, still attempting to distract him, the doctor launched into an explanation of the psychological mechanism involved in the forgetting of the luggage. While they prepared to leave the funeral parlor, he moved on from subconscious motivation to the pros and cons of Freudian translation of trunks, valises, and their

delivery chutes into wombs, vaginas, and other female appur-
tenances. "Surely it seems obvious, at minimum," the doctor
croaked in his frog's voice, "that you didn't want to stay, that
you wanted to be put back on the plane with your suitcases."

"I don't think much of that kind of theorizing," Ralph ob-
jected, even though he was pleased that the doctor should go
to so much trouble to shield him from the other mourners.
"My feelings would be obvious even if I hadn't forgotten my
bags in your car." He could not refrain from adding, "In fact
you forgot them too. Did you want me to leave town?"

Dr. Stark replied foxily, "You fail to consider the possibility that my behavior was deliberately calculated. This
way you can decide your future course of action for yourself.
You can get on a plane after the interment, you know, and
wash your hands of a very messy business. Marty and I
will do our best to settle things up, and see if we can't get
Raymond into a nice quiet rest home." Without giving Ralph a
chance to reply to this, he tacked back to an earlier course.
"I don't mean to insist that you drive my car. If you prefer
you can drive in one with the Kadin cousins."

Ralph glanced over the shoulder of the doctor, whom he
was helping into his overcoat, to his mother's two cousins,
last remaining links to a common ancestry which meant less
than nothing to anyone. The women, both safely past the
change of life, both squat, heavy-cheeked and earringed, both
heavily powdered and corseted into their black dresses and
Persian lamb coats, both moving painfully and awkwardly,
like barnyard fowl, bore no resemblance to his mother, who
had been tall and rawboned and extremely shy. Why have
they come, he wondered, they who never once came to the
house after Mama's death, they who had no regard for any
of the Lands? Was this the same kind of "respect" for the
insentient corpse (for whom they had had no use during his
lifetime) that was so repugnant to Ray? Or was it that they
sniffed an odor stronger than the discreet incense masking
the mortuary stench of corruption: the smell of money, of that

considerable fortune that the doctor had spoken of earlier in the day? In any case Ralph could not bear the thought of being cooped up with them in the velour depths of a rented limousine for the long ride to the burial ground.

"No," he said to Dr. Stark, "I'll take you up on your kind offer."

The doctor unclipped his car keys from a large ring and handed them to Ralph, who observed before slipping them into his pocket that they were attached to a silver fob, which bore a caduceus on one side and a small reproduction of the Hippocratic Oath on the other.

"A present from my son, a little reminder." The doctor grinned. "I'll just let the man in charge know that you'll be driving my car. And Ralph . . ."

"Yes?"

"Good luck." The doctor pressed his hand and was gone.

Ralph had wanted to ask him about the Kadin cousins, but there had been no opportunity. Now they bore down upon him. But Ralph kept moving toward the door, forcing them to trot on their black suede platform shoes, like hobbled Chinese women.

Cousin Lillian said, "What an occasion for a family reunion! Just the same, Ralph, you're looking well, after so many years."

Cousin Henrietta said, "We should be grateful. Your father didn't suffer like poor Max, that's a blessing."

"How true," Ralph replied. "I must go now. I'm sure I'll see you later."

"We'll be there!" they both cried ambiguously, waving their crumpled little handkerchiefs as Ralph shouldered a path to the doctor's car.

"You are first, sir, as the nearest of kin," whispered a hired servitor whose glossy black shoes shone astonishingly against the slush of the entranceway. With caressing obsequiousness he delivered his daily commercial as though he were stroking Ralph's back: "Stay quite close to the hearse and keep your

dims on. Then you can go right through all the traffic lights."
What a treat!

He had not reckoned that one day he would be jouncing along these raw snow-packed streets behind the body of his father. Nor that he would be leading the way to the family plot for the prosy interchangeable Kadin sisters, paid-up no doubt in their sites but far from ready to bury each other. They were, each of them, plump and overstuffed like tearoom luncheon tomatoes packed with creamed goodies, still running with the juices of life. It was more than familial piety that drew them out on a holiday along this dismal trail; it was more even than a grim satisfaction that they had outlasted both of the Land brothers and so earned that secret pride which culminates, after the deceased has been laid away, in heavy eating and semi-hysterical merriment. Ralph was convinced, cruising cautiously behind the hearse as though he had been commissioned to pick up the body if an unexpected jolt were to bounce it stiffly out of the hearse, that the Kadin women—and whatever other connections by marriage or common assumption were rolling along behind them—had sniffed the intoxicating scent of an inheritance, and were announcing by their presence that they stood ready to cut themselves in—particularly since the sons were alienated, dispersed, and undeserving. We'll see about that, Ralph said to himself grimly; through Dr. Stark's tinted rear-view mirror he could see not only the weak yellow head beams of his second cousins' limousine, but also, right in the car, his own valises, resting on the cushioned upholstery and ready to be opened.

The air was bitter, bitter at the graveside. In the declining sun the final obsequies were pronounced with as much haste as was seemly, to an accompaniment of feet discreetly stamping and hands wrung together. Ralph was quite numb, in body and in spirit. There was a moment when, staring with his eyes only half focused on the velvet cord pulls that were to lower the casket into the yawning hole and that glistened stiffly, half frozen, with speckled crystals of ice, Ralph felt that he was still high in the sky, on the morning airplane, staring down through the little window at this little hole as though it were an excavation for another monument to progress, an eighteen-lane bowling alley or a drive-in movie.

But then someone pressed a handful of crumbled earth on him, he sprinkled it on the coffin that the Mackinawed gravediggers had lowered into the hole, and the sudden reality, the actuality, beat against his bare temples so fiercely that he stumbled away to prevent himself from crying out.

To the left of his father's grave lay the heaped-up clumps of earth, still coarse and lumpy, but fortunately blanketed with recent snow, that marked out the six or seven feet of Max Land's reluctant return to the dust. And to its right was the spot which he knew so well, the stone that marked his mother's grave, together with a small urn in which he had once planted a pot of salmon-colored geraniums, her favorite flower. IN LOVING MEMORY OF JENNY KADIN LAND, 1906–1950, it read, SORELY MISSED BY . . . but the rest, the bottom line of engraving, was covered with snow.

Ralph dropped to his knee and wiped away the snow that clung to the stone: HER LOVING HUSBAND AND SONS. What a laugh. But he was not laughing as he knelt in the drifted snow, any more than he had laughed when he knelt before Sasha, the half-blind servitor and guardian of husband and sons as well as cracked brother-in-law. These were his connections now, an incontinent, cataracted hound whom no one could bear to put away, a bearded half-mad brother who had put himself away, and another who . . . He glanced up through a blur of icy tears (whether caused by the raw twilight wind off the lake or by the memory of the poor woman, neglected in life and forgotten in death, who lay beneath his hand, he did not know) at a pair of stout black galoshes, clipped about heavy tweed trousers, that had suddenly appeared beside him. What gave him pause was that one leg was shorter than the other, so that the left overshoe seemed to be standing on tiptoe, straining, aiding its owner to grasp for something just beyond his reach. Ralph raised his head and smiled.

Yes, it was Martin Stark. Still with the clubfoot, which he would drag to his own grave one day, doctor father or no doctor father. But in all other respects he had changed, and much more than his father, who was simply the same cynical old man he had always been. Ralph remembered Martin best, not from the last few times they had met, perhaps ten years ago, but from long before that, maybe twenty years back, when he himself had been a wretched boy, ashamed of himself and his family, and Martin a college student, limping down to the Settlement House two blocks from Land Bros. Pharmacy on Saturday mornings to give violin lessons as his civic duty to children who were not only without money but also without talent. In those days Martin had seemed always tentative, always groping (perhaps because of the short left foot which, even after two operations, threw him always a bit forward and upward), his dark intent eyes absorbing everything from musical notations to the stingy faces of small boys, the fleshy bag of a nose which he had inherited from his father saving his otherwise delicate features from prettiness. Now his hair was quite gray above the ears, there were two grooves carved above the nose, and he looked every bit of forty; but more than that, his youthful air of wonder and uncertainty had completely disappeared, replaced by a mature self-assurance that sat strangely on him to one who remembered him as a youth.

Martin too was smiling, as if he in turn were assessing the changes in Ralph. He held his hat in his left hand and extended his right. Ralph grasped it, shook it, and allowed himself to be hauled erect.

"Thanks," he said. "You were kind to come on a holiday, and such a bitter day."

"I liked your father." Martin's voice was pitched considerably higher than his father's, but was so mellow and confident that it was easy to imagine it ringing out in a class-room or court of law. "I have very pleasant memories of those hours when he and my father used to argue in the drugstore while you and I practiced fiddle. I don't suppose you play any more."

Ralph shook his head. Pleasant memories, indeed; if only others could say as much.

"My wife plays cello, so we butcher some Schubert and Haydn every once in a while . . . Ralph, there are a couple of reporters here who would like to talk with you for a bit."

Martin indicated, with a wave of his raglan-sleeved arm, two men standing discreetly to one side—the others of the cortege were already trudging back to their cars (thank God it was too cold for even the Kadin women to renew imaginary happy associations). They were, he saw, the two strangers whom he had wondered about in the funeral parlor.

"I happen to know the older one, Jenkins of the *Chronicle*. I think that if you were to see them now and get it over with, you might have more peace in the next few days. Otherwise they may keep after you."

"What do they want to know? What should I say?"

"Play it by ear. I can stand by, and maybe give you a hand."

"All right, Martin." Actually it was not all right; he could feel himself tensing as if, alone in a darkened hotel room, he had suddenly heard a strange alien sound. The hair of his forearms rising away from the flesh, he stood quietly and waited where he was, at his mother's graveside, while Martin Stark summoned the two men.

"This is Stan Jenkins of the *Chronicle*. And—I'm sorry, I don't know your name."

"Ed Burgholzer, of the *Inquirer*, Mr. Stark." This was the shorter of the two, a grinning stumpy-legged type, barrel-chested but shivering inside his overcoat. "I'm also a UPI stringer, Ralph. I can see you don't remember me—I was a year behind you at Warren G. Harding High."

"You do look a little familiar. But why should you be interested in my father's funeral?"

"It's not just the funeral. You've been out of town a good ten years, it must be. Maybe you don't realize what a character your uncle was—the dog, the rent collecting, the junk collecting, the whole bit."

"My uncle was an eccentric. You know what an eccentric is? A nut with some money. But I don't see what that's got to do with my father."

Burgholzer had the grace to look embarrassed. His companion looked nothing more than bleak. Barely opening his long jaws, as if words cost money, Jenkins mumbled, like a true miser, "Your father lived with him. Rumors tend to collect."

"Such as?"

Braced by the cold and the moment's respite, Burgholzer bounced back. "Collections of precious stones, see? Jewelry and Liberty Bonds. Even illegal bullion."

"What crap! You yourself said my uncle was a junk collector. Well, that's what he left—junk. My father never had a dime. He simply lived with his brother—in the junk. Is that what your readers want to know?"

Jenkins looked sad, almost wounded. "We've checked out every bank in the city, including branches. Not one Land safe deposit box."

"I've never had one either. How about you?"

"It was your uncle that made money, not us." Burgholzer beat gloved hands together. "You can't do much on a Guild salary. But you can if you got all those rents coming in. Care to comment?"

Ralph saw that Jenkins, on his other side, was scribbling on a memo pad. He said carefully, "I was told that Max Land bought two things with his rental income—junk and more rental properties. The junk is crammed into the house and the store. The real estate is scattered around the Thirteenth

Ward. For all I know he went into hock to the banks to buy it."

Martin Stark had been walking along behind the three of them, stepping delicately with his left foot on tiptoe, as always, on the path that led back to the parking lot. He said casually, "There won't be any great mystery about the property holdings. I believe I have some of the title deeds in my office safe. No doubt the others will turn up in the house."

"Got any idea, in dollar figures, what the estate will add up to?"

"Not the faintest. How could anyone guess, least of all Ralph Land, who hasn't even been home in ten years?"

Dr. Stark's shark on wheels came into view as they rounded the last turn, its long-toothed grille bared to bite into the cypress sentinels before which Ralph had parked it. It seemed to him that he had never been so glad to see a dark untenanted automobile; once he had regained it he would be free. Not even the most eager beaver could poke and prod indefinitely for information with his claws freezing. Meanwhile, though, Burgholzer persisted.

"Max Land's will left everything to your father. That's another reason we're here today. Now that your father's passed on, who are the heirs to the estate?"

"How can I know, without having seen his will?"

"When are you going to see it?"

"When I find it. If I do."

Jenkins remarked sadly, "Eccentric people do eccentric things. Suppose there isn't any will?"

"Mr. Stark is the lawyer, not me."

Martin said, the words coming from his mouth in short bursts of vapor, "If Leo Land died intestate, which we doubt, the estate would be divided among his direct descendants."

"And where are they? That's the question!" Burgholzer cried happily. "For your uncle's funeral, Ralph, except for your father, only collateral relatives turned up. Where were the boys? That's what I asked your father, see? But he was upset, he didn't want to talk. I said, I knew Ralph in high school, I hear he's in New York, but what about—"

"I wish you hadn't gone after him. You didn't make his last days any happier."

"Did you?" demanded Jenkins lugubriously.

Ralph lurched toward him, but Burgholzer put out an arm. "No offense, Ralph. A job's a job. Here we are, and—"

"And here is our car." Martin Stark took the keys from Ralph's fist. "Let's not freeze to death. You'll be able to get in touch with Ralph again."

"Where?" Burgholzer leaned in through the open window as Ralph slumped into the front seat. "Are you going to stay in your uncle's house, Ralph? Going to hunt for the will there?"

Dry-mouthed, Ralph nodded. The icy wind had risen off the lake once again; above them the dry cypresses swayed, shook and moaned hungrily, badly nourished by his mother's bone and marrow.

"If nobody else turns up, you'll get the biggest bite, right? You and Uncle Sam? If I was you I wouldn't look too hard for the will. Or for my brothers."

Ralph forced his lips open. "Leave me alone."

"Maybe you're in touch with Mel and Ray already? Then why didn't they come back for the funeral? Can we say there's bad blood?"

Martin Stark had the motor coughing, then running, and began to back slowly out of the lot, leaving the two men, tall and small, stomping beside their dented and rusty Volkswagen. Jenkins, more the cemetery gatekeeper than the reporter, raised his arm gravely.

"See you again."

Ralph closed his window. The vicious air had struck him on the forehead, and as he raised his hand to his brow he encountered great beads of sweat which had detached themselves from his scalp and were coursing down toward his eyes. Hastily he pulled out his handkerchief and dried his face.

"I think you could use a drink." Martin was very calm. "My home isn't far, but I imagine you'd rather not meet anybody else."

"If you don't mind . . ."

"We'll find a quiet bar. Everybody's nursing hangovers today."

Neither spoke until they had parked once again and were seated in a dark corner with bourbon in their hands. Ralph drank deeply. His legs trembled still from the funeral and its aftermath. Dr. Stark himself would have been cooler, for all his seventy-odd years.

"I'm sorry about those guys, Ralph. I didn't think they'd be so rough. We should have discussed beforehand what to say about Mel and Raymond."

Martin Stark was cleverer than this, Ralph thought; then why had he allowed the reporters to sandbag him? Was it to give him a taste of what was in store for him? He said, "They won't be the only ones. How much do the Kadin women know?"

"I suppose you mean about Raymond."

"Let's start with him."

Martin smiled slightly, a lawyer's smile. Whose side was he on? His father was old enough to be disinterested; besides, it was his father, not Martin, who had been Leo Land's friend and companion, and who mourned him now. But the son had axes to grind, all lawyers did.

"They know of course," Martin said slowly, between sips, "that Raymond is in the house."

"But the reporters didn't find that out from them."

"They're ashamed to talk. I'm afraid your cousins have mixed feelings. No doubt they hope for a share of the estate. At the same time they're terrified of the publicity. You can imagine how they'd feel if Mel were to turn up."

And how about me, Ralph wanted to demand, how do you think I'd feel? Or was Martin deviously indicating that he knew the real basis for the kinship between himself and the overstuffed bourgeois sisters?

"First thing, though," Martin was saying, "is to get Raymond out of that firetrap. Obviously he can't stay there alone, any more than you can keep people from knowing about him—and Mel. Then the will must be found and probated. Of course, you're going to have to take in stride a whole series of unpleasant experiences, like the one you just had with the reporters."

"What's my alternative?"

"To clear out—today—and wash your hands of the whole thing. The house, the property, the probate, Raymond. I understand that you've been trying to do just that for years, but you never have gone all the way, have you?"

"No man can cut his ties all the way, not even Ray. What was I supposed to do, disappear? Change my name?"

"Mel did." Martin's eyebrows came together, as though it pained him to point this out. Actually, he was probably enjoying himself, which was even more infuriating.

"He was a bum!" Ralph cried out. "Are you comparing me to that traitor? He had no option, he had the cops after him."

"I'm only saying that neither of you ever came home after you'd both left. As far as most people in this town were concerned, all three of the Land boys had disappeared, until you showed up this morning. They're not going to distinguish among your various motives."

"What do I care? *I* know why I stayed away. Wouldn't you have done the same, if you'd been me?"

"When you appeal to one other person, you appeal to the total community. Didn't you just recognize that Raymond's isolation is impossible?"

"All right, supposing I don't clear out. Can I see the will through and settle the estate without having Mel come into it?"

"Just as with Raymond, it's only a matter time until the reporters track him down. He's in the pen now, isn't he?"

He said this as coolly as his father would have said, He's got cancer now, doesn't he? Were all professional men so cold-blooded, or were these two simply determined to retaliate for his having moved in on their closed stewardship of the Lands' affairs?

Without looking up from his glass, Ralph muttered, "He's doing three to five for breaking and entering, under another name. That's the last I heard."

"With luck we could settle everything before he gets out. On the other hand, if he's mentioned in your father's will, it might be impossible to do it quietly."

Ralph raised his head. "The bastard doesn't deserve a penny."

"That may be. But offhand I'd say that the only thing that could keep him from profiting as a legatee would be evidence that he had contributed to his father's death."

"He contributed to his mother's death, isn't that enough? And I'll never forgive him for it."

"I understand. Nevertheless, you may as well face it: if your father died intestate, Mel would have a very good claim to a third. And if it should turn out that there is a will and that he hasn't been mentioned, he could contest."

"I'll take my chances."

"I don't blame you." Martin Stark had been stuffing his pipe. Now he lit it and drew on it, remarking between puffs, "The prize . . . is worth it."

Your father thinks so too, Ralph was on the point of saying; but the old man had not implied by this—as his son might be intending to—that Ralph had come back simply to feather his nest.

He said sharply, "I didn't know that when I came home."

"So my father observed." There was nothing objectionable in the words themselves, or even in the tone. Perhaps it was just the affectionate way in which Martin caressed the shank of his brier pipe, with its handsomely embossed sterling silver band, that quickened Ralph's mistrust. When Martin inquired, "Another round?" he declined.

The older man insisted nevertheless on chauffeuring him all the way back across the fringes of town to the crumbling mansion where his young brother awaited him. The housing development had come to life, the spectral gray-blue eyes of the TV glowed through the picture windows, children were crying out mutual farewells before tossing aside the ropes of their Christmas-present sleds and going in to supper, eggnog guests were departing as storm doors sighed shut and motors coughed into action, even the Happy Valley delicatessen in the shopping plaza had opened for an evening's business. Only the Land house, forty feet higher than anything else in sight, brooded darkly from its wintry battlements on the domestic scene beyond its black and looming shadow.

"You'd swear there was nobody inside," Ralph said uneasily.

"I understand Raymond has blackout curtains in the attic."

"And my father actually helped him crawl up there." Ralph could not keep the bitterness from his voice. He twisted open the door and began to haul out his valises.

"Your father wanted him to be happy. The only way he could think of was to give him what he wanted. After all, Raymond gave your father what *he* wanted."

"And what was that?"

"He didn't leave home."

"The more fool he." Ralph slammed the car door behind him.

In some alarm, Martin called out, "I didn't mean it that way."

Ralph came around to the driver's side and extended his hand. "Neither did I. Thanks again, Martin."

But Martin was reluctant to let him go before he had made himself clear. Still holding Ralph's hand in a farewell clasp, he said, peering out into the darkening sky, "I think it was more your Uncle Max than it was your father who got what he wanted from Raymond. It's true that he didn't understand Raymond. Who does? But he loved to dominate, and he felt that in his own way he was taking care of Raymond, especially after you older ones had left."

"But he never cared for me anyway. I wouldn't humor him with his collecting mania."

"Yes, Mel was really his favorite, even though he was supposedly disappointed in him," Martin said ruminatively, releasing his hand. "Even your father was surprised that Max didn't specify Mel in his will. That's why I wouldn't bet that your father has left Mel out of his own will."

"Good night," Ralph said then, picking up his bags and heading for the dark immense porch.

"Ring me up," Martin called after him, "as soon as you find anything."

Ray was waiting behind the door to unbolt it; he must have heard the car come up the driveway.

"It's all over," Ralph said heavily, dropping the bags in the front hall. "Papa is buried, next to Uncle Max and Mama. Now our troubles begin."

"Don't feel that way, Ralphie." Still in his carpet slippers, his eyes red as though he had been weeping alone, Ray stepped forward and placed his hand on Ralph's forearm. Once again Ralph was astonished at the strength in the boy's finger tips, steely as a concert pianist's. "We'll stick together, and we'll make out."

Ralph laughed shortly. "That's hot stuff."

He shucked off his storm coat, threw it on the valises, and turned to face his brother. "I'm ready to get to work. I don't want to spend my whole life looking for Papa's will. How about putting some lights on?"

"If they saw me . . . Some of the neighborhood kids might start throwing rocks. Sasha's too old to keep them away. They're nice enough kids, but all kids take advantage, and if they—"

Ralph strode into the living room and clambered over the bundles of newspapers and magazines stacked atop the couches to get at the blinds. "I'll draw the curtains. But this hiding will have to stop."

"All right. Here's the bulb. But you haven't eaten, and we have to fix up a place for you to sleep."

Ralph considered. "You could go with me to the delicatessen for a bite. It's opened again."

"I thought I might make us an omelet. And you could start clearing one of the upstairs bedrooms. I'll give you a hand as soon as I have the food ready."

"That sounds like progress. I'll start now. Which bedroom?"

"There are four on the second floor, and two on the third floor, but those are impossible, they're full of circus posters and Ann Sheridan, and no beds anyway. Papa's and Uncle Max's rooms are in reasonably good order. Papa's is at the head of the stairs, Uncle Max's was the one to the left of it, beyond the bath. If you'd prefer one of the others, one has birdcages and beauty shop equipment—"

"Never mind." Ralph was already mounting the broad, curving staircase, which was now a repository for bottles of all kinds—a case of siphon dispensers, empty gallon jugs of bleach and cider, beer bottles both large and small, family-size Cokes, a Canadian stone ginger-beer mug, a liter of vin rosé, liquid shampoo and vinegar bottles, and others unrecognizable beneath layers of grease and soot.

"I'll take Papa's. I'm not superstitious. You let me know when you've got something ready to eat. Why the bottles?"

Ray touched a switch. A massive bronze chandelier hanging in the stairwell, a great hammered circle and a series of smaller forged circlets, lit up the entire hallway; like an Elizabethan prop left over from an old Laughton or Olivier movie, it was at once too good for the house and too wrong for it. Surprisingly, all the bulbs worked.

"The milk bottles were being held in case the deposit went

up. Uncle Max thought it would, on account of a glass short-age."

"What glass shortage?"

"He always expected shortages. The other bottles he was going to sell to a lamp maker. Well," Ray said more cheerfully, "I'll start supper."

Ralph had chosen his father's room because here he might begin at once to search for the will. First, however, the bed had to be stripped (it seemed to Ralph that he could still discern on the sheet the imprint of his father's body) and the room aired. Now he knew that he had also chosen this room to test himself, for suddenly he was breathing badly, his chest constricted and stabbing with every inhalation. He flung open the single window, not without effort; apparently it had not been opened for years.

The freezing air moved in. Its draft was a knife laid across his bent back as Ralph moved about the room, gathering up his father's miscellaneous personal belongings. None were familiar to him. He dragged in a carton from the hallway, lined it with newspapers, and proceeded to fill it with shirts and socks and underwear from the bureau drawers, old suits and hats and neckties from the closet, several pairs of shoes from under the bed. Raymond would have gone all weepy over every bunion bulge in the shoes, no doubt.

On his knees, Ralph cast about at the bedside, and among the fluff under the springs, for those objects which had fallen from his father's tired hands during the last week of his life. A paperback, cracked in two, on the social life of the animals, a Black & White Scotty ash tray with four cigar butts (his father liked to smoke his self-imposed ration before going to sleep), a child's spiral notebook with a row of dates adjoining a column of indecipherable figures (rents, perhaps?—he slipped it into his shirt pocket), a Number 2 Eagle pencil stub, George Sarton's *History of Science,* and two or three copies of the previous week's *Inquirer.* Ralph's eye was caught by his own name in type.

Still kneeling, he read Ed Burgholzer's account of Uncle Max's funeral. His father had not only folded the paper back to the story of the "aged eccentric," he had cut one side of it with a penknife. Why he had not then removed it from the paper—whether because he had been too shaken, or too weary, or had realized that he had no one to whom to send it—Ralph would never know.

But he could imagine all too vividly his father lying in this outsize four-poster, no longer with even the terrible consolation and reproach of hearing his older brother moaning between clenched teeth next door, and reading the lurid account not only of the bleak funeral, but of the deceased's oddities and the disappearance one by one of the three nephews who had been his only blood kin beyond their father, his surviving brother. The fact that the brother still survived had been apparently the only restraint on Burgholzer or his superiors. At that, the story was seasoned with hints that Max Land's nephews had taken off, one after the other, as his eccentricities became intolerable to them, and had left their father (himself no paragon) to carry on alone.

Ralph read it through twice, stung with the fury of impotence, pounding his fist hollowly into his father's mattress. How miserable and ashamed the old man must have been! And muzzled, not even free to say that it wasn't so, that Ray had never left home and Ralph had always kept in touch. But no, not in touch. That they had never been; one wrote, and if the other answered, it was only, Ralph knew, because he, like a cowardly lover, had lacked heart—or maybe guts—to let it die.

Earlier, kneeling before the dog Sasha, it had been his dead uncle, that horrible man, whom he had suddenly . . . not missed, but recognized once and for all to be alive in himself. And in Mel. At the cemetery, sprinkling soil on the lid that covered his father's closed face, and wiping off the snow from the gravestone beside him, it had been his mother who had suddenly risen up before him once again, in all her silent sweetness and despair. But now, beside this bed, his knees on the stained hooked rug, clutching in his fist the very newspaper that his father had stared at just four nights before, he felt for the first time, all the way to the bone, the harrowing reality of his father's presence—and absence.

Ray coughed. He was standing in the doorway, a tray in his hands. "Are you all right?" he asked. "It's freezing."

Who was solicitous? Who was worried about the other's behaving unnaturally?

"I was just airing the room," Ralph explained hastily. "I'll close the window now. You're sure you don't mind my staying in here?"

"No, no! I'm very pleased. It'll help keep things as they were. I could hardly have suggested it to you, but I thought, now that you've done it, why don't we seal it by eating here tonight? I'll set up the card table—Papa used to play solitaire on it—and you can sit in the old armchair."

This suggestion of an entry into permanence was as unsettling as Ray's gratuitous approval. Ralph was suddenly struck by the incongruity of his labors. He had been gathering up his father's effects with a cool efficiency which would have been beyond Ray, but for what end? To see that they would go to a suitable charity, when all eleven other rooms of the house were crammed with enough junk to keep any charity, suitable or not, occupied for months?

"What are you smiling at?" Ray asked, hopefully.

"I was just thinking that I'm a slave to orderliness, when there's no proof yet that it will do me any good. Never mind. You make a delicious omelet."

"I didn't forget that you like strong coffee, Ralphie. I only made it weak this once because I didn't want you to be sleepless after such a terrible day."

Was there no end to the boy's kindness? Ralph began to suspect that if he did not challenge Ray's implicit claim of moral superiority, every effort to help him and to close out the estate could be paralyzed.

"Now that Papa's gone," he said casually, "I think it would be a good idea for you to come down from the attic. I'll help you fix up any room you like."

"I'd rather not, thanks."

Ralph prided himself on his self-control. With all the fraternal charm he could muster, he murmured, "This bed is big enough for the two of us, buddy. You can bunk in here with me."

How much more could one offer? Did he want to be carried down, like a bride?

Ray stared at him in puzzlement. Then he smiled. "If you're nervous about staying, you're perfectly welcome to share the attic with me. I've got it insulated, and we can bring up a sleeping bag and an air mattress."

The boy was grinning gently through his tangle of beard. Staring at him, Ralph began to sweat. Spookiness, even the hermit's terror induced by moral paralysis, was one thing; but how could you cope with someone who insisted on being pitying instead of pitiable?

"Never mind," he muttered, "we'll talk about you and that attic tomorrow. Let's get started on the papers."

But he had not bargained either on Ray's motive for rummaging: a passionate curiosity about the family history, and the motives of its members in choosing their partners and their professions. Ray was in love with all the Lands, or so it seemed to Ralph as they finished eating and began what Ralph had hoped would be a systematic inventory, starting with this room. The principal object of his immediate curiosity was an oak bookcase with glass doors that was stuffed to the hinges with photograph albums, ledgers, diaries, loose-leaf notebooks, bridge pads, score cards, receipted bills, photostats of birth certificates and naturalization papers, and compositions written ten, fifteen, and twenty years earlier by the three brothers.

"Look, here's a book report on *The Life of the Spider*. Papa's influence, but I don't recognize the handwriting. Must have been Mel's. Wouldn't it be interesting to learn how Mel feels, not just about bugs, but about people too?"

Ralph snatched the yellowing sheets from Ray's hand and pitched them into the wastebasket. "Forget the scraps—let's find the will."

"But, Ralphie, how can you find the future without the past? In order to find the will, we have to go through all this." He waved his hand to include the bookcase, the room, the house. "Even if we do find it, we'll still have to figure out our real heritage."

"You're talking philosophy, I'm talking dollars and cents. I have to think of your future as well as mine, so you can afford to play at philosophy. At least until we find the will, do me a favor. Stop worrying about the past."

"But I have to worry about it. And about you. You're my brother."

"Are you going to help me, brother, or aren't you? Because if I have to do this alone, it may take so long that the district attorney will come busting in here, and the U.S. Treasury Department, and God knows who else. Would you like that?"

Ray shook his head, smiling deep in his beard. "No more than you would."

It was like trying to run through a quagmire. No matter which way you turned, the ground slipped from under you; as confidence oozed away, panic moved in like quicksand.

"Ralph, I do want to help. But can't we get some pleasure, or at least some knowledge, out of the search?"

He was exhausted. Ray had an eager question for every scrap of paper. The fear began to grow in him that even in the morning he would not be any better equipped to master the boy and exert his will upon him.

Over the card table his brother was opening a limp leather photograph album, embossed "Souvenir of Saratoga Springs" above a brave bearing a tomahawk. It could not possibly contain anyone's last will and testament. On the other hand, why couldn't it? And if that was possible, anything was; and he faced the appalling prospect of weeks of poring over family photos and letters better burned unread, while Ray babbled about bombs and brotherhood and hounded him, like one more reporter, for the inside dope.

Staring first at his dead mother's frightened, tentatively smiling countenance as she posed, gawky and rawboned, before Grant's Tomb, beside her husband on their honeymoon, then at his brother's rapt expression as he regarded the photograph, Ralph knew the sinking fear that comes to the man who has taken on too much. This was what Dr. Stark and Martin had been trying to convey to him—that he was in beyond his depth and would never be able to make it on his own to his goal.

"Poor Mama," Ray was saying, "that's almost the way I remember her, don't you? She never had the chance to become old, like Papa or Uncle Max."

"Whose fault was that?"

It was not that Ray wanted to be quarrelsome, he warned himself, it was only that so much had happened when he was very small, or even before his belated accidental arrival (he had been only eight when Mama had died), that he was as eager to visualize it as a small boy who pesters his father for news of what it was like when Daddy was young.

But how much that I have been trying so hard to forget will I have to tell him, Ralph thought despairingly, how many photographs will I have to stare at until my heart bursts and the blood veils my eyes—and all for a piece of paper that may not even exist?

He arose, knocking over the chair behind him. "I've got a foul headache."

Ray was at once contrite. "I should have insisted that you turn in, after such a day. Wait here, I'll hunt up some aspirins. I never take them, I never seem to have headaches."

You wouldn't, Ralph thought vindictively. Waiting for Ray to return from the bathroom, he prowled the room in an agony of weariness and restlessness. In the corner, atop the

filing cabinet, was an old-fashioned telephone, the stand-up
kind with a pronged hook. He lifted the earphone idly and
was surprised to hear a live drone.

"The thing works," he said aloud.

"I connected it." Ray, returned with the pills and a pitcher
of water, glowed with pride. "Papa and Uncle Max had a lot
of old phones, from the drugstore and from the properties. So
I set up an extension system." He hesitated, then blurted out,
"I'm very practical, I'm not as crazy as you think."

And I'm not as tough as you think, Ralph wanted to reply.
How soothing it would be to pick up the telephone and permit
himself to be comforted by Kitty's low, reassuring voice. But
the danger—he knew this so well that it had thus far protected
him effectively—was that he would lose his head, which was
what women counted on, and say something to her that he did
not mean, in order to gain her compassion. In this sense the
telephone incited as much temptation as a plastic bomb, lying
on the same cabinet, would have to a terrorist.

"Now I'm going to clear out and let you get some sleep."

Ralph did not protest. He was determined to resist the temptation alone.

"I'm glad you've come, Ralphie." Ray paused, his hand on
the knob. With his next words he destroyed Ralph's determination as surely as if that had been his exact intention. "We'll
have some good times together, you'll see. I'll make your coffee
strong, and I'll help you look. I'll come down for that, I promise. And we can argue"—he said this as if he were a thirteen-
year-old talking about God—"about all the really important
things."

When the boy had finally mounted to his loft, Ralph strove to
forestall the inevitable by rummaging furiously through his
valise in search of pajamas, shaving equipment, slippers, like an
adolescent trying to exorcise erotic fantasies with gymnastics.
As he did so, he carried on the silent and losing argument. To
confound loneliness with love was worse than stupidity, it was

a crime, it was surely what his own father—and maybe his mother too—had done. Why compound the prescription once again? Wait, wait, he cried to himself, she'll be there. Bring her the will first, bring her the money first, then you can do it on your terms.

But in the end it was no use, as he had known when he had first cast eyes on the phone, or perhaps even before that, when he had begun to see that there stretched before him something even worse than the dead-end job and the insanely sullen boss to whom he had been tied like a penniless husband to a rich nagging jealous wife—days of being trapped here in this dying house with his bearded brother, the two of them poring over letters, diaries, and photos of the dead, infecting old memories as do those who pick over sores, while the press and the public waited on the porch, gloating at the ludicrous spectacle.

He slammed out of the bathroom and stumbled through the hall. If he was going to go through with it he had to be supported by someone who could warm him with the reassurance that what he was doing was good, just, and right; someone whose very presence would serve as a living reminder of a goal that might otherwise be dissolved in his balmy little brother's overheated mixture of bathos and bewilderment. He ran to the phone.

Summoned with a twist of his index finger, Kitty Brenner's contralto, saying hello twice, with that familiar rising inflection as though she were French or still in the finishing school which she had never attended but wished she had, made him as weak with relief and gratitude as if she were already beside him.

"Kitty," he said, "it's me. Ralph."

"As if I didn't know. And long distance, too!" Then, more seriously, "Was it terribly rough?"

"It was rough," he said. "But that doesn't matter. I called to tell you that I'm not coming back."

There was silence at the other end of the line.

"Kitty," he said tensely, "I want you to come here."

"You're joking."

"I need you," he whispered. He felt himself growing hoarse, as if he had been too long in a smoky room. "You must come. There's a fortune waiting here. But I can't do it alone, do you understand?"

"I'm afraid I don't."

"I have to find my father's will. But it may take time, do you see? And it's too hard, I can't go into it now, but my brother is half cracked, and it's in the papers already, and I need you, for God's sake, I need you!"

Kitty said, very slowly, "Ralph, you mustn't talk to me as though I were an old friend. I'm not an old friend. I'm not your roommate, even though I've been sleeping with you, and I won't pack my bags and throw everything over just because you're down in the mouth."

"Then you won't come."

"I didn't say that."

"What do you want? Do you want me to tell you I love you, is that it?"

"That wouldn't hurt, considering what you're asking of me. I'd like to know how much you love me."

"More than I ever thought possible." Hearing no reply, he said loudly, desperately, "Enough to marry you. I mean now, as soon as you can get here."

It was then that he heard her crying, muffled but unmistakable. "How can this happen in one day, if it didn't happen in six months?"

"You find things out. Sometimes it takes a lifetime. If you're lucky, it takes a minute. Do you love me?"

"I do. You know I do."

"You'll come?"

"Yes," he heard her saying faintly, "yes, I'll come. Tell me what to do."

Now he could relax his grip on the telephone, which he had been clutching so tightly that his palm was wet and his knuckles

ached. Now that he had put his chips down, he who hated
gambling, on the longest odds of all, he felt suddenly enormously cool and self-possessed.

"Try to get a seat on the six o'clock plane out of Idlewild
tomorrow night. That should give you time to pack. Wire me
care Dr. Solomon Stark, Coolidge Building, and I'll reserve a
hotel room and meet you at the airport. Do you have enough
money for the ticket and immediate expenses?"

"I have two hundred and twenty dollars in the bank."

"Draw it out. We'll need it. I'll pay you back later, with
interest."

"Jokes, at a time like this!"

"I want you to go into the office tomorrow morning and tell
Wollenweber about my father's death—I haven't had the chance.
Tell him that I had to come out here for the funeral, that it
will take time to settle the estate, and that I'd like a two-week
leave. Actually I never expect to see the place again."

"Does that go for me too?"

"In spades. Tell him simply that you're leaving at the end
of the day and that you'll send him a forwarding address for
your check."

"And my parents?"

"Phone them from here. They'll give you their blessing. Wait
until they hear that I'm coming into money."

"Is it that sure? I couldn't care less, I swear to you, I'll come
even if you tell me it was an invention, a trick. But for you to
throw over your job . . ."

Ralph winced. It was bad enough to be baited by an old man
like Dr. Stark, but to be reminded by the girl whom you had
just proposed to that she thought of you as cautious and careful
—that was too much. A petulant response, however, could only
make him lose momentum, so he said quickly, buoyantly, "The
money is there, but it's frozen in chunks of real estate. The
trick is going to be to unfreeze it, with speed and without
publicity. You must say nothing to anyone—"

"I won't." Kitty's assurance was almost humble.

"—and we'll make out somehow, until we find the will and probate it. I promise you, Kitty, you won't regret it."

"I don't care if I do! I don't care, because I'm coming anyway. And Ralph . . ."

"I'm still here."

"Happy New Year, darling."

Then he was no longer there, but back in his father's room, alone and barefooted, his belongings instead of his father's scattered about the room, the door ajar, the silence closing in upon him once again like fog.

He stuck his feet into his slippers. There was nothing more he could do this day, even though it would be a coup if he could find the will alone. But the odds were too great; better to search for a sleeping pill instead, to keep the aspirins company. He stepped quietly into the hallway.

A sense of presence, not a noise, simply a feeling that he was not alone, made him stop before he had taken two steps toward the bathroom. His flesh shrinking inside his pajamas, he swiveled his head slowly to look up and down the hall. Nothing. But there, at the head of the darkened stairway, on the landing of the third floor to which he had not yet ascended, glowed a pair of blue eyes, luminous as a cat's in the sepulchral gloom. His brother was sitting, listening, watching.

"Don't be afraid, Ralph," he whispered. "I'm on guard."

3: KITTY

THE CITY OF HIS BIRTH, Ralph had told Kitty, was as dull and paltry as hers, but as she closed in on it now, winging in so unexpectedly from the science fiction world of Idlewild, it rose up for her out of the night like a fairy capital, a Venice, a Peking, a Lhasa.

The bridal lights winked on for her as the plane banked over the braceleted boulevards, arms flung out from the burning body of the glittering city. Tiny seed pearl rows of pinprick lights crisscrossed the brilliant columnar avenues, and in its heart the steady glow erased the night for her. Kitty caught a glimpse of her own peering face, reflected momentarily in the tilting window; she was as flushed as a virgin. But why not? Why not?

Motors went out, music and lights came on, and the bride was making her way unsteadily down the aisle and the freezing gangway to the arms of the man who had so suddenly, so unexpectedly, declared himself.

Kitty buried her face for a long time in the thick, damp fur collar of Ralph's storm coat before she raised her head to gaze at those familiar, forbidding features: the hooded eyes with the thick single brow that overscored them; the solid stubborn forehead; the unhandsome but powerfully assertive nose, highly ridged down the middle like stone; the drawn and secretive mouth. How much it must have cost him to make that telephone call!

"Darling," she said. She hugged him hard. "I did everything you told me to."

"I knew you would." Against her temple she could feel the muscles move in his jaw as he spoke. "I was sure you would."

"Wollenweber said—"

"The hell with him. Let's jump in a cab before you get pneumonia."

In the back of the taxi, nestled protectively in the crook of Ralph's right arm, reality returned to her comfortingly. The street names were different, the days would be chancy and unregulated by office hours or pay checks, but it made sense because of Ralph.

"First thing in the morning, we'll go for our blood tests and marriage license. In three days you'll be Mrs. Land." He uttered one of his infrequent, abrupt laughs. "Lucky girl."

"Don't joke about it," Kitty protested. She twisted around to look at him. His guarded countenance was creased into a smile that hid, she suspected, the wretched uncertainty of the man who asks himself, Was I a fool? She said insistently, "I *am* lucky. I have great faith in you."

"Why?" he demanded.

He wants an explanation of why I've come, she thought; love—or their kind of love—wasn't enough, and in this he was quite right. Meeting in the office they had liked each other, and after a few dates had fallen into bed together. It had been convenient for them both, but at twenty-five, Kitty was beginning to be frightened, and so through the months of their intimacy she wondered uneasily whether, if she had been a little less complaisant, a little more reserved, Ralph might have

been less inclined to refer to her as his girl and more inclined
to think of her as a possible wife. Not that he ever foreclosed
the latter possibility. Indeed that was one of the troubles with
their relationship: in exact proportion to Ralph's tacit concession that one day—when he had produced a feature film or
struck it rich or liberated himself in some other way from the
white-collar class—they would be married, Kitty had found her
doubts multiplying about the wisdom of marrying a man who
regarded her as an item on his agenda. It was the other side of
him, dark, troubled, immoderately ambitious, that made him
appealing as a lover; like a slumbering volcano, he gave
promise of an eruptive power that could very well engulf her
(she knew that she too possessed this quality—a married man
with whom she had yielded to a brief and deadly binge had
assured her of it—and it increased her uneasiness to think that
perhaps Ralph measured her as she did). That power kept her
from breaking with him and trying her luck elsewhere.

How was she to tell him that it was his subterranean sexual
attractiveness, and not his office exterior, that had impelled
her to tie herself to him on his terms, at the cost of talk in
their place of work and loss of opportunities for her elsewhere?
Nevertheless, she had to try to explain what it was that had
happened the night before, if their marriage was to have any
prospects for success.

Somewhat frightened, but with a determination that approached obstinacy, she said, "My faith in you comes from
love. If you must know, I think it was only last night, when
you telephoned, that I really fell in love with you for the first
time. Does that sound strange? Remember, it was the first
time you ever said you needed me. I've had lots of men tell me
they wanted me, and I guess they did, because in some cases it
was mutual, but no one, until you, ever insisted that he needed
me."

"I meant it, Kitty."

"Maybe I wouldn't have believed it if we hadn't been intimate, and if I had less confidence in myself, but I know I

can give you what you need. As soon as you asked me, I knew
the answer was yes. And when you started telling me what to
do—my God, I've been aching to be told what to do! Does
that sound so awful? Because it's the truth, and it's why I would
have come here from New York on my hands and knees, if
you'd ordered me to."

Ralph replied, in a queer, choked voice, "It was only when
I discovered that I needed you . . . and you responded . . . that
I felt I could talk to you in a way that I never presumed to
before, not with any woman." He wrenched about convulsively
and blurted out, "You know why I was sure I could count on
you? Because underneath that flip New York manner you're
passionate, like me."

Kitty felt a sudden twinge in her loins, a wonderful stabbing
pain as though Ralph had violently, shockingly, gripped her
there. She said nothing, but stared unseeingly out the fogged
window of the taxi, her eyelids drooping. He does know, she
thought, he does know.

"You want what I want," he whispered. "Not the ten-dollar
raise or the ten-dollar bet at the bridge table. The real ambition, to break away from what we've had, the real gamble,
to reach out for what we want. There is no one else in the
world to whom I could have said, Pack up, come to this lousy
town, for something I can't even tell you about on the phone.
Most women are jelly, in the spirit as much as in the flesh.
You're strong, you're firm, you're passionate."

In an agony of pleasure, Kitty pulled open her plaid coat
and tore aside the knitted scarf folded over her chest. Grasping
Ralph's free hand, she pressed it to her bosom and covered it
with her own. "Feel my heart," she cried softly, "feel how it's
beating for you."

It was not alone her heart that she wanted this stranger, so
suddenly exciting, to feel, but the flesh that covered it, soft
and curving but not jelly, not mush. Her breast was as firm
and proud, as sharply thrusting, as her will: she heard a voice
whispering this—her own, Ralph's? Her lips apart, panting,

the breath catching in her throat, she kissed him deeply, for the first time since he had asked her to marry him. Let him take me tonight, she thought blindly, I won't need to say yes, I'll show him.

But by the time they had arrived at the hotel, they were both somewhat more composed. Kitty stepped sedately from the taxi, holding her coat collar almost to her lips against the raw January air, more bitter than New York's, and waited under the marquee while Ralph paid the driver and passed on her valises to the doorman.

"Eight dollars for that crazy ride," she said, staring after the departing cab (suddenly she missed it terribly, that warm dark nameless shelter in which they declared themselves), "and I never saw a thing. But I don't care."

"Come in out of the cold."

Obediently she followed Ralph into the hotel lobby, which was vast, impersonal, like a movie palace or an interdenominational church, and decorated in the manner of the twenties, with much stainless steel and brass used in severe geometrical patterns to suggest a straining toward the infinite.

"Cozy," she murmured.

"Don't knock it." Ralph led her to the register. "We're not buying it. Just check in, it's your last chance to put your maiden name on a hotel register."

"You make me feel like an undergraduate."

Actually he made her feel momentarily uncomfortable. They had slept together in hotels once or twice, but always under his name; why did he now place the burden of identification upon her? The answer could only be that this was his home town and so a place where he dared not use his name carelessly —and surely not now. Somewhat abashed, Kitty followed him across the carpet to the elevator and, after he had brushed aside a bellhop, up to the eleventh floor.

There he opened the door of her room and set down her valises. But instead of turning on the lights he led her to the window in the darkness and drew aside the curtain.

"That's why I didn't want a bellhop. He'd have flipped on every switch and showed you how the shower works."

"It's beautiful, the city, even more so here than from the plane."

"It's ugly."

"I don't believe you. Is that why you wanted me to see it like this? That boulevard below is the one I saw from the plane, I'm sure, with all the streets radiating off it. I can't wait to see it in the sunlight, with the snow on the boughs of all those trees. It must be even more beautiful in the summer, with the sun shining through the leaves."

"You won't be here then. Oh, I suppose I did want you to be impressed. It's true, the boulevard is stately. It's still lined for a dozen blocks with the stone houses of the barons who made it here, seventy and eighty years ago, in chemicals, paper, printing, power. None of us has ever laid eyes on any of those people. They're long since gone, to Paris and Palm Beach and Newport. They come back once or twice a year, some of them, for a board meeting or a ball, but for the most part they've disposed of their mansions to the Archdiocese, the Red Cross, the Welfare Board, the Girl Scouts."

Ralph turned from the window in disgust, his saturnine features immediately in shadow. "The rest of the slobs, the Germans, the Jews, the Hunkies, the Polacks, the Italians, the blacks, have been jammed into their ghettos, grubbing away their stupid lives in the plants and the mills, paying rents to people like my uncle—who wasted his stupid life with my father in their cruddy drugstore."

This was not what Kitty had expected when Ralph had led her by the hand into the darkened room. She came to him at the writing desk, where he stood tensely folding and unfolding the hotel blotter in his hairy hands, and she said, extending her hand, "But this is no different from Syracuse."

"Does that make it good? You left there, didn't you? And I left here—or at least I tried to."

"But your inheritance . . ." Kitty withdrew her hand. Better not to press him. Ralph was a moody man, a sullen one according to some in their office; but this was, she recognized, because there warred in him two conflicting elements—an eagerness to be not simply like everybody but like the most substantial people (like those, she began to see, of whom he had just been speaking with such envious bitterness, those who had inherited money and manners and the consequent liberation from having to compete and to compromise); and a desire to be more ruthless than they, to be able to ignore the ordinary rules of conduct that governed the lives of ordinary people.

Then suddenly, once again self-possessed, he stepped behind the club chair and bowed like a headwaiter, but sardonically. "Sit down, Kitty. You're right, there's the inheritance. But it's going to be tricky, and I want you to know the odds before we start. You still have the opportunity to change your mind."

Kitty started to protest, but Ralph waved her to silence as he seated himself on the edge of the bed, after having turned on the lights. He began to outline the situation as though they were back in the office. She listened obediently, knees together and skirt tucked primly beneath her.

Ralph had never spoken much of his family or his past. She knew that he had left his city college to go into the Army, and that after returning from Korea he had come to New York to finish school and make a fresh beginning. She knew too that he never visited home, the way people usually did, because for unstated reasons he wanted to be reminded of home as little as possible.

Listening to him now while he sketched his childhood for her with the cold fury of disgust—the dusty drugstore in a deteriorating neighborhood, the obsessed uncle trotting about tirelessly, collecting his rents and his roomfuls of garbage, the mother overborne by squalor and seediness, cold sores and sties, the father pottering, inventing, allowing himself to be dominated by his brother—Kitty felt herself melting once again, yielding in the innermost corners of her being to the plea that was all the more demanding for being unstated. She craved as never before to hold that dark troubled head to her bosom until his voice had fallen silent and his rigidity had relaxed in her arms.

"But all of that is past," he said. He glanced across at her briefly, then returned his gaze to his knotted hands. "I wanted you to know where the money will come from. First, there is Raymond. My number-one hangover from the past. Everyone thinks that he's cleared out, the way"—he hesitated for an instant—"I did. But no, he's playing hermit, perched in the attic of Uncle Max's castle like a butterfly on a garbage heap. In a sense, he's sitting on the estate, do you see? And that's why I've got to find the will before I pry him out of the attic. Maybe he even knows where the will is, but wants me to hunt for it in order to keep me in the house, so he won't have to stay there alone. And I have no alternative—at least not until I locate the will. Or establish that there isn't any."

"He knows that I'm coming?"

Ralph glanced up, his eyes hooded. "He eavesdropped on my call. After that of course I told him. He claims to be delighted—and maybe he is. After all, he's playing for time. You'll be sorry for him, I know you, you might even like him. But don't let him con you. We've got to get him out of there as quickly as possible, or . . ."

"Or what?"

"There'll be a public scandal much worse than what we've already got."

"But, Ralph, I don't care about that." Was he worried for her or for himself? She added insistently, "I really don't. So if you're concerned on my account—"

"I'm bringing you into what's left of a miserable family." He arose and knelt beside her chair. "I have hopes for you and me, but first we're going to have bad trouble. You've never known real shame."

"If you mean family shame, no. And I never expect to. We're

ready for more important things, and if you have to find the
will and do something about your brother first, I'm going to
help all I can. I swear it, Ralph."

"I promise you," he whispered, his lips moving against the
palm of her hand, "that you'll never think twice again about an
eight-dollar taxi ride. I promise you style, Kitty, the kind you
deserve. Style, and—"

Kitty bent her head and put her lips to Ralph's to silence
them. They seemed to throb beneath hers, and the thick
pounding began again in her bosom, almost like a message.
But this time he would not have to ask her, there would be no
need for words.

She strained to lift him from the carpet into her arms, but
he held off stiffly, as if he were an embarrassed stranger.
Alerted, she desisted, and then was startled to hear him saying
thickly, "Kitty, listen to me."

She withdrew her arms and waited, in a suspension of
motion and of thought. She stared down wordlessly at the top
of his head and its coarse powerful mat of short-cropped wiry
black hair, electric in its springiness.

"I've made you my promise," he muttered. Then he gathered
strength. "Now I want you to make me one. I know why most
women marry. I've nothing against children. But not yet. You
must promise me that there will be none until we've gotten
what we came for. Later you can have whatever you want,
but we mustn't trap ourselves."

Kitty placed her hands on his head and turned his face up
to hers. "I promise," she said. Her heart was still beating fast,
but in a different rhythm; it was not the oath Ralph had
exacted which unnerved her so much as it was the circumstances, both obvious and implicit, of the exaction.

Ralph arose rapidly. "Then you must understand too," he
said, "that until we're married you must stay here and I must
stay with Raymond. I don't dare . . ." He hesitated, then finished wryly, "And that's the first of our troubles."

He walked to the door with his customary brusque swift

stride. "I'll pick you up first thing in the morning," he said, and was gone.

In the sudden silence, Kitty jumped up and flung a cushion at the door which had just closed silently on her lover. But it made no noise either, and she was alone with herself as she had not been since the buoyant hours of packing and leaving her job, preparing to descend the ladder held up to her window by her impetuous fiancé. The insensitive bastard! To bring her here and then to walk out, virtually to sneak out without a kiss or a caress, as if her very eagerness had brought to the surface all his latent stuffiness, reminding him of peeping hotel detectives and of his obsession, here in his home town, with shame.

But even as she stooped to retrieve the pillow, she knew that she was wrong, she was unfair. If Ralph was too preoccupied with what people would think to be the perfect un-self-conscious lover, he was not a pig or a boor either. Surely the abruptness of his departure had been occasioned by his reluctance to leave—and by embarrassment at revealing that reluctance.

Just the same, what was she getting into? Maybe Uncle Max and Raymond weren't the only crazy ones in the Land family; what had Ralph's mother really been like, or his father, not even cold in his grave? And for that matter, what was Ralph himself? What did he want so desperately, that he couldn't even put a name to— Did he know? Or was he only dreaming dreams of dreams?

The full-length mirror on the back of the bathroom door, to which she turned now, revealed her as slim, blond, sulking. A lie: she was none of these. Her body was fuller than it appeared in sweater and sheath skirt, without help her hair was mud-brown, and her pout was in reality an expression not of petulance but of fear.

As an only child, Kitty had lived before the mirror since the age of eight or nine. First, as Judy Garland, Judy Holliday, Elizabeth Taylor, Lynn Fontanne, laughing, smoldering, singing, simpering, always with one eye turned, trying to see how she looked. Then as an eyebrow plucker and adolescent black-head squeezer and tooth examiner, lips drawn back against her gums. And now as a narcissist, presumably full-grown but still unmarried, disappointed in the men to whom she had given herself.

Teetering on her toes, back to the mirror, head twisted over her shoulder, she considered her buttocks and the two dimples just above them that were said to be so important. If it was not to be Ralph, who then would avail himself wholeheartedly of this ripeness? She rotated nude, her hands covering her heavy breasts until the nipples swelled and she felt the erotic fumes like incense rising to becloud her consciousness.

In a spasm of self-disgust Kitty threw on her nightgown and kicked the bathroom door closed. Ever since her earliest posturings before the glass, whether as chanteuse or as admirer of her own teeth and nipples, she had imagined a grand passion, a dark powerful man who would drag her away from her parents and her job. Now that he had come, she reverted to pre-adult behavior simply because he would not—and perhaps really could not—honor her every sensual whim. Worse, she had to charge him in her mind with being strange because of the very intensity which had originally drawn her to him.

Still, it had been odd, the way he had balanced promise against promise. Such talk she might have expected from her college dates, not from a man of thirty. Or did all men, when you had gotten to know enough of them, talk and think in this weirdly romantic, hopelessly impractical way, becoming even worse when they were married and the fathers of families? She thought suddenly of the last man in her life before Ralph, married with three children, who could imagine nothing more splendid than that she run off with him to Puerto Vallarta, where his in-laws (no less) had a beach house. Oh, if only Ralph could have stayed, just for a little while!

It struck her that she and Ralph had quite neglected—or forgotten—to ring up her parents and inform them of the news. They would be worse than hurt, they would be wretched, if she were to go off and marry without so much as letting them know. Kitty padded barefoot to the phone and sat down on the edge of the bed. But what do you say, that in three days your name will be Mrs. Ralph Land (Mrs. *Who?*), Kitty Land on the stationery, K.B.L. on the luggage . . . No, it was still three days too early. This was not exactly going to be a catered affair, with her parents haggling over the guest list. Anyway the time was past for doing things alone, Ralph had recognized it when he had phoned her and asked her to join him; she could only tell her parents with Ralph at her side.

Stretching herself out at full length on top of the neutral blanket and staring up at the seamless ceiling, Kitty had a bride's-eye view of the hotel room. But she was more alone than she had ever been since her first night away from home, lying on a narrow cot at Girl Scout camp and feeling the onset of her first period. This was the opposite of what she had expected when she had flown here, like a bird trying its wings in fear and exultation; but then from now on nothing would be what she had expected, of that alone was she certain.

In the morning she was awakened from a deep dreamless sleep by the ringing of the telephone.

"I knew you wouldn't be up," Ralph said cheerfully. "I hope you got a good night's sleep—you're going to need it. I'm downstairs."

They took breakfast together in the hotel coffee shop, and then hurried out onto the icy street.

"It's sunny." Kitty clung tight to Ralph's arm. "That's a good omen, isn't it?"

Without troubling to answer, he led her self-confidently through the business streets. "Nervous about the blood test?"

"I think I'll pass it. And if they had to take a quart, I'd still do it to marry you."

She was a little taken aback, though, to learn that the doctor was an old friend of the family, Leo Land's oldest friend, and that Ralph had known him since he could remember. She could not explain why, certainly not to Ralph, but she would have preferred it if he had arranged for this rite to be performed by a complete stranger, a businesslike young professional man. Nevertheless she was pleasantly surprised. The waiting room walls were lined not just with diplomas but with sensitive photographs of men at work—fishermen, glass blowers, cowboys—that the doctor, an enthusiastic amateur, had taken at Pátzcuaro, Murano, Big Bear Lake, Martha's Vineyard; the magazine table was stacked with the bulletins of half a dozen peace organizations. And Dr. Stark himself turned out to be a most kindly man, gentle as an old hound, with sad dog's eyes, a drooping, half-inflated bladder of a nose, and large ears whose pendulous lobes were almost concealed by tufts of graying hair. Beneath his white jacket he wore a baggy English tweed.

He was sizing her up, but politely, almost sweetly, putting her at her ease while he swabbed her finger tip and prepared to withdraw the blood. In his hoarse bullfrog voice he asserted, "You don't look the fainting kind, Miss Brenner. Usually it's the big mean ones, like Ralph, who keel over."

"I never have fainted," she assured him. "But then, I've never had the occasion."

"You don't need the occasion if you're the type. After forty-four years in practice, I can spot them all, the fainters, the yellers, the whiners. I have a hunch that Ralph has done very well for himself."

"You're very sweet."

Because of what the doctor had said Kitty could not turn aside her head while he drew the blood. He had a mother's touch.

"This is an occasion. Only two days ago Ralph gave me no indication that marriage was so imminent."

"I didn't know then that Kitty would accept me." Ralph laughed readily, but Kitty observed, and was afraid that the doctor had too, that the laugh had been preceded by a quick grimace, as if Dr. Stark had done something painful to him.

"Going back to New York after the wedding?"

Ralph, scowling at the doctor's scrubbed and freckled hands, replied deliberately. "It depends. I've taken a leave of absence from my job. Ray says he'll help us hunt up the will, if there is one, and that he'll try to cope with the idea of moving, if Kitty and I will stay on there with him as long as is necessary."

"I see, I see," the doctor mumbled, and then, just as he jabbed into Ralph's thumb, he added, "Say, Ralph, since I saw you last, it came to me, I'm almost positive your father did leave a will. Because that was what I witnessed."

Ralph's eyeballs rolled upwards, and he tottered away from the vial of his blood.

"Whoops!" The doctor cried. "Miss Brenner, reach me that little tube, if you please."

But Ralph did not faint, he was only momentarily dazed; he quickly waved away the ammoniated spirits from under his nostrils. "Sorry," he said. "Too much strain lately, I'm afraid."

"Don't apologize, perfectly understandable. Anyway, as I was saying, if you people stick at it, you'll turn up a will. Because I'm sure the document I signed was headed 'Last Will,' even though I have no idea what it said. It was just a matter of doing your father a favor. He was a notary public, he did many such for me."

Ralph's eyes narrowed as he replied, shrugging into his overcoat and barely troubling to smile, "You wouldn't be stringing me along, would you, Doctor?"

"Now why would I want to do a thing like that?" The old man gazed at them both innocently. "Well, best of luck in your quest. And of course your marriage."

In the corridor outside the office, waiting for the elevator, Kitty demanded, "Why did you make that crack?"

"Because he asked for it. He knows more than he lets on."

"Why shouldn't he let on to you?"

"Maybe he wants to play God. Maybe he wants to make sure that I won't stop hunting, or taking care of Ray. At least now he knows that I know. The only thing I'm sorry about is that I got dizzy."

"Maybe that was because you're afraid of getting married." Kitty grinned at him in the empty elevator.

Ralph replied quite seriously, "That could very well be."

Somewhat abashed, Kitty kept wordlessly to his side while he led her the two buffeting windy blocks to City Hall. There, in the basement, still breathless, they took their place in line before the clerk's window at the marriage license bureau. Kitty stared in consternation at the couples who had preceded them; they looked as though they had been carefully selected for their inappropriateness, like bit players from an old Laurel and Hardy movie. A little mustached man dangling from a big dominating woman, two skinny solemn young people, he with baggy pants, she with baggy stockings, a middle-aged pair of rubes, ruminating with the dumb patience of resigned travelers waiting to buy coach tickets from noplace to nowhere.

"This is romance?" she stage-whispered to Ralph.

"Don't knock it." Ralph repeated the phrase he had used about her hotel. "These people are in love. It's the squares, not the sophisticates, who believe that only beautiful boys and girls can fall in love."

It was only when they were in the taxi, riding out to Max Land's house, that Ralph again began to seem a little nervous, as he had been in the doctor's office. Alternating between tension and reassurance, he was overly talkative, pointing out landmarks with bitter comments on the barren scene, as though he were a cashiered tour guide getting back at his former employers.

"It's no wonder," he said, "that the new generation has deserted the center of the city. But before they left they should have blown it up, like a retreating army."

Then: "You mustn't be uneasy about Ray. We'll manage him."

And then: "In its day Uncle Max's house must have been

something. Even now, surrounded by the new suburbs, it could be fun to live in. Not for three peculiar bachelors, but for people with vision." He added, with evident self-satisfaction, "You have to know what you want from life."

Is that us, Kitty wondered, can he really have such ideas about us? He had her by the arm and was demanding that she duck down so that she could look forward and see the house over the taxi's hood before being thrust inside of it.

"You see?" Ralph demanded. "The nut who put it up wanted something facing away from the city. That's understandable, but nothing else about the house is. You know what all this used to be? Swamp and muck. Who else would have found it appealing, deserted and run down, but another nut like Max Land? Then one night came the biggest joke of all—the suburbs. And the Lands were sitting on something worth ten times what Max had paid for it just before Pearl Harbor."

The taxi pulled up to the old mansion's carriage drive, the only place where the snow was trampled down enough to make the house approachable. Kitty was surprised that it was not surrounded—as she had more or less envisioned it—by a six-foot wall topped with broken bottles set in mortar. There was a stone fence, to be sure, around the entire corner occupied by the house and grounds, but it was no more than waist-high even with the accumulation of snow and, at points, where it must have crumbled away, not even that. The lawn, or whatever ran around the three exposed sides of the house, had been allowed to go to seed, judging by the irregular hillocks of crusted snow (probably concealing clumps of crab grass) that arose here and there like white ant hills. But what was sinister about the place? It was just a big old house. Ralph, she began to suspect, had to construct a set of attitudes toward every situation he confronted; he was in truth much more of a romantic than she had ever realized.

This impression was reinforced when Ralph let them in to the dark foyer with the key she had not known he possessed. Filthy, yes; jammed with unspeakable junk that was not only dirty but totteringly dangerous, surely; but frightening? No more so than the tattered young man who came bounding down flight after flight of the winding stairs in response to Ralph's falsely hearty cry: "Ray, oh, Ray! We're here!"

She saw a terribly timid boy, heavily bearded, unkempt but not unclean, with great beautiful eyes as light as Ralph's were dark. What Ralph had not prepared her for was the extraordinary strength of his handclasp, which was not that of a recluse but of an athlete. His fingers were supple and well developed too, cool and pleasant to the touch, but most of all manly. Despite his timidity, he seemed to know instinctively that a woman likes to be taken firmly, even in a handshake.

"I'm very happy that you've come, even into such a terrible mess." His manner of speech was tentative, very different from Ralph's. "I don't know that I can help, but at least I'll stay out of your way."

"You can do better. Even from here I can see obstacles that will require strong backs and stout hearts. Surely you can give Ralph a hand, moving things while I dust?"

Raymond touched his beard with his finger tips, as if seeking reassurance in its curly fringes. Why should someone so strong be so uncertain?

"I suppose so."

Kitty refused Ralph, who was attempting to help her off with her coat. "No, no," she said, "I'm on my way out to the shopping center across the street to buy a housedress and an apron. In the meantime you can hunt up a mop, a broom, rags, soap, scouring powder. We'll clean one area, then you can bring stuff there to examine it."

Ralph had no intention of bringing in an outsider to clean. Even an illiterate might stumble on something, to say nothing of hearing Ray up in the attic. Apparently Ralph had hoped that she would pitch in at once, to riffle through rows of files with her New York office efficiency, but he made no complaint against her choice of priority. So, with a scarf knotted around her head, she attacked cobwebs and heaps of rubbish while the brothers grunted and sweated at her command.

Perhaps Ralph had dreaded carrying on the hunt without her practical presence to assure him that the search was sensible, and that he was not simply digging to distract himself from the hopeless reality of his situation, like a prisoner dutifully but senselessly chipping away with a sharpened spoon at the bottomless stone floor of his cell.

What was even more likely, Kitty thought as she watched Ralph poring over mountains of papers, discarding each as reluctantly as if, a true Land, he feared that he might be tossing aside the very object of his quest (who knew, maybe written with invisible ink?), was that he could not bear the prospect of being alone with Ray.

For herself, when she could pause long enough to think of it, Kitty was astonished only at how quickly one's daily life could be organized into an established routine around an unforeseen (and more than a little preposterous) set of circumstances.

After the first day she did not believe that Ralph would ever find the will, and indeed shared his suspicion that the doctor had made up the whole story to get Ralph to stay on and shoulder his responsibilities. After the second day she did not even care. And on the third, whistling "The Wedding March" as she tied cord around bundles of *Popular Mechanics* to be put out on the porch for the Salvation Army truck, she felt as though she had been intimately involved in the rhythm of this house for years. What was more, she didn't mind it. One more night and they would be married, yes. But more than that, it was apparent in Ralph's slightest gesture that she was fulfilling his highest expectations. Will or no will, he would have to demonstrate this gratitude when finally they were alone as married lovers. Because of this she was happy, and the housework—not despite its seeming endlessness, but rather because of it—was a daily task that she took up with more pleasure than she had ever greeted her office work.

It was fun to be doing for two men. They took to being bossed just as she, to her surprise, took to being maternal, calling them brassily for lunch, insisting that they wash up before sitting down to her pancakes. Even Ray's inability to eat meat, which could be an irritant to a permanent cook, was at the moment a challenge to her ingenuity.

What would she make them tonight? Spaghetti? That was last night. Vegetable plate? The night before. Kitty paused in the middle of the kitchen, thumbnail between her teeth, and gazed absently about her. Her eye lighted upon an old-fashioned wooden recipe box on the shelf next to the throbbing whale of a refrigerator, whose guts rattled and groaned as though Jonah were inside pleading to get out. Nibbling at the varnish on her nail, Kitty wondered whether the box could have belonged to Jenny Land, the dead mother whose rather horse-faced, sad-eyed photo she had discovered only this morning on the mantel behind an Optimo cigar box stuffed with Kirkman soap coupons. Would the boys like something that their mother had made many years ago?

Kitty lifted the lid cautiously. Yes, it was Jenny Land's. With schoolteacherly neatness she had written her name and address in Palmer penmanship on a shipping label and pasted it on the inner lid. The label was curling loose but the box was not particularly dusty. Kitty began to flip through the three-by-five cards, but they fell open at B: Birthday Cakes. A folded oblong sheet, closed with a paper clip, was holding the cards apart. She pulled off the clip and opened the sheet. Block letters: LAST WILL AND TESTAMENT OF LEO LAND.

Kitty clutched at the breadboard. Groping behind her, she sat down on the kitchen table top and stared at the paper which rattled in her hand. She had resisted the immediate temptation to cry out in triumph. Now as she read the erratically scrawled statement her ears were drumming and her mouth was dry, so dry that she could not have called out had she wanted to.

But she did not want to. The simple two sentences were

what they had been looking for. There could be no question. Below Leo Land's name was the hastily scribbled signature, typically messy, like all doctors', of Solomon Stark, M.D.

Kitty sat so still that she could hear an entire chamber orchestra of sounds about her in the house. The circular whir of the failing electric clock on the wall, the marine gulp-throb of the refrigerator, the thud-thud of poor ancient Sasha rousing up from his post under the dining-room table to claw feebly at his balding hide with a palsied paw; and, in the living room or the parlor or the front room or whatever the builder had called it, the two brothers shuffling papers, muttering, even chuckling, searching for what she held in her hand.

On the edge of the stove, no further away than her hand, was a blue and white cardboard box of Ohio wooden matches; she could strike one without anybody hearing, without anybody (not even Dr. Stark) ever discovering what she had done. One day she could tell Ralph—he would believe her, he knew she was capable of it—and it would be over with, done. But would he be grateful? Was this what he would do in her place? I don't know him that well, she realized in sudden fear, I don't know if he would do what I would do. Nor was she sure—she cursed herself for her idiot ignorance of the law— what Ralph's legal position would be if she were to reduce the paper to ash.

But of course, of course, there was Ray. And as soon as his name had formed itself in her mind, together with the image of his blue eyes, transparent as clear glass, she realized that what she had been contemplating was, quite simply, impossible. What has Ralph done to me, she marveled, that I should think even of holding it back for his private decision? She had already given him substantial proof of love. There was no need to start fires; he knew that she would be with him in whatever he had to do as a result of her discovery. She kicked free from the table and strode down the hallway with the paper in her hand.

In the pillared entranceway to the living room she stopped. Ray and Ralph were squatting, facing each other, in the cleared area before the hideous false fireplace, their faces sharply highlighted by the fringed floor lamp they had lit against the waning winter day. Ralph held a legal folder in his hand, which was dirty, as was his face. He did not look up at her entrance.

"No bankbooks," he was saying, "except for the current checking account?"

"Everything went into mortgage bonds, or more properties."

"What about Papa's life insurance?"

"I heard him say something once to Uncle Max about cashing in his policies after Mama died. There wasn't much anyway, just a couple small ones from that fraternal organization with the long name, the Rumanian one."

"Ralph," she said. "Ray. I've found it."

"Just a minute, Kitty," Ralph said impatiently. "What do you mean, Ray, just a couple small ones?"

"Ralph," Kitty repeated insistently, "I've found the will."

She stared in fascination at the face of the man she was going to marry in the morning. Ralph was squinting up at her uncomprehendingly, the line of the razor along his cheekbone perfectly clear in the lamplight, his firm secretive mouth gone a little slack, agape, as though he were having difficulty breathing.

"Will?" he demanded. "My father's will?"

"Yes. It leaves everything to Ray." She paused. "And one other thing. Who is Mel?"

4: RAY

January 6

Not surprised about will. Wasn't even particularly complimented that Papa left everything to me. He was grateful that I didn't leave home. Didn't leave him, rather. But more likely he was worried about what would happen to me, afraid Mel and Ralph might cut me out or hold up my share. So he figured he'd make sure. But how could I say this to Ralph? Wouldn't make him feel better to think that Papa trusted him so little.

Was more surprised last week to learn that Uncle Max left everything to Papa. Thought surely he'd leave something substantial to Mel. He always worried about Mel like Papa worried about me. That really floors me, no bequests for Mel or Ralph in either will.

Couldn't explain my feelings to Ralph, because in each case it comes down to Mel.

Supposedly there was no love lost between them. But there had been love between Mel and Ralph when they were kids,

I'm convinced, and somewhere it got lost. Isn't that worse?

What did surprise me was Kitty asking, "Who is Mel?"

I knew Ralph was not proud of us. That's his business. But to conceal your older brother from the girl you're going to marry and bring into the family! Can't understand his reasoning. Wasn't she bound to find out sooner or later?

Then, when Kitty read the will aloud, he gave us both a horrible look, as though in that instant we had done him some physical violence. Made a lunge for Kitty.

Tore the paper out of her hand and glared at it, while she was asking, "Who is Mel?"

Shouted at me, in sudden, irrational rage, "What do you know about this?"

"As much as you."

"Did you put Papa up to this?" he yelled. "Is that why you locked yourself in this nut house with him and Max? So as not to let him out of your sight?"

Kitty said, "I asked you a question."

So he turned on her, asked her why she came running in with the will, why she didn't talk it over with him first. She froze. Asked him if he thought she'd have behaved any differently in that case, and hidden the will from me.

That stopped him. Kitty asked, it must have been for the third time, almost in a whisper, "Who is Mel?"

He shoved past her, desperate to get out of the room, as though the very sight of us sickened him. As he went he cried over his shoulder, "Ask him! Ask Ray! He knows everything, he'll give you all the dirt."

Kitty looked at me uncertainly. I wasn't used to giving advice, but finally I suggested that she should let him go, that he'd cool off.

"Will you tell me about Mel?"

So I did. Just said what she would find out sooner or later anyway, such as that Mel and Ralph had been very close when they were kids, two against the world, that they had a falling out, that Mel had the reputation of being a tough guy just as Ralph had the reputation of being ambitious and thin-skinned, that Mel had gotten into some trouble and run away from home when he was eighteen, and that none of us had ever seen him since. And that when we did hear of him it was always because of some new trouble. Like now, convicted of burglary.

"The poor guy," Kitty said. "The poor guy."

I thought she meant Mel. Didn't envy Ralph the explaining he was going to have to do. But then I realized it was Ralph she was thinking of!

So I started by not understanding Ralph and wound up by not understanding her.

When Ralph came back he was cleaned up, clothes changed. Looked to me as though he had been soaking his head, especially his eyes, with cold water. Gotten himself under control, too, but barely.

"You win all the marbles, kid," he said. "You'll have enough to keep you in comfort for as long as you want to hole up. So I guess you won't need me."

Kitty scolded him, but gently, for not telling her about Mel. "Do you think I care?" she asked him.

"I'm holding you to nothing," he replied.

Kitty stared at him.

"You came here on specific terms. I can't fulfill them, so you're free to leave."

She called him a horse's ass then. And an idiot. "Idiot," she said, "do you think I came here for the money? If Raymond is going to be rich, let him. What's it got to do with us?"

I was so embarrassed for them, I wanted to crawl up to the attic. Gritted my teeth, stepped between them, said to Ralph, "I don't need the money, I don't want it. I need you. Don't go away. Don't feel you have to do anything on account of me. Stay here, both of you, and I'll go on up to the attic."

I hate to say it, but a very calculating expression crept into Ralph's eyes. He nodded coolly, picked up Kitty's coat, told me to sit tight while they went out to eat.

I made another mistake, asked Ralph if he was going to be back.

He told me not to wait up for him. And that was that.

Made myself cheese sandwich, came back up here. Haven't eaten it, have no appetite, it's drying on the table. I know why Ralph took Kitty away—he was afraid I'd eavesdrop. All because I was listening that first night, when he called her on the telephone.

What was so terrible about that? I just wanted to make sure he wouldn't call a cab and go away for good.

11:15 P.M. The Late News is finished, and the last of the lights are going out in Happy Valley. I am so alone!

January 7

Slept late. Made no difference, nobody came back. Can't keep to a schedule when I don't know what's going to happen next.

Did the usual. Rolled hammock, 15 min. setting-up exercises, 30 min. weight-lifting (press and jerk only), policed attic, called in W3RS as per schedule, discussed neutral subjects. But couldn't concentrate on reading, much less studying or memorizing. 11 A.M., am at a standstill.

How much longer will I be here? The 3-in. fiberglas insulation batten that I stapled to the ceiling, the random tile floor covering that I put down using the odd pieces Uncle Max dragged home, the pictures I shellacked to the celotex walls, even the steel rod chinning bar that I screwed into place between studs, all my improvements will go to waste. To say nothing of my radio rig, books, clippings, the ledger books for this diary.

Mel and Ralph would both laugh at me for being so attached to things. That's another of the attitudes they've always had in common. Which is more important, property or people? They're right, of course. Neither of them would give a second thought to what's in the attic, or to the whole house, if it stood in the way of progress.

But the whole story of our family is right here, under these eaves. Why tear everything down without finding out about ourselves first?

Anyway, what's so terrible about my being scared? Isn't everybody scared?

Maybe if I look at people for a while it will help.

Later. Hunkered down behind louvers in customary catcher's position. Mailman came on schedule, pushing one-handled gocart along shoveled walk, wiping nose with free hand, bringing the usual: *Life* magazine, announcements of private sales to public customers, delayed New Year's cards, also birth, death, marriage, communion, bar mitzvah, and removal of dentists' offices to new locations. After him, clumsy chocolate-colored United Parcel Service truck. Driver is coward. Sat in truck honking for housewife to come out, afraid of her little girl's dachshund. Then a young doctor, new in the neighborhood, broad-shouldered and blank-faced like a professional athlete, lifting his little bag from his Buick and stepping fussily over the snowdrifts. Went into corner house, first time I knew anyone was sick there, scuffing his rubbers on sisal mat, then ducking indoors past outstretched arm holding open storm door. Must find out what's wrong there.

Looked across to A & P, hoping that the Jehovah's Witness would be back on the job again in front of it, but no such luck. Knew she wouldn't be there, she's been gone so long, but all the same I kept watching.

Then the phone rang. It rang so many times I almost screamed. Had to jump up with my hands to my ears. Maybe it was Ralph, couldn't take a chance. After I finally lost count, it stopped. Found myself doodling, three linked circles, like the Ballantine ad. Purity—body—flavor, which am I? Stuck my initials in the inferior circle, junior partner in firm of Max and Leo Land, Drugs and Sundries, Nuts and Bolts. Then made three more circles, me in bottom one again, clinging member of a new trio—Ralph, Kitty, and unwanted me.

Nobody has to tell me that I can't just sit here forever. But Ralph is liable to stay away as long as possible, to make me as dependent on him as possible.

He'll be back, it was written all over his face. He's as hungry for what I am going to have as I am for what he is going to have. So why should I bear him a grudge for what he said? Instead, I'll make a surprise.

11:50 P.M. Third entry today. The surprise took all afternoon to make, and still no one came.

I *know* he'll come. Not just because of the estate. Because of me. He's always thought that he could wipe out the past, Papa, Uncle Max, Mel, me, the store, this house, by being what none of us has known how to be. For him that means not only having so much money that you don't have to get up in the morning to make more. It also means behaving not like a Land, but in high style. Noblesse oblige. He'd be humiliated if the newspapers said that he had neglected me. Especially if they printed my picture! So I have weapons on my side too, if only I don't lose my nerve. If things drag out, though, time might be more on his side than on mine. He's more mobile, more used to planning than I am, and he's more ruthless.

But if only he'd come back!

January 8

What a day. In the A.M. tried to pretend that nothing had changed. Fiddled with ham rig, recalibrated, checked call letters. Tried to memorize some more constellations. Read three articles in *Britannica*. All worse than useless. Because I kept sneaking looks in hopes of seeing a Yellow Cab pull up. I was being punished, it didn't make any difference whether it was by Ralph or by the Almighty, for the sin of pride. Once I said aloud, "I want to be good!" but right away I was ashamed of myself.

Then the front door slammed, with no forewarning. Ralph shouted up, "It's us."

There they were, helping each other off with their things, Kitty tottering on one foot and laughing while Ralph tugged at her overshoe. Ruddy-cheeked, completely unlike the two who had left the day before yesterday. Scattering snow all over the hall, shaking themselves like Sasha, who stood by dumbly. My heart leaped when I saw Kitty's bags standing beside her.

She is very quick. "Yes," she said, "I've come to stay for a while. You won't mind?"

"Mind?" I could hardly talk.

"In that case you might as well congratulate us. It's legal now."

Ralph looked wary as we shook hands. I knew I was supposed to kiss my new sister-in-law, but I couldn't. I stood there like Sasha, with my head hanging. So she took the initiative, placing her hands, pinkish from the cold, on my shoulders, and kissing me on each cheek. Her breath was delicious, she smelled wintry and fragrant.

Then I remembered my surprise, and insisted that they come back to the kitchen with me. Ralph wanted to know whether I was going to pull something else out of Mama's recipe box, and I had to laugh, because when I turned on the kitchen light, there was the wedding cake on the table.

Kitty's eyes filled with tears.

"How sweet," she said. "How sweet."

I set out plates and coffee cups, and while the coffee was perking, Ralph wanted to know how I was so sure that he was getting married, when he wasn't even positive himself. I admitted I had taken a chance and Ralph winked at Kitty and said, "Don't we all." I think he was really pleased about the cake. He said now he had a wife and a brother, and responsibilities to both of them.

That was what I'd been hoping to hear, and I asked him what he thought we ought to do about the will.

"As soon as we agree on the way things ought to be arranged," he said, "give it to Martin Stark and tell him how you want to dispose of the estate."

I wasn't sure that we ought to keep it to ourselves even that long, but Ralph argued that the reporters would start hounding him as soon as it became public knowledge that the will was being probated. Besides, he said, I wouldn't be of age for some months, and Martin probably wouldn't be able to do anything until then.

It sounded reasonable, what more could I have wanted? We shook hands on it. But I was thinking (not aloud, because I didn't want to spoil things) that it was to Ralph's advantage not to let on to anyone that Kitty had found the will. All I said out loud was, I still didn't want anything for myself.

Ralph held up his finger confidently, warningly, like a schoolteacher. Even before he spoke I felt the menace in his gesture. "That's not quite true. You want us."

That was a brutal thing to say. Next thing I knew Kitty had her hand on my arm and was telling me how Ralph wanted the best for me.

"If I can live on here quietly," I said, "I'll divide up everything that comes in from the estate. Share and share alike. Half for you two, half for Mel."

"The fact is, brother, you can't live on here indefinitely. No more than you could on a desert island, if the island happened to be where they wanted to test bombs."

I started to protest, and Ralph held up his hand to stop me.

"So I chose a bad example. But you know what I mean. I've had a long discussion with Kitty about Mel, and she agrees that he's not entitled to participate in the inheritance."

I turned to her.

She colored a little, but she stuck by Ralph. "I can't see rewarding him for the suffering he's inflicted on the family. Besides, he wouldn't have any conception of what to do with the money."

"That's not for us to say. I don't say what Ralph and you ought to do with your share."

Ralph smiled patiently, and remarked that I wasn't being very practical.

But when I explained that I wasn't trying to be practical, simply principled, like Ralph himself with his protests that Mel should get nothing at all, his face contracted, so I tried another way. "If you'll agree that it's nobody's business what we do with our shares, then I'll agree to forget about Mel. We'll divide the whole works, fifty-fifty."

Ralph burst out laughing. "You're so transparent! You'd just turn around and give your share to Mel. Sorry, pal. That's out. You'll have to give me a written promise not to sign anything over to Mel."

"I could just as well demand the same thing from you. How do I know you wouldn't turn around and make a deal with Mel against me?"

I wanted to find out just how much Ralph had told Kitty, so it was her I watched while I said, "Mel was the one you were close to when you were a kid, not me. I found the secret oath you both took when you became blood brothers, when you were eight and he was nine, and I wasn't even born. No wonder you can't stand each other now."

Kitty sucked in air through her teeth, but she didn't say anything. I could see the muscles going in Ralph's jaw when he answered me.

"I'm trying very hard to be reasonable. If you want Martin Stark to give Mel a nominal sum in return for a quitclaim, that might do it."

"A nominal sum isn't what Papa specifies."

"He doesn't specify anything."

"Papa specifies in the second sentence—"

"The will, the will!"

I knew the will by heart, and I recited it aloud, fast: "I hereby bequeath all of my possessions and worldly goods to my faithful son Raymond, to be held in trust for him until he becomes of age by my brother Max; in the event of Max's death by my friend Solomon Stark, M.D.; in the event of Solomon's death by his son Martin. I bequeath also to Raymond as the executor the task of apportioning to my sons Melvin and Ralph a share of this bequest, as he sees fit, depending on the relationship existing among the three at the time of my death."

"If you keep whining about that bastard who shortened your own mother's life, I'll flush the will down the toilet."

Ralph's features had grown even darker, and his cheeks were startlingly red between the bluish planes of his heavy beard and his grown-together eyebrows. He was pressing down hard on the table, near the remains of my wedding cake. When he stopped speaking I could hear his chair squeaking horribly behind him on the worn-out linoleum.

"You're not the only one that's been thinking, Ralphie," I said. "If there's no will, they'll split up everything between you, me, and Mel."

Kitty jerked her head nervously.

"Don't bet on that," Ralph replied harshly. "They won't be in a hurry to hand money out to one nut sitting in the can and another sitting in an attic."

I hadn't been intending to say what I did next, but he forced my hand, didn't he?

"If that's how you want it, I'll be glad to oblige you with lots of publicity for the reporters. So will Mel in his cell, I'm sure."

"What's your price, Ray? What do you want?"

"A *détente*."

Ralph looked a little baffled, so I explained, "Stay on here with Kitty. We can argue it out—I'm not twenty-one yet—and maybe one of us can convince the other."

I extended my hand. Ralph's rose slowly to meet it.

But then the phone rang. Ralph shook his head rapidly, like Sasha leaping from the washtub after a bath, and reached for the extension phone before Kitty or I could move.

It was Dr. Stark. After that, of course, everything happened. He and Martin came, and the Kadin cousins, but I'm just too tired to go on with it. Tomorrow.

January 9
Can't. Too busy getting back on schedule.

January 10
Here we go. The rest of what happened 2 days ago, on the 8th. Was quite calm while Ralph talked to Dr. S. and Kitty asked me to be patient with Ralph and his ferocious temper. She sounded proud of it.

When I learned that not only Dr. S. and his son, but also our cousins, were coming, I had all I could do to keep from turning and running up to the attic. Told Ralph and Kitty that they'd have to get along without me, I was going upstairs.

"No you don't," Ralph said. "Those people are the only ones who know you're here, and if you want to keep it that way for a while you'd better stay put." Kitty tried to soften it, but it still sounded like a threat.

The cousins knew about me, but they had only come once since Mama's death, and then they had practically held their noses as they fled. Once, too, they had gone to the hospital—to make sure that Uncle Max was dying, was the way Papa put it, and he was not a spiteful man. They had gone to Uncle Max's funeral too, to make sure that the lid was screwed down tight. I am as hungry for family as a cat for fish-heads, but I felt about them coming into this house as Ralph did about the reporters. No good could come of it.

Ralph urged us to stick together against the cousins. He and Kitty had me lifting and hauling while they cleaned up the parlor for the company. Then, when Kitty went back to the kitchen to prepare some food, Ralph went to work on me some more.

"You look awful," he said.

I ran my filthy hands up and down my trouser legs. "I'll get washed up," I said.

"It's not that. It's the pants. And those slippers. Shuffling around like an old man. Haven't you got any pride?"

I felt my throat filling. I could hardly talk. I whispered, "I'm in mourning."

"So am I. Out of respect for Papa you ought to get out of that sweater and pants."

"I'll try to find something," I said. "It's been years."

"And shave while you're at it."

Ralph wanted to march me out like a clotheshorse. For what? Suddenly I was certain that this was to be the first push in his big drive to dislodge me from the attic. I had to resist.

"No, I can't shave, Ralph," I said. "I don't think you ought to ask that of me."

And I didn't. But once I was upstairs I dug up the clothes I had worn three years ago for my high-school graduation. Blue suit with wide lapels, white on white shirt, black shoes. I didn't mind trying to look neat, like the husbands and fathers of Happy Valley whom Ralph despised, or even like Ralph himself; but Ralph wanted more, he wanted to cut me down and destroy my potential for bringing him shame, by making me indistinguishable from all the rest.

It was only when I tried everything on that I saw how ludicrous I looked. White shirt couldn't button, neck three sizes too small. That meant no tie. Couldn't even get my arms through suit-coat sleeves. Feet had spread from wearing slippers. Had to remove laces so I could squeeze my feet into the graduation shoes, which had green mold on the welts that I couldn't wipe off.

When I came down to lunch Ralph considered me carefully and decided that I would pass. We were still eating when Dr. Stark and his son arrived.

Dr. S. is one person I am always glad to see. At least he tries to understand me. Besides, he really loved Papa, and he knows the history of our family from before I was born, in fact from before Papa and Mama were married.

He came marching right into the kitchen with Martin. They insisted that we finish our bananas and cream, and congratulated the newlyweds.

"Tell Kitty some of your stories about Uncle Max and Papa, Doctor," I urged him.

Ralph was uneasy. "Let's go into the living room."

I was supposed to be the uncomfortable one, but Ralph was more anxious than me. Afraid that the doctor or the lawyer would start asking questions about the will, what Ralph was going to do with me, etc., etc. As simple as that.

"I'd like to hear about Ralph's father's inventions, Doctor," Kitty said, "but I really want to know the truth about him and his brother."

"The truth? That's one hell of an order. Even to start, I'd have to go back well before your time, even before Martin's. The two Land boys arrived here early in 1911, I believe it was, from the old country. It was Max who made the decision for them to come out here. They were young, they weren't afraid of hard work. They shoveled snow, they worked on junk wagons, they ate beans and rice.

"Besides the dream of pharmacy school, which was more practical than medical or dental school, they were saving up to pluck their parents out of that benighted corner of southeastern Rumania, I think it was, where they still clung to their little grain and feed store.

"But in 1914, after the years of struggle, they learned that their mother had died in an epidemic. A tough blow, but it made them work twice as hard for their father. When they'd succeeded finally in sending him the passage money, their old man wrote back that he had already remarried and was raising a new family."

By now the doctor had us.

"Six years of overwork and deliberate semistarvation had

had their effect. Even though the supposed motivation had been removed, the same life rhythm continued, like a watch that keeps running on a man's wrist after he has stopped breathing. They graduated, they rented the drugstore—in which they had originally hoped to install their parents. The flu epidemic got them over the financial hump and enabled them to buy the building. By the time I met them, which was 1920, they were already confirmed in their neuroses. At any rate, isn't it clear why Max Land should never have married? Why he should have preferred the shadowy consolations of Ann Sheridan? Need I labor the point?"

"You'd labor the point, Dad," Martin remarked dryly, "if we'd let you."

"Fortunately for me," Kitty said, "Leo Land married. But why did he, if his brother didn't?"

"He wasn't hooked until he was pushing forty. And at that it was my doing. The brothers were very different, and re-acted differently to the same stimuli. About all they had in common, in truth, besides upbringing and education, was their pyknic bodily structure. Both men were small but long-armed, they did look a bit simian, but that was the end of the resemblance. All I'm suggesting is that their diverse neuroses had a common origin."

"What happens to your Freudianism," Martin demanded, "if you admit that their peculiarities came not from their infancy but from events when they were already grown?"

"You're being simplistic," the doctor retorted. "Those events in Rumania circa 1916 must surely have aroused dormant memories of what the old man had been like when Max and Leo were tots, of how he had behaved with their mother, and all the rest. Isn't that obvious? Boy," he addressed him-self to Ralph and me with youthful enthusiasm, "I'd give a cooky to have known your grandfather. That old bastard must have been something."

"Does that bring us to the inventions?" Kitty asked.

"Well, I always felt that Leo was ashamed of himself, because he didn't dare be ashamed of his father. What's more, I told him so, just as I'm telling you."

Ralph stared curiously at the doctor. "What did he say to that?"

"He laughed! Because in his own gentle way he had to work at being good to others, whether to his brother or to humanity in general, in order to expiate his own feelings of shame and inadequacy. So came the inventions, do you see?"

"I don't know that I do," Kitty replied.

"All of his inventions, even his feeble attempts to patent and market them, were grounded not in a desire to make money—in which he wasn't really interested—but in an irrational desire to make other people happy. The obverse, in short, of his brother's anal propensities. In a parallel way he went through all that suffering as a young fellow not to liberate himself from his father, which I think we can say of Max, but rather to put himself under his old man's domination again, under the guise of getting the folks out of Europe."

"But the inventions?"

"Anybody tell you about his pillow for the weary traveler? A self-inflating and deflating rubber spheroid with a bulb that you squeezed to force gas into the bladder, and unscrewed to release the gas, like a blood-pressure apparatus. He spent considerable dough on it, and time too, back in the twenties, and then someone beat him out with a simpler gadget." The doctor sighed. "Then there were a series of anti-nail-biting devices inspired, I regret to say, by my son's bad habit."

Martin was sitting negligently on his spine, but it pleased me to see a forty-year-old lawyer blushing.

"Martin, Leo used to say, it's not nice for a violinist to chew his nails, his hands are on display. So, because he felt sorry for my boy, he made up a pocket kit, including scissors, file, orange stick, buffer, and a little bottle of some odious mixture that you were supposed to smear on, to make your gorge rise every time you brought your hand near your face. Do you think I could convince Leo that you can't cure nail-biting with toys, any more than you can thumb-sucking or enuresis? I gave him books to read, I argued. No use. How he used to plead with me to let him paint Martin's nails with that rat poison!

"But Martin gave up the habit. Or rather he substituted a pipe. Leo's other preoccupations grew out of his own childhood, his mother's desire for a daughter, his father's deafness. I'll tell you this much, a shady character on the west side fleeced him out of fifteen hundred bucks on a promise to market Leo's litmus paper test for determining the sex of unborn babies. He got clipped good on his cure for deafness too, based not on amplification but on some kookie fenestrating chemical, like a universal solvent. This one he claimed to derive from Benjamin Franklin's Autobiography, Beethoven's letters, and I think Goldoni. Or was it Manzoni? I can never tell them apart."

"I hate to break in on your reminiscences," Martin said pleasantly, "but don't you think we ought to take up more current matters?"

Ralph glanced across at me warily. Kitty was smiling fixedly, like a young lady at a dull tea party. I had a feeling all hell would break loose.

Just at that moment the doorbell went off, like a rusty alarm clock. I was relieved to see that I wasn't the only one who jumped.

Can't write any more, my arm feels like it's falling off. Will try to put down the rest of it tomorrow.

January 11

January 8th, cont.: Ralph brought in Lillian Kadin and her sister Henrietta, and Henrietta's husband, Ben Lurie. My intestines were tied up in knots. Was dying to run to toilet if not to attic. Visitors tense too. And funny-looking. The sisters are small, roly-poly, overdecorated, like loud souvenir pillows. Too much hair, even under their little veiled hats, and too many clothes. Sweaters over dresses, scarfs over sweaters, etc.

Mr. Lurie has a smile that is artificial even when he means it—when his face opens it looks painted on, like a circus clown's. When he stands next to his little wife they look like Mutt and Jeff.

Ralph suddenly became like them. They brought out in him the same gestures, the same gentilities.

"Ralph, you were wise to marry right away." That was Henrietta.

Ralph put his arm proudly around Kitty. "Don't I know it?"

"Life is too short." Lillian this time. "Your father would have wanted it this way. It doesn't pay to wait. Nothing lasts forever."

Even Mr. Lurie got into the act. He shook hands all around, showing two rows of teeth and a row of ball point pens. "Life has to go on, doesn't it, Doctor? These young people should take advantage of it. You and I have learned that from our professions."

The doctor grinned like a fox. I was hoping they'd ignore me in favor of the newlyweds. Did my best to be inconspicuous, sat on edge of piano bench at the fringe of the semicircle we'd arranged. But Mr. Lurie sat down next to me, gripped my thigh, addressed me in his disagreeably penetrating voice.

"Young fellow, you're looking good, all things considered."

I didn't know what things he had considered, but right away I knew what he had been put up to by his wife and his sister-in-law.

"Don't you think it's about time you started making plans for getting out of here?"

I looked to Ralph for help, but he was pleased that the heat was being turned on me, and looked on unblinkingly with a mocking smile. I told Mr. Lurie that Ralph and I had a lot of things to talk about first, but he wouldn't let it alone.

"You can talk, who's stopping you? But you can't keep on hiding. You can't expect us to cover up for you indefinitely. People get suspicious, it's not normal."

"Then why not tell them?" I was getting tenser every second. "For my part, I don't care. Just tell people that I'm here and that for the time being I want to stay here."

"Once word gets out that you've been here all along, they'll besiege you and your brother. They'll bombard all of us."

"But that's going to happen whenever—"

"Not if you leave discreetly." Mr. Lurie looked very wise, as well as buddy-buddy. "Then you can turn up here just like Ralph did, and it's nobody's business where you've been."

Henrietta and Lillian moved in on me.

"You've got your whole life ahead of you," Henrietta said.

"Only part of it," I pointed out.

"The best part," Lillian insisted. She nodded so hard that the bird's nest wobbled dangerously on her little hat.

"How can you tell beforehand?" I asked. "Maybe I've already had the best part. Maybe we all have."

"It doesn't pay to be morbid," Mr. Lurie said. "What if everybody talked like that?"

"Questions like that," Dr. Stark said in his leisurely way, "are of no particular help to Raymond."

Ben Lurie persisted. "Ray, look at your brother. He didn't let any grass grow under his feet."

"We're different," I said in desperation. "No two people are alike."

Martin Stark surprised me by saying quietly, "We can't expect other people to do exactly what we would, if we were in their shoes. On the other hand, if they want to be helped, we ought to be ready to help them."

"I do want that," I said. "Ralph knows it. If you'll just give me a chance, I'll try not to disgrace anybody."

Dr. Stark put his arm around my shoulders and squeezed me. "Nobody can ask any more of you than that. You have to make allowances for us. Remember, everybody isn't concerned simply with your welfare. They're worried too about how your behavior is going to affect them. Not just in publicity but also in dollars and cents."

It was as though the radiators had suddenly cut off and the

living room had turned to ice. Only Martin didn't seem chilled by what his father had said. The two sisters puffed up furiously, and Henrietta's husband, Ben, let his face go long and slack again. Ralph threw a warning glance at Kitty. Or maybe it wasn't warning but beseeching.

Whatever it was, she jumped up and said, "I'm going to heat some coffee. Would you ladies care to join me in the kitchen? I'm going to slice up the beautiful cake that you brought."

Henrietta and Lillian waddled off eagerly after Kitty. They were glad to get off the hook.

Then Martin took it upon himself to smooth things over with Ben Lurie. They talked politics, which has never interested me, and then ice hockey, which I don't follow. The doctor pulled down his jaw in a comical way and winked at me.

After the women came back with the trays I was out of it, I was able to sit in the corner and watch them all, the next best to being back in my attic. Lillian's chapped mouth opened like a pecking bird's whenever she wanted to talk. Henrietta, I saw, was much heavier than her sister (because she was married, or because she ate up her skinny husband's portions too?). She was hovering over the cake, eating too much and pouring too much cream and sugar into her coffee. Deep creases in her back where the girdle cut into her flesh.

Ralph was calm again, outwardly, but he didn't finish his coffee, and his fingers were drumming nervously against his ankle. Maybe if he hadn't shown me how much he felt he had to gain by my silence about the will, the afternoon wouldn't have wound up as it did.

As it was, the doctor shuffled his thick brogues and got up to go. He growled in his sardonic way, "There's something to be said for family get-togethers. The bride shows us how she has made this god-awful house look homey, and we show her how polite we are—*de mortuis nil nisi bonum*."

The Kadins didn't know exactly what he was talking about,

but they were uneasy. The man of the family spoke: "We said good-by to a way of life the other day. Let's hope these young people are saying hello to a new way of life."

"Life isn't that discontinuous," Dr. Stark replied. "You couldn't sell me on the idea that these boys' father really enjoyed living in the middle of this mountain of junk any more than Kitty would. He wasn't that acquisitive, but he allowed himself to be dominated by someone who was."

Suddenly he turned to me. "Ray, you're the direct link. Wouldn't you agree that we're surrounded here more by the smell of old Max than by the sweeter memory of your father?"

I felt my face getting hot. "You can't blame everything on Uncle Max. Something about this life and this house must have appealed to Papa too, or he wouldn't have put up with it. The same goes for me, I don't deny it." I swallowed, and added: "What's more, the same went for Mama. If she didn't find the Lands appealing, she wouldn't have stood for them."

Then, because everyone started talking at once, I had to yell, "She wasn't such a weak sister!"

"When you were born," Ralph said loudly, "Mama kicked Uncle Max out of our flat. That's how he wound up in this house with this junk. She was an angel to put up with him as long as she did. So why try to make out that she was like the Lands, or found them appealing, for God's sake?"

"You're absolutely right," Henrietta said.

"Not absolutely." The doctor shook his head as he shook himself into his bulky overcoat. "The fact is simply that the flat behind the drugstore was too small to hold Max too, after the unexpected arrival of Raymond."

Ralph turned on him. "I'll bet you one thing: If it had been Papa instead of Mama who died twelve years ago, you never would have caught her moving into this rat's nest with her boys."

"That's hardly logical." The doctor bundled his hand-knitted scarf around his neck. "It sounds more like an unconscious preference. Or a suppressed wish."

Ralph was livid. In the front hall, while everyone was putting on galoshes, Ben Lurie tried to step into the social breach again by inviting Ralph and Kitty to spend a family evening at the Luries real soon.

Then he tapped me on the chest. "Don't forget what I told you, young fellow. It's up to you to make something of yourself. Your life is in your hands alone."

"I wish that was true," was all I could say.

"What do you mean?" Mr. Lurie reared back. The little half-moons of his bifocals glinted. "Thirty-one years I'm selling insurance, I come in contact with all kinds, I speak from experience. Let me tell you, you're the master of your fate, you're the captain of your soul. As a student of life, I can assure you that the only thing about your life that you can't control is when it's going to end. And even that you can protect your loved ones against."

It was at that moment that Martin Stark proceeded to ask the question that no one else had had the nerve to ask. He did it so innocently that it had to be calculated, he being a lawyer and forty years old.

"I assume," he said to Ralph and me, "that you've already begun to look hard for the will?"

Mr. Lurie started breathing hard, like a firehouse dog. His wife and sister-in-law, grateful to Martin Stark for having asked what they dared not, paused avidly in their farewells. Lillian stopped in the middle of drawing on a black kidskin glove, one long finger of which hung free like a dark teat from the plump udder of her hand.

It was Ralph who decided me. He pursed his lips judiciously, as though Martin had asked his opinion about the chances for more snow. He wasn't kidding me. He had been hoping against hope that the afternoon could be gotten through without anyone's raising the question of the will. Here he had been laughing at me for not wanting to come down and mix, when he had been more worried than I.

And here I had been waiting for the company to go away

so that I could sneak back where I belonged. Suddenly I was terrified at the idea of their leaving without knowing what only Ralph and Kitty and I knew.

"We have some ideas about that," Ralph said ponderously, desperately.

"We've found it," I said. "You mean Ralph hasn't told you? We've found the will."

January 12

Ralph's reaction to my springing the news wasn't just immediate—burned up, naturally, counting on me keeping my big mouth shut—but long drawn out. It is still going on, or maybe even just getting started. No end in sight. For us to come to terms Ralph is going to have to change at least as much as he expects me to.

January 14

Snowed all night. Still coming down. According to the experts, a real blizzard. Lovely to watch. Kids having great fun. But their fathers are struggling with shovels and stuck cars. When I think how much worse it must be in other places I do feel guilty at how snug and cozy I am up here. Ralph has been bearing down on that ever since I let the cat out of the bag. Every time he comes up the ladder with food or books he gives me a dig.

January 15

Ralph reminded me this morning how many people have starved and frozen to death since the storm began. He's not going to let me alone. Better take it for granted and assume it as part of my problem. Doesn't make any difference to him that since Dr. S. knew about the will, he probably knew what was in it. If the doctor was keeping quiet for the time being, he wanted to know, why couldn't I?

In the middle of all the hubbub that day, although the doctor had insisted blandly that he didn't know the contents of the will which he had most likely witnessed, nobody believed him. Not that he cared.

If Dr. Stark knew Papa's intent and still kept his mouth shut, it was understandable. He thinks people should be free to arrange their own lives. Still, it's a little devilish, like giving a man enough rope.

But of course Ralph had very little rope left. He couldn't very well deny that the will had been found, or even that Papa had left everything to me. He was stuck with the situation, which was what I was counting on. At least it gave me temporary protection here.

Henrietta and Lillian and Ben Lurie looked bruised. They couldn't wait to get out, as if they were saying to themselves, Why did we come, why did we bring cake? Not Martin Stark, who had precipitated the whole thing as much as I had. He must be accustomed to hearing terrible confessions: that people have committed crimes for which they want to go unpunished; that they hate their wives and wish to be rid of them; that they hope to buy something for less than it is worth or sell it for more than it is worth; that they intend to cheat, or already have cheated, the government; that they desire documents binding their heirs by means of the goods that are their final weapon, even from beyond the grave.

Martin must be accustomed too, that's lawyers' business, to making deals, compromising, feeling out the opponent. As far as I was concerned, he was a representative of the world in this house, and it frightened me to see him turning over the whole new situation in his mind.

Ralph didn't see any of this. No reason why he should have. He had to keep smiling and saying his good-bys all the while he was furious with me, and letting it be understood that of course the only reason the will hadn't been mentioned, aside from his marriage, was that he and I had a number of things to settle before my twenty-first birthday.

"Raymond may not be quite a man yet in the eyes of the law," Dr. Stark said, standing on the porch. "But you know,

Leo had a point when he made out his will. Because Raymond acts like a man."

On that he stomped off, followed by his silent son, who left behind him a fragrant blue haze from his pipe, thin but sharp like wood smoke in the wintry air.

Only then did Ralph turn on me. I wanted to run back up to the attic but he literally wouldn't let me. He had me by the arm and was shouting, "I hope you're proud of yourself for going back on your word!"

There was no way out, I tried to explain to Kitty as well as to him. "If I hadn't spoken up," I said, "you'd have found a way to do something about the will, as long as nobody knew about it. You know you would."

Ralph started swearing. I tore loose, and took the stairs two at a time. He was going to come after me, I looked over my shoulder, but Kitty was at the newel post pleading with him. The last sound I heard before I got up here was my brother's panting breath.

January 17

Just heard on the 7 o'clock news that a 20-year-old girl, identified only as the daughter of a prominent military expert, walked into a police station and said calmly, "I have just declared war on the world. You have thirty minutes to give yourself up." The desk sergeant gave her a cup of coffee and then had her carted off to the hospital, where she is "under observation." Which means that the world declared war on her. How about me? Who has me under observation?

January 18

Haven't been finishing anything I start. Keep trying to get caught up on the situation with Ralph and Kitty, don't seem able to. Never used to write such interminable entries. Why should it take more time and trouble to write about yourself than about the people you watch through a window?

Maybe I have been studying the wrong subjects.

If only the Witness hadn't disappeared.

January 19

Must try to put down what happened when Ralph and Kitty got me to come down for "a talk." Not even sure which day it was. Within the last week.

Started with Ralph saying to me, "For a would-be saint, you certainly know how to look after yourself."

His attempt at self-control was a failure even before it began. Kitty could barely bring herself to smile.

"Come on, Ralphie," I said. "I never claimed I was trying to be a saint. All the saints I know of got there by doing penance for their sins or by overcoming great temptations. I'm not like that."

"Why not?" Kitty was staring at me, puzzled. Almost fascinated.

"Because I'm a coward. I never even expose myself to temptation. I know beforehand what would happen. I wouldn't be able to resist, I'd be as bad as the worst."

Ralph made a noise with his mouth.

"I had to tell the others about the will. You'd have done the same. Now we can start over. It's months yet until I become twenty-one. I promise you that before then we'll come to an agreement. Isn't that fair?"

"For you. You can hop back into the attic and sit there laughing at me. But what am I supposed to do in this filthy dump? I've stayed on too long already."

Kitty stood apart, her face shadowed by the chandelier. Even so, her pallor was plain. I knew what she knew, that Ralph had taken a tremendous gamble, and that for days he had been thrashing about, trying to figure out a quick way to recoup. If only I could make her see that I was doing this for her and Ralph as much as for myself!

"What's the matter," I asked, "aren't you enjoying your honeymoon here?"

Ralph was shocked.

Kitty said, "Ralph has been doing everything he can to make you comfortable and to make you confront your situation. Don't taunt him. Not when he's making such sacrifices."

I refrained from pointing out why he was making the sacrifices. She knew as well as I. (Besides, maybe there's something to what she said? I do begin to feel that Ralph is oscillating in his feelings. One day genuinely friendly, anxious to help, to come to terms with my "situation" as well as his. The next, mean and suspicious, convinced I'll screw him if he's not extra careful.)

"This could be a great house," I said. "If you don't like it now, you will when the weather gets better."

"You should live so long. Kitty doesn't know a soul here and I don't intend that she ever will. We're running out of money, and if we're going to have to live on love, we'll do it in New York. From now on, you can communicate with me by mail."

I didn't want them to see how I was trembling. I crossed my arms over my chest. "I'm telling you now, if you pull out I'll have the will probated and divide up the estate my own way."

"I'll have you declared incompetent."

"Try it. Dr. Stark knows I'm all right, just ask him." I was astonishing myself with my own boldness. "Martin will stick with me too. All you'll get out of it will be a lot of bad publicity."

Ralph cried out in anguish, "Ray, what do you *want* from me?"

That hurt. I knew what I wanted, I think Ralph did too, but how could I put it into words? It was ambitious, romantic, maybe it was even wild. He knew, he knew, but I didn't dare answer.

Still, he wanted me to speak, so I said, "Just for you to stay. You and Kitty. We'll help each other."

"I told you. My dough is almost gone already."

"Can't you take out a temporary loan? As soon as I come of age, you'll have all you need. All this will be yours."

"I never borrowed money in my life. Should I start now"— he was practically sneering—"when the word is getting around that my father cut me off? What do you take me for, one of the poor slobs in Happy Valley, mortgaged from balls to brain?"

"But this is different. It would only be for a short while. I promise."

"What good is your promise?" Ralph added cruelly, "Look at yourself in the mirror. Who'd give me a nickel with you as security?"

"Dr. Stark would. I bet he'd be glad to loan you enough to tide us all over, until we can probate the will."

My brother turned to his wife. "Can you fathom it? He insists on sharing the estate with someone like Mel. But he has no compunctions about sending me to beg from a man who doesn't even particularly like me." Then he turned on me. "Is that your morality? To mooch off Dr. Stark on the long shot that you and I will get together?"

"It can't be a long shot. We have to come to an agreement. Otherwise what is there to live for?"

He didn't answer that, any more than I had answered all of his questions. He simply turned his back on me and stood rigid, as though he was at attention before the flag or the national anthem. Kitty was biting at her lower lip again and again, as though something on it tormented her.

I went on upstairs.

January 21

Something special about this day? Can't remember.

Those noises downstairs in the dead of night! Haven't been able to bring myself to write about them. Still can't.

January 22

Outside, a slight thaw. Not inside. Ralph came up this

morning and dumped everything at me contemptuously, all my groceries. I think he cares more for Sasha than he does for me.

January 27

It has changed my whole life, having Ralph downstairs. And I have changed his whole life too. Whether for better or for worse is not for either of us to say—we're too dependent on each other.

Except for two people, he would surely have walked out, renouncing any hope of sharing in the estate, even though he yearned for it.

1. Kitty. His marriage to her a losing gamble. I mean losing only in the sense that Ralph had been counting on a quick killing, not on having his nose rubbed in 500 Happy Valley examples of what happens to losers. And regardless of how he claims to despise their rabbitlike conservatism, in at least one respect I'm convinced he'd behave exactly like them: if worst came to worst he would never desert Kitty. He would make the best of a miserable bargain.

2. Me. I see it more every day, how he vacillates between contempt for me and a funny kind of admiration (the remains of childhood affection?). Here too he is trapped. He can't even make the grand gesture of renouncing the estate, because he knows I'll just turn around and split it up between him and Mel. On the one hand he fears what I will do if he doesn't come to terms with me, on the other he honestly fears for what would happen to me if he walked out and left me alone.

So we coil in upon ourselves, one upon the other, as we recommence our lives together.

January 30

Ralph has bought a car! Was watching a dishwasher being delivered, truck surrounded by preschool kids, when Ralph came skidding up the slushy carriage drive in a little white

Triumph. It has a knock, I heard it clearly up here while it was idling, but it is stylishly battered and has more class than the VWs and Chevys in the Happy Valley driveways.

He didn't seem excited. Didn't even call Kitty out to see it, simply clumped up the steps and on into the house.

It must have taken the last of his money. Worse than that, it is a confession that Ralph is stuck here.

He brought me up a couple of books that I had asked him for from the library. When I congratuated him on the car, he gave me a sour look.

January 31

This morning R. was all turned around. Came up with some canned vegetables. Instead of hurrying back down the ladder, he said, very friendly, "I'm ready to take you for a spin, kid."

Was taken by surprise, could only stammer. He told me he counted on my tuning it up and fixing the timing. I could hardly talk him out of it. I can see, his new campaign to get me out of here has begun.

So far, I think he's been improvising, more or less like me, trying first one approach and then another, just as I try everything I can to soften him up on Mel (I don't think I've even written down anything about that, and I won't, not until something *works*). His hard line hasn't worked. I've got news for him. A soft one won't either.

But he's not basically an improviser. He's been meeting with Dr. S., and Martin, and consulting lawbooks on his own. And I hear him and Kitty talking, arguing, talking until all hours of the night. I think he's decided to quit playing it by ear. I think he's working out a plan.

My best countereffort will be to play for time. This morning I said to him, "Ralphie, the newspapermen don't bother you any more, do they? They've forgotten all about us, we can take our time and work things out. They won't come back until we're ready with a final decision about the will."

An odd expression came over his face. It was almost as though he was in pain, and was trying to conceal it from me.

"Take our time?" He repeated the phrase I had used. "But I'm ten years older than you. I know you'd like me to wait forever, but I just can't."

February 1

If Ralph only knew it, what weakens me most in my resolve is not fear of him. Not even fear of myself. It's pity for him in his present situation and guilt at my part in it.

Here he is, caught up in the most banal of American dilemmas. He's broke, so he has to have a car to hunt work, and he has to go to work to support the car.

I hear him phoning up, answering ads, making appointments for interviews, hunting for a job which will carry him and Kitty (and me too, I might as well admit it) through the uncertain winter. There's nobody here for him to turn to, no "contacts," the way people in New York City move from one job to another. And he is not going to let Kitty go to work. That wasn't part of the bargain. He has his pride.

February 3

Ralph has a job. Area representative for distributor of short subject movies. He'll be busy, out of the house. I should be building my own plan. Maybe somehow the job, which will involve traveling around his home town, will soften his feelings about Mel? If he would only be *reasonable*, what wonderful possibilities there would be for us!

I know he must be saying the same thing to Kitty . . .

And Kitty, what will she do now, all alone, all day long?

February 12

Every morning, on my knees, I peer through the window and watch Ralph going off to work. Sometimes I can hardly keep from crying out, "Stop! I didn't mean that, come back!"

The movies he peddles show audiences, mainly kids, how

lead pipes and chocolate bars are manufactured, and demonstrate the incomparable working conditions in the factories and the kindliness with which the owners operate their enterprises.

Same kind of films that Ralph was associated with in New York. He never cared for the work, he made no bones about that. It was always a makeshift occupation, a temporary substitute for real life.

But now he really *hates* it. Not so much for what is in the cans of film. That he ignores. No, it's for what they symbolize, and he practically spits when he says it. A cheap hack routine job in a provincial town, a facsimile of all the jobs of all the mortgaged husbands of Happy Valley.

The misery is his, but if he only knew it the guilt is mine. I watch my brother grimly backing his little car into the sluggish stream made by the car pools of Happy Valley. No bus for him, no fraternizing with the commuters. (He is a great democrat, he is all for the people who did the dirty work of building the development, but he'd rather die than mix with them.) In the dark end of the day he comes home, his face older each evening, his new hat drawn down over his dark furrowed brows. Who would know, encountering him on his rounds, that he is any different from the husbands across the street?

This galls him as much as the job itself. And because it galls him it hurts me.

I have the temporary security of the two below me, the comforting sounds of their comings and goings, and the hope that maybe the entire ambience—this funny old house that Kitty is struggling with, the emerging sense of a common past not totally shameful and worthy of more than scorn or concealment, the recognition that I, me, up here in the attic, am not just a nut but someone with a claim on my brothers' consciences—all these—may be exerting an emollient influence on my jagged and abrasive brother. Maybe instead of destroying each other we'll come to understand each other?

What I don't have is Ralph's freely accorded respect and confidence. Much less his love.

As I stare down, condemned to watch, at my older brother angrily leaving the house and tiredly returning to it, I begin to feel like an old man I once read about, who desperately desired a young girl. The old man managed to get her to marry him by threatening her parents with disaster. He had won the girl, her constant presence, her prettiness, her soft warmth beside him in the sheets, but none of what he had dreamed of beforehand—whistling in the sunny kitchen, willing eagerness in the darkened bedroom—and in consequence the very sight of his prize became more and more bitter to him until at length it became utterly intolerable, and he committed a terrible deed . . .

5: KITTY

KITTY HAD TRIED TO IMAGINE, as everyone does, what love in marriage would be like. She found it far different from anything she might have guessed, for there was very little tenderness. She wondered, though, whether this might not be a hangover from girlish daydreams of masculine gallantry on the part of a faceless someone both fierce and kind, demanding and gentle—or whether she had wishfully believed that a husband would be absolutely different from the four or five actual lovers with whom she had grappled and groped her disappointing way toward self-realization. If one had not been tender, it was all too obviously because he was in terror lest tenderness be interpreted as readiness for marriage. If another had been enervatingly soft, it was because he was pathetically grateful, horribly grateful, for the small favors accorded an unhappily married man with no intention of divorcing his wife.

Ralph was neither soft nor gentle. Even when he said nothing, but simply bore down on her, bore her down onto the bed that had been his father's, against her ear she could hear his jaws working, clamping and clenching; and later, when he slept, his teeth grinding, relaxing only when she wormed her way under the wing of his arm.

It was terrible, the hard metallic sound, but it came to be associated in her mind uniquely with Ralph, with their act of sex, and after a while she began to accept the grim collision of his opposing jaws as one of their shared private sounds.

She began too to realize that she did not know or understand her husband at all. If she could not recall that Ralph had ever ground his teeth in his sleep before their marriage (hadn't he had as much frustration and provocation then?), Kitty had also to remind herself that in those days of presumably "getting to know each other" they had seldom spent an entire night together. But it wasn't only the comparative brevity and abruptness of their premarital experiments that rendered them unmemorable. What she had done, she realized now, was to range Ralph—even while she was admitting him to her bed—with the other men who had come and gone, his predecessors (whom she had neither gotten to know nor allowed to get to know her), and so with some success to push him and his love-making out of her mind, simply because he had been quiet and cagy and had never, any more than the others, permitted her to hope that one day he would plead for permanence.

Far from disturbing her, this feeling that she was in certain substantial ways still a virgin, wedded not to someone with whom for months she had been working by day and making love by night, but to an exotic man who had swept her off her feet, gave to their nightly physical encounters an added spice—the thrill of violation by a stranger who took her not because he cherished her or wished to make her love him, but because she smelled tempting and felt hot. Gradually she would learn (in fact was learning) about him, and what sort of person he was; right now, however, she could only be

astonished at her temerity in running off with a man about
whom she had known little more than that he was reticent
about his background, surly with strangers, aristocratic in
his tastes, and brutally attractive, from the thick brows that
grew together over his piercing prow of a nose down to his
quick decisive tread.

She did not mind that he was not tender like the gallants
of her high-school daydreams; she had enough tenderness,
she discovered, for them both. Nor did she mind that he had
reneged on his assurance that they would never lead an ordinary life, and thrust her without warning into a housewifely
existence in the same kind of community from which she had
fled to New York in hopes of finding someone different, someone like him. It would have made no difference to Kitty if
Ralph had installed her in a Rivington Street tenement or a
call girl's kittenish cubicle on Central Park West; and she
barely gave thought to her long solitary days of housework
in the Lands' mausoleum, with only an occasional creaking
board to remind her that Ralph's odd brother was crouched
up above, watching over her. She would have been as content
—or as mindless—if Ralph had insisted that she go to work
every day to support him, scrubbing endless corridors or
mountains of pots and pans.

All that mattered was that his brooding physical promise
had been fulfilled. How did I live without this, she marveled,
as she wandered about the house, dust mop or garbage pail
in hand, in a feverish erotic haze. Before, her evenings and
her nights had been spent in a fashion so blandly inane, so
depthless, that she could think only that it must have been
another person, the Kitty Brenner who had sat dumbly before
the television with a towel around her drying hair and a box
of Loft's butter crunch at her finger tips; who had sat in the
art movies with whichever uneasy date, dreaming of what it
would be like to be undressed and loved like Jeanne Moreau,
Sophia Loren, or Brigitte Bardot; who had sat with her
roommates doing each other's nails and hair and talking fret-

fully about men. Men! Ralph was a man such as she had dared to imagine—without really being able to visualize—he might be.

There was no quenching the fire that burned in his loins. He had no need for, no interest in, amusements, distractions, television, radio, magazines. In the evening he ate rapidly and then proceeded to take her at once, sometimes not even waiting for supper, absolutely ignoring her protests that dinner was cooking and would be spoiled if it were not eaten before love, shoving her up the stairs into the bedroom, rapping her on the flanks to make her move faster, forcing her to disrobe hurriedly while he yanked at his belt buckle and kicked off his shoes.

Ralph did not even attempt to be gentle. He tore at her underwear, he ripped the straps on her nightclothes, he left his saliva on her shoulders and her breasts as well as in her mouth, and his hot seminal fluid on her thighs, while she cried with pleasure. Once she was sure that he would not be disconcerted, she responded in kind, worming her hand inside his waistband to dig her nails into the black mat that covered his belly, nipping him while he undressed her, biting him until she could taste his dark red blood. She loved to wait until he had fallen asleep on his back, sweating and momentarily exhausted, his mouth a trifle ajar, his lax arm lying upturned across her, but his teeth grinding, faintly at first and then louder; then she would begin to caress him, to tickle him, at the very source and fountain of her straining delight. Until, in his sleep, without knowing who or what, there would come that resurrection more thrilling and more awesome than anything she had ever known, giving her such a trembling exquisite sense of her own power that she bent unbidden, her hair falling about her face, to touch her lips to the soft but surging source of her ecstasy. It was then that Ralph would rouse to consciousness, his lips drawn back over his teeth, the muscles working behind his gangster's jaw that was already turning blue-black, and, unable to bear any more, would push her off him, fling her face down into the mattress, and mount her, muttering, groaning between his teeth, "You, you, you!" The while she pressed her mouth into the tumbled pillow, to suppress her own cries, morsels of words (half fainting, she no longer knew), "Ralph!" or "Husb—" or "Lover, lover, lover!"

It was the memory of these moments that would overcome her when least she expected to be reminded of them—when, a kerchief bound round her head, she shook out a carpet, or wiped moldings, or rubbed furniture polish into neglected wood. Suddenly she would be lost in an erotic confusion, lost in the woods like Goldilocks, with no one to help her but herself. Swooning at the recollection of what Ralph had done the night before, at what she had dared to do, at what she would do that she had not yet done, she would have to subside into a chair, the backs of her thighs trembling, the sweat suddenly beginning to pearl her neck and her bosom.

This had to be brought under control. Not just because it interrupted a businesslike house-cleaning schedule, but because it struck her as perverse to be at the mercy of such desires, as if she were a deserted divorcée or a love-starved castaway on an uninhabited isle, rather than someone who only awaited her husband's return that very evening.

Kitty tried, with increasing success, she felt, as time passed, to understand not just the lover in the bedroom but the human being who was revealing himself to her almost in spite of himself. Not that he did it quietly, reasonably, seated beside her on the sofa, or driving about in the little white auto on one of their rare evenings out. No, at those times he was as impersonally businesslike as he had ever been in the days of their courtship, or still was for that matter during the daylight hours. It was only between their acts of love that there spurted from his lips, like the jets of his fierce sex, the ferocious phrases that began to expose to her the depths of his involvement with the family from which he had fruitlessly attempted to flee.

Ralph had to explain why it was that he hated his older brother so much. In the process he disclosed to her, although still refusing to admit that there had been a time when he and Mel had dearly loved each other (and that fascinated her most of all—what lay behind his refusal?), something of the sort of person he himself had become in the stifling atmosphere of the Land household.

"How would you feel," he had asked bitterly in the dark, not really asking, even rhetorically, simply justifying himself to himself for speaking aloud at all, "if your brother was in and out of juvenile court, half the time for things that probably your own uncle had egged him on to do? And your mother sat home and cried?"

And (was it the same night or another?): "I was almost relieved when he ran off. He never came back, not once, to see what he had done to his mother. Not even to her funeral."

Kitty began to see, dimly, uneasily, that one of her attractions for Ralph had been not her legs or her liveliness, not her bust or her brusque firmness, none of the things he praised, so much as the fact that she was an only child. If she had been an orphan to boot, unencumbered by a father who tapped out gratuitous philosophical advice on a gummy Smith-Corona, and by a mother who glanced up from Ayn Rand only long enough to sign, Love Mother, Ralph would undoubtedly have been tempted to carry her off at once, unconstrained by his own poverty and lack of prospects.

For he was nourished by hatred of family, which fed his self-pity as much as it explained to his own satisfaction the unhappy turns his life had taken from childhood to marriage.

"When you graduated from high school—how long ago, only seven years?—you must have been one of the most popular girls in your class. Tell me."

Laughing in the dark, innocent of what he was up to, she had said, Yes, she had been popular, not sexy or even unusually attractive, a clown in fact, but popular with girls as well as boys.

And her parents had come to her graduation, no doubt? Had closed the store early to dress up and hear her valedictory speech?

"Well, of course. They came to my college graduation too. It wasn't as if they had far to go, just across town."

"Or as if they had other children to worry about."

Not that her mother hadn't tried to have more, until the doctor had told her it was dangerous.

"If Dr. Stark had told my mother that from the outset, we all would have been better off. You included."

What a horrible thing to say! She protested vehemently, asserted with the warmth of her own body her happiness that he had been born, but in vain, for now he came to the point, teaching her—who had had no way of knowing—what desolation could mean in a family where there was not enough love to go around.

"Mel ran off six weeks before my high-school graduation. May, nineteen forty-nine. I don't know whether he was sick of hanging around, banging around. I think they were after him. It makes no difference. Five weeks after he left, Raymond came down with polio, and my mother nursed him. We didn't know that she was the one who was going to die, we thought it was Ray. My father was stuck in the drugstore, my uncle was no help—he was a lost soul after Mel ran away. The night before my graduation the crisis came."

"But Ray shows no traces of polio."

"Some people are lucky, aren't they? It was in the hip, he had to start exercises afterwards. That's how he went on the physical culture kick. I'm convinced Ray never would have gotten polio if it hadn't been for Mel. Ray went swimming, Mama would never have let him go so early in the season, he came home at suppertime shivering, I remember, his lips blue. Mama didn't pay any attention, only because her eyes were swollen from all her crying over Mel. When she realized about little Ray, it was almost too late. The next night, after Dr. Stark had seen Ray safely through the crisis, everyone in the family was too exhausted to go with me to high school. There were a hundred and seventy-six in my graduating class. I was the only one without a relative in the audience.

"Even Vinnie Barbera, whose parents had been killed in an auto accident that winter, had his aunt and two cousins there. No one was supposed to applaud the individual recipients, but they did anyway. When the principal came to the L's, nothing but silence for me. I tripped and dropped my diploma. Somebody laughed. I had a crush on a girl named Olivia Tagliaferro. For months I'd been hoping to dance with her in the gym on graduation night, and maybe ask her out afterwards. I never even said good-by to her, I went right home instead, to see how Ray was doing. I found everybody dead asleep. My father on this bed with his clothes on, my mother in Ray's room sitting up on a chair beside him. Uncle Max was drowsing over solitaire in the kitchen. He'd done without food to go to college. He glanced up and said, 'So you got the diploma.'

"And that was all. My parents didn't even wake up until the next morning."

Pressing him to her breast, Kitty had forborne from questioning Ralph about Mel and his mother, knowing that more would come out one night. Certainly the lonely graduation from high school had crystallized all of his envy and dislike of his older brother. After that there was good and sufficient reason to hate without stint.

And Ralph had suffered, unquestionably, no matter if his hatred seemed a little excessive to another human being, even to a wife. With a young brother too small for friendship and a big brother whose games were tricky and adult, with no real home to which to bring his friends, he had stopped trying to make friends, and had made his own retreat to a world walled with hate, but commodious within and furnished with the unostentatious luxury of a comradely but disembodied aristocracy that he must have learned about from books and movies. This had served him well, at least it had gotten him through Korea, through college, into the business world, partway therefore to success even as it was measured by those he admired. But now it could serve him so no longer; trapped in his uncle's lair, it could not be a goad, only a painful dream reminding him that in actuality he had fouled it up somewhere along the line, so badly that he was back where he had started from.

Back, but worse off than when he had had a big brother to blame everything on, a little brother to pick on, a crazy uncle, and a weakling father. For now all the excuses had crumbled away, leaving what he himself in his darker moments called only the keel and ribs of a personality. At the age of twenty he had been able to imagine that he could turn his back, sail away from all of them, and one day by the force of his own proud and solitary ambition become whatever it was that the world would most respect. Now he *had* to stay, he had to play games with his brother (neither of them knowing for sure which role was his, or whether perhaps they were interchanging parts, internal emigrant becoming external immigrant as the days wore on), he had to mime the wife-enwrapped suburban junior executive—or everything would collapse, including the last shored-up remnants of his self-respect.

He could not stay indefinitely, that was the rub. Raymond's deadline was his; and Kitty began to feel communicated to her, through the very sweat of her husband's heaving rib cage, his lonely terror at what faced him if he could not come to an accommodation with Raymond: He would have to face it out like some doomed figure in a Shakespearean tragedy, make common cause with his mother's cousins, break with Solomon and Martin Stark and incur their contempt, and do his very damnedest to have his own brother publicly branded as incompetent and committable. The kind of total war that he shrank from, including making public the connection between himself and Mel, and making public the hatreds he had cherished through the years partly because they *were* private, he would have to undertake brazenly, to blazon forth as a moral act, the responsibility for which he not only admitted but gloried in.

There began to grow in Kitty, so strangely, unfamiliarly, insidiously, that she was not sure whether it resembled more a fetus, fruit of her womb, or a malignant tumor, result of some poisonous misbehavior, the conviction that to be truly Ralph's partner she must become more than his receptacle. For she knew now—and the knowledge degraded her—that despite his nocturnal assaults upon her (or perhaps even because of them) Ralph was coming to regard her as yet another of the encumbrances that weighed upon him like an albatross. Without her, *perhaps* he could have fled; without her willingness to share his last stand, he would probably never have undertaken to play the dual role of Ulysses and Telemachus.

The best that Kitty could say for herself was that from a man's point of view during this perilous time she was a repository of confidence as well as of passions and effusions. But the idea that she was nothing more than a vessel did not suit her. This was something that almost any woman could be; there was nothing particular enough about it to make it a uniquely sufficient undertaking, in short to make it fit her own notion of herself—even if she were to think of her husband as being the most important man in the world and of herself as his indispensable safety valve. That was almost nothing, not even a feminine image.

So she decided, one morning that bore with the wind through the open window the hint that winter had blown itself out and another northern spring was in the air, to present herself to Raymond in order to discover whether there might be a way for her to achieve what her husband had so far been unable to gain. She picked up a jar of olives, she regarded herself long and carefully in the mirror (she was wearing—and it did seem to her a little odd that she should have dressed this way before making the conscious decision, in fact even before thinking about it—a candy-

striped blouse with pushed-back sleeves and deep V neck, no
brassiere, pink corduroy pants, and leather and cork sandals
through which her toes showed, pink also), and she began
to mount the stairs to Raymond's retreat, her heart thumping
loudly in her ears with each step.

Since Kitty had moved into the house Raymond had kept
very much to himself. She had no way of knowing whether
this was his habitual practice, or whether he was being particularly considerate during these early weeks of her marriage.
Perhaps too he was making himself as inconspicuous as possible in order to impress upon her and Ralph the practicality,
even the viability, of an unnatural arrangement.

Just how reasonable he could be she would find out now.
Up until this day she had never entered his attic; it had
always been Ralph who had gone up, or Ray himself who
had come down, for his books and the food she bought him
several times a week.

Arrived at the third floor, panting a little, she walked down
the narrow corridor that had still not been thoroughly cleaned,
and paused at the foot of the attic entrance, which was simply
a closed trap door, the underside of a flight of steps that
could be lowered only from above or from a dangling chain.
Kitty held the jar to her breast for an instant, allowing the
glass to cool her warm flesh, and then reached up to pull
firmly on the chain.

In the attic a bell tinkled. She heard Ray's slippered,
muffled footsteps, and then his resonant, calm voice: "Kitty?
Groceries?"

The stairs emerged from the ceiling, then Ray's head.

"I can't get this jar open. Could you help me?"

"Be right down."

She said coolly, "Would you mind if I came up, just for
a minute?"

Ray smiled and extended his arm. "Watch your head."

He was wearing his undertaker's trousers with the satin

stripes down the sides, and the same carpet slippers, shredding so that his stockinged toes looked as though they too were made of the same stuff. In place of the army sweaters, however, since the attic was very warm, Raymond wore only a white T-shirt on the breast of which was stenciled in green CAMP WA-TUM-WA, in a circle around the silhouette of an Indian with headdress, like the one they used to put on pennies.

There was nothing funny, though, about Ray in his T-shirt. His pectoral muscles stretched the cotton, and how had he gotten his massive upper arms through the skin-tight sleeves?

Fascinated, Kitty stared at his biceps as Ray plucked the jar of olives from her grasp and twisted it quickly. The lid turned with absurd ease.

"Next time," he said, "let it soak for a minute in hot water."

"Yes," Kitty laughed, "but I can never remember whether it's hot water or cold . . . What an extraordinary place you have here."

"It is a little different from the rest of the house."

Kitty stood at the head of the stairway, facing Ray's desk, which was surmounted by what seemed a gray wall with myriad little eyes and knoblike protuberances. On either side of it, like sentinels, stood two old-fashioned wooden filing cabinets, each of their four drawers neatly labeled.

"That's your radio station?"

"I hope it doesn't disturb you. I'm on mostly quite late at night."

"I never hear a thing."

Where did he sleep? She glanced down at the floor, which Raymond had tiled from the very edge of the steps to the eaves which came steeply sloping down to meet it on two sides. He had covered the tiles here and there with threadbare Oriental throw rugs which his uncle must have dug up somewhere. But there was barely enough clear floor space in the center of the attic with the steep slope of the peak, for a single bed. And there was no bed.

A skylight threw a rhomboid of sunshine on the rug at her feet, but the ventilating window at the front end of the house, facing the street, to the right of the radio set, seemed to emit light rather than to admit it. Through the tilted slats of its louvers Kitty could see, perhaps sixty feet below, the border of the driveway, with its gray cones of melting snow, and by cocking her head to the other side, the life of the street, the development houses of Happy Valley, even the blacktop parking lot of the shopping plaza dominated by the neocolonial supermarket. But no one there could very well see up here, which was rather exciting.

Raymond had covered the two sloping eaves and the blank back wall (which must once have had a window looking down on the junk-heaped backyard) with maps, prints, working drawings, and charts scissored out of books, magazines, newspapers—all neatly trimmed, Scotch-taped, and then shellacked to a pale brown. At a glance the garret had the atmosphere of a rather unusual laboratory, or college workroom, except that when you looked again you saw signs that someone not only worked but lived here—a hot plate, a sweater flung across the one chair before the desk, two cans of Campbell's vegetarian-vegetable soup and a jar of French's mustard atop the left-hand filing cabinet, a handkerchief and a towel both neatly folded on the desk itself, and, next to them, a stack of ledger books stamped ACCOUNTS PAYABLE. One of these lay open, with a ball point pen across its face, and as Kitty approached it, her husband's name leaped up at her, not once but two, three times, from the page where it had been written in his brother's surprisingly firm, bold hand.

It was obviously Raymond's diary, all six volumes of it.

Surely there would be things about her in it, about her and Ralph? Feeling Ray's uneasy eyes upon her, she forced herself to look away from it, like a young girl fighting not to stare at the nude Apollo in a museum. Instead she examined an iron chinning bar that Ray had screwed into the beams near where she stood, and a matched set of barbells that lay neatly stacked on the floor beside the desk. What a funny boy, to build up his body and then hide it so that no one could ever see it! The sudden unbidden memory of his brother prowling after her, naked, but hairy and grappling as you never saw a nude in a museum, made her flush in the presence of this innocent boy. She smiled at him.

"Where on earth do you sleep? Not curled up on the little rug?"

He indicated what she had taken to be a laundry bag, dangling from an eye hook on a two-by-four. He unfolded it. "Here, see, nothing more than a plain old hammock. But it's adequate."

"Looks a little skimpy."

"Oh no, it's quite comfortable."

"For two, I meant," Kitty persisted, looking at him sidelong.

"I never expect to have anyone else stay here," he protested seriously, and then, seeing her grin, began to stammer. "I mean . . . there are such things as Mexican double hammocks . . ."

"It's all right. But I've been wondering about you. You and Robinson Crusoe, Ray. Mind if I sit here?" She indicated with her thumb a neatly stacked pile of magazines on the carpet before the filing cabinet.

"No, no, please," protested Ray, "take the chair."

"Nonsense." Kitty seated herself on the magazines. "Sit in your own chair, come on."

Reluctantly Ray lowered himself to the chair, on which he poised himself stiffly above her, his arms hanging. He placed his fists on his knees, elbows defensively rigid, a nineteenth-century youth posing for a daguerreotype, and as Kitty disposed herself almost at his feet, she was tempted to reach up and tickle him in that dense thicket of beard, or tell him a dirty joke, to see if it would make him laugh.

Instead she remarked, "I don't think it's at all queer, your wanting to live like this. Especially now that I've seen the place. I wondered about how you spent your time, but now I can see that you're kept busy."

"You've been to college, you know how much I've missed. It's not easy to educate yourself all alone, but I think I'm making progress. I haven't got a systematic disposition like Ralph, but I'm trying to keep to a regular schedule."

"A schedule?" Kitty rested her chin on her fist and gazed up at him.

"With radio you have to be punctual. I've learned a lot about electronics and physics from my ham operation. And I'm in touch with some very interesting people, with whom I can discuss scientific problems."

"And never have to see them."

"But we are friends, in a way. Except that it never gets personal, we simply discuss matters of mutual interest."

"You don't like things to get personal, do you?"

"I don't think I have the right . . ." Ray clenched and un- clenched his fists on his kneecaps. "You see, my interests either have to help me directly, like radio and astronomy and math, or indirectly, like my program of exercising, by keeping me from going stale, or getting stoop-shouldered and anemic."

"You have a wonderful physique." Kitty stared into his face until she caught his eyes. She held them. "I don't think I've ever been so close to such a powerful man. But what good does it do you, all this studying and body-building? Can I be frank? It seems to me a terrible waste."

"What you have to understand, Kitty, is that I'm committed to this." He indicated the attic around them. "Wouldn't it be even more of a waste if I didn't try to better myself during this time, to make as much of myself as I can?"

"But for what?" And what did he mean by "during this time"? How could that be a permanent commitment?

"I'll tell you how I feel. It's hard even to explain it to myself, although I've tried to write about it in my diary."

Ray hesistated, then leaned forward eagerly. "I'm in training, like a fighter. I know, you're going to ask again, for what? I can only say, for a purpose that hasn't been revealed to me yet. But it will be for life and not for destruction."

He bent so close to her that Kitty could feel his warm breath, fresh and scentless, on her cheek. "I do something else. I look down out of this window, through these louvers, for several hours every day, to see how much I can learn about people's lives from this distance. That is, without participating in them, simply as a spectator at specified hours."

This wild dive from her own bourgeois regularity into the murky waters of diurnal voyeurism was both frightening and exhilarating. Kitty asked unsteadily, "Ray, you haven't been doing that with me? Studying me?"

He was too naive, and at the same time too intense, even to try to lie. Instead he tried, crudely but charmingly, to disarm her by diverting her attention.

"A girl used to stand down there by the parking lot, in front of the supermarket, every Thursday and Saturday evening, when the stores are open late. Partly because her own schedule was so regular, I watched her more closely and more regularly than I've ever watched anyone in my life. She was selling the *Watchtower*, out of one of those little canvas bags. Yes, a Jehovah's Witness. She was smaller than you, dark, very beautiful. I always knew just when to expect her, and she showed up, no matter if it was raining or hailing. Her life had purpose, she had courage, she had a message."

"Some message!"

"I know, I know." Ray sighed. "I was curious, so I asked Papa to get me some of her literature. What mumbo jumbo! But that's the point, that's the difference between me and the people down below. I don't want to plunge blindly, like Uncle Max, or because—like that girl—someone else handed me the message and told me to pass it on. I'm preparing myself, but I can't leave until I'm sure."

He had given her an opening with his talk of leaving, but Kitty could not forbear to tease him first. "And whatever happened to your girl friend?"

"She stopped coming. So I'm free to imagine that she got sick, or moved away, or got married."

"But not that she changed her mind?"

"No, I doubt that. She was too firm."

"Now, that I must object to."

Kitty was certain that the boy was lying, and that in reality he had had a movie-fan crush on the girl he had been watching, but even so she was annoyed by his dogmatic tone. She said sharply, "No one can tell that much about a person without ever so much as speaking to her. That's not a simple observation made in lonely humility, it's presumptuous arrogance."

"Forgive me." Ray lowered his head. "You're probably right."

"Oh, come on. That's even worse, to mumble something you don't really believe, just to avoid an argument. I believed you when you said you admire people who stand up for a principle, even a false one. What's more, I think I understand you, but it's not simply from watching you, as you watched that girl—or me. Until I met Ralph, I was living like you, in almost complete ignorance. Because I supported myself, and knew various men, I thought that I understood something about people, even myself, when actually I didn't understand the first goddamned thing. You know when I found that out?"

Ray shook his head dumbly.

"When I got married. When I moved in here. When I started sleeping with your brother."

Ray made as if to rise but Kitty restrained him. She placed her hands firmly over his, feeling the arteries of his wrists pulsing under her finger tips.

"Wait. Little Crusoe, you're missing the touch of another human being. There is no substitute for passion. You wouldn't think the way you do, you wouldn't talk the way you do, if you weren't terrified of the touch of human flesh. You talk about your feeling for that little Jehovah's Witness, but you have no conception, no conception! Do you know what you'd do if you really loved her? You'd run out of this house after her, you'd lick up her footprints in the mud, anything, just to be able to be close to her, to hold her body against yours!"

Ray was staring at her in silent fascination, his mouth half open. Kitty continued to hold his hands under hers, but his gaze faltered, following the downward course from her cheekbone to her throat. She was hotly aware of her open blouse and of the way her breasts hung free, like fruit dangled before Ray's parted lips. His lips, his brilliant eyes, made everything swell within her. An artery in her neck began to pulse. She moved her hands up along his bare forearms, knowing as she did so that her shoulders were drawn even further forward, presenting her pendent bosom to his dazzled gaze.

Kitty slipped to her knees before him. Her pants were straining at her thighs, but so were Raymond's, the muscles of his legs bulging even as he sat motionless. She was uncomfortable, even in pain, but so was Raymond, and she determined to press her advantage, to go all the way, to succeed where Ralph had failed.

She whispered rapidly, almost frantically, her lips running faster with each phrase, "You'll never learn by yourself what you want to know. What you must know. You'll never understand your family, you'll never come to terms with Ralph, until you know what he knows. First you must discover the meaning of passion. To have to possess someone, desperately, over and over and over . . ."

She thrust herself forward, releasing her hold on Ray's arms the better to clutch him round by the hips. Her breasts were flattened against the backs of his hands; she could feel him struggling to free his hands, but her weight would not allow him to withdraw.

"Little brother, come down out of the attic. You have to take the chance, you have to learn to hurt and be hurt. It's good, I'll show you, I'll help you. We both love Ralph, isn't that a good enough reason? Isn't it?"

"Please," he whispered.

Kitty ignored his plea. She turned his hands over, palms up, so that he should feel her more directly through his fingers, then refastened him under the pressure of her upper body.

"It's the only hope. The only way out. Join your brother, join me, join all of us that you peep at from your hiding place. Once you do, you'll never want to come back up here again. You won't be able to."

"I know that." Ray was groaning; the small sound, so different from those his brother made, only goaded her on.

"Then come. You'll see why Ralph feels the way he does. You'll understand him!" Intoxicated with what she was saying, Kitty raised her voice. "If you do something bad, Ray, you'll suffer, and you'll understand what Ralph has been going through. Not just for me. For you, too! Do you believe that? Do you?"

"I do! I do!"

Kitty pulled at him so fiercely that he almost toppled from the chair in which he sat as rigid as if he had been nailed to it. She was burning, choking, dying to destroy this innocence which heated itself to the melting point at her heart. If I had a knife, she thought wildly, I'd cut our clothes off; her breasts were so hard and aching against his palms they might have been distended with milk. She swooned at the thought of tumbling on the attic floor, of being tumbled in this lonely virgin's hide-out with no one to know what they were doing or even that they were here. To initiate him as she had been, to show him what to do, to make him groan not in frustration but in fulfillment . . . And not just for either of them, but for Ralph, for Ralph!

"Oh God," she cried, "you're harder than your big brother. Be stronger, use your body, own your body, be a man!"

Suddenly Ray had wrenched himself loose. With a bound

he leaped from the chair and backed against the desk, hands clasped behind his back, face aflame, pale bright eyes glowing like jewels.

"In my own time," he said. "In my own way."

Her arms still clutching the chair where he had sat, Kitty stared up at him unseeingly from her kneeling position, unable to believe anything—what he had done, what she had said . . .

"I told you," he said. "I told Ralph and you, but you didn't believe me. I'm not a saint, I'm a coward."

Except for their labored breathing, the silence was absolute. In the street below a young mother shouted in exasperation, "Stevie, I said *stop* it!" A moment later, the long-drawn wail of a small child.

"Everything you say is true," Ray muttered. "But that doesn't make it right. I know as well as you that once I start I won't be able to stop. That's why I don't start." He drew a deep unsteady breath. "When I do, the decision will be mine, not Ralph's. And it won't be with his wife—whether he's aware of it or not."

"I assure you that he's not," she said through lips that had suddenly shriveled and gone parched. "You must believe that."

Ray smiled at her, self-possessed once again. He brought his hands out from behind his back and clasped them loosely before him.

"It's all right," he said in his customary voice. "It doesn't make any difference."

"But it does," she insisted. "You mustn't think that Ralph . . . That would make things even worse."

"No," he said. "Really. I believe you."

"In that case," Kitty replied, astonished at her own sudden composure, particularly since she had no reason to accept his assurances, "I'll take my olives and be on my way."

She picked up the jar from the desk and swayed across the attic, feeling Ray's gaze on her as she made her way to the stairs, which still hung suspended to the floor below. Let him look; she hyped herself with artificial boldness, trying the same self-persuasion she had used more than once, going home alone late at night, with sodden drunks sizing her up on the subway, or making vile remarks at the corner candy store; let him see what he missed, he'll be sorry.

But she was the one who was sorry, she knew that without even looking back at her brother-in-law. Now he could feel more superior than ever; he could even take pride in the fact that he was above terrorizing her with the unspoken threat of revealing to her husband, in the guise of charging Ralph with complicity, what had happened this morning.

Even at this moment, she was the one, not he, who had to negotiate the steep awkward steps, knowing that he was still watching and perhaps even laughing triumphantly to himself. Now she hated her impractical, absurdly provocative clothing, the unbuttoned blouse in which her oversized breasts jiggled like a chippy's, the skin-tight pants which cut into her crotch as she made her way down, the slippers which before had seemed sexy but now were merely obscenely treacherous, slipping on each step as she fumbled for the next; and her body beneath the clothing, broad, ungainly, made for carrying babies, not for seductively acrobatic leaping up and down ladders.

"You're all right?" He half called, half spoke the words.

Kitty dared not glance back to see if he was peering down at her fleshy awkwardness. She replied, in a rather clipped voice, "Quite, thank you. You can retrieve the ladder, Ray— you'll be safe now."

She descended another flight of stairs, went directly to her bathroom, and removed her clothes quickly. Stepping into the shower, she turned up the hot water as high as possible. But then she found that she could not stand, her legs were weaker than they had been when she had slipped to her knees before her brother-in-law; the trembling became so unbearable that she started to cry.

She sat on the floor of the shower stall, back pressed against the slimy tile, knees drawn up to her chest, hands locked tight around her legs, the hot spray beating down, plastering her hair onto her forehead, over her welling eyes. Finally, when the drumming water had drowned out the beating of her heart, she allowed herself to go lax and receive the benison of the water, both tears and shame washed away by the stinging cascade.

After a long time she arose and turned on the cold water, gripping the tap until she cringed. Then she stepped from the shower, reached for a towel, and began to whistle as she rubbed herself dry.

6: RAY

March 16

Ever since the morning Kitty came up I have lived in such dread that I didn't even dare write about it. Thought she'd feel constrained, awkward, with me. Don't know how to talk to people, it always comes out wrong. Don't know how to write to them. Even if I did, how could I have talked to Kitty, or written her? Tried to compose words in my mind, assuring her of my continuing regard. Stupid!

Saw her yesterday for the first time since her visit. Ides of March. She was bringing me my groceries. I let down the ladder when she pulled on the chain, but didn't come down to the third floor to take the package from her arms. Held back and kept my face in shadows. A needless precaution. She was brisk! cheery! businesslike! Exactly as she had been before, only more so.

How will I ever learn to understand people?

March 18

Today logged Titusville, Council Bluffs, Fremont (O.),

Michigan City. Studied physiological psychology, international trade, astronomy. 45 minutes each. 50 push-ups. Chinned myself 10 extra times. But Ralph is right when he asks, How long can it go on? We're living on borrowed time, but whom are we borrowing it from? The people I watch are bound to catch on that I'm here. Maybe they know already.

Much quieter downstairs lately.

March 22

Martin Stark came yesterday. He and Ralph conferred. Invited me down. I declined because of my radio schedule, which was true. Still, I was curious when I heard their muffled voices way below.

Kitty was right, that day—the one torment for me would be the suspicion that her overture (clumsy word) had been calculated. And not by her. She tried to deny it, I passed it off. But actually it was her very attempt to reassure me that sharpened my suspicions. Sometimes I think my mind must be a cesspool. If I mistrust people (worse, imagine them capable of the lowest perfidy), what must they think of me? And with more reason—look at me.

It is disgusting to be 20. Impossible to play at being a boy. Don't want to be grown, too easy an ambition. Even so, if others my age puff on pipes or stuff themselves into phone booths, I take on the worst traits of adults.

Just the same . . . It *is* quieter downstairs, it has been ever since that day, I think. Not just my imagination. But why? Those first weeks, I was torn between relief that Ralph and Kitty could feel so uninhibited by my presence, and fear that some of their sounds were exaggerated, deliberately, to torment and shame me. Which only shows what an egomaniac you can become when you don't have to accommodate yourself to others. But if those were the honeymoon noises, does it mean that now the honeymoon is over? And if so, why? Is it something that happens to all couples, or does it have a special meaning for Ralph and Kitty? Could it be partly my fault, because of what happened between Kitty and me that day? I know she only wanted to help her husband, it was for love of him. But now, I wonder, does she love him less? Or he her?

March 27

Watched Kitty from my observation post today. She often shops across the street, swift, efficient, impersonal, as though she were in a hurry in a strange neighborhood, had an exact list of what she needed, bought it, went home. But today was different. She was leisurely. Saw her buy the first spring flowers (jonquils? have to look them up) from a coppery old Indian lady, then was very surprised to see her chatting with a broad-hipped young housewife I've noticed going into the A & P and Woolworth's. Girl with cheerful but vulgar face, always wearing figured scarf around her hair (always has it in curlers). Couldn't make out what they were talking about, but they got on well. Smiled and nodded vigorously at each other on parting.

How I wished the Jehovah's Witness had been there, next to the Indian woman with the yellow flowers. Another sign of spring. Maybe Kitty was right about my feelings for the Witness. I always delude myself.

March 29

Could there be a connection between my ignorance of flowers (see above—not knowing jonquils from daffodils) and my ignorance of people? Have spent 2 years trying to repair my ignorance of basic science and technology. Thought I had no time for other pursuits. But Dr. S. is a man of science, more than Papa was, and he finds time for all sorts of things. Can a person really get knowledge of others from reading novels? Just made-up stories? N.B.: Make up list.

April 1

April Fool's Day. That's my day. Last night, *Walpurgis-*

nacht, my night too. I went downstairs, they were anxious for me to.

R. looks older. Parentheses engraved around his mouth. My fault? Not like a newly married man. Again my fault? The ground keeps shifting. I state my case, he his, both of us are belligerent, both basically uncertain. I'm sure of that.

(To be sure only of uncertainty, what a fate! The hell of being 20. Never again, that's the only consolation. Sometimes I admire those who can do away with themselves. I could *never* do that.)

One minute he acts persuasive, as if we were reasonable politicians trying to work out a compromise. You give a little, I give a little, we both make it look good for the folks back home.

Next minute he stares at me as if I was something he'd never seen before, a new kind of bug maybe, bearing strange diseases, completely unpredictable and unreasonable. A menace to humanity. So he, self-appointed spokesman for humanity, starts threatening me with DDT: he will dust, spray, bomb me out. He will carry his wife away from my contaminating presence. (If he only knew!)

I try to tell him that I know what he is going through. Which only infuriates him.

"What do you know?" he yells. "You've got it made, you don't have to lift a finger!" And of course he is right, in a way.

Then he becomes super-reasonable all over again, he tries to tell *me* he knows what *I* am going through. Why should I believe him any more than he does me? He knows what hell it is to grow up, he says. If I was left alone by the deaths of Uncle Max and Papa, he had the same experience, he points out, first with Mel's disappearance and then with Mama's death.

"You go to college right here in the attic, I bring your books, Kitty brings your groceries, and still you suffer. Well, I went to the city college, nobody brought me anything, Papa was wrapped in his own misery—you were too young to know

—then another war broke out. Do you think I don't know what hell it is to grow up?"

No, you don't, I say, nobody does. When you're a child you can't imagine, when you're an adult you can't remember. Nature is kind, the wound closes over, the scar is hardly visible, painful only when the weather turns bad.

This seems to make an impression. Ralph is thoughtful. I can tell he's reflecting that maybe I'm not completely nuts. I press my advantage. I take up the case of Mel, our bone of contention. Let's start by recognizing that neither of us actually knows him. If we still don't know each other, how can we know him, a stranger and a fugitive? Since I was seven, I haven't laid eyes on Mel, I have no special ax to grind for him that I wouldn't have for Ralph, if their situations were reversed. Or for any other brother.

Ralph responds that he isn't interested in abstractions. If I want to go on about justice and equity it's because I'm young and haven't suffered at Mel's hands. Supposing it was Mel who was responsible for Uncle Max's and Papa's disappearance, then how would I feel?

I tell him he's operating with abstractions at least as much as I am. Hatred is more emotional, maybe more satisfying, but it's just as much an abstraction as equity or justice. Or am I wrong? When I say to Ralph that you can't resolve your life by blaming its miseries and failures on a single human being, I have the feeling that I'm arguing with myself too, trying to persuade myself as much as him.

Funny thing. All through this, Kitty sat quietly, hardly moving or even breathing, but very cool, not at all eager like she was when Ralph first brought her here. She didn't say one word, didn't try to persuade me. Last night for the first time, I had the feeling that she was more a spectator than a participant.

April 3

Watched Kitty again today, talking to that kerchiefed housewife in front of the supermarket. She seemed more vivacious with the girl than she was with Ralph and me the other night.

Made up list of books for R. to get me. Passed it down to Kitty—looked at me queerly when she saw the fiction. Said nothing for a moment, then asked, "Have you ever read *Madame Bovary?*" When I admitted that I hadn't, she said, "I'll bring that too."

April 7

Ralph came up with my books and made a crack: "Any time you're ready to climb down off your high horse, the Baby Carriage Brigade will welcome you with open arms."

I didn't understand until he explained that the young women of Happy Valley were culture-hungry, with even a Great Books course going.

There are so many meetings in the development that you can't tell which is which. Sometimes they go up the driveways with books under their arms— Those must be the ones Ralph was kidding me about. Funny that he should complain about the continual get-togethers of those young married couples. Hard for me to understand his bitterness. Doesn't he want our neighbors to be as happy as the rich? Why does he mock at them so? Is he afraid that once he relaxed he'd be just like them? I don't dare say it for fear that he'll fly out at me.

April 11

Much less barbell work today. In fact have been unable to hold to my schedule for weeks. Am spending more time with the books, and watching what goes on outside (see Kitty quite often), and less with the weights. Who needs all those muscles? Right now I need more brains.

Note, about Kitty: saw her yesterday with two young women. The regular, who always wears the scarf, and another one pushing a blue stroller with a baby boy in it. Talked animatedly for a while, Kitty pointing over here at our house.

Thought for a minute she was going to point up here directly at me—I'm sure Kitty knows I'm watching her. Hamming it up for my benefit. Then they began writing something on their shopping lists, laughing. Even without binoculars I could tell they were exchanging phone numbers. What next?

April 14

Ralph was mean to me, about the books. Am trying not to be childish, but to put it as simply as I can. He told me that he was sick and tired of running back and forth to the library; that the branch library didn't have everything I wanted, and sometimes he had to go to the main library, and got a parking ticket there, and almost ruptured himself lugging the books. If I don't leave the attic, meet with him and Kitty to negotiate seriously—now that my twenty-first birthday is approaching—he'll cut off my library privileges.

He is putting the squeeze on me. If I don't come down he won't deliver my next batch of books. I said, "If I come down and we talk some more, will you have the books for me?" He said, "Yes." So I said, "What about in the future?" He replied, "That's one of the things we'll talk about."

I think I can see what's coming.

April 16

Went downstairs to pick up my books today. Amazed to learn, from something he let slip, that Ralph has been reading my science books after I have finished them. He majored in literature at college, read many novels, is very bitter because all the reading didn't do him any "practical" good. Now he feels that if only he knew as much science as I, he'd do far more with it than I have.

Then he said flat out, "No more books unless and until you see things my way. Your birthday is little more than nine weeks off. That is our personal deadline. Everything must be regulated well before then."

I said, "Ralph, you are blackmailing me."

He drew his eyebrows together tight in that way he has. But then he smiled, as if he was reminding himself of how firmly he had the upper hand, and he shook his head slowly.

He said, "Kid, I don't care any more what you think about me, or even what you say about me. As long as you do what I want."

He turned to Kitty to ask her if she agreed. Instead of replying directly, she simply shrugged, as if she couldn't care less.

I said, "Ralph, I have an encyclopedia in the attic. There's enough in it to keep me busy for a long time. Don't do me any more favors."

He bent back his fingers and cracked the knuckles. "Reading is a habit, like smoking."

I said, "I can write for books. The mailman will bring what I want."

He smiled. "No more mail. I can't take chances on arousing the postman's suspicions. Everything for you goes back marked 'Address Unknown.' You might as well face it: I mean business."

I almost started to cry. "Ralphie," I said, "what do you want of me? Why did you pretend that we were going to get along?"

He became very stern. "Things can't go on like this. You've got to get out, you've got to turn up again as though you've been away, you've got to probate the will. If you read the papers you'd know they're still looking for you. Nobody can understand why you haven't shown up to claim the estate. Burgholzer phones me at my office. So do the radio and TV people. They ask me questions: What are you going to do about the estate? Where is your brother Raymond?"

"Why don't you tell them and get it over with, if you feel this way?"

"It's too late. I'd look like a fool. Or worse, people might accuse me of locking you away like a Mongolian idiot. They might even say I've been in cahoots with you against Mel.

No, it's going to have to be done right, and you're going to have to do your part. You knew the hermit routine couldn't last forever. The picnic is over, kid."

"All you have to do is be reasonable," I said. "Then I'll sit down with Martin Stark and work out the whole thing. Otherwise I'll give out the news, not you. You'll look mighty selfish and small if I tell it my way."

"I don't believe you." Ralph sucked in his cheeks as though he had just bitten into something sour. "But what hurts is that you'd rather have me suffer than Mel. You claim to love your family. Which of us did more to harm the family?"

"That's not for me to judge. I only want to give Mel his share and you yours, as Papa wanted. I don't want him on my conscience. Or on yours."

"My conscience will take care of itself without your help. Can you get that through your head?"

All of a sudden I was tired. I said, "Just don't take it for granted that I won't do it, Ralphie."

What I'd said before hadn't made him lose control. But now he flew into one of his sudden rages.

"You wouldn't be able to do anything on an empty stomach, would you?" He shoved his face up against mine. "Don't look surprised. Kitty will do what I tell her to. It isn't just your food for thought that'll be cut off if you don't grow up."

He couldn't have meant that. And he must know that I couldn't have meant my threat. What gets into us, that we're able even to think such things!

I can't write any more tonight.

April 17

Still convinced that morally I am right, even if practically Ralph is right. And I think he knows that too. But neither of us dares admit it to the other. Because if you admit half the proposition, the game is almost up. Besides, I suspect that each of us can see some merit in the other's attitude. After all, we're not completely crazy. That's the worst of all, to be aware that you are drifting toward catastrophe, paralyzed by knowledge and by fear of the consequences of what you are capable of doing.

April 19

Tried to resume exercise schedule. Must keep in shape for whatever lies ahead, but it's hard. I'm too worried. Still have come to no decision. Stare out the window for hours. Spring. Kids with kites, window washers working, women airing out rugs, trucks picking up coats and furs for storage.

April 20

Surprise. Watched Kitty going across not to supermarket but to Happy Valley itself. Dressed quite chic, not in slacks but in spring coat. Visited her new friends there for several hours, came out in time to cook supper for Ralph. Bet he'd be surprised if he knew. But what should he expect her to do all day while he's out making money? Scrub floors in a house they'd just as soon would burn down?

(With me in it?)

I wonder if Ralph hears the clock ticking as I do.

April 22

What a turn I got this morning. No sooner looked out window than it seemed to me the Witness was standing in front of the A & P, radiant and humble, just as she used to. I felt like shouting for joy. Strangest sensation of relief and peace. But it turned out to be someone else entirely, a girl who bore no resemblance at all. She unfolded a card table, propped a poster against it, then set herself to collecting signatures on a petition. Something about the Bomb. Completely different-looking girl. How could I have confused the two?

Can't even read the last batch of books Ralph brought.

Keep thinking about his deadline. Almost wish it could be taken out of our hands by an act of fate. Do others feel that way too, sometimes?

April 25

Thinking all day yesterday, and half the night, about Mel, Ralph, me. But was I really thinking, or simply scurrying about purposelessly like a rat in a maze? Compared to Ralph, I should be in a good position to concentrate. Healthy, alone, no distractions, regular mental and physical exercise, etc. As he says, I've got it made. But all I could come up with was a note to him, a sorry makeshift. Recopied it this morning, sent it down to Ralph via Kitty.

(She is more brisk and impersonal with me than ever. Am absolutely convinced that by now she has no memory whatsoever of that disastrous morning, in fact would be affronted, maybe even amused at my overheated imagination, if I ever alluded to it. Now how do you explain that?)

Copy of note to Ralph:

DEAR RALPH:

I have given much thought to our difficult situation. I believe there is room for compromise if we don't lose our heads. I must say I am suspicious that you are trying to pry me loose when you insist that our talks take place downstairs. On the other hand I know you wouldn't come up here, because you regard this as an abnormal place, a hothouse which ought to be eliminated. Maybe for the next little while we ought to try to communicate through Kitty at least to get our separate positions clarified. So here is my first attempt.

#1. I don't think I ought to come down to bargain with you under threat of things being regulated one way or the other, as you put it, by the time of my twenty-first birthday. You wouldn't come up here to negotiate under such conditions, would you?

#2. I will not be insistent on Mel sharing equally with you, if you will not be insistent on my ignoring him. Maybe we could do something like this: Try to find out his circumstances, his plans and hopes, and see if a portion of Papa's and Uncle Max's estate can be set aside to help him fulfill them in his own way.

Don't say No offhand, think about it first.

YOUR BROTHER

April 26
No answer.

April 27
No answer.

April 28
Much coming and going today. Poor old Sasha roused to howl, *how-oo, how-oo.* Strange man at the door, obviously not a salesman. Fat, not young, driving a huge car. Was in the front hall with Kitty quite a while. After he left, she promptly made various phone calls—couldn't help listening, but couldn't hear much—to Ralph, I'm sure, and afterward to Dr. Stark, I think, and to Martin.

Later on she came up to talk to me. Can't explain this easily, it's only an impression, but Kitty seemed to be blooming, as though the coming of spring had brought new color to her cheeks, or maybe she and Ralph have reached new understanding. Their honeymoon is certainly over—I guess I'm vulgar to think of it so much—there was surely some connection between this and Kitty's other visit to me.

When I complimented her on her appearance a very secretive look came over her face. Sly, but satisfied. And I don't mean that she was behaving at all as she had the other time. In fact she passed it off by thanking me politely, not with embarrassment, but as if it was her due.

Then she said, "Ralph has asked me to tell you that he was not displeased with your note."

Imagine. Took him three days to produce an upside-down, inside-out answer like that! Not only couldn't he reply in writing, as I had asked him to, he couldn't even reply positively. But at least it was an opening.

Kitty added, more spontaneously, that Ralph wanted to discuss my last sentence, but that it couldn't be tonight, because someone was coming. How about tomorrow afternoon?

I was confused. If Ralph agreed with my note, why should he expect that I'd come down just to get into another fruitless argument? "During the day? Ralph works."

"Tomorrow is Saturday." Kitty laughed. "Don't you even keep track of the days of the week, Raymond? You should, you know. After all, you're going to be a man soon."

She said it nicely, but just the same, it was a dig. Even more upsetting, it was a reference to Ralph's deadline, which I thought we were going to cast aside.

But she turned swiftly and hurried down the ladder, giving me no chance to complain or comment. Over her shoulder she called back something about having to fix up the place for their company.

Whom was she referring to? They never have company, the way most young married couples are supposed to. It's weird—they live almost as privately as Uncle Max and Papa did. As I do.

Whoever it is, the company should be here any minute. It's half-past eight already. Could it be those women from Happy Valley? I can't believe Ralph would stand for that, or that he's even aware of their existence.

April 29

Much to say. Best to put it in order. First, the company came last night just after I finished my last entry. Turned out to be same man who'd come earlier in the day and talked in the front hall with Kitty. Recognized him the minute he stepped out of his car. Obviously he had made a date to see

Ralph. That must have been what the telephoning was about too, although no one else came last night. Didn't stay long, but after his car pulled out there was much conferencing, and some phoning back and forth. Was convinced that this had some connection with me, but had no way of knowing for sure until this afternoon.

Soon after lunch Ralph called up to me, casually, but still peremptorily.

"Ray, come on down!"

I thought it over. There was nothing to be gained by stubbornness. Besides—I was curious. So I came. They were waiting for me in the kitchen, Kitty had made extra coffee. Everything was almost as pleasant as it had been on our first day. But I had barely settled myself at the table with the coffeecake (Kitty was outdoing me in the homemaking department) when Ralph went to work.

"You said you wouldn't want to negotiate under threat of a deadline like your birthday."

I started to get up. "If I'd known you were even going to mention it, I wouldn't have come down."

"Relax." Ralph was freshly shaved—denim slacks and sneakers, no socks, sport shirt instead of business suit. I hadn't seen him look so well-rested and self-assured since his arrival.

"Things are moving rapidly, kiddo. It isn't a matter of my mentioning it or not. Things may be taken out of our hands. We may be forced to negotiate and get it over with."

My heart gave a leap. I was sure that at last he was ready to do what I had been hoping he would: recognize Mel. No doubt there would be conditions. Certainly the recognition must be made to look not as though he was giving in to me, but as though he was responding realistically to what was best for everybody. And certainly he and Kitty would have to get enough out of the estate to enable them to realize whatever dreams had been sustaining them.

It's not that I thought of Ralph as uniquely willing to bargain off his ideals, as he conceived them. But I'm beginning to think that that's the way people are. Look at me. If I could have done it with good grace, I would have been ready to abandon my insistence on a share for Mel. That is, if some way or other Mel himself could have turned up and said: Forget it, Ray, I don't want any. And if I could have had some assurance that Ralph and Kitty wouldn't abandon me.

No such luck. Meanwhile, however, here was Ralph, his eyes glittering, and Kitty, looking sleek, very blond, terribly self-assured in tight black velvet trousers and pearl-gray blouse with red scarf.

"The man that was here last night was a builder. He wants to put up a professional arts building here. A block of offices. He's ready to pay a substantial sum for this corner. Cash, no haggling."

He looked at me expectantly.

Finally I said, "Well, what about it?"

Ralph clenched his hands. I could almost hear him counting to himself. "Ray, listen carefully. Without clear title it's no sale. Who's the legal owner? he asked. Where's your brother? How soon does the will get probated? I said, Soon."

"Well, I guess that's true."

"It had better be. Once we give Martin Stark the green light for your twenty-first birthday, this builder, this de Angelis, will carry on from there. The search and everything will be taken care of, between his lawyer and Martin Stark."

"And where will I go when they tear this house down?"

"With Kitty and me."

I glanced across the table at Kitty. Her face disclosed nothing. She sipped her coffee quietly (she was the only one not having cake) and tipped her cigarette ash into the saucer. I said, "But nothing will have been resolved."

"We'll have the cash. We'll have liquidated Uncle Max's worst legacy. Once this dump is pulled down, and we move away, the reporters and the creeps who cruise by here and stare in our windows will forget about us. Then we'll see if we can work out something fair on Max's other properties. There are a lot of them, you know. Plenty of room for argument with them."

He was smiling at me with all his might. His charm was almost radiant, but I was sick with disappointment.

"I'm sorry, Ralphie," I said. "I'm really very disappointed. I thought you had something tangible to offer."

"Tangible? What do you call ninety thousand—"

"You're just using Mr. de Angelis as another crowbar to pry me out of the attic. First we have to understand each other, we have to come to an honest agreement, without trickery or duress. Then the properties will be no problem. The world is full of de Angelises ready to put up professional blocks."

"I warned you, Ray . . ." Ralph was already on his feet.

"No threats." I got up too. "It'll be better if we talk to each other through Kitty. We made a start that way, we should have stuck with it. She can deliver our messages while we work it out between us, can't you, Kitty?"

"No, I'm afraid not."

We both turned. Until that moment both her husband and I had taken Kitty's presence for granted. She was sitting motionless at the table between us, her hands folded in her lap, the same secret smile on her lips that had appeared the day before, when I had told her how attractive she looked. This time I was afraid to say anything. I left it to Ralph, who was gazing at her distractedly, a bit puzzled.

"You chaps might as well know. I'm going to have a baby."

It was too silent, too breathless, as though we were in the eye of a storm. Something terrible was going to happen.

But Kitty was very cool. She smiled at us impartially.

"And I am very sure. I went to see Dr. Stark."

Ralph's lower jaw had fallen. He looked both stupid and menacing, like a wounded beast. "You mean now he knows too?"

"He was very happy for us."

For an instant I was sure that Ralph was going to attack

her. He had forgotten me absolutely, it was as though all the fury he had been building up against me now found its outlet in his wife. He said venomously, "No doubt you've also made sure that it's too late to do anything about it."

Kitty nodded gently. "Dr. Stark did say that I may have a difficult time. I'm going to have to live as quietly as possible for the next few months."

It is extraordinary—the power of suggestion—how Kitty changed before my eyes. Even while she spoke, I marveled that I hadn't recognized her pregnancy earlier, her body was taking on the peculiar contours of the mother-to-be. Her chest seemed to have sunken in somewhat, so that her bosom, which before had been large for her frame, now appeared to have melted into the concavity of the upper torso. I thought I could see already, beneath the thickening waistline of her tailored slacks, the pendent globe which women carry before them in their late months like a precious vessel slung over the loins. I have watched many, many of them moving in their stately way through the Lanes and Drives of Happy Valley.

But now, how special: a new Land at last! And I thought of how many years Papa must have waited, with his hopes diminishing, first in Mel, then in Ralph, at last in me.

I turned to Ralph, thinking that if I were to say something of the sort, it might hearten him by reminding him of his role as sole continuator of our line. But he was exhaling audibly through his nostrils. Suddenly he reared up, his eyes dilated and his head flung back as if he could not bear to look at either of us, and pivoted on his heel. The crepe of his tennis shoes squealed softly on the linoleum as he ran from us, careening blindly out of the kitchen.

A moment later the little Triumph fired up in the driveway, then roared away, rubber screaming as it hit the street and swerved about for a wide-open take-off.

Kitty had still not moved from her placid position at the table. As I stood staring down at the light sparkling on her blond hair, I tried to reconstruct for myself what must have driven her to this action, and her husband to this despair.

The conception must have taken place very soon after that morning up here with me. It must have terrified her, much more than it did me. Maybe she became frightened at the pleasure she was experiencing from what had probably started as an act of extreme marital devotion. Could be that she felt she had the same potential for becoming a bum as the lowest woman.

Then the pregnancy would be a shield against such a terrible degeneration. With it, she can be more supremely self-possessed with me than ever. She has wiped the incident from her consciousness for the sake of her unborn child. No wonder she has been wearing that secret smile. She thinks she has won. But Ralph? What of Ralph?

That was why I couldn't resist asking her, "Why did you do it?"

She chose to interpret my question as referring to her having taken this particular moment to announce the pregnancy.

"If I told him when we were alone, I don't know what he might have done in a burst of temper. Not to me, but to the baby. You understand, don't you?"

Kitty gave me a leisurely smile. I felt as though she were patting me on the head.

"Ralph will get over it, you'll see. Men do."

Maybe. But things will never be the same.

7: RALPH

Why did she do it? why? why?

Ralph skirted the perimeter of the city, driving unseeingly past the offal of his fellow citizens. Slag dumps, twisted mountains of rusting auto bodies, bloated oil storage tanks, abandoned lumberyards. Like an ant making its blind and painful way across an endless expanse of kitchen toward its half-divined goal of sugar, he was groping half-consciously for roads that would wind away from the dead level and up into the hills where he and his car could come alive.

Surrounded by ugliness, he could only repeat the question, without even attempting to answer it. Only after he had found a way out of the junk-laden plain, up into the foothills of the mountains that hid Happy Valley from all the other happy valleys, was he able to formulate for himself some of Kitty's arguments.

"I did it because you wouldn't talk to me."

"I did it because you proved that you couldn't master Raymond."

"I did it because you broke our contract."

176

But I didn't break it, I didn't! If we haven't yet gotten what we had hoped for, I haven't broken my word as you have yours.

Even as he framed the replies in his mind, he knew that he was constructing an imaginary dialogue now because before he had been afraid to engage in a real one.

I trusted you more than I ever allowed myself to trust anyone else. You betrayed that trust.

"Your trust wasn't enough. If you'd given me more, you wouldn't be in this state."

But no amount of trust was ever enough. It hadn't been for his mother, who had persisted after nearly a dozen dismal years by making yet another Land, only to wind up behind the eight ball.

And if nothing had done for his mother, what chance had he had to succeed with those two men where she had failed? Nothing had helped—not running errands, getting good grades, delivering parcels, or collecting his uncle's goddamned string, wax, and tin foil. Uncle Max had only glanced at him shrewdly, cynically, from those tiny but terribly bright eyes, as if to say, I know what you're up to, kid, and you'll never get my stamp of approval, not as long as Mel walks the earth in my footsteps. As for Papa, how could he understand if he never looked up from his silly gadgets? And Mel himself, king of the traitors, knowing perfectly well that no one would ever be as devoted as his year-younger blood brother, had turned on him as you would on a pest at a party and casually, heartlessly, cut him out of his life, then had gone off and left him holding the bag.

"But it's always the other person who betrays you, isn't it? And now it's your wife. Do you really think I came here and took up an unnatural existence, hiding a half-mad boy in the attic as an unmarried girl hides a baby in her belly, just so I could betray you?"

Just the same, you did. Whatever the reason, whatever the provocation, you did.

"Self-pity. The most destructive emotion a man can experience."

How pitilessly feminine! You never catch a woman yielding to self-pity. She may fall in love with a man who does, and she'll feel sorry for *him* because he's weak, as if he were a drunkard, or a failure. It gives her an unearned superiority. But to feel sorry for herself—never.

"A woman has more important things to do with her life than to waste it in self-pity."

Such as making babies.

"Precisely."

Was that the logic that had led her to pregnancy? Winding the wheel hard as he wove his way through the sweet little hills which, arising from the filth of his native city, reminded him of an order of nature that he might otherwise have believed to have vanished forever from the world, Ralph fought to remind himself of the classic simplicity of his situation.

In a way he was behaving exactly as if Kitty had told him that he had been cuckolded. You betrayed me, you betrayed me! That was the howl of the standard mass-produced American jerk, whom Ralph as a soldier had gotten to know and hate, when he discovered that in his absence his wife had been serving him precisely as he had been serving her.

Yes, it was true that he had not kept his promise any more than Kitty had hers. So far he had given her nothing more than the most dismal complications. Treating Raymond as a stubborn donkey, first with the carrot, then with the stick, he had wasted precious weeks, months even; for Ray was no four-legged beast, but an odd bird, resisting every enticement to leave the building that trapped them all.

And who had set Kitty the example? Who had fallen into the trap, taking up a wretched "temporary" existence worse than the one he had left behind in New York? Having allowed himself and Kitty to be taken captive by the captive, he had opened before her not the enchanted prospect which had enticed them both into marriage, but instead a routinized, predictable existence of the kind that had always made him shudder, with every little trail blazed for Kitty: Diaper Service, Nursery School, Open House, Den Mother, Car Pool, College Endowment, Disneyland Tour, Retirement Dinner, Monthly Pension, and a quiet death sponsored by Blue Cross and cushioned by Ben Lurie's Twenty Payment Life.

There was reason for Kitty to have done what she had. Her deliberate pregnancy was a warning flag run up for him.

"The baby won't be born tomorrow. Long before it arrives, matters will have to be arranged between you and Raymond. Your own deadline still stands. I have simply reinforced the necessity of coming to a final decision before Ray's twenty-first birthday."

But you did something irrevocable. And you did it as unilaterally as a woman can.

"What did you expect, a perpetual honeymoon? Or that if your magic trick with brother Ray wouldn't work, I would pull a disappearing act, like a woman sawed in half? Did you really think that you could annul me like a bad dream? Nothing can be like it was again. Never."

You could have given me a sign.

"Would you have preferred it if I had turned sullen?"

It might almost have been better. At least I could have been alerted.

"That may be your way. It's not mine. I wasn't resentful, I was happy. But there came a point, didn't there, when you stopped talking, when we settled into a routine of sweating it out and praying that something would happen. Well, now I've made something happen. Over to you, Ralphie."

Maybe she did intend to firm him up, to urge him on toward their goal with more speed. But I won't quit in any case, so why couldn't we have talked, why couldn't we have planned together?

"You withdrew, you forced my hand. You need me, so I've forced yours."

It was true, his silent self-pity had preceded the pregnancy, aroused again by the realization that Raymond had the power to force at least a temporary stalemate, and that in consequence he himself had to play the part of the returned rebel, come home to make his peace with the going order of things. At first he had taken it out on Kitty in a violent wordless sensuality, which she had welcomed with such passion that his own had redoubled. But after some weeks (was it after he had gone to work?) his more natural moodiness had reasserted itself even in the bedroom. This too Kitty had accepted as if it were a part of their difficult bargain, if not an inevitable concomitant of married life. When all the time she was planning to break their compact, knowing that Ralph would not dare to scuttle the marriage—not because he was incapable of it in reprisal, but because of how one more desertion by a Land, this time of a pregnant woman, would be taken by those whom he still needed in the contest with Ray.

Besides, he swore to himself, I still intend to win, I still want to do it with her. And that was what would matter long after the dialogue had worn itself out.

He turned the car about, backing its tail into a dirt road and aiming the nose at the unseen city below. Confusion, confusion. He drove downhill, going home more slowly than he had left, arguing with himself on the way back as he had argued with her on the way out.

He knew what would happen when he entered the house. Dinner would be ready and Kitty would be smiling enigmatically. Not acidulously, not demandingly. She would not even pretend surprise that he had returned. And he, feigning weariness, as unable to talk as always, would wind up lying silently at her side in the dark, and wondering whether despite everything he had come back because he still wanted her, or because he still needed her to fulfill his dream. Or did one imply the other? She would go on being pregnant, he would simply have to accept that. But she would also go on doing what he had to have done. And that was essential, that made them truly married.

The young laurel, seemingly springing from the very hill-side stones, glistened in the strengthening sun, and above them the curving whips of forsythia swayed and shook, bursting with yellow-gold blossoms. Sorely troubled and no longer positive that he controlled his world, or that it would change for him in accordance with his plans and predictions, Ralph drove past the laurel, the forsythia, and the reddish holes gouged in the mountainside for more happy valleys, too intent on his own pain and his own altered prospect, as he descended once again to Kitty and Ray, to feel for the disappearance of the natural world into the jaw of the bulldozer.

The game was not up. Driven forward by Kitty's boldness, Ralph set himself to tightening the screws on Ray once and for all. First he withdrew library privileges. Then he refused to honor his brother's requests for small items. Next he took to editing Ray's shopping list, scratching from it everything but the barest necessities for survival. Already Ray, unable to secure replacement parts for his ham radio, was being cut off from his last links with the outer world, and deprived of the threat that he would transmit anything damaging. Soon he would slip below the subsistence level. After that he would have to decide for himself whether to go hungry or to come down and rejoin the human race.

This gradual program of withdrawal was for Ray's good, Ralph was convinced, as if he were withholding drugs in order to break the boy of an addiction. But with Dr. Stark and Martin nudging him, asking what progress was being made, Ralph found it increasingly difficult to keep firmly to his purpose. The Starks would think it cruel if they knew. I do myself, he thought; but it must be done.

Without Kitty it would have been impossible. Not only was she his agent, supplying or denying in strict accordance with his instructions, so that even when he had to be away from the house the reduction of Raymond went on. Much more important, she supplied the moral sanction.

Not that he talked with her about Ray, any more than he did about anything else. It was simply that when he told her what he wanted done, she did it without making a face, efficiently and effectively, immediately and unquestioningly. If there remained on her clear blooming features the traces of that enigmatic smile with which she had announced to him her one unalterable violation of their contract, Ralph dared not refer to it or even analyze it. It was hard enough to face the lonely truth that he himself had doubts about what he was doing to Ray, doubts which arose in part from fraternal admiration for the boy's stubbornness, in part from the suspicion that, but for Kitty, he would himself be tempted to toss in the towel. But if Kitty were to reveal that she too harbored doubts, everything would be impossible.

Not only did Kitty say nothing. She revealed nothing. The only indication that she held in her womb a creature formed in the likeness of the Lands was the banal fact that she had become a hearty eater. And Ralph, peering covertly at her apparently contented housewife's face, could only marvel that there had ever been a time when he and she had accepted each other's gifts. In a nightly frenzy of possession and repossession, he and this strange complacent woman had kissed, sucked, chewed, and bitten at each other. Was it possible?

Maybe, though, this was what happened to women when they were bearing their young. How was he to know? Never having slept with a pregnant woman before, Ralph had no basis for judgment, and there was no one whom he would dream of asking about the matter. After all, he himself had lost most of his ardor too. He could only assume that there was nothing any more final about this than there was about his job, or about this house and his hidden brother.

So the spring weeks slipped by, his own will weakening along with Ray's, and with them the pretense that he had flown in like a bird of passage, alighting only long enough for

a swift conquest before flying off. He had built his own nest,
if he had not exactly feathered it, and the fact that the weather
had turned mild only infuriated him.

What good was all this false sweetness? With the top of the
Triumph down and the lake breeze ruffling his hair while he
made his business rounds with the stupid cans of stupid film,
a con man among the yokels, he felt as though he were playing a charade of the happy suburbanite. It's not so bad, the
wind whispered; there are worse existences than cruising with
the auto radio playing Cole Porter, a hint of summer in the
air, and a few dollars in the bank. Home to a hot supper, an
uncomplaining wife, and the six o'clock news, which concluded every day's smoke screen made by the international
dragons breathing their interminable fire with a consoling
Panglossian vignette of an absent-minded professor (driving
away from the Last Chance gas station at the desert's edge,
he left his forgotten wife in the ladies' room) or a bouncing
baby (tumbling from his sixth-story tenement window, he fell
unharmed onto a truckload of mattresses).

No. It had been better when the weather had matched his
inner climate, when his nose had run, his lips had cracked,
and his hands had chapped and bled clenching the steering
wheel. At least then, in February and March, he had the sense
of combat, the bitter exhilaration that grew from pride in
his own stoic courage. Now the spring sun was melting it all
into mush, and Ralph was invaded by terror lest the trap he
had spent these lonely months preparing with such patient
care would spring (maybe it had already sprung!), only to
leave him, its designer, caught beyond any possibility of release or rescue. For every evening when he came home there
awaited him not only the same sights and sounds that made it
all worth while for his similars in Happy Valley—the sizzling
roast in the oven, the baby in the belly, the news of other
people's troubles on the radio—but above his head, rustling
softly like a squirrel rousing himself and his rattling hoard

from the winter's hibernation, the unique brother who stuck in his throat, choking him with the knowledge that de Angelis the builder was not his, but Ray's to command.

What was more, there was no quarter of the city that did not bear an immediately recognizable emblem of his youth. For most people the very word childhood was supposedly nostalgia itself, transformed by the gentle miracle of selective memory into a synonym for happiness, in which even rare moments of deprivation or grief were mollified by the lenitive ointment of parental love. For Ralph it was the reverse. Childhood was a hateful word, and the city (which he thought he had pulled down in his mind) rose up before him once again in all its ugly actuality, reminding him at every street corner of the despair which he had never succeeded in eradicating.

Here, at this intersection named for dead presidents, the trolley line he had taken to high school from the pharmacy had been abandoned, and the tracks pulled out as if the curving street were a deveined shrimp. But within arm's reach of his open convertible was the same newspaper stand before which he had jumped up and down every winter morning for years, first on one foot and then on the other, his hair freezing to the roots as he awaited the lurching dismal ride to school. The same girlie mags still dangled like fish on a string, the same movie stars and princes too, or nearly; if Rita's swelling bosom had been replaced by Brigitte's, King Farouk's bemedaled bosom by the Shah's, no matter. The interchangeable Communist and Free World Spacemen confronted each other in their cereal-box bubble suits. Over them all presided the same Polish newsdealer who had lurked in this same cavern fifteen and twenty years earlier. The same cigarette butt depended from his stubble-fringed lips, the same leer played across his wizened and cynical countenance. My sentinel, Ralph said to himself, the guardian of my erotic daydreams; he will outlive me yet.

In the old Eighth Ward, at an intersection named not for

dead presidents but for dead German poets, there still stood the tavern called The Spot, where he had drunk his first beer, read Pierre Louÿs to a girl who made him tremble, and studied a whole new vocabulary. In the merciless spring sunlight, peering from the car as he waited for a signal to change, he could see the phony knotty-pine paneling, and to the side the alleyway down which he had staggered at sixteen to vomit up everything, his ears ringing with the mocking laughter of the girl who had repaid him for *The Songs of Bilitis* by making fun of his wacky family.

In the old Thirteenth Ward, he cruised by the Settlement House where he had sawed away his Saturday mornings under the tutelage of violinist Martin Stark, whose limp was as distinguished as his University Shop tweeds. If it had been a miserable place under its original name, with the runny-nosed children of the poor tripping each other in the corridors and passing dirty books under the ping-pong tables, it looked no better now as the Boys' Club, with a new generation of Afro-Latin brats, black now and brown, some seemingly as haunted and wretched as he had been, others as conniving and shrewd as Mel had been.

That too was trapped inside himself, unexplainable to any other living soul but one, and he locked away. The city was a monument not only to what he himself had been, but also to Mel. If one street, one Spot, one Settlement House, was irrevocably his until the moment when it should be bulldozed and pulverized, the same could be said of Mel and innumerable corners and moments in the life and death of the city.

What would pass through Mel's mind if he in his turn were to come back and walk these streets? Would he too be frozen at those intersections where his own life had crossed that of his brother and of all those others who had taught him hate?

Walking, brief case in hand, through the collapsing business district, in a neighborhood now as then crushed under crumbling loft buildings tenanted by tanneries, jewelry repair depots, plastic toy wholesalers, broom and rag dealers, and furtive employment bureaus exploiting pearl divers, bus boys, migrant laborers, and field hands, Ralph came upon Commerce Alley. There he stood with his eyes unfocused for a long moment, at the very spot where sixteen years earlier he had frozen at the sound of Mel screaming in pain. Here, transfixed, the beauty parlor handbills he had been stuffing into mailboxes dropping from his fingers like so many petals, he had watched helplessly while Mel was kicked and beaten senseless by three vengeance-seeking hoods.

Two blocks ahead bulked the soot-blackened mass of the County Courthouse, a battlemented monstrosity surely designed by a demented architect in the fashion of an earlier Teutonic bedlam. Up its forbiddingly endless steps trooped the innocent in search of dog licenses and title deeds. But for Ralph it would forever be the hell where he had escorted his silently weeping mother, past lounging bail bondsmen and small-time fixers, unshaven elevator starters, and other weeping women, to the juvenile court where Mel, again Mel, always Mel, was to be produced, questioned, prodded, poked, and catalogued for another of the acts which defined him as antisocial.

There was, finally, at the fringe of Agassiz Park, the Sisters of Mercy Hospital, another turreted relic of Victorian horror. For Ralph it was the worst of all. If I owned it, he thought, if it had been willed to me, I would ram the earth-mover into it myself, I would raze it with my own hands and let the flowers of the Agassiz Botanic Garden grow over the spot where it had been. In the pebbled courtyard the chimney of its outbuilding, not even decently concealed with ivy, smoked constantly with the burning placentae of religiously fertile mothers, the tonsils of their wailing children, the tripes of trussed-up collision victims, and the amputated digits of careless employees of the Agassiz Car & Foundry Co. Here Jenny Kadin Land had been taken much against her will, hands pressed to her face in the ambulance, to spend her final weeks, only the stubborn refusal of her heart to go on working finally stilling her feeble cries for her lost pride, the runaway oldest son, deserter of a foundering family. Here, waiting for Dr. Stark in the bile-green corridor under a cheap polychrome statuette of Mary Mother of Jesus, dying for a smoke and learning to hate his brother, Ralph had been accosted by a stranger, an intern in rumpled white who approached silently on rubber-soled shoes. Ralph had been astonished to see that he had tears in his eyes. The young doctor had stammered awkwardly, "Your mother is gone," and Ralph's only immediate reaction had been confusion: how come it was not he himself, but the doctor, a stranger, who was crying? And why?

In the years that had followed his mother's death Ralph had been positive that he knew what was wrong with this world, as it shaped itself in his native city, and what kind of world ought to replace it. Now that he was back, though, and now that his temporary winter had gone on to look like a permanent spring, always promising but never fulfilling, he was tormented with the suspicion that—while he was firmer than ever in his hatred of what he saw about him and felt as a menace that would continually encircle him until he himself wiped it out—maybe he did not have the unique answer any more than did Mel or Ray. What if the answer was not an apocalyptic bulldozer appointed by history to push aside the city's heaped-up rubble, but an evolution of the city in ways unforeseen by any of the Lands? What then? Who would control and master it?

Oddly, his uncertainty took the outward form, not of humility, but of a heightened determination to win through, and of a cold arrogance toward those who seemed to feel that he had slipped back almost imperceptibly into their provincial lives. Upon his arrival childhood acquaintances had regarded with open envy the traveler returned to claim his birthright. Now they nudged each other knowingly when they saw him, prosaic like themselves, in a barbershop or drugstore.

He still found his name in the paper from time to time, but no longer as a man of the world briefly returning home. Now he was simply part of a running story as the only visible survivor of a line of peculiar people, whose peculiarity was hardly less newsworthy than their whereabouts.

On the first prematurely hot day of the season there was flung at Ralph, like a taunt, the sense of what he had become for the locals. Characteristically he responded with the harsh and bristling self-protectiveness that he had learned during his adult years of struggle in New York.

In the elevator of a downtown office building he suddenly found himself face to face with Billy Bauer. Back in the days when things were going bad between himself and Mel, when he was being ostracized because of Mel, and when he was unusually receptive to any rare appeals for his comradeship, Billy had insisted despite the lack of reciprocation that Ralph was his best friend. Billy, a lout who had sat behind him in his high-school home room, had befriended him because he was himself friendless, and because he had sensed in Ralph a vulnerability lacking in all the others. Ralph had had to accept the fat boy's offerings—the Milky Ways, the *Spicy Detectives*, his father's press pass to the pro football games— because to reject them would have thrown on Ralph the ultimate responsibility for Billy's being quite completely alone, embedded in fat and misery. For two long years Billy had clung to him with the obstinacy of a snail fastened to a wall, phoning when he couldn't come (and who else would enter the Land flat behind the pharmacy?), writing when he couldn't phone.

In the elevator Billy, sweat still beading his upper lip, pants still too tight around the belly, squeezed Ralph on the arm. He exuded his horribly familiar mixture of damp armpits and Pinaud hair tonic. His manner was exactly what it had been during their adolescence—at once fawning, jovial, and calculating.

"You're looking good, boy. Better than your picture in the papers. Come back for a cut of that dough, didn't you? I guess it hasn't been as easy as you thought, or you wouldn't have settled down in the old house and taken a job. Well, they all come back sooner or later. It's not such a bad town, you've got to admit. Especially compared with New York. I was there last year—Christ, nobody speaks English there any more."

Ralph was unable to protest even to this slob, whom he thought he had eliminated from his life so long ago, that one ought not mistake appearance for reality, expedience for change of heart. He dared not indulge himself with boasting that he was playing a part, and would be on his way as soon as the accounts were settled. But he did have the learned ability, acquired in the hard years since high school, to be ruthless.

"I've been expecting that you'd give me a ring." Billy Bauer blocked the elevator exit, clutching Ralph's forearm with his gross fingers, grinning hopefully in his idiot innocence. "Wouldn't you and your bride like to get together some night with me and my wife?"

Ralph freed his arm, looked Bauer up and down, and replied deliberately, "I think not."

Lying naked in bed beside Kitty that night, Ralph re-experienced the grandiose satisfaction that had been his at the sight of the frozen fat man, unable even to stammer a reply to Ralph's calculated rebuff. But then, remembering the flush that had crept over his former friend's slowly comprehending features, Ralph could no more sustain the cheap satisfaction than he could disregard the heat which, like Billy Bauer, had appeared as unexpectedly as a creditor demanding payment for a forgotten debt.

With his father's pillow propped behind his head and his hands locked at the nape of his neck, Ralph lay semirecumbent beside his swollen sleeping wife, staring up into the darkness. Kitty had complained about the unseasonable weather, and he had reassured her that it would not last. Then she had turned over, in the pajamas whose buttons she had already reset for greater comfort, assumed the fetal position, and given herself over contentedly to a profound plunge into unconsciousness.

At last he too, thinking of the smell of his mother's lap, warm and fragrant when she rocked him after he had come in freezing from sledding with Mel, felt exhaustion invading his system. He eased himself down silently alongside his wife, in order not to rouse her to the querulous demands of pregnancy. Only then, closing his eyes, did he release his clutch on what passed for reality and allow himself to be transported to other deeper regions.

His dreams were first of four ragged children he had known by name in Pusan, and a toothless crone, somebody's mother, gumming sunflower seeds by the roadside and crooning at him when he dropped PX parcels into her lap. As she tore open a box of Uncle Ben's rice, the kids took wing and flew up into the sky, waving good-by as they disappeared. Then Grandma herself was suddenly a hostess at a faculty-student get-to-gether, her shaggy white hair the only reminder of her previous incarnation. She offered him a plate of Uncle Ben's rice and inquired kindly after his progress as a young man of letters under the G.I. Bill. "I have been liberated from my uniform, just as you have been liberated from yourself," Ralph replied, and walked through the college wall behind her. He scratched his face and hands on the ivy, but it was more than worth the discomfort to find himself in a paradise where he needed neither discharge papers, identity card, nor ticket stub. A city boy, he had no idea where he was, nor even whether he was indoors or out. But he had arrived after much travail at his ultimate goal, that much was sure. The air was filled with fragrance and the faint sound of soft music. Strollers, moving neither languidly nor agitatedly, greeted him as though they knew him and accepted him. The sense of being at once adventurous and at home, discovering a terra incognita and returning to the green fields of childhood, was actually voluptuous. This sensuousness alerted Ralph to a new presence, as a lover will quickly feel the threat of a rival.

Ralph tried to contain himself, much as one waits impatiently for the passage of a presumptuous little cotton wadding of cloud which has the audacity to blot out the sun and, in the sudden chill shadow which follows, can even cause the dark wind to rise sullenly and the paling leaves to shudder violently. But then this shapeless nameless intrusion grew a cloak, as the Lamont Cranston of his boyhood had changed into The Shadow, blotting out light and warmth, making Ralph's paradise dark and horrid. For a moment he was paralyzed with horror, as much at the disappearance of his Eden as at the gloomy Oriental apparition thrusting itself between him and the light, like those earlier Orientals who had swarmed over the 38th parallel, eclipsing the sun for Ralph and the other innocents of his age and company.

If one dream ended, so did both dreams—and if both, then all. The apparition was real, and so was the intent: not only to kill the dreams but to extinguish consciousness as well. Arms extended like an organist, the shadow groped for Ralph's windpipe. An animal sound of fear and outrage welled up in Ralph's throat, as he reared back to avoid the hands, plunged suddenly into a reality more terrifying than a nightmare, more naked than his own body.

The form was upon him in the dark, pressing him down into the damp twisted sheets, panting and grunting over and over, like a wild pig, "Where? Where? Where? Where? Where?"

Without answering Ralph wrenched free and hurled his assailant away, the adrenalin flowing through him like wine.

"Ralph!" Kitty's cry was breathless and frightened. But she was not numbed with terror, and already she was reaching for the bed lamp at her side.

"Leave it off," Ralph grunted, crouching on one knee to ready himself for a renewed attack.

Then the intruder was at him, still faceless, but smelling of beer, sweat, and fury. Ralph gripped hard. A wet T-shirt gave way beneath his fingers. They had each other by the upper arms, rocking and tumbling across the foot of the bed, staggering like a marathon dance team drunk with exhaustion, each supporting the other not from love but from hatred of his partner and of the watching world. Half falling, they swayed across the room in slow motion to the open window, then to the bureau. A loose knob of the top drawer hooked the torn T-shirt; as Ralph lurched back, his assailant's saliva trickling down hot and wet onto his own bare chest like a slow stream of piss, the drawer came along, crashing loudly to the floor.

They were both entangled in the debris of the overturned drawer, their feet catching on Kitty's scarfs, panties, stockings, suffused with Miss Dior perfume. Ralph kicked frantically at the snakelike silks and nylons, but his bare foot skidded on the plastic case of Kitty's abandoned diaphragm and he fell down hard on his behind, his antagonist leaping on top of him like a rapist, both of them enveloped in the characteristic sweetish odor of vaginal cream.

They fell to hugging, fighting to prevent each other's hands from clawing or closing into fists. Clumsy wrestlers both, they rolled over and over on Leo Land's carpet, panting, sweating, unable to release each other—they might have been ardent lovers. Once again they brought up against the bed. Ralph stared up into Kitty's clenched teeth, gleaming even in the darkness. The breath was hissing through her parted lips.

"Now get the light," he muttered.

At once it was burning his eyeballs. Blinking, he made out a bulky rolled-up magazine that Kitty was thrusting at him. It was no real weapon, but he grasped it like a pikestaff and rammed its end with all his force into the spit-flecked squinting face, suddenly as horribly familiar as though it had always been there before him.

"I'll call—"

Ralph slapped Kitty silent with the back of his hand.

"Don't call anybody. You hear?"

Blood beading the bridge of his nose, the invader smashed Kitty's lamp with the flat of his hand and threw himself heavily onto Ralph's back. Ralph tried to roll out from under, but he could not. The only way he could bear the weight without collapsing and being smothered was to hump over on his knees, his hands clutching desperately at the sideboard of the bed frame like a drowning sailor clinging to the gunwale of a half-swamped lifeboat.

"Just tell me," the voice whistled in his ear, almost sobbing, "where—"

"Up your ass!" Ralph cried in fury, releasing his grip and with a quick jerk throwing his hands high above his head, as he straightened his back. The weight fell away and he whirled about, free again. "That's where, you bastard!"

He grabbed up his father's heavy old ceramic ash tray, which Kitty was pressing on him, and brought it down squarely on his attacker's head as it advanced, lowered, bull-like, the features obscured by the straight hair hanging loose, wet, from the dripping forehead. The china shattered in his hand but did not even slow his assailant, whose skull blasted like a ram into Ralph's chest, sending a sudden stab of agony into his lungs. Sick with pain, he raked downward with the shard that remained in his hand.

Whimpering, his assailant staggered back, his hand to his cheek. He lurched through the open door, his naked dirty shins protruding below ragged and oil-stained chinos. Ralph sucked in air and ran after him.

He caught up in the hallway, but the pursuer, now pursued, the left side of his face open and running blood from temple to neck, halted suddenly and turned to confront him. Lips drawn back over his teeth, supporting himself with a hand that smeared blood down the floral wallpaper as it sought a purchase, he flexed his knee and drove it at Ralph's dangling unprotected sex.

Instinctively Ralph cringed, his hands flying to his groin. The other whirled and made for the stairway, racing not down but upward, two steps at a time. He was bound for Ray, either by foreknowledge or by inspiration. Cursing, Ralph struggled up the stairs and on the third-floor landing managed to grasp a flying end of T-shirt. The cotton tore loose in his hand, but his fleeing foe, thrown off balance, tottered forward, the force of his movement carrying him on into the first room at the head of the stairs. Ray was safe from him here, and he from Ray, if only he could be kept in the room, whose single window gave out on a three-story drop.

They began to circle warily, face to face in the feeble moonlight that filtered through the cobwebbed window, Ralph trying to keep the doorway at his back.

This was the room that had been consecrated by Uncle Max for his movie posters and signboards. Here one madness served as excuse for another: only the total stranger could be so naive as to believe that this roomful of Hollywood—which gave you the sensation on entering it of having fallen into a deep smooth-sided well filled with honey instead of water—represented nothing more than a final extravagant extension of Max's collecting mania. The contrary was the case: it was as if here at last that mania served to fill in the emotional blanks in the life of the mad bachelor.

For here, even if the crammed room was the battle site of your fight for life, you could not but be overwhelmed by the shrinelike testaments to youth, to romance, to the myth and mystery of a world populated by the eternally young, the perfectly beautiful, the unwaveringly magnetic, all of them regally amicable and even affectionate.

For Max, With Sincerest Best Wishes From Andrea Leeds, someone had written across Andrea's provocative shoulder. *Fondly Yours, Ann Sheridan,* the Oomph Girl had stamped on her glossy eight by eleven. *Heartiest Greetings,* Lyle Talbot had inscribed over his Adam's apple with a blunt pen. Leo Carillo, Johnny Mack Brown, Sonny Tufts, and their fellow gauchos, halfbacks, and navy officers jostled one another, winking and grinning from the cut-glass frames of their dime-store photos, from the curling covers of defunct fan mags, from the life-size cutouts salvaged from the storerooms of since destroyed movie palaces. Beside them, propped on flimsy wooden frames, the silhouettes of Maria Montez in harem trousers, Alice Faye in black silk stockings and tails, Mary Carlisle in bobby sox, and Lana Turner in sober WAC uniform (blouse stuffed with goodies, though), looked out with limpid-eyed emptiness on the dusty combat. At the far corner, by the window, Deanna Durbin, at once regal and winsome, presided over the slow-motion struggle in her grown-up evening gown and tiara, a Hollywood-teenager version of the Goddess of Justice.

The two men circled before her as if performing a fraternal rite which demanded a blood sacrifice. There was no longer any other motive for this confrontation.

Surrounded by the pantheon of those they had themselves once worshiped, benevolently regarded even by the shades of May Robson and Edna Mae Oliver, they closed, felt each other's hot and furious breath, grappled, staggered, and fell to the barren floor. The dust touched their tongues and, as they slid, blackened along the bare boards, Ralph cried out in pain from the splinters which pierced the flesh of his thighs. Rocking together beneath the window, they toppled Deanna, who came crashing down on their heads. They paused to kick her aside, as soldiers will declare a Christmas truce, and then made for each other again.

Ralph crooked his right arm and jerked the elbow upward into the gaping mouth, gulping air, that mirrored his own. He felt a tooth splinter as it struck his elbow and collided with the bone. But the other, far from relaxing his grip, drove Ralph to the floor once again.

The tendons of his neck stretched and twanging, his eyeballs starting from their sockets, Ralph saw first Kitty's feet, bare and pretty, and then the rest of her, still clad in her pajamas. From the floor, she had a statuesque aspect. What was astonishing—it made Ralph think he was going out of his mind—was that she bore a pitcher over her head in a theatrical attitude mimicking one of the more queenly movie marquee cutouts, Ann Harding or Elissa Landi. But then she moved her arms forward, at first ever so slowly, measuringly, lowering the amphora in a pantomime of grace, and thereafter with power and precision, bringing it down unerringly on the skull of his antagonist, who collapsed inertly on Ralph. Just as Ralph shifted his hips on the creaking floorboards, anxious to ease himself out from under the dead weight, the weight refused to die, but belched with a terrible inhuman sound, and heaved itself together in one final spasm of defiance.

Enraged at this insensate refusal to accept obliteration, Ralph rolled until he could mount the maniac and punch him in the pulpy face as he had never punched anyone, punish him as he had never punished anyone, grabbing him by the hair and pounding that head against the floor until there should be nothing left of it, no reminder, no voice, no belch, no protest, no question, no demand, no teeth, no mouth, no eyes, no nothing nothing nothing . . .

Kitty was tearing at him, trying to restrain his flailing arms. He brushed her aside and kept at it methodically, no longer seeing, only doing, she was scraping and pulling at him to no effect, she was crying in a non-Kitty way, like a small animal trapped under a beam, or was the sound coming from the face beneath his that was becoming a non-face, a no-longer face . . .

He was only vaguely conscious of being lifted as if by a hoist, restrained, dangling, facing away from what was on the floor.

Kitty was not there, but then she was again, wrapping him in a bathrobe and pressing compresses on his face, laving him and protecting him too from the policemen who had finally pulled him loose. There seemed to be two of them, or maybe there were more, he was not sure of anything. He thought he asked them what time it was, but the answer of the older one seemed to bear no relation to his question.

"Prowl car. Lucky for him and you both. Another five minutes and you would of killed him."

"He almost killed me."

"Could be. Hetzel, call in for an ambulance."

The younger cop hurried, stumbling, out of the room.

"Looks like a nut house. All these pictures." Still breathing heavily, the cop was squatting on his fat hams, his thumb on the limp blood-smeared wrist. "Now if this guy broke in, we can book him at the hospital on a felonious assault. On the other hand, if he was a friend, or like that, you may need a lawyer yourself." He sucked saliva through his teeth. "Especially if he dies."

"I can't talk." Ralph wiped blood from his lips. "I'm sick."

"I can talk, Officer," Kitty said. "He entered our bedroom and attacked my husband."

The policeman gazed at her emptily. "What do you mean, attacked? Did your husband catch him going through his pants? A second-story man generally doesn't go looking for trouble. Was he armed?"

"You must let me put my husband to bed and get help for him. After that, I'll gladly go over everything with you."

"The medic on the ambulance will be here in a minute. Now in the meantime. When did he enter? In what manner? What time were you aroused?"

Ralph spat blood into a towel. "My name is Ralph Land. It was my father and my uncle that lived here."

The policeman gazed at him steadily, then glanced about once more at the smiling Hollywood faces. "The ones that collected all the—"

"There's been plenty in the papers. Maybe if there hadn't been so much, he wouldn't have turned up tonight."

"Searching for treasure?"

"Something like that."

"Well, I still got to file my report."

Ralph felt Kitty gathering breath beside him. "It will have to be tomorrow," she said, her voice breaking. "I must call our doctor."

"No, no, no," Ralph mumbled. "Nobody else. You hear? Nobody else."

Kitty ignored him and turned to the policeman.

"I think something happened tonight. I am afraid I've lost my baby." Her hands smoothed out the fabric of the pajamas, outlining the little bulge of the fetus. Her knuckles, Ralph observed with dull surprise, were knotted and trembling, as though it were arthritis that had suddenly affected her. "I have started to bleed. You must let us try to take care of each other until the doctor arrives."

As if in a new dream, this time stolen from Shakespeare, with his strong-willed Lady having gained him a new reprieve after participation in much carnage, Ralph moved in noctambular fashion under Kitty's arm away from the suddenly quiet policeman waiting, like them, for reinforcements, and out of the grotto, stepping over the cracked form of Deanna Durbin and the huddled form beside her that lay snoring horribly in its congealing blood while it dreamed its own broken dreams.

8: KITTY

If kitty had frightened an obstinate cop unnecessarily, she felt no guilt about it. Quite the contrary. She had wisely protected her unborn child, so Solomon Stark had assured her; she had at least temporarily pulled Ralph out of a hole; and she had given herself a badly needed respite.

How good it was to be relieved of the round of responsibilities! She had been drawn into that routine insidiously, like a donkey which is first gently blinkered and then brutally beaten to make it tread a continuous circle. So it was delicious to lie on her back between crisp sheets, to sip ice water through a bent straw, to be served breakfast (no matter how dismal the food), and best of all to be freed from the necessity of making petty decisions. They were the worst; compared to them even the larger decisions—which men made so much noise about but which seemed to her to mature almost spontaneously, growing like flowers once you had planted the seeds and watered them—were simple. Becoming a mother, say, or settling in your mind the nature of your marriage.

Yet this freedom was merely provisional. Even though
Ralph had not yet come to see her or phoned her for that
matter—whether from a compassionate feeling that she should
have a period of absolute tranquillity, from shame at having
involved her brutally in a murderous revelation of his real
temper, or from hatred because she had called in outsiders
against his express injunction—Kitty was perfectly aware that
she had to make new decisions for herself and Ralph. Indeed,
now was precisely the time for calm analysis of the blood that
had flowed from the two antagonists, as well as from her own
womb; yet she preferred to temporize, to enjoy these last
precious hours of luxurious mindless solitude.

Dr. Stark had installed her in a semiprivate room and
promptly put her under sedation. At dawn two attendants had
removed her aged roommate, from whom she had been separated by a screen anyway and who had probably died during
the night. Now the other bed was stripped and bare, and
through the open window (the heat had broken during the
night) came the pleasant muted sounds of the city. Trucks,
delivery wagons, children in a school playground across the
way. A delicious sun warmed the dull green walls of the
high-ceilinged old hospital room.

There was a rap on the door. Before Kitty could speak an
elderly nun entered. Smiling, she shook her head on observing how Kitty was hastening to smooth out the bedclothes.

"Don't disturb yourself, my dear. You have a visitor, but he
can only stay a few minutes. Doctor's orders."

Before Kitty could inquire as to who was coming, the old
nun withdrew. Hastily Kitty combed out her hair. She had
just finished making up her lips, and was blotting them with a
folded piece of hospital tissue, when there was a knock on the
door once again. This time it did not open.

"Come in," Kitty called out.

The stranger who stood before her was heavy-set but sallow, with straight blond hair cut short and square and brushed
upward, which still managed to look too thick about the ears.

He was perhaps thirty-five, his muscles bulging here and there, like a weightlifter (like Ray?), in his plaid summer suit. He wore no tie, but had his open shirt collar folded out over his jacket. He would have looked more comfortable in army fatigues, Kitty thought, or grease-stained coveralls. Gesturing apologetically with his summer straw, he fetched a leatherette card case from his breast pocket and extended it as he approached her bedside. It looked absurdly small in his thick-fingered paw.

"Detective Lieutenant Karpinski," he said, in an unexpectedly high-pitched voice. "Sorry to bother you. I won't take long." For bother, he said bodder. He spoke English as though it was a second language, one that he did not speak at home but had learned, painfully, at school.

"Harold Karpinski," Kitty read aloud, examining the little identity card for a longer time than her caller seemed to like. She was frightened suddenly, irrationally, as one is by the arrival of an unexpected telegram, so she stalled. "The picture doesn't look like you."

"They never do." He retrieved the identity card rather brusquely. "Mrs. Land, I'm sorry the boys in the prowl car gave you a hard time."

"That's what we pay them for, isn't it?"

Her smile had absolutely no effect on the detective, whose fleshy lips were seemingly fixed in a permanent pout. She was reminded a bit of Charles Laughton.

"Please sit down, Mr. Karpinski."

He seated himself at her side, his hands, thumbs pointing toward each other, resting squatly on his muscular hams.

"According to their reports, you were a witness of the fight."

"A participant, too."

Harold Karpinski's solid neck settled a little more heavily into his shoulders. His features, now that the light from the open window struck them obliquely, were so strongly Slavic as to be almost Oriental, the eyes shallow in their sockets and lightly lidded, the cheekbones beneath them jutting bleakly out of an otherwise doughy countenance. Kitty was suddenly reminded terrifyingly of the sweaty panting face of her husband's assailant.

"Then you understand why I'm here."

Kitty's insides began to ache again. "How is he, that man?"

"He'll live." Detective Lieutenant Karpinski smiled, thinly, for the first time. "He got some going-over. With your help."

"I was afraid—"

"Concussion, broken nose, seventeen stitches, two teeth, some hemorrhaging. But he's a tough customer. Almost as tough as your husband."

"It was horrible."

"We're trying to figure out why they fought like that. A second-story man beats it when he's surprised. And a man who finds a housebreaker calls the police. I'd say that if either one had had a firearm, the other one would be dead now." He squinted at her. "Wouldn't you?"

Kitty had no place to flee. She said faintly, "You don't know how much my husband has suffered from all the publicity about his family. He's desperate for privacy, he didn't want the police unless it was absolutely necessary. And then he lost his head, I suppose because he was afraid for me. As for that man, I don't know why he was so aggressive. He was like a cornered animal. But I don't even know his name."

"Marc Lafarge. At least there's a set of prints and a record under that name."

Kitty's laugh rang hysterical in her own ears. "It sounds like a name out of E. Phillips Oppenheim."

Karpinski was not smiling. He stared at her rather dully, uncomprehending.

"A man who used to write books about spies and jewel thieves. That's what Marc Lafarge sounds like."

"Could be. Whatever his right name is, his record isn't strong-arm. Just the same, somebody could have hired him to beat up your husband. Or to attack you."

"But why?"

"That's what we want to know. Maybe you can help."

"Surely all the ridiculous stuff in the papers about hidden wealth, crown jewels, Confederate bonds, was an invitation to housebreakers. It's a wonder it didn't happen before."

"Maybe. But if it was only grab and run, why the violence?"

"I'm sorry, Mr. Karpinski. I can't think of anyone who'd want to hurt me or my husband. It might be better if you talked to him about it."

"The trick is to find him. Nobody answers at your house. So I figured, if he was able to get out of bed himself, he'd be here, with his wife."

Kitty smiled, but said nothing.

"I left word at his office for him to get in touch with me. Would you tell him when you see him? I don't want to have to send out a tracer for him."

"Of course."

"Mrs. Land, did you hear the man entering your house?"

"No."

"Are you a heavy sleeper? Pregnant women don't sleep good."

"This one does." Kitty slipped her hands under the bed-cover in order to conceal their trembling from Karpinski. "What was I supposed to hear?"

"A heavy-set man forcing open a pantry window. Then jumping through it, avoiding a whole bunch of obstacles. All this in a strange house. And they tell me that it's not the neatest house in the world."

"It's not. I assumed he had a flashlight. I only wish Ralph or I had heard him downstairs. It would have saved us a lot of grief."

"You'd have called the police at once?"

"Of course." Avoiding his gaze, Kitty fixed her eyes on the shaving line around his naked Adam's apple. Why didn't he wear a tie? And how had she allowed such a sullen brute of a man to entrap her so easily, only moments after she had asserted that Ralph wanted neither publicity nor police?

"Mrs. Land, don't it strike you funny that he should force a window, push through all that piled-up stuff, climb a flight of stairs, and attack your husband—without waking up the dog?"

Kitty laughed in relief. "Oh, Lieutenant, poor old Sasha isn't good for much, I'm afraid. He's more dead than alive."

Harold Karpinski gazed at her unblinkingly. "That's not the way he behaved when I stopped by your house this morning. He barked from the minute I hit the front steps until I got back into the squad car. Besides, when I rang the bell he jumped up against the inside of the door and started clawing. Some reception. Maybe he's half dead, but I'm glad it wasn't me coming in that window at two A.M."

While she stared at him in fear, he arose, stooping to retrieve his hat from the floor.

"Well," he said, "I'll be on my way. I promised the doctor I wouldn't tire you out."

The glass of ice water rattled in her hand. "I'm afraid," she said. "Lieutenant, I—"

Karpinski chose to misunderstand her. He gestured reassuringly with the straw hat. "I wouldn't worry. Lafarge is in no shape to hurt anybody right now."

I wonder, she thought. But she did not say it aloud.

"And we'll get to the bottom of it soon."

Now she asked what before she had not dared to: "Do you have any theories?"

The detective's peasant face contracted. It was as though she had asked him how he felt about atheism. He said deliberately, in his high-pitched, coarsely-accented voice, "I don't go in for theories. If you stick to the evidence and steer clear of the high-brow stuff, you get results. That's been proved."

He took a step toward the door and stopped, as if he had just thought of something. "Folks like yourself, that don't get in trouble with the law, can't imagine what people will do. I could tell you about some, they'd make your hair stand on end. And it isn't the psychiatrists that crack them, it's the cops that go by the evidence."

"For example?"

"Last year I had one, it was in a new house in Happy Valley. The whole family was practically wiped out. When I got there I found the father dead, the mother dead, the little daughter dead, the young son beat up and bleeding. Fine people, all the neighbors said so. They were scared a maniac was at large, so we had to post a detail around the development.

"When we checked out the case, I saw there was holes in the boy's story. How come all his injuries were on the front? We went over his medical history. A-one. The school psychologists had him down for brilliant, top student, no problems. He never yelled in the neighborhood, never made trouble, went to Sunday School like clockwork. So the highbrows started in with race theories, politics theories. Me, I followed the book. I went over the boy's story with him twenty-six times. The twenty-seventh time, he cracked."

"You mean he did it?"

"On his sixteenth birthday he got his driver's license, like they all do. Then he bought one of those motor scooters on credit. He was afraid he'd get bawled out, so he took down the twelve-gauge, waited till they were all asleep, and while his father was laying on his back with his mouth open he shoved the gun down his throat and pulled the trigger."

Kitty put her hand to her mouth. She wanted to stop him, but she could not speak.

Karpinski went on remorselessly, "The mother woke up with her husband's brains all over the pillow next to her. The boy said she got crazy and he had to knock her down with the butt of the shotgun and then shoot her too, although he hadn't meant to. His little sister came running in and started to cry. He was afraid she'd disturb the neighbors—that's just the way he told it to me—so he shot her too. After he signed a statement, he took me out to the creek to show where he'd thrown the shotgun in, weighted down with an old truck battery.

"As soon as we had the case sewed up, the psychiatrists came up with all kinds of theories to explain it. Maybe they were right. But why didn't they predict what he was going to do before he wiped out his family instead of after? I never heard a dirty word out of that boy's mouth. The only thing was, he didn't have any feelings about it when he described the killings to me. So you go figure it out."

Karpinski demanded rhetorically: "Who knows what goes on inside a family? Just because the neighbors never heard bottles breaking, does that prove anything? I had a case, they were the happiest family on the block. The old man mowed the lawn while the old lady knitted on the porch. Sundays they took their old-maid daughter for a ride. Except that the man and wife didn't talk to each other, not one word, for seven years. They used their daughter for a go-between. 'Tell him to pass the butter,' 'Tell her I won't be home till late.' One night they had a suicide pact, turned on the gas. The daughter saved herself by jumping out the attic window and breaking both legs. She was the one who told me, and I believed her—but not till she proved it. So who knows? I just go by the evidence."

He smiled at her in farewell, a fleshy, unfriendly smile; what made it horrible was that it was obviously the best he could manage. "That way I'm prepared for anything."

After he had gone, Kitty found that she was shivering, as though the sun had gone behind a cloud. But in fact the sun continued to pour through the window, and the piping, unquenched children's voices arose reassuringly from the courtyard. Of one thing Kitty was more certain now than she had ever been: Ralph had not confided in her as she had had the right to expect.

Just the same, he had accepted her pregnancy. That overbalanced everything else—especially since she had violated a pledge. He acknowledged the speck that clung precariously to the wall of her womb. Nothing else really mattered.

She did not resent his staying away from her bedside. In fact, it rather pleased her to lie here quietly and feel his passion—whatever it was, whether love, hatred, or shame—even in his absence. Ralph might plunge ahead blindly without consulting her, but he would always be hers, without being merely a husband, merely stuffy, merely dull. Regardless of what he would do next, Kitty knew now, more than she had known during the highest moments of their shared passion, that she and Ralph were henceforth committed to each other—and as they had never been before. Quite simply, therefore, she would have to do everything humanly possible to help and protect her husband. Fortified and calmed by these reflections, she dozed off, briefly.

When she awoke she discovered to her relief that she had not dreamed at all; what had disturbed her was yet another knock.

"Come in!"

The door was opening already. Dr. Stark padded in as silently as old Sasha.

"I thought I'd find you here," he said. Despite his grin, he looked disheveled and weary, as though he had been up all night. Everything hung on him, more than ever. His pendulous earlobes, his wiener of a nose, the bags under his eyes, the jacket pocket from which his stethoscope dangled.

"Don't ever bank on me," she said. "You never know."

Solomon Stark laughed his dry, old man's laugh. For all his vivacity and sophistication, he was old. "Even if you don't care about yourself, I'm sure you do about the baby."

"I'm a little more wicked than you give me credit for."

The doctor had seated himself on the sole chair, at her side. He regarded the boxy toes of his wrinkled leather shoes for a moment, then folded his arms and stared at her frankly.

"I knew you didn't really think you were losing the baby. But from a medical point of view you were well advised to check in here anyway, after all the excitement and the exercise that you indulged in."

"Do you think Ralph was needlessly brutal?"

"I think he lost his head." The doctor paused, and then added deliberately, "I don't think you did."

"I was frightened," Kitty said in a rush.

"Who wouldn't have been? But you didn't phone the police very fast."

"Ralph told me not to. In fact he knocked the phone out of my hand."

"Later you phoned, though."

"I couldn't stand to see anyone get killed, no matter what Ralph had ordered me not to do."

"Perfectly understandable. As I said, you didn't lose your head. Still, I expect that's what the cops wanted to talk to you about. I gave a detective named Karpinski permission to see you briefly."

"He's already been here. But he never even raised the question of my phoning."

"Sometimes those guys are devious."

"He did want to know how somebody could get in without Sasha's barking his head off."

"A good question. I was struck by the same thought myself. Weren't you?"

Kitty was disconcerted by his gaze and decided against meeting the issue head-on. "How is that man?"

"His mother wouldn't recognize him. He looks like he walked into a meat grinder. Fortunately he can be patched up."

"Ralph was sick about it. That's why he was so insistent that you treat the man."

"Is that why?" the doctor said innocently. "I didn't know he cared."

"Cared about him, or about you?"

"Oh, I'm sure he was upset about the beating he administered. Who wouldn't be, if he had any human feelings at all? Your visitor is going to be weeks having his head grow together again. Also he's got a deviated septum, and he'll need work on the nasal cartilage. No, it was me I was thinking about. Do you really believe Ralph trusts me that much?"

"Why else would we have called you? You're always the first one he thinks of, from my pregnancy to this thing."

"As I recall," the doctor said dryly, "it was you who came to me about being pregnant, before Ralph got the good word."

Kitty felt herself flushing.

"I can think of other reasons why he'd turn to me. For one thing, I'm handy. Ralph never knew the other medical men who used to send their patients' prescriptions to Leo—let's face it, there were damn few anyway. Besides, he feels he can rely on my discretion. Faithful friend of the family and all that. You can always rely on the old boy to keep his mouth shut."

Kitty demanded boldly, "Well, can't we?"

Dr. Stark laughed and patted her leg. "Before strangers, yes. But among ourselves? That's when I shoot my mouth off. After all, some advantages should accrue to the aged. You know, young women like you don't find me so terribly decrepit, but men of Ralph's age think of me as more dead than alive. Curious, isn't it?"

"Not so curious. Women make more fuss about not looking old, but they don't live in terror of death like most men. So they don't judge men simply by their age. But the fact is that Ralph respects you."

"Between you and me, Kitty, I think Ralph would respect me more if psychoanalysis was my profession instead of my reading matter. If I had the diploma . . . As it is, he figures I must be a little phony, and who am I to say I'm not? But you see, after forty years of it you get a little sick of sore throats and fractures. So the great psychiatrists have been a kind of escape valve for me. Maybe I'm getting to such a point of senility that I'd prefer Ralph's feeling sorry for me to his looking down his nose at me."

"But he doesn't! He likes you a great deal."

"That would surprise me enormously." Slyly, he squeezed her knee. "I didn't know that Ralph liked anybody a great deal—not even himself."

Kitty withdrew her leg. "Now you're just being catty, Doctor."

"Who are your friends here in town?"

Kitty looked away. "You know we're in an unusual situation. Ralph's been in no position to make friends. I've met a few of the Happy Valley women—they're pleasant enough."

"Does Ralph know that you know them?"

Stubbornly Kitty compressed her lips. A man like Dr. Stark should know when his probing was taking him too far.

But the doctor did not look at all discomfited by her silence. Rummaging through the pockets of his vest for his thin gold watch, he remarked affably, "And Raymond, how is he faring? Who looks after your secret boarder now that you're temporarily out of commission?"

"I suppose Ralph. Frankly, I'm not particularly worried about Ray's care and feeding. Not after he didn't lift a finger to help us when he might have made the difference between life and death."

"I'm sure he didn't enjoy staying up there through the whole thing. If he's at all the boy I know, it was a very painful experience for him."

"Painful! Compared with what his brother was going through?"

"I'm not just referring to the fact that he saved you from having to explain his presence to the cops, on top of everything else. If you spoke to Ralph about it, I expect he'd agree that Raymond was trying to do what was right, keeping himself uninvolved. For all I know, Ralph may even be feeling grateful. Ask him."

Again Kitty was invaded by fear. She shivered convulsively and withdrew her hand from the doctor, whose fingers had been pressing the pulse at her wrist.

"O.K., O.K.," he said. He plucked at her bedcovers. "Now if you'll just let me have a listen, which is presumably why I'm here . . ."

After a moment, he arose, smiling as he stuffed the stethoscope back into his pocket. "Junior seems to be doing all right, no thanks to any of you. I think it would be wise, though, if you stayed in the hospital a few days just to be on the safe side. I'll leave instructions that you can sit up tomorrow and maybe go into the solarium in the afternoon."

She waited until he had reached the door before she called after him.

"Do me one favor. Tell me where Marc Lafarge is."

The doctor swiveled in surprise, his composed countenance suddenly gone pale. He declined to answer but instead waited expectantly for her to go on.

"I want to make amends. It's the least I can do, considering his condition."

"He's in no condition for fun and games, I warn you."

"There's been enough of that already, hasn't there? I can't hate him, even though he tried to murder Ralph. As you say, Ralph lost his head. But if I can make up for it, in some way, won't you let me?"

"If you'll promise not to start roller-skating around the hospital . . . He's in A-115. That's a flight below you, on the other side of the building. Ring for a nurse's aide, she can deliver messages, or presents—short of arsenic. First you crown him with a vase, then you want to send him flowers. That's hot stuff!"

Pleased with the conceit, he nodded a chuckling farewell as he pulled the door to behind him.

Kitty glanced at her watch to fix the time and picked up the morning paper. She tried conscientiously to focus on the latest military-scientific stuff about the moon and the stars, but her eyes kept returning to an article titled "Violence At The Land Mansion." Breathing slowly and deeply, she read Burgholzer's piece through three more times, surprised at how little the public could understand a situation, when once you knew it yourself from the inside. Finally she permitted herself to check her watch again, and was relieved to see that the ten minutes she had allotted herself had passed. She pressed the buzzer at her side and sat up to await the nurse's aide.

Instead it was the same Sister who had announced the arrival of Harold Karpinski. Her smooth but mannish chins creased tightly above her habit, she demanded Kitty's pleasure.

"Do you know if Dr. Stark is still in the building?"

"You were his last for today, I'm quite sure. In fact I saw him go out to his car. I'm sorry, dear, but short of an emergency, he won't be back before his usual hours tomorrow morning."

"It's all right. I'll see him then, thank you. By the way, Sister, the detective you brought in earlier—"

"Was that man a detective?" The Sister looked at her with sublime innocence.

You know damn well he was, Kitty said to herself. Quickly she repented. Am I getting to be like Ralph, suspecting everybody of everything? But then: Is Ralph really like that, or am I allowing Dr. Stark to sway me against my own husband?

"I was just wondering if he's left the hospital too."

"I showed him out the moment he was through." The Sister smiled and Kitty could see a gold molar halfway back in her mouth. "Doctor said he was only to have ten minutes— I was about to tap on the door when he came out."

"Thank you so much."

Puzzled and disappointed, the Sister retreated. The moment she had closed the door, Kitty swung her legs to the floor, stepped into her slippers, and reached for her dressing gown.

She was so wobbly that she had to grab hold of the foot

of the bed until the dizziness subsided. Don't panic, she urged herself, it's nothing but nervous tension. If it had really been the baby, I simply wouldn't be doing this, it would be unnatural. But supposing something *was* wrong? Supposing Dr. Stark had been trying to put it to her as gently as possible? Maybe that was really why he wanted her to stay on for several more days?

Nonsense, she said to herself, nonsense; fear always invents excuses not to do what has to be done. If the doctor had his motives for immobilizing her, she had hers for moving ahead. For each of them everything started with Ralph and the baby, but for her the two were inextricably commingled, in her blood as in her conscious concern for them, the two Lands who were utterly dependent upon her. She pulled open the door decisively and peered up and down the hall.

The fat Sister was just stepping into an elevator. No one else was in sight. Kitty closed the door quickly behind her and walked unhesitatingly in the opposite direction. She gained the end of the corridor unremarked, but at the head of the stairway all but bumped into a young intern, who pivoted smartly on his rubber-soled white shoes to appraise her, fortunately quite incuriously.

On the floor below it took some wandering about—she dared not ask anyone or even look uncertain—before she could find Section A. The duty nurse at the entrance was busy at her switchboard and did not notice her. But a uniformed policeman stood at the desk beside the nurse. Kitty could feel his eyes on her back all the way down the corridor until she reached 115 and put her hand to the knob. Even as she strolled on past him with false casualness, she remembered that he was the young one, Hetzel, who had been hustled out to summon the ambulance.

Then he called out to her, "Hey, you can't go in there."

She smiled at him, brilliantly. "Don't you remember me?" She reassured him. "I'm Mrs. Land. Dr. Stark said I might see him for a few minutes."

While he hesitated she pushed open the door, calling over her shoulder, "I'll be out before you can say boo."

At that moment two men came out of the toilet between her and the policeman. They had been having a quick smoke —the blue haze still curled over their shoulders—but they both stiffened when they saw her.

"Wait up, there's no visitors allowed."

"But it's Mrs. Land. Ed Burgholzer, Mrs. Land." The smaller one smiled a terrible smile, as obligatory and anticipatory as Karpinski's. "We'll wait right here for you."

Quickly Kitty squeezed the door shut behind her. She turned, leaning against it, panting a little, and faced the man lying in the bed.

He was prone, his head wedged like a raw hamburger between two doughy sandbags. A tube, taped to his mouth, brought nourishment directly to his stomach from a bottle clipped to a stand. His forehead bulged like that of a fetus; his skull was strapped, but had not been shaved. His eyes were Slavic, as she had remembered them, almost as blue as Raymond's, but shallow and slanting like Harold Karpinski's. His blond hair, leaking here and there from the bandage, appeared still damp and shaggy. Oh yes, I remember that too, Kitty said to herself. The eyes showed no more emotion than hers, neither surprise nor fear, as they gazed up at her patiently.

"Do you recognize me?" she asked. "I'm Ralph's wife Kitty. I've come to settle up."

9: MEL

Roused by the soft thump of rubber meeting rubber, the clean connection of iron clasping iron as his door clicked closed, he rolled his eyes as far as he could, but was still unable to see even so much as the feet of his visitor until she had advanced to the middle of the room. There she hesitated for a moment, waiting either to be invited to take the only chair, or to give him a chance, immobilized as he was, to look her over before she stated her business.

"Excuse me for not getting up," he said. His voice was at once rusty and muffled. Well, this was virtually the first occasion he had had to use it since she had crowned him with the pitcher. "I'm not used to entertaining with a tube in my stomach. And they've got my head wedged in between these two things like lox in a bagel. Thanks to you."

"I'm here to apologize."

"Not to finish me off?"

She shook her head seriously, but smiled then, and began to laugh, low in her throat.

Mel stared at her. Yes, he had recognized her at once, as if she had been someone he had known, or even slept with. But in a different guise. Three different guises. It was confusing. His head ached. He motioned her to the chair.

She sat with her hands folded composedly in her lap, just beneath the thickness of her pregnancy, looking not demure but, rather, maternal and statuesque. The folds of her dressing gown concealed the close outline of her figure as if they had been sculpted. But her eyes, bluer than his, shone with a charitable humor. She might have been some distant relative of the different aspects of her that he had already encountered in the dark of night. An older sister, perhaps, of the disheveled barefooted young woman in the rumpled blue pajamas, her nostrils flaring and her blond hair tumbled about her forehead, who had thrust into the bloody hands of her naked husband a whole junkyard of weapons with which to belabor him. Not an older sister, though, more like a mother to the strange young blonde he had encountered for the first time, sprawled in sated sleep alongside Ralph, so black and hairy and satisfied in his own sexual sweat that Mel had been overcome with rage and had flung himself upon him with insensate fury.

Peering between his outspread feet at this poised mother-to-be, who for all he knew held in the folds of her robe a butcher knife ready to plunge into his gut, Mel was willing to grant her handsomeness as well as controlled intelligence, if not erotic appeal in the mind of someone she had helped to beat into senselessness. But then, he thought as he gazed into her smiling, patiently attentive eyes, you couldn't hold that against her. It was just funny that after all those months of institutional saltpeter, he had returned to the highly seasoned world of women only long enough to be bashed over the head by one and carted off to still another institution.

He laughed, and instantly regretted it, as a sharp sinoidal stab cut through the strange unknown space behind his eyes. He pressed his hand to his nose, and to the tube.

"I hope it only hurts when you laugh."

"Ever try laughing with a tube down your throat?"

"Why start now?"

"I was thinking that you don't look very sexy. Isn't that comical enough, considering you practically killed me?"

"At this moment," she replied, "you don't look like Valentino yourself. Since that's partly my doing, I've come to apologize."

"The point is that I don't look like a Land. That's why you're here, isn't it? Because nobody knows yet, except for you and Ralph? And maybe Doc Stark? So never mind the apology crap."

"I'm not here stooging for Ralph. He doesn't even know that I know who you are."

"Prove it."

But the door opened again before she could reply. Mel turned his neck as much as possible until he could make out a pair of sturdy white-stockinged legs. They belonged to the little Italian student nurse who had been in and out ever since he had come to.

"I'm sorry, there can be no visitors here." She was so stern that it was obvious she was scared. "You'll have to leave, Mrs. Land."

Kitty arose with infinite leisureliness and began to rummage in the pockets of her dressing gown. She might have been hunting for a handkerchief, but Mel would not have put it past her to try to slip a bill to the nurse.

He said hastily, "Give us ten minutes, kid."

"I can't. It's not me. It's orders. You're not to see anybody, not even—" she stopped short, in confusion.

"The cops, you mean. It's all right, you can say it."

"I meant the reporters, too, that are hanging around the corridor."

"Don't get your bowels in an uproar. I promise I'll tell you all about them later on. Now run along and leave me alone with the nice lady that beat me up."

"I just don't have the authority—"

"But Dr. Stark does, doesn't he?" asked Kitty.

"Well, yes. He was the one who told the detective he'd have to wait before questioning you."

"He's my doctor also, Nurse. And he told me less than ten minutes ago that I might visit here. Check with him and verify it."

"But he's left the hospital."

"Oh Christ, don't be so square," Mel grumbled. "Go ring his office. Go ahead."

As the door closed behind the reluctant nurse, Kitty was already drawing her chair to his bedside. "So you do want to talk."

"You started it," he said hoarsely. "You got an offer, or do I unload?"

"Unload what?"

All right, he thought, you asked for it. "I'm going to file assault and battery charges. I was no burglar. Ralph attacked me in a house where I've got as much right to be as he does. Now toddle on home and watch him turn purple."

"Why do you hate him so?" She was leaning forward, hands clasped under her chin, as though she were listening to a lecturer.

Mel shifted the tube. "You better give me your proposition. The nurse or the cops will be breaking this up soon."

"I'm here to see that Ralph doesn't ruin his life over you. He's sick ashamed over what happened. He can't face you. He can't even face me. He hasn't been here since Dr. Stark signed me in. You can check on that. And remember, you're going to need me more than I need you."

Once again he found himself drawn, tempted to take her at her word, to tell her his sad story. A nice plump shoulder to weep on. That was fine for Ralph, the social-climbing sellout artist, it was just what he had been after, all these years. Not for me, Mel swore to himself, no band-aids for battle wounds. Supposing what she said was true? She'd fight

like a wildcat for her baby, if not for Ralph. That alone put
her on the wrong side.

"Whatever I can do," she pressed on, "to bring this crazy
business between you two to an end—"

"First, you can stop claiming he hasn't told you who I
am."

"But he hasn't."

"Balls."

"You're in enough trouble," she said severely, "without
threatening suits. You ought to be giving thanks that I haven't
lost my baby. Now start talking sense."

"All right, where's Ray?"

She blinked. "He's in hiding."

"I think he's someplace right in that house."

"It's his own idea, not Ralph's."

"Tell Ralph I want to see Ray. As soon as possible."

"That's not up to me. Or Ralph."

"Are you going to deliver my message or not?"

"I said I'd do anything I could. But Ralph doesn't control
Ray. In a sense it's the other way around."

"You still think, don't you," he said, his tongue sliding
around the tube, "that you're going to walk off with Uncle
Max's dough."

She frowned, furious, and her eyebrows came together over
the bridge of her nose. Married only months and already she
had Ralph's mannerisms. Fascinated, he raised himself on his
elbows as high as he could and gazed at the newest member
of his family. The grimace gave you a hint of what she would
look like in her middle years: her face etched with the
years of struggle to guard those whom she loved. She must
have been a knockout when she was a girl, people would
say.

"I couldn't care less about the Land money," she was saying, in a voice that had become a little hoarse, like his own.
She added passionately, "Ralph did. He cared. Now he knows
better, but he's so ashamed the knowledge is killing him."

She fixed him with her handsome eyes. "I asked you before, why do you hate him so much?"

His head was beginning to ring. He pointed shakily at the glass on the night table. "Let me have some ice water. You're giving me another headache."

"We've got to break the circle. The money is an excuse for the hate. Nothing more."

Mel passed the back of his hand across his cracked lips, touching his cheekbones gingerly, then rubbed his bare biceps, where the faded tattoo of a dragon, foolish product of his fire-breathing youth, was roughened by goose pimples on flesh still white as a skinned fish from the months of confinement.

"Ralph is struggling in his mind to confront you as a human being. Not just as the reason for his troubles. As a brother. If only you would too!"

"I know him better than you. He's always been desperate for respectability."

"And you were always desperate to be an outlaw. Isn't it time you both got over it?"

"Got over it? When he went and married you in order to borrow respectability?"

"What a lousy rotten thing to say."

"He was buying time. He had to be a solid citizen while he was getting his hands on the Land money."

Now he had broken through. Her nails, he observed with interest, were digging into her palms. She leaned forward, disregarding her robe as it fell open at the bosom, and whispered in a rage, "He was in love with me. What would you know about love?"

"I loved him when we were kids. Did he ever tell you that?"

She stared at him in astonishment, her face suffused with fresh blood. At the base of her throat a pulse tapped, filling and emptying the hollow. "He told me other things about you. Never that."

"Why do you suppose he hates me? I protected him at the Settlement House because he was younger, he didn't know the score. It was always the two of us—until I found out that he was willing to sell his own brother down the river. He talked big about revolting, but in the end he was the biggest Babbitt of all. You want him? You're welcome to him. I've had no use for him ever since he stood and watched while I got the shit kicked out of me."

She was no longer looking at him. She managed to mutter defiantly, "What do you mean, watched? It's typical of you to use a word like that."

"Ralph has snowed you, hasn't he? This is what really happened.

"I'm backed into a blind alley. Three dagos are trying to cool me. I'm bent over double to protect my crotch from their cleats, my hands are on my head to protect my ears from the knucks on their fists, my arms are across my face, my spine is grinding the mortar out of the brick wall behind me. I hear another noise, I squint out of the corner of my eye. It's Ralph, with a sack of handbills over his shoulder.

"Help me, kid, for God's sake, I call out. He's big for his age, all he has to do is throw his sack at them and come in swinging. They're cowards, the dagos. But Ralph stands with his mouth hanging open, you'd think he was watching his sister putting out, and then he takes off. I'll get Pops, he yells over his shoulder, or maybe I'll get cops. What difference does it make? He left them to finish me off.

"When I crawled home that night, so banged up I couldn't lie down—I was hemorrhaging through my ass for two days—I found Ralph sitting at the dining-room table, calmly doing his algebra. The miserable creep, I grabbed him by the neck. I said, You let a bunch of hoods work me over so you could get back and do your homework? I could have drowned in my own blood, it's your blood too, did you ever think of that? I'm not proud of it, he said, and ducked his head back into his book.

"That was the kid I'd protected. That's your husband, the man that's got me sandbagged here."

Ralph's wife had gone very pale during this recital. Where does all that tide of blood flow, Mel asked himself, to the brain, or the belly? Or maybe to the new baby?

In any case she was not about to give up, much less change sides. She said coldly, "This time I was there. You were the instigator, you were the aggressor, you were the attacker."

"Maybe I wanted vengeance, mostly I wanted information. But Ralph? He had murder in his heart, and you know it. That's why you're here."

"The vengeance, that's what gets me. You bitch a lot about Ralph. Considering that you just had your face sewed up, and you've still got a glass tube in your esophagus, there's no stopping you. But where did you earn the self-righteousness?"

"If it makes you gag you can always shove off." Mel put his hand to his eyes to blot her out. "In fact I wish you would."

"Not so fast. I'm not going to have Ralph tormented for the rest of his life simply because he didn't mix into one of your gang wars when you were kids."

"That was only an example. Who is entitled to the loot, Ralph or me? Who made the dough? My mother, the old-maid schoolteacher? My old man, who couldn't even make change from the register? If it hadn't been for Max, there wouldn't be any estate for Ralph and me to be fighting about. And I was Max's boy. Not Ralph."

To this Kitty made no reply.

"It was Max who looted his old man's till in the first place for the passage money to the States. Did you know that?"

Kitty shook her head. "Their father never got here."

"I suppose Ralph blames it on Grandpa marrying again, while the boys were struggling to get started."

"It wasn't Ralph who told me, it was Dr. Stark."

"They got started by Max helping himself to the old man's

dough. It was Max who made the decision to shove on past Rivington Street. It was Max who made the decision for pharmacy school."

His throat felt as though he were still swallowing blood, but he could not stop. "When Max and Leo went to work for the post office, it was my old man who took the inside job sorting mail, but it was Max who went off with the heavy horsehide pouch on his back. It was Max who was willing to buck that mean icy wind off the lake. You know why?" He was falling into the very trap, trying to make her understand, trying to convert an enemy into an ally, against which he had been trying to stay alert. Nevertheless he went on. "He told me himself. It was to learn the city, and the real-estate market. It was to find where to open a drugstore, at a time when he and my old man were living on Silvercup bread and peanut butter.

"It was always Max who took the initiative, from the time they both were kids. It's easy enough for the newspaper writers, your husband, all the Rotarians, to say that Max turned prick after he had made his pile. But he was the one who made the pile. The difference between them and me is that they're hypocrites and I'm not."

"You're still satisfied with yourself, after all the beatings you've taken."

Kitty said this wonderingly. In a way that made it all the more cutting.

If he was more entitled to the old man's loot than those who hated Max or were ashamed of him, by the same token he—*not Ralph*—had been the one most tormented by Max's stepping on his mother and father. Instead of them teaching me, he thought, I tried to demonstrate to my parents not by precept but by practice, by conning, looting, lifting, and hooking, what really lay below their life, to spade up the manure in which it was rooted. And to reveal to them what was going to happen to us all, even to little Ray, if they didn't stand up to that mad old man who trotted around town after his rents with his crazy eager laugh and his falsely forbidding hound at his heels.

"My mother knew the score. But she was too weak to go back to the schoolroom she'd left for that great catch, Leo Land. She was so grateful for being married that she had no spirit left.

"I know how Ralph has taught you to think of her. A character, pining away, going into a decline, because her oldest son, the slant-eyed wild one, had hit the road. What crap! She knew me. When I left she knew I intended it as a last warning, the only kind I could give, that unless she cleared out too she would bring worse on the boys who remained.

"She couldn't clear out, so she paid the price. Whom could she turn to? Her mother the overstuffed widow, all tits and no milk, with whom she had been living like two spinsters, until Dr. Stark came along with Leo Land? But Grandma Kadin had already gone and died in an apoplectic rage at Jenny's having left her for a spooky pair. Then who, her only relatives, the female cousins? But they were turds, the two of them. They washed their hands of her, after she went from decent schoolteaching to raising a crank's brats in a moldy flat. Her husband, maybe? But poor old Leo had long since burned out.

"Naturally she gave up without a fight and let herself die. She must have known what was in store for your Ralph, who was already a Sunday morning fiddler and a Monday morning cheat. And for little Ray too. If anything brought her down besides what Dr. Stark wrote on her death certificate, it was that she couldn't face the future for Ray.

"See what a laugh it is, Max's final joke, that the most hopeless son should be the one to pick up all the marbles? The one that your husband the hypocrite plays big brother for?"

It was so quiet that he could hear the pulse in his temple thumping against the sandbag.

"Ralph has never been a hypocrite with me."

"Has he told you what I just told you?"

"You're a fool if you expect his version to be the same as yours."

"That's not what gripes me. It's his gall in claiming Max's dough. Everything Max did was beneath him. He was too busy sawing away at his fiddle and bucking for the Honor Roll to give us a hand."

"What do you mean, us?"

"I was saving string and bottles for Uncle Max before I was out of kindergarten. By the time I was eight I was covering the city, picking up empty cigarette packs for him. I'd start at seven on a Sunday morning, the best time because everyone'd been out the night before and the sweepers hadn't cleaned up after them yet."

"What good were cigarette packages?"

"Tin foil. I worked all the streets with the Indian names. Mohawk, Chippewa, Niagara, Seneca, Genesee, Iroquois, Delaware, Ottawa, Algonquin. I'd stop in Agassiz Park for a hot dog and strip down the packs and smooth out the tin-foil sheets. Max had a ball of silver foil out behind the drugstore as big as an Italian cheese, hanging on a cord. It must have been worth something, but the crazy bastard liked the look of it too much to sell it. And Ralph? You'd know what I mean by hypocrisy if you'd seen the look on his face every time I picked up a cigarette pack stuck in a sewer drain. The shame of it, the shame of it."

"If you tried to understand that he was different, instead of sneering—"

"You didn't listen. I still loved him then, I covered up for him with Uncle Max. When I got bigger, Max used to take me along to collect his rents. Not Ralph. Me. By then Max was getting scared to go through the bad neighborhoods with dough in his pockets. It never bothered me, I went any place, that was one of my assets. But one day he decided that he needed protection, so he went to the pound and bought Sasha for a buck and a half, plus license. Then he and I and Sasha would go out together, rent-hunting. There were even times when we tried to beat each other out, to see who'd collect first, sometimes on different floors in the same tenement."

"A very peculiar relationship." Kitty spoke coldly. She was pulling herself together.

"That's exactly it. I knew him for what he was, he knew that I knew, and we got a bang out of each other—to a point. He realized that when I cut out, it was partly because I had to get loose from him. But what makes you think I'll hold still while Ralph does me out of Max's money?"

"I don't recall that Max Land left you a dime."

"Can't you see why he left it all to his brother? Don't play dumb." His head ticked like a bomb, the tube was like a sausage in his mouth, and his throat was parched again, but he dared not break off to ask her for more water. "Not only did Max have to cover his brother, my father had to cover Ray. But I know what my father intended, and I know what Max intended."

"What a pity no one will believe you."

"Don't bet on that. There's still such a thing as evidence, baby."

Weak and stinking as he felt, it gave him genuine pleasure to see her face go blank and guarded.

Before she could reply, the door had opened again. The little black-haired nurse with the student cap. Her voice was startlingly high and clear, almost childlike, after Kitty's.

"Mrs. Land, you're going to have to leave at once."

"And none too soon," Mel said, following with his eyes the lower portion of Kitty's figure as it made for the door.

"You've been very considerate," she was saying to the nurse. "I realize I've taken advantage. Are the reporters still there?"

"The policeman sent them away." The student nurse added tensely, almost in tears, "Please go now. Please. I'll get in awful trouble if you don't."

Kitty turned to address Mel. "If we let this go on any longer, it won't be just you and Ralph who will be at war. You'll drag down the whole—"

"If you're worried about the whole human race, you can't be all bad. I look forward to meeting you some day with your clothes on." Gratified at seeing her turn red, he concluded, "Don't forget to deliver my message."

But would she? Caught between blowing his horn and playing softer violin music than Ralph, he had produced for her a jumble of sounds that could have had almost any effect. If she didn't tell Ray, or at least Ralph, there was no way for him to get at them short of staggering out of here on his own.

Ray was still the key. He would have to be shown that Papa had willed everything to him because he feared for him, helpless as a guppy, and hoped that the responsibility of parceling out the estate would increase his self-reliance.

To cut Ralph down to size would be worth almost any gamble, bigger than the one he had already lost with Ralph, or the one he had just taken with Ralph's wife, and probably lost.

What could those two know? As far as they were concerned he was an outlaw; he wanted to overturn everything they had been painfully building after their own little rebellion; he refused to abide by Ralph's rules, according to which people lived together in hypocritical respect. No matter how much they apologized, for them he would remain a psychopath who had all but murdered his mother and would have further dishonored the family if he hadn't mocked at it by spurning its very name.

"What's your name?" he muttered to the little nurse, who was hovering over him gently, gently moving him to ease the soreness.

"Leone."

"Leonie what?"

"No, that's my last name. Laura Leone. Comfortable now?"

"Considering that people have been jumping up and down on my face. Take this goddamn tube out of my head, will you, Laura?"

"It comes out after the noon feeding. Isn't that good news?"

"Don't baby me. What about the real news, can I see the papers?"

"Sorry." Then she relented. "Don't blame me. I just work here."

She had an open face. It wasn't just professionally kind— she couldn't have seen too many people die so far, or even suffer. And yet she wasn't just another kid. Her violet eyes were young, but there were shadows under them. On her own she had already suffered, in some way, of that Mel was sure. He began to wonder.

"What's the matter," he demanded, "is that Polack cop still hanging around?"

"After he couldn't get in here, he went to see Mrs. Land. Then he left."

"At least you know who I'm talking about."

She flushed, then began to bustle. "I don't mean to seem nosy."

"It's only natural, I'm in the papers, I'm a crook and all the rest. Doesn't that make you nervous?"

The girl regarded him frankly. "You're in no condition to make trouble, for me or for anyone else."

"Never bet on that, Laura. You have no idea how hard up I am. It's been a long long time."

She did not color at this, or even become annoyed. Instead she took it straight. "You must have had it rough."

Touched, he mumbled, "By and large I've asked for it . . . If it wasn't for these cement earphones I'd be grabbing for you. You're a sight for sore eyes."

The girl hesitated, then spoke nervously, rapidly. "They're going to ask for an indictment as soon as you can be released to police custody."

"I'll beat the rap, Laura. In fact with your help I can do even better than that."

Amused, she crossed her arms over the crackling breast of her uniform and showed him her small irregular teeth, the canines squeezed like a kid's over the molars. No wonder she hesitated to smile. What a number she would be if her teeth were fixed! She was a giving girl.

He pressed on. "I'm out of commission for the time being. But I need a friend. I need help. I need someone I can trust."

"You need a good lawyer."

"Don't make jokes. I'm asking you something. What do you say, kid?"

She replied, consideringly, in her high girlish voice, "I took an oath. I'll take another when I graduate. You can't even imagine what that means to me. I won't jeopardize it just because I feel sorry for one patient."

"But feeling sorry is progress." He said quickly, "Now listen to me, Laura. I'm not going to ask you to do one thing that would violate your oath. If you're not supposed to pull out the tube from my insides, don't. If you're not supposed to give me a newspaper, don't. All I want is for you to deliver a message for me."

"In the hospital?"

"No. Just listen. I can't telephone. I can't go myself. I'm so cross-eyed I can't write a note, even if somebody'd give me pencil and paper. So it's got to be you."

"I don't go off duty until four-thirty." She added hastily, "I mean—" but it was too late.

Mel said jubilantly, "It's the Land house. I know it's far, but there are buses. It's where we had the fight, you know?"

The young nurse gave him an odd sidewise glance that he could not interpret. "I know it all right. I've known it for years. It stands kitty-corner from the shopping center of Happy Valley."

"Exactly. Now if you can go there as soon as you get off

duty . . . The person to see is Mr. Land himself, nobody but Mr. Land. Capeesh?"

Looking hard into her eyes, which were enlarged in the pupil and fixed on him unblinkingly as if she were an actress and he her director, he thought delightedly, She isn't a stranger any more, I've done it, the old Oriental magic still works!

Still staring at him, she nodded.

"Then you give him this message: If he doesn't produce Ray at once, I'll tell them who I am."

"If he doesn't produce Ray at once, you'll tell them who you are."

"Right, right, right! Don't change a word, or you'll get mixed up and you'll mix him up."

"But it doesn't make sense."

"Let me worry about that, O.K.?" When she did not reply he repeated, "O.K.?"

At last she said weakly, "I must be crazy."

"You're one of the few uncrazy ones, that's what you are." With all the strength he could summon he pulled at her wrist, until she had to sit beside him if she did not want to fall on top of him. "Anyone else would have refused, or tried to find out what it meant, or said, Why not telephone? You renew my faith, kid. What am I to you besides a beat-up bum and a jailbird?"

"For one thing, you're persuasive." She tugged gently until he had released his grip so that she could arise. "Besides, the Land house isn't all that far. It's practically on the way to my house."

"I must look even worse than I feel."

"Why do you say that?"

"For you to feel so sorry for me."

"But I'm not that sorry for you. You'll heal up all right. And it isn't as if this was the first time you've been in trouble. It's just that I think everybody ought to get an even break."

"Just that?"

Self-contained again, Laura Leone nodded and laughed a little, as she walked to the door bearing his urinal, nicely napkined, like a precious amphora. Observed from the back, her calves, efficient and serviceable as they were in their snug white nylons, were slightly bowed. Peasant stock. Many generations of women with too much pasta and too many burdens. Carry the jar on your head, he wanted to call after her, it'll be more natural.

Instead he repeated hoarsely, "Don't change a word, you'll only confuse him. Say it again to yourself on the way. I'll be waiting here. I won't go away."

Her laugh floated over her shoulder and ended with the closing of the door. So did everything else about her. Twenty seconds away, and already he couldn't remember exactly what she smelled like or looked like. No, what was paining him was not the long months of deprivation.

It was, rather, that there was no single human being to whom you could really say everything, not even yourself. The price of bachelorhood? More likely a portion of the grief every human being had to expect, after his parents had conceived him without being able to conceive of his reality, and the hired midwife, their impersonal agent, had dragged him, reluctant, into the world.

His head rang from talking so much with those two women. But how little he had told them! Ralph's wife's amends supposedly stemmed from sympathy as well as from fear. Yet he had come closer to the quick of it, and in a shorter time, with the little nurse.

But even with Laura Leone he hadn't ventured beyond the clearing at the edge of the jungle because, wild as were the chances he took with himself, he didn't dare take them with anyone else. Such were the cautions that thirty years of disappointments imposed on you, even at the hands of those presumably of your bent or your blood. How could he be sure that Kitty wasn't working both ends? Or that Laura wasn't

working for the enemy, the Polish cop? The world was jammed
to overflowing with self-seekers and double agents. Everybody's secret heart, when you saw inside it, yearned to bring
you down. Far from being exceptions, women proved the
rule, especially when they were sold on the fiction that their
behavior was patriotic, kindly, noble. And cops—cops were
capable of anything.

It was inevitable that Karpinski would discover very soon
who he was. Maybe he knew already and was holding off for
his own reasons. In any case he'd be bound to make his
move soon. So would Ralph.

Shifting slowly and painfully onto the other haunch, feeling
all down his side the hurt that Ralph had inflicted on him, he
turned again to confront the brother he once had loved. It was
Ralph who had drawn him back to the scene of the new crime,
breaching his parole the moment he was able, after reading
the new myth of the missing will.

To this very minute Ralph was living in his cheaply tailored
lie, filling his wife with babies and with fairy tales of re-
pentance and amends, denying the truth, feeding her a
faked-up version of the Lands' history, with himself as the
responsible revolutionist and his brother as the guilty sub-
verter.

The simmering hatred rose yet again in Mel's throat like
water coming to a rapid boil. Remembering now how he had
come upon Ralph naked in their father's bed, lolling with his
blond wife on the lonely old bastard's dream-soaked mattress,
Mel had to remind himself that the rage which had overcome
him then had not been simply hateful envy of his brother's
sexual prosperity.

And in reality he had wanted to find Ray no more than
he desired Max's loot. Both were only ostensible goals, excuses for outrage, extensions of the self-deception that Ralph
practiced so habitually that he had become incapable of
honesty, like a cellmate who confessed that during an earlier
imprisonment he had gone to bed so long with pictures

of naked girls that upon his release he had been incompetent, even incurious, when confronted with a living girl.

What was the honest living actuality that he was determined to confront? This he could not define. But it was worth staying alive to discover it.

Exhausted, he lay back on the sheet that Laura had smoothed for him and fell into a dreamless sleep.

10: LAURA

ALL THE WAY OUT to the Land house, Laura had the feeling that people were staring at her. Old workingmen peering over their *Polish Dailies*, waddling wives carrying live ducks and white cauliflowers in shopping bags, little girls licking lollipops, jacketed repairmen toting gray tool kits all seemed to be sneaking glances her way, first on the platform in front of the hospital and aboard the bus, then while she waited, transfer in hand, for the second bus, and finally on the last long ride to Happy Valley. She was startled to realize that she had never felt so uneasy before, never, not even during all the bleak joyless trips she used to make to Happy Valley on a far more conspicuous errand.

It would be embarrassing to be recognized by those who would remember her as she used to be, sacrificial and glumly determined. What would they think of her now, in this new incarnation, self-conscious and more conspicuous than before? For she had not taken the time to change out of her uniform, she had simply unpinned her student nurse's cap and tossed a cardigan over her shoulders, not even slipping her arms into it, merely buttoning the top so that the breeze would not blow it off her back.

It wasn't as if she was doing anything even ethically reprehensible. She was just stopping off for a minute. She might have been bringing a patient one last glass of ice water, before continuing on home to her parents. At first she had been a little excited at the idea of attending a patient written up in all the papers, but that was hardly why she had agreed to run his errand. It hadn't taken her long to realize that he was no more an inherently criminal type than was anyone else. He was a man, a human being, vulnerable, variable, desperately hoping to prosper.

Laura knew now that this was what had drawn her to nursing. People who understood nothing about it, or about the practice of medicine, usually had the thing completely inside out. They had the notion that caring for the ill must turn you into a cynic. They thought that when you became involved with bodily dysfunctions, patients had to shrink to ciphers, or at best to file numbers, case histories, charts, graphs. They conceived of the shaving of vulvas, the extraction of urine, the removal of feces, the laving of bedsores, and the rubbing of reddened rectums as degrading to the attendant and dehumanizing to the attended. How foolish! Every day Laura understood a little better how the confronting of pain, nakedness, birth, death, tightened the bonds of your human connection.

Never before had people been so sharply distinguishable, so appealingly unique, as when she moved among them doing all the little drudgeries demanded of her. Not only was this true of the ill-smelling old women whose pustules she anointed and the incontinent old men whom she shaved and cajoled, each become a part of her life, her being, her own singularity, as they smiled, shuddered, wept silently, or touched their finger tips to her finger tips in gratitude; but her comrades too, and her superiors, the head nurses, and even the Olym-

pian doctors, bloomed for her like flowers that she could not
only see but smell and touch too.

She was happy. She was happy even when she cried in her
room from weariness, from looking hopelessly at death, and
from the humiliation of being bawled out before the others
by a heartless older woman, as though she were a child who
had wet her pants or stolen penny candy. She had tried to
explain to her father and mother—no luck, they didn't get it—
how it was more than worth all the misery and pettiness just
for the opportunity to be in the same sickroom with someone
like Dr. Stark. To see him approach a fevered child, calming
frightened eyes with his gentle assurance, radiating sympathy
for the suffering that he probed with his infinitely experienced,
immaculate fingers, was for Laura a revelation of the religious
experience that had never been vouchsafed to her through
works or through dogma, despite her adolescent years of
straining and her mother's endless assurances. So this errand
was simply an extension of what she defined as duty.

To deliver the message was no more than to hold Dr.
Stark's hat and coat. (Maybe a little more. She hadn't said
so to the patient, but there had been a maddening poise about
Mrs. Land. The idea of conveying word to Mr. Land unbe-
knownst to his wife had given her a shameful thrill.)

And yet . . . Was it because of the house, then, and not
because of Mrs. Land or the banged-up patient, that she was
so nervous?

How many times had she stood here in baking sun and
pelting rain on the shopping center blacktop, her eyes fixed
on the looming anachronism that resisted the grunt and push
of the bulldozers only through some strange internal stubbornness? Seeing its windows dusty and uncurtained, the broken
panes covered with the wrenched-off ends of packing boxes,
its clapboard siding, curling shakes and weather-beaten
dadoes too bleached and furrowed for any more paint, its
porch billowing here and sagging there like a blowzy, un-
corseted old lady, its lawn become a nesting place for moles

and a bed for dandelions, the track of its carriage drive as cracked and crumbling as a weathered face across which a razor has been scraped, she had never dreamed that one day she would cross the street and see it from the inside. The spook house, the kids of Happy Valley had called it, and along with them she had wondered, not when it would be pulled down, but who it was that could go on living there (living? better, rotting) while another world was growing up around it.

Now as she approached it from the same vantage, the colonial A & P where the bus dropped her off, she saw that the spook house (in all the earlier days she had never known the names of the men living there, and she still had little interest in current news) had changed. Certain signs bespoke a new determination, like those on an aging woman who has determined to take herself in hand. Paint had been applied to the casements, the lawn had been trimmed, the privets cut back, the weeds burned out of the carriageway by oil and exhaust, if by nothing else, the downstairs windows washed and decently covered. It still loomed, but no longer as a temptation to housebreakers, or wild high-school kids. It was perfectly plain that if her patient had indeed broken in, he hadn't been motivated by common vandalism.

Laura went steadily up the walk to the creaking porch, found the iron thumb screw in the middle of the front door, set in a round protuberance like the corroded breast of a copper statue, and twirled it firmly, undismayed by the high dull *whanggg* of the clapping bell within.

She waited for what seemed like a long time. Then, hearing nothing, she reached forward and gave it one more turn. Rummaging in her purse for pencil and pad, she wonderd whether she could entrust the message to paper and slip it under the door. It was annoying not to have foreseen that there might be no one at home. She began to arrange in her mind an order of priority for the other stops—dime store, drugstore —before going home to her parents for dinner.

The door opened suddenly. Laura sucked in her breath involuntarily.

Before her stood a thickly bearded young man in purple boxer's trunks with an elasticized waist and a white stripe on either side. His bare legs ended in frazzled plaid carpet slippers through which his little toes protruded like snails peering from their shells. The upper part of his body was somehow jammed into an outmoded sport shirt several sizes too small; at least his biceps and triceps burst from it rebelliously, and lengthwise it was considerably short of meeting his trunks. In between there was only skin, ridged with muscle, but pale. Through the buttonholes of the undersized sport shirt he had crisscrossed a white tennis shoelace, the ends of which lay open on his chest.

The shoelace fascinated her in a horribly embarrassing way. It was as if their sexes were reversed and she were unable despite herself to give up staring at the taut expanse of breast before her, on which the shoelaces rose and fell in an unusually rapid rhythm. This astonishing-looking person (could he really be Mrs. Land's husband? or anyone's husband?) might have been catching his breath after a race. Indeed, his nostrils were dilated, and his pale cheeks were flushed above the curly prophet's beard. His lake-blue eyes, bright with intelligence, were staring with what seemed to her to be amazement and admiration.

"Hello," she said, pleased.

He did not reply.

Taken aback and suddenly sweating with uneasiness, she felt her self-confidence melting at her feet. What if he were a mute? Then what?

"I am looking for Mr. Land. I have a message for him."

The young man continued to stare at her in silence, but her words were knuckles rapping him to recognition of his situation. His lips began to tremble and for a moment he looked ready to flee.

What did I do, what did I say? Caught by the contagion

of his fear, Laura dabbed at her damp face and took a step backward, recoiling from the implicit rebuff as if she had been a peddler who had inadvertently insulted the man of the house.

But before she could pivot on the rubber sole of her white shoe, he held out his hand beseechingly and opened his mouth.

In that instant she was forcibly reminded of the swollen-faced, bandaged philosopher who had sent her on this errand. Didn't his eyes too give off this haunted gleam, or was there some closer resemblance, the attempt to define which confounded her . . . Or was it simply maleness and a need for her that they both shared? Anxiously she leaned forward to assure the young man that she was waiting.

"Yes," he said. His Adam's apple moved first up, then down, as he swallowed saliva. He gestured clumsily, boyishly, for her to enter the house. Then he spoke with startling decisiveness.

"Yes, yes, I am Mr. Land. I've been watching for you."

Laura followed him unhesitatingly into the gloom.

"Please sit here, it's comfortable." He indicated a velour couch, and stood beside it until she had settled herself. "Can I bring you a cold drink?"

When she shook her head no, he said in a rush, "This is truly remarkable. I never really thought you'd come back."

For the first time, Laura felt that she had made a mistake in coming. "But I've never been here before. You must be confusing me with someone else."

"Oh no. I wasn't referring to this house. I meant, you know, across the street."

I had to come all the way back, she thought resignedly, to be recognized. "You saw me there?"

"Many times. You're the Witness, aren't you?"

Laura nodded slowly. Then she qualified the nod: "That is, I was."

"You've been away so long! I've turned it over and over in my mind, trying to guess what happened to you."

"I lost my faith, is all. One day I couldn't face handing out any more literature, and I knew it was finished, my belief was gone. My mother was always the religious one. She still is. My father was brought up Catholic, like her, but he says in the old country it was a woman's religion. He says his religion is poker. Seven card stud."

But why am I saying all this, she wondered, why should he care? To her further astonishment, she heard herself asking the question aloud while she stared into his eager innocent eyes.

"I don't know why you should care."

"But I do. I do! You can't imagine, I used to wait every day for you to show up." He must have read the confusion in her face, for he hurried on. "I work in the attic, that was why it took so long to let you in just now. And that's where I used to watch you from. Believe me, I waited for you like a drenched man waiting for the sun to come out. I can explain why, but first you have to tell me some more."

Seated on a small stool at her feet, he looked up at her beseechingly, and yet with an innocent confidence in his persuasive powers. Like a child he pleaded, "Go ahead, you first."

"No one has ever asked me about myself quite like that. I don't know where to start. How much is there to say? My mother brought me up as a Witness; she kept telling me that I was going to be saved and the rest of the world wasn't. For a while, when I was in my teens, I was sure the light had entered my soul. All of a sudden I was ready to go anywhere, do anything, to prove it, even if I had to ring doorbells or stand on street corners. Snubs or insults meant nothing to me, less than nothing. I wasn't ashamed. After all, at that age it's a privilege to suffer."

"I know, I know! And it doesn't make any difference why, or what for, does it, as long as you're one of the privileged."

"Finally, though, it did make a difference. Instead of

bothering strangers for something I stopped believing myself, I thought it would be more honest to go where people really needed my help. That's why I'm studying nursing. My mother hasn't changed. She really believes. I'm sure she always will. I wouldn't have said this a while ago, but maybe it's best that she does. She's happy, she's harming no one."

"And that was all? That was why you stopped coming with the *Watchtowers?*"

There was an unidentifiable note, almost of disappointment —or was it jealousy?—in his question.

"My mother almost died when she learned that I was going into a Catholic hospital, the devil's lair. She can't understand, she can only think of her own childhood, and those immoral priests. It's no use explaining that before, I did nobody any good, not even myself, but now everything I do, even the dirtiest little job, helps somebody. Including me—especially me. You know something? It's only lately I've discovered how selfish I am. Who knows, maybe I'm kidding myself now as much as before—when I used to stand out in the rain with the *Watchtowers!*"

"Probably not. But it meant a lot to me, your being there."

"I don't understand. How much could you have seen me . . ." she hesitated, ". . . unless you were watching me all the time?"

"That's just it. I was. I've been a witness myself. Let me try to explain it to you. When I've tried to straighten it out in my own mind, or to write it down in my diary, I've been encouraged by the feeling that you were reading over my shoulder, or actually listening. Sometimes you can say things to a stranger that you can't to your own family. I felt we wanted the same from life, you and I. That it should be more pure, more disinterested. We called what we did bearing witness. We protected ourselves, or thought we did, by hiding, or, what amounted to the same thing, by warning others that the world was coming to an end."

Hiding? Who had done that? Laura was not so much offended as confused. No one had ever spoken to her with such penetration. With her hands folded in her lap, she waited quietly and expectantly for him to go on.

"How did it start? For myself, when I think about it, it brings me always to my family. Just as it brings you to yours. In my case, the family is bound together by hate. That can't be right, not even when we protest that it's love which makes us do what we do.

"I'm the biggest hypocrite of all. You know about women who seal their wombs because they're afraid of an imaginary hereditary taint? Or men who refuse to become fathers because they say they don't want to bring more childern into a terrible world? What I did was even worse.

"Out of fear that I would do things like those already done by my family, I refused to do anything. And I called the refusal by such fancy names that I wouldn't even have the nerve to repeat them to you. Look at me!"

Tears had sprung to his eyes as he talked. With his hands he gestured helplessly at his figure.

"A clown! Don't think I don't know how funny I look. But I didn't dare stop to change. It would have taken too long, I'd have missed you."

"I don't care. Believe me. I didn't change out of my uniform to come here."

"That's different. You've earned it. Just like you earned that funny sack when you were peddling your magazines. But with me it's a fraud. I took a vow of simplicity like monks take a vow of silence—and what do you think I've been living off? The same money that's been willed to me. The same money I pretended not to care about, just like my brothers pretended not to care about each other."

"Willed to you?" Laura was stunned. My God, she thought, it's the other one, my God, what have I gotten into? She cried again, "Willed to you? Then you're the brother everyone has been looking for. You're—"

"I'm Ray Land, you mean you didn't know? *Mister* Land,

you called me. You're the first person who ever called me that. I assumed—"

"Is that how you watched me so much? You've been in this house all along, just sitting here?"

"More than just sitting. That's what I've been trying to explain. I've been in the attic, it's true, but I've followed a stiff schedule to keep me from rusting physically or mentally. At least, if I didn't accomplish anything else, I was preparing for the sign that would tell me when to come down."

Laura held her head in her hand. For the second time in one remarkable day, she was being drained of her energy, almost hypnotized; first it had been one strange man, now another. But if the first had radiated, even from beneath his bandages, a potent durability that was almost overpowering, this one emanated a sweetness as innocently exhilarating as a wild flower. Why do I want to stroke his cheek, she thought in panic, when I hear him talking such foolishness?

As coolly as she could, she demanded, "And you've never had the sign? What makes you think you will?"

"Because I have already." His smile was dazzling. His teeth, so much whiter and straighter than hers, gleamed in the thicket of his beard. "I had it this afternoon. A bell rang."

Get up, run away, she still knew enough to say it to herself. Go home where you are merely expected as a daughter bringing ordinary news and an ordinary appetite, not desperately wanted, not awaited as a sign. But she could not move.

She said faintly, "I think you're very arrogant. Even more so than most men."

"What's your name?"

He was the second to ask in one day, but this time she did not willfully answer the question backward, like an army nurse reporting for duty. She said her name as she wanted to hear him say it. "Laura. Laura Leone."

"Laura. It's true. You're right. I am arrogant. I would have been ashamed to admit it a while ago—now I'm not. But I am ashamed of the cowardice that drove me up to the attic in the first place. I kidded myself that it was a virtuous refusal to become involved in evil."

"I don't think it's cowardly to resist evil."

"It is when you let other people do the dirty work for you. Too easy, too easy. I only wonder now how I could have believed that any good would come of it. I should have known that my brothers would use violence to try to win an impossible victory. And that I would stay perched like a parakeet, not knowing the right words to keep them from destroying each other. I guess we're all ashamed now, but wasn't I the worst, secretly hoping that my brothers would bleed each other to death?"

"Did you say, your brothers?"

"Of course. I knew perfectly well that the man who broke in was my brother Mel."

I am such a fool, she thought. Her fingers were aching from gripping her purse. "You mean that the patient, the man who sent me here . . ."

"I'm positive he's Mel. He had to come here. First Ralph, then Mel." His voice trailed away, his blue eyes glowed strangely; he reached out and took hold of the white material of her uniform. She felt only wonderment at the touch of his fingers, so unlike those of his brother.

"But wasn't it Kitty who sent you?"

"It was your brother. And I thought you were Kitty's husband!"

"What was his message?"

Laura hesitated. "I don't believe he intended it for you. He said Mr. Land. He must have meant—" She stopped short; now she knew *what* he had meant too.

The boy removed his hand from her skirt, stiffly, almost as though she had asked him to. "Just the same, you must tell me."

"I never should have started this."

"That's like saying you shouldn't have been born."

So she told him, in an instant, without moving her hands

from her lap. His head was lowered and she looked down into his tense tangle of black curls; she had almost physically to restrain herself from reaching out with her fingers to touch the curls just beyond her knee.

"When I go back, what shall I tell him?"

He lifted his head and looked into her eyes. "Tell him nothing. He doesn't expect an answer. He expects a visit."

"Then you'll come?"

He shook his head. Almost apologetically he declared, "There's nothing between him and me. It's between Ralph and me. When Ralph and I have settled matters, we can see Mel together and arrange everything."

This was so outrageous that she could not keep the tremor from her voice. "Then you're afraid. You talk a lot, but you're still afraid."

Ray Land arose as if he had been uncoiled—he was as graceful as a snake—and turned away from her. Don't take it back, she said to herself, don't take it back.

He said over his shoulder, "I didn't think of it that way. It's probably true, what you say."

Freed at last from the demand of those dazzling eyes, she got up too. "Forgive me. I think I'd better go now."

At that he lurched around with uncharacteristic awkwardness and grasped her by the left wrist.

"Oh!" she cried out in pain. "Oh! My watch, my wrist!"

"I'm sorry." He released her at once. "I'm not used . . . You had every right, there's nothing to forgive."

"Then tell me what I should say when I go back."

"Say that you delivered the message. I swear to you that when Ralph shows up I'll tell it to him, just as you told it to me." With hope in his voice he added, "Then we'll all be on an even footing, won't we?"

"No. You and Ralph will be way ahead. But the other—he's flat on his back, he still won't know about you two what you both know about him."

He smiled faintly. "You don't know the Lands. You're

learning, but you don't know us yet. Mel wouldn't have turned up without an ace in the hole. He's aware that the police are bound to find out who he is. Or that Ralph himself might decide to tell them. You think Mel will quit that easy? Watch and see."

"Just the same . . ."

"Ah, just the same. You're right, that's no reason to take advantage of him. The point is, you've done what he asked you to. And now maybe I can persuade Ralph. I pleaded with him, all this time, not to be vengeful." He shuddered. "But he said just what you're thinking. That I'm afraid, that I'm weak."

Laura's heart was thumping. She moved to the boy's side and put her hand on his wrist to restrain him, as he had done to her, but gently.

"It's not true. I believe you. You want the best for everybody."

"I never knew how to go about it. I sat up in the attic, telling myself that I was preparing, while you stood out there, offering yourself with those crazy papers. But believe me, believe me, this is the moment. Don't think I'm simply afraid to go to the hospital. I did come down to let you in today, didn't I? I did say, Yes, I'm Mr. Land, didn't I?"

The silence was close about them. They stood together, holding hands, their mutual warmth flowing between them thick as blood.

He said, "Ralph is shocked, he's afraid Kitty will lose the baby he didn't want. He's afraid he would have killed Mel if he hadn't been stopped. Isn't this the time to bring them together?"

Who am I to say? she asked herself in terror. She was astonished to hear herself reply, "Yes."

"If I go to the hospital alone Ralph may get suspicious again. He'll think Mel's making a deal with me. Maybe I can get Ralph to go with me."

"Ray—" It was the first time she had said his name. It

was exciting. She said it again: "Ray, why do you need me?"

"Better ask, Why should I let you go? You must come if I call you."

He held her with his eyes as as she held him by the hand, his pulse thudding against her fingers. Blue, blue, his eyes searched her as she had never been searched, they demanded what had never been demanded of her.

"Yes," she said at last, "of course I will."

Now he was jubilant. "I knew it! Ever since I used to watch you, so obstinate and forlorn with your papers, like a wild flower that no one pauses to admire, I knew it. I called to you without daring to open my mouth: Look up! Look up here! And now you have."

He had her by the waist, holding her close to him, so close that the pulse was no longer at her finger tips, but beating against her breasts. She looked up, as he had predicted and commanded, and was surprised at how well she already knew his features. His lips were red as raspberries in the wild thicket of untrimmed beard; between them his small teeth, hard and white like his body, gleamed as his flesh gleamed between his oddments of clothing. Through the length of her body she could feel the tension of this obdurate youth who had said no to a bad world and set himself to await a better one, staring down at her from his high sanctuary; he was the same boy who yearned for her.

He wants to kiss me, she thought vaguely, wonderingly, no longer in the least astonished at herself; and she put her hands to his head and drew his red lips down to hers, drinking from his warmth as she felt everything grow dark and heavy about her, borne down by the fine fixity of his purpose.

When at last she opened her eyes she discovered that he was gazing at her, marveling at what had happened. He continued to hold her by the waist. She drew back her head and smiled at him, slightly. She wanted to say nothing, only to feel forever what she felt now.

"We're practically strangers. I don't even know you, in the ordinary way. Isn't that what they'd say?"

"Who?"

"Ordinary people."

But that's what I might have said too, Laura thought confusedly. Does that mean that I am only ordinary? She shook her head, frightened, and just then felt Ray Land shudder against her.

He bent forward, his face averted, and put his lips to her ear.

"I'm trembling," he muttered. "Can you feel me trembling?"

She was afraid that her own voice would sound coarse and ordinary, no matter what she was to reply. She nodded silently.

"It's because I'm not used to being with anyone." He clenched his teeth. "It's because I'm a virgin. I don't really know anything about anything."

Laura experienced a sudden surge of strength. It was as if she had been swimming beyond her depth, exhausted, panicky, but then with the sudden appearance of her objective had gained her second wind, and plunged ahead rejoicing in the power of her lungs and limbs to take her forward as far as need be. She hugged the boy to her, running her fingers through his dense upspringing curly hair.

"You know a lot. You know how to be kind. And wise. Besides, you might as well know, I'm a virgin too. They don't believe me at the hospital, but it's true. I've had other concerns."

"But now me," he blurted.

"Oh yes!" she cried exultantly. "And now you!"

Finally she released herself. "Now I'm going to go." She rummaged in her purse. "I want to write down my address and telephone number. And the number at the hospital."

"You do trust me then, even though I'm half crazy?"

"After this afternoon, we must both be crazy. When I think how I used to stand out there blowing my nose, telling myself that the Lord would number me among the sheep—and all the time you were watching me from up there!"

Actually she was close to tears, and she had to blink to write down the information legibly. As she handed him the paper, she said matter-of-factly, "I did see your sister-in-law this morning, you know. I had to ask her to leave your brother's room; he's not supposed to have visitors."

Ray stared. "Kitty was with Mel?"

"For quite a while. But she may not have known who he was—I didn't."

"Believe me, if Kitty was there, she knew. So she must have told Ralph."

"Not necessarily. There are things some women don't tell their husbands."

"You're right, there are." Ray was suddenly pale.

"Did I say something wrong?"

He started. "No, I'm glad you told me. But I must talk to Ralph as soon as possible."

"You won't go back to the attic?"

"Not to stay. Not any more. Soon everyone will know I've been up there. For myself, I don't care, but what have I gotten you into? Laura, if you threw yourself into the world when you threw away your *Watchtowers*, that was nothing compared with what you did when you rang this bell. If I had it in me to urge you to stay away, I would."

"It wouldn't do you any good. Good-by, Ray, good-by for a while."

Outdoors, on the porch steps, on the spongy lawn, on the dappled sidewalk, the entire day had altered. Had the sun been shining so when she had entered the Land house? It did not seem possible. From its hiding place in the lilac bush by the carriageway, a bird sang. Laura wanted to sing back at it.

Across the street, a lineman, straps wound round his pants, lounged at the base of a telephone pole. Who could blame him for not wanting to work on such a day? When he saw that he had her eye, he winked boldly. Half tempted to wink back, to run across the street and share her secret with him, the first person she had seen since it happened, Laura laughed to herself and walked on. I have changed, she thought. Here's proof. They never used to wink at me when I stood there crying to myself with the *Watchtower*. Only Ray knew, in his watchtower, only Ray.

On through the brightness of the June afternoon she hurried, not frightened, despite Ray's warnings. Hastening home to her parents, whom she loved in their own way, she felt now that she had only the slenderest of ties to them, ties she was about to sever with hardly a pang. Leaving the mysterious house of the Lands, she sensed that she had entered their life for good, how fully only the passage of time could prove. She accepted all, all, her heart thumping gaily, wildly, as she quickened her pace through the afternoon dazzle.

11: RALPH

ONLY NOW, when it was too late, and everything was crashing down around him, could Ralph assess the depth of his attachment to one abiding belief: that planning, executed with reason, constituted an exact science, unlimited in its potential. Until now he had experienced nothing that could shake this belief. Not the brute unreason of war (itself susceptible of explanation if you took the trouble), nor his own years of disillusionment in New York (where if no doors had opened it was because he had lacked the key), had in any way weakened his conviction that those who planned succeeded. So there had been no reason why the behavior of either Ray or Kitty should have sapped the roots of that conviction.

Ray was trying and tiresome, it was true; he was even a menace, as long as he persisted in hiding in the attic like a time bomb; but behind his pleas for recognition of the importance of the spontaneous and the wayward, he too was a man who planned. Ray detested the word, but what else had he been doing in the attic, if not mapping out a campaign?

Therefore you could counterattack, you could devise a series of alternate courses of action, with a reasonable expectation that within a limited period, more or less defined in advance, you would succeed in neutralizing him, in frustrating his schemes, in making yours prevail.

Kitty, on the other hand, was vehemently female and moon-driven behind her businesslike and pragmatic manner, swept more than she commonly revealed or even realized by sub-terranean currents and tides. But that didn't mean that you couldn't plan for her and with her, or that you couldn't count on her as an integral part of your own expectations. Even when she had gone ahead on her own and committed him to parenthood, it had been at least partially a result of his own lack of foresight; when he had finally overcome his panic, after those hours of erratic driving about the countryside, he had been able to improvise a speeded-up timetable based on what she had done. What was more, after constructing an imaginary dialogue with her, he had persuaded himself that Kitty—although she never said so—might in actuality have been using extreme means to force him to confront a new reality.

Why, even Mel, considered in the abstract, had been under-standable—no, that was a little ludicrous. Better to say that the emotions Mel had aroused in you—first the admiration and love, then the uneasiness so readily transmuted into hatred—were susceptible of being understood. And mastered. That very hatred, the basis of which seemed quite clear, and hence reasonable, had appeared to Ralph as the motor force of his ambitious conception of what should be done with the fortune of the Lands.

All very fine. Until the moment when, pulled by main force from his murderous position astride his smashed and gasping brother, he had had to face the truth: that he too was domi-nated by base passions beyond realism, beyond practicality, beyond planning—passions such as Mel had personified in his flight from respectability, such as Ray had pleaded underlay their irreconcilability, such as Kitty had simply demonstrated, coursed beneath the frail raft of human planning and maybe even provided its essential current.

Ever since, he had wandered around the city, planless, aimless, trying to exhaust himself, wondering—beyond all the wondering about the collapse of the bridge he had built to the future, with himself midway across it—what kind of life he could go on living once the rationale of his existence was gone. It did him no good to think about those brought up in a faith who had suddenly discovered themselves bereft of belief in the tenets of their church; the only names that would come to mind were of those who had switched from one faith to another.

He dared not visit Kitty, much less discuss this with her, because he could not yet face her, no matter which of two suppositions was correct. Either she had almost lost the baby as a result of the struggle, in which case the responsibility was doubly his. Or she had not, but in a moment of inspiration had faked the onset of miscarriage. The idea of her pitying him was unbearable, when she had seen with her own eyes how his cool self-mastery had turned to wild and bloody despair at its first real collision with fraternal implacability. She had won them both a brief respite, yes. But for what? What difference did it make at this point whether the cops left them alone a little while longer? When they knew who Mel was, when they wanted the whole story, they'd come for it.

Meanwhile, the respite provided only space for himself to chase his tail; he was unable to confront himself in a hopeless situation. For if he could not visit Kitty, no more could he bring himself to visit Mel and look upon the wreckage of his brother's face, of his own pride, of their common code: privacy, secrecy, victory.

Ray he had seen, more than once, over the wandering weekend; but each time he had come in—never for more than a moment, only for long enough to show that at least he could do this, enter his own house without flinching—Ray had tried to waylay him, to cajole him into conversation. From Ray too, from this brother who could not conceal the satisfaction of the man proven right, he had fled.

Finally, as it had to, it wore itself out. Ever since the fight with Mel he had been cringing like a child away from a confrontation of his situation. But neither booze nor NoDoz pills, swallowed during his dull miserable drifting from bar to gas station to bar, to phone the hospital or the doctor, could obliterate the memory of what he had done to someone he once had loved. Mel, blood streaming from his nose onto his neck and the floor beneath his battered head, one eye smashed closed, the other rolling about horribly like an agate or a ball of quicksilver, unrecognizable and recognizing nothing. He had repeated it to himself so many times that, while losing none of its truth, it had become boring, as even cancer can become boring for its moaning victim and those who love him: I would have killed him if they hadn't pulled me off him.

Supposing a palmist, or even someone who knew not just the lines of his hand but the metallic grinding of his teeth in his sleep, had predicted to him: Ralph Land, someday you will try to kill your own brother with your own hands, and the memory of it will haunt you. He would have laughed aloud. There were times when men had to die violently. He knew that, he had been in a war. He had fired at distant fleeing figures stumbling through the snow, but that had never troubled his nights afterward, any more than does the memory of a maddeningly painful illness that has run its course. After all, if it were otherwise, the world would be one vast congress of hysterics, unable to screw their wives or to make a living because their endless nightmares persisted through their waking lives as well. Then why was he so horribly certain that the vision of Mel bleeding beneath him would never fade, not as long as he lived?

Was it because of the physical pain he had inflicted, the capacity for behaving as Cain that he had suddenly demonstrated, or the bloody ineradicable proof in the deed itself that he was as much a creature of his glands as the most wretched death camp sadist? No matter why. Worse than a war, worse than a wasting disease, it weighed on him, this crushing memory which he would never find the means to lift from him, any more than Mel had been able to summon the strength to push him from his chest.

Here was Monday morning, and the executioner awaited. Not with cyanide, ax, high voltage, or firing squad, but with the whips and scourges of his own conscience, and the desolate awareness that he had gone beyond infallibility into a murderous new land where the old rules and regulations on which you based your expectations were meaningless and dangerously misleading. Infinitely weary, he allowed the Triumph to stall in the carriageway, and stumbled up the steps for news of Kitty and Mel, both of whom had taught him things about himself that he had never wanted to know.

Ray was waiting for him in the front hall. Ralph had found him there each time he had returned, ever since the battle, and had brushed past him impatiently. Now, however, he felt neither the need nor the desire to side-step his younger brother, whose eyes were glowing with a strange new light.

Ralph crammed his fists into the pockets of his zipper jacket. "You look different."

"I am different."

"You've trimmed your beard."

"It's not just that. I've left the attic. It's time, Ralph. We've done terrible things, all of us."

Ralph removed one hand from his jacket pocket and passed it across his mouth; it grated over the stubble sprouting around his lips, and it trembled noticeably. Thrusting it back into his pocket, he said, "I'm not going to argue with you."

"If we make a start, each of us, no matter how—"

"What's your start?"

"This."

Ralph saw then that Raymond had put on a fresh shirt, and

combed back his hair. And he was panting a little, not from any physical exertion, but as though the utterance of every word was a great expense of moral currency. Am I responsible for this, Ralph wondered? It came to him—gradually, but none the less with enormous force—that Ray had at last been moved of his own free will to do just what he had been so bitterly resisting. Who could have guessed that he would been impelled to it not by any concessions to his demands but rather by the converse, a vile attempt to drown Mel in his own blood? It was borne in upon Ralph that he had not yet seen anything like the final consequences, so unpredictable as to be unimaginable, of his acts, both the premeditated and the passionate.

He said to his brother, "What do you expect of me?"

Ray shook his head. "I lost the right to answer that when I let you two fight it out. I knew it was Mel, and yet I couldn't—"

"*You* lost the right? How do you suppose I feel? This is as fruitless as our old arguments used to be, in reverse."

Oh, I am so tired, he thought, if only I could lie down and forget for a while.

"You did come down, though, Ray. You made the move. All right, tell me what you think we ought to do."

His young brother's eyes lightened and hardened, jewel-like. "There is no more my way or your way. Whatever we do from now on, I think we ought to try to do together."

At that moment Sasha tottered erect, hackles rising and a rusty growl issuing from his throat. The doorbell rang behind Ralph, and he started, feeling his face contort involuntarily.

"Quick," he said. "Get upstairs. Or into the kitchen. Quick."

Ray did not move. "It's too late, Ralph. I can't hide any more."

"Will you get out so I can answer the door? It may be reporters, my car's in the drive, they won't go away. It may be—"

"It makes no difference. We have to start now."

The bell rang again, Sasha's growl was rising to a bark. Ralph shoved his brother in the chest, pushing him back toward the kitchen.

"For God's sake," he cried, "get back. Go!"

"You were the one who wanted me here. You pleaded, you threatened, you starved me. Now open the door."

Ralph felt the tears of frustration springing to his eyes. "What do I have to do, get down on my knees? Maybe you're ready. I'm not. Give me a little time. I can't get a megaphone and yell. Here he is, here's Ray, it's just a little game we've been playing. I can't, I can't, I—"

Abruptly, wordlessly, Ray turned and slipped back to the kitchen. Ralph looked briefly at his expressionless countenance in the hall mirror. Nothing might have happened, nothing at all. Calmly he opened the front door.

For a moment he thought Mel had come back again. The man before him was also blond, also high-cheekboned, also narrow-eyed. But his face was unscarred, marked by nothing more than the souvenirs of adolescent acne and a fresh razor cut above the Adam's apple.

"Detective Lieutenant Karpinski." The man presented a leatherette case which Ralph declined to examine. "I saw you the other night. You were probably too shook up to remember."

"I remember now."

"Can I come in for a few minutes? It won't take long."

"Of course. Let's go in here." He led the way to the parlor. "A cup of coffee?"

Karpinski displayed his vertical palm in refusal, like a traffic cop. "Well, your wife's coming along. I guess you'll be glad when she gets home."

"Naturally."

"That's right. It's been rough all around. I had a long talk with her in the hospital. She's pretty smart. Good-looking too, if you don't mind my saying so. I can see how you'd miss her. Still, it isn't like she'd left you here all alone, is it?"

And suddenly, shockingly, a sickly shit-eating grin spread across the detective's face. It was a face unaccustomed to smiling, it seemed to Ralph, except at the bought and paid-for agonies of others: football players piling one on the other in a muddy heap of bloody jerseys and clotted cleats, television gladiators grimacing as they wrenched at each other's extremities. What stunned Ralph all over again, though, was not Karpinski's obscene happiness at springing a trap, but his own irrepressible desire to smash the man's face in—just as he had with one brother, and had almost done again with the other not five minutes ago.

He demanded, "What are you getting at, Karpinski?"

He would not have been surprised to hear the man charge him with having brought a mistress into the house while his wife lay bleeding in the hospital; it was an offense commonly attributed to expectant fathers. The detective allowed his face to relax into sullen somberness as he shifted his heavy haunches on the sofa.

"Police investigation is like house cleaning," Karpinski said sententiously. "It's not always exciting, but it's got to be thorough. We were interested in the whereabouts of your brother, Raymond Land, just like lots of other people. You were supposed to be too, but nobody saw you doing much about it. Well, the Federal Communications Commission granted Raymond Land an amateur radio operator's license a while ago. Want to see it?"

It was Ralph's turn to raise his hand, palm outward, in negation, as the detective made a casual gesture toward his jacket pocket.

"His home address and the address of his transmitter are the same. This house, this house right here. We believe your brother never left here, and that for your own reasons you've been concealing him. Now are we going to have to bring a search warrant to prove it?"

"Supposing he was here, whose business is it that a man stays put in his own house, if that's what he wants?"

"If that's what he wants. There's other reasons why it's our business. According to the Bureau of Vital Statistics, Raymond Land is still a minor. According to Martin Stark, he's the inheritor of the Land estate. We want to hear from his own mouth that nobody's holding him against his will."

"Oh, for Christ's sake! If he decided to be a hermit, he decided years ago. And I only got here New Year's Day. You ought to know that much."

"We know. We haven't pressed you. But like I say, lots of people have been interested in Raymond Land. One of them broke in here the other night."

"You think so?" Ralph asked carefully. It was no good. The man was playing with him.

"Mr. Land, I thought so from the time this here dog first barked his head off at me." He indicated Sasha, who raised neither chops nor tail from the hearth on which he was snoring fitfully. "If he barked like that at the housebreaker, how come it didn't wake up you or your wife? And if he didn't bark, why not? Another thing. When you started to get the better of him, the man didn't run down here and try to get out of the house. He headed upstairs, to the third floor, where as I remember there's two more bedrooms, and an attic entrance too. That's where the boys found you. And stopped you from killing him. Why did he go up instead of down?"

"By that time I don't think either of us knew what we were doing."

Karpinski shook his head. A strand of long straight blond hair fell forward across his forehead; he brushed it back.

"Nobody's that crazy. And he wasn't after a bunch of old movie posters. If you want to convince me different, you'll have to let me take a little tour of the upstairs."

Ralph pressed his upper arms to his sides; sweat was trickling icily down his ribs. Take it, he said to himself, take it a little longer.

"If you'll just give us a while to straighten out the family affairs, I can assure you everything will be all right. There's been no intention on anyone's part to violate the law."

Karpinski leaned back and regarded him smugly. "You and your family have been giving the Department an awful lot of trouble."

He said this with pride, as though he were reciting statistics on traffic fatalities caused by speed violators. But it was worse than that. His tone was not official but personal, and it struck Ralph suddenly that he had come not so much on police business as to batten off the misery of others; he might have been pursuing a private grudge against the Land family. They were kookie, they were foreign, so they were dangerous to those taxpayers who were not, and who hired the cops. For the first time since the death of his mother, Ralph was drawn to the defense of his family, against this brute in a business suit. A thousand years of pogroms lurked behind his shallow Slavic smile; he gave off the smell of one born to the pursuit of the odd and the uneasy, heir to the pleasures of countless generations of drunken hunters of the dispossessed.

Ralph said coldly, "We didn't have you in mind when we went to settle our affairs. Was there anything else?"

"You figuring on pressing assault and battery charges?"

"Certainly not."

"I didn't think you would. But supposing *he* does? If it turns out that he had as much right to be here as you, then what?"

"I'll worry about that when it happens. You might do the same. I've already said that everything will be straightened out shortly."

Dismissed, Karpinski arose. But he could not resist a grinning threat. "It better be. Except for those things that take a lifetime to straighten out. Those are your own problems."

In the hall again, at the door, he put on his cheap summer straw and turned for a final word.

"Some people might take it for kindness, having your family doctor take care of somebody that attacked you and almost made your wife lose her baby. Then again, others might take it for collusion. Especially with nurses running back and forth between the hospital and here."

"What the hell are you talking about?"

Karpinski was patient. "If you stayed home more, you'd see that it's getting pretty lively and popular, for a haunted house."

He opened the front door. With his thumb he indicated the telephone lineman across the street.

"We've had the place staked out ever since the fight. One of the nurses that's been attending your housebreaker dropped in here yesterday. Somebody let her in. Maybe it was a ghost?"

He added reassuringly, "I'm taking that man off the stake-out now that you've turned up. You sure now there's nothing else you want to tell me?"

Still shaking his head no, Ralph closed the door on him, weak and trembling with anger, and turned to confront Raymond.

"You heard that Polack. You were listening from the kitchen. He said you let some nurse in here yesterday."

"That's right. I was just going to tell you about it when the detective came. She brought a message for you from Mel. Let's have a cup of coffee in the kitchen, and I'll tell you as best as I can. I waited up for you last night, but I didn't hear you come in or go out. And every time I've tried to talk, you've brushed me aside."

"I've been in no shape. But tell me now."

Ray repeated the message carefully while they sat at the kitchen table, with the coffee perking on the stove and the birds singing in the apple trees in the backyard. Not only had Ray changed physically; he had never talked with such vivacity, and with such an absence of that beggar's dolefulness which afflicted him even at his most cheerful.

"That nurse seems to have made quite an impression on you."

"I kissed her."

"You *what?* Tell me more."

"She's the same girl who used to stand across the street when she was a Jehovah's Witness, selling the *Watchtower* in front of the A & P. That's what was so remarkable."

"Remarkable? It's preposterous. A Jehovah's Witness!"

"Why? It's no more preposterous than being a Democrat or a Republican. And if I hadn't recognized her, I never would have found the courage to open the door to her. You remember, don't you, I told you about her one day."

Ralph searched his mind. He was blurry with fatigue. "No, I'm sure you never did."

Raymond blushed. "Then it was Kitty." He went on quickly, "I guess she thought it wasn't important enough to mention to you."

There was something wrong about this, but he was too weary to put his finger on it. It was hard to visualize Ray and Kitty chatting companionably in his absence. And about girls? He gazed speculatively at his brother.

"So that's why you came down. Why you cleaned yourself up. Why you're not going back to the attic."

"Only partly. It was the fight too. When Laura came I was sitting up there crying, I admit it, thinking of Mel in the hospital and you wandering blindly through the city just like Mel used to. And of Kitty trying to keep her baby, after the three of us almost took it away from her. Me included. I was as responsible as if I had taken part in everything. What's the difference? None, in my mind."

Glancing up from his steaming coffee cup, Ralph saw that his brother was transfigured.

"And when I looked down at the street below and saw her approaching the house, so human, so substantial, a plain ordinary Italian girl, but so beautiful and hesitating, all in white, in the bright sunlight, I went racing down the stairs. I almost broke my neck to open the door before she should go away, and when she asked was I Mr. Land I just looked her in the eye and said yes."

"Fine. But what do we do about Mel's message?"

"It was for you, not me. It's for you to say."

"Are you going to start evading all over again? Speak up, I'm dead on my feet."

"Forgive me. I'm ready to go. I'll say to him . . . First I'll take his hand, then I'll say . . . Mel, tell me what you want."

"Don't be surprised if he still wants the world. I doubt that you can change him."

"Maybe I shouldn't try. But I should find out, shouldn't I?"

"Yes." Resting his forehead in the cupped palm of his hand, Ralph added, "Listen, kid. I'll go along. I don't know what to say to him, or what he'll say to me, but—"

Ray broke in eagerly, "Don't you think that people usually respond to what you expect of them?"

"No." The boy would always be a fool. And yet, Ralph thought, if you pitch your expectations too low, won't people respond by giving you less? Instead of my ally, I offered only to make Kitty my accomplice—and hasn't she behaved like one? Still he persisted, "Don't expect a cannibal to discuss philosophy with you just because you'd like him to. Now let's call up Martin Stark."

"Why Martin?"

"If we want to settle with Mel, who else is there to tell us what we can and can't do?"

He closed his eyes and saw orange flashes and green circles. With his hand over his eyes, he muttered, "Who else but the Starks could keep us from killing each other?"

Ray replied, slowly, "I thought maybe we could work it out among ourselves. But if you think we need Martin, go ahead."

But when he dialed the lawyer's office, it was all wrong. Mr. Stark was already in court. He would be there the entire morning. He had a two o'clock lecture at the Law School. Thereafter a series of office appointments which could not be canceled. He would not be free until the end of the day.

"Ralphie," Ray pleaded, "let's try it without him."

"Won't work."

"Please."

Ralph shrugged. He dialed the hospital. "This is Mr. Land, L-A-N-D," he said. "I'm calling again to inquire about my wife."

He was switched to Kitty's floor. After a moment he recognized the already familiar mannish voice of the duty nurse.

"Dr. Stark left instructions for your wife to be discharged tomorrow morning." Her tone was impatient and barely civil. "Do you want her sent home in a cab?"

"I'll come for her first thing in the morning. About eight-thirty? Very good. May I have the switchboard again?" When he was reconnected, he demanded, "I'd like some word on the condition of Marc Lafarge."

"Out of danger."

"I wish to visit him. My name is Ralph Land."

He could hear the woman suck in air. He counted to twenty-two, waiting, looking across the kitchen at his brother's bowed head. Finally the voice said, "Sorry, no visitors. This is not a hospital ruling, it's a police matter."

He hung up. "It's no use, without Martin. They won't even let us in to see him."

Ray blurted out, "But Kitty saw him!"

"What are you talking about?"

"Laura found her with him—"

"Who's Laura?"

"I told you. The student nurse, my friend. In fact she had to ask Kitty to leave."

Ralph sank into a chair. So Kitty knew too. It figured. The only ones who were deluded were those who, like himself and Ray, had clung to the childish belief that you could keep secrets. What he should do was to go to Kitty at once and learn from her what Mel had said. He should go to her *anyway*, that was what Ray was thinking, you could see it in his eyes. Partly to forestall him, partly to persuade himself, he said aloud, "It doesn't matter what Kitty was doing there.

Maybe even apologizing. I'll find out from her in the morning. The point is, we're stymied at least until then. And in another day, who knows, maybe in another hour, it's all going to be out in the open. We've had it, and we can't even get to Mel."

"I think we can get to him. Through Laura. Won't it have been worth while, then?"

What was the boy talking about? Ralph mumbled wearily, "Nothing has been worth while. The price for everything is too high. If you want to try, go ahead. You need the practice. But I can't talk to anyone any more, not even you." He arose. "I have to lie down."

"Please, go ahead. I'll see you're not disturbed."

Ray had extended his hand as if to touch him on the shoulder in passing. No, Ralph thought, not that, I'm not ready yet for fraternal caresses; and he maneuvered around the kitchen table so as to avoid any touch on his shoulder, even at the cost of embarrassing his brother.

He went on through the hall and up the staircase to the room which he had pre-empted, the room which had been his father's. He kicked off his shoes, and lay down heavily on his father's bed. It was strange. With Kitty gone, the bedroom had already reverted to masculinity, lonely and monastic; once again he felt his father's presence, even more strongly than before.

Although he was exhausted, sleep would not come easily. But it was not his dreamy father, any more than it was his ill-used mother or his driven uncle, who kept him awake; the dead were well dead, and over these last six months he had exorcised their ghosts. Even if he had not, this weekend's supposedly aimless driving (in actuality he had been startled at the number of times he had passed the Land Pharmacy) had drawn most of the sting from his memories of those three. He had crossed their tracks, and his own too, so often that finally he had felt nothing—no pain, no grief, not even any lingering traces of disgust—at the sight of the house where he had passed what passed for his youth while his mother wept dry-eyed over her darning, and his father the alchemist concocted Land Sea and Air Sick Pills. Even Max's castle, last way station for the Lands before dissolution into eremitical eccentricity, was now just an old house engulfed by suburbia. Its ghosts were gone, including the defeated widower who had retreated to it with his one remaining son, thereby dooming him to deformation that he just might have escaped had they clung to their own home, the three and a half dark rooms behind the fusty drugstore.

It was not the dead who troubled him now, nor even his own dead youth, which he had buried at New Year's with his father. No matter whether you bemoaned your own wretched childhood or the twisted lives of your forebears, it was all mere wasteful self-pity. A living trio concerned him more now: his brothers and his wife.

As a result of what he had done, in his blind thrashing way that he had thought of as being rational and calculating, not just their faces but their futures were altered. There was warrant enough, you might argue, for him and Mel, who had once been devoted, to beat each other to death, to battle with fists, feet, spit, and blood, presumably over their inheritance, but actually to destroy the past and to avenge their common separation from it.

As for Ray, he was enough to make anyone itch to starve him slowly, to give him the excuse and the basis for honest-to-God martyrdom. The prize alibi of all time: If I hadn't done it to him someone else would have, or he would have done it to himself. And who could be held accountable for that? Answer: A brother.

But weren't there brothers who hated each other with good reason? And brothers who ignored each other's existence with what you could only describe as perfect propriety? So, although his guts still pained him for what he had done to Mel and to Ray, it was still reasonable to cling to the belief that they owed him redress perhaps as much as he did them.

With Kitty, though, it was another matter. Men made

apologetic jokes about a stiff prick having no conscience, but they flinched from recognizing the responsibility that followed their demand for commitment. A roll in the hay was one thing, but when you pleaded, even wordlessly, for a woman's love, the best thing she had to give, then you had to accept the consequences.

On this bed on which he lay staring, desperate for a few hours of forgetfulness, he and Kitty had writhed night after night, and as he made her twine her limbs about his in absolute abandon, he had drawn from her the orgasmic confession that she was his once and for all, she was his, she was his, he could do with her as he pleased. And he had. If she had filled her belly in violation of their compact, it was because in the end she had come to believe that he would give her nothing else. She hadn't wanted a god, or a father. Like most grownups, she had already had those. She had wanted a man.

That was the one thing, in his obsession with the future, that he had not reckoned with. Lost in his dream of retribution and of a vaguely roseate life thereafter, he had perhaps succeeded for a time in persuading Kitty of its inevitability. But mostly he had moved through this dream-filled house like one more Land in a dream, draining his wife of her best in the vain hope that the dream not only would become the truth but was in fact the immanent truth.

Perhaps only Kitty knew where his somnambulism had taken him. Had she already recoiled so far from it that she would no longer want to tell him? It could be that, like his mother who had rocked Raymond to sleep while her hopeless husband did his brother's bidding, she was no longer even interested. She might already have written him off in favor of his unborn offspring.

No one was wholly right. What a discovery! His brothers had been wrong, as wrong as their uncle, as wrong as their parents. Kitty was wrong too, to think that without a husband she could have a baby who would turn out to be anything other than one more variation on an already overplayed

theme. And he had been wrongest of all, fixed and frozen in
his conviction that to deprive Mel of his portion was to vindi-
cate their mother and thereby to render his own life worth
while, regardless of what it did to Kitty. What if Mel had been
everything he accused him of? What had he himself achieved
in these long months other than poisoning the innocent?

At last he fell asleep. In his sleep the argument continued,
for a while, in the form of stale and rancorous discussions with
his father in a familiar saloon, Land's Spot. The two of them
were served by a silent drooping waitress. At first he hadn't
recognized her but then he looked up from the reddened
hands to the black uniform and the tired homely face, and
he cried out gladly, "Mama, I'm so happy to see you, I
thought you were dead, they said you were dead!" She looked
pleased, but said nothing in reply, only caressed the nape of
his neck with her rough hand in the absent way he had been
yearning for without realizing it. His father muttered, "She
was sick for a long time, she was upset about you boys, that's
what you're thinking of." He was filled with an enormous
sense of relief, but it did not last long because after that he
became involved in a panoramic drama which he knew would
be endless but was nevertheless fascinating, like reading a
picaresque novel with himself the hero.

Two people kept reappearing, Solomon and Martin Stark,
only now they were not father and son but brothers, constantly whispering comments to each other about Ralph which
he could not quite catch. They had come down in the world,
which pleased him, and were rooming together in a creaky,
creepy old house that faced the back of the saloon, Land's
Spot. From his bedroom window he could look across the way
directly into theirs, which had no curtain, and in fact had no
furniture at all other than two empty chairs. He nudged Kitty,
lying comfortably in bed beside him, and said, "Look, see how
those two exist, and they make remarks about me sleeping
with a girl when I'm only sixteen!" But then a noise roused
him further and he arose from his bed, glancing at his watch

(it was six-thirty in the morning), and peered down out of his window. He saw in astonishment that an immense funeral cortege was forming in the street before the Starks' rooming house. That's why their room is so bare, he said to himself, and motioned to Kitty to join him at the window. Even though it was barely dawn and the street lights were still on, a line of cars filled the street, and pedestrians in their Sunday or mourning best filled the sidewalks. There was a great coming and going, and all the houses on the block were decorated with strung-up Christmas lights, neon tubing, or Chinese lanterns, as though it were some great fiesta. Directly below stood the horse-drawn hearse, the European kind, blacker than the night, with much baroque silver scrollwork. A uniformed employee of the funeral parlor, who was directing the activity, had painted his top hat a luminescent orange. The effect was ludicrous but it was sensible, because he was constantly darting out into the street to direct traffic, and might otherwise have been run down by one of the throng of dark automobiles. Suddenly he did something odd. He clapped his gray-gloved hands together smartly six times in a rhythm of five, then one: clap-clap-clap-clap-clap . . . Clap! It was embarrassingly like a conga. Besides, as Ralph murmured to Kitty, the uniform, the jerky movements, and even a light rain which had begun to fall, imparted to it a highly stylized quality. They might have been watching a German expressionist movie of the twenties. Six honorary pallbearers, all of them distinguished, and all in formal mourning wear, sprang up from under the very hearse, clapping their hands in unison with their director. What Ralph suddenly realized, very belatedly, and with considerable uneasiness, was that the director was none other than Martin Stark. For a while he had managed to disguise his limp with his rigid jerky movements, but as the pallbearers took their places he moved among them with a brisk authoritative brutality, and was therefore unable to conceal the clubfoot which threw him forward with every step he took. He was particularly brusque when he discovered that one rank of the double line of pall-bearers was lame. One man had a short leg and a huge built-up boot, a second wore an aluminum brace over his shriveled leg, a third lacked a leg completely. "It takes a cripple to be really cruel to another cripple," Ralph said over his shoulder to Kitty, and watched in fascination as a coffin, rather small for a grown man, perhaps large enough for an adolescent, was hoisted from the hearse on the shoulders of the pallbearers and carted into the house with the empty rooms. The coffin tapered sharply at one end and was painted a bright yellow, as if it were meant to decorate a kitchen or a playroom, but more disturbing was the thought that if Martin Stark was running the funeral, he could hardly be the one they had come to bury. Nor could it be his brother, the doctor, for there he was too, standing in the wan artificial light beside the bright yellow coffin, shaking his head pityingly, with agonizing slowness. Invaded by a quick surge of nameless terror, Ralph whirled about and demanded of Kitty, in a trembling voice, "If it isn't either of the Starks they're coming to bury, who can it be?" Kitty fixed him with her glittering eyes. "You," she whispered, and Ralph lurched up and away in terror, his throat cracked and his lungs screaming for air.

Ray was shaking him gently by the shoulder. Ralph blinked and sat upright rapidly.

"What is it? What is it?"

"I hate to disturb you, but you were sleeping restlessly anyway and I thought you'd want to know."

"Know what?"

"That Laura has a message for us, from Mel."

Now he was awake. He swung his legs over the side of the bed and demanded impatiently, "Let's have it."

"But I don't know what it is."

Sometimes Ray invited violence. Ralph slipped his feet into his shoes and said, "When you're ready you can go ahead and explain it to me. Take your time, we've got all our lives."

"You see, Laura got hold of Martin Stark, I guess through Dr. Stark—she couldn't get to a phone—and Martin called us. He says it's most urgent and he'd like us at his house by five o'clock."

"So what's your rush?"

"It's almost that now. Ralphie, you've slept the day away."

12: RAY

LEAVING THE HOUSE, Ray discovered, was simple. Far simpler in fact than leaving the attic, repository of his few clothes, his tools, his books, his barbells, his radio station, and most of all his confidant: the ledger books in which for nearly three years, ever since he had decided to remain in the attic, he had carried on a running battle with himself, setting down what he saw and heard, and trying furiously to make some sense of it. He would be returning to the house, of course, and to the attic, to clear out the little accumulation of objects he would no longer need. But he would never write in the diary again. Of that he was so sure that he bound the books round with twine and stacked them in a corner; still he could not quite bring himself to destroy them.

Ralph, oddly enough, was far more nervous than he. On the front porch he first peered, scowling, every which way. Then, as if it were raining heavily, he scuttled rapidly out to the carriageway, neck hunched forward, and began to tug at the canvas top of his little sports car.

"Come on," he grunted, "give me a hand." When they were settled in the closed car and backing out of the drive, Ray was emboldened to protest.

"What's the point in hiding any more, Ralph? It's all up, you said so yourself."

"I still have to play for time. Bad enough to have to explain to everyone about you. What could I say about Mel, when we don't even know ourselves how things will work out?"

"But from now on everyone will have to see what we're doing."

Ralph replied only, "One of these days everyone will have other things to think about," and then fell silent.

Ray was free to look about him as they cut across Happy Valley on the straightaway leading to the village of Emersonville, where Martin Stark lived with his family. Most exciting was not what Martin would have to say, but what lay on either side of them now, thanks to the low little car, not only within earshot but within arm's reach too. How wonderful it was not just to see people talk, but to hear them as well, not just to see them walk but to move with them. Watching, he had been unable to hear; listening, he had been unable to see. How beautiful this was!

At the curbside, bordering an empty lot—no man's land between two warring worlds—an elderly veteran, his gray hair tousled and wind-ruffled, a cigarette butt wet and brownish depending from his lower lip, propelled himself slowly in his motorized wheel chair. Beside him, a kid (his grandson?) in polo shirt and stained dungarees, the front of his face distorted by pink bubble gum, skipped seriously, avoiding the cracks in the cement. For the suspended moment when the auto drew abreast of them, pausing for a light, Raymond was suddenly one of them, he was both of them, resting his powerful old forearms on the tiller, skipping over the asphalt with his springy young legs, lipping a damp cigarette and inflating an elastic morsel of sweet gum.

"Isn't it a wonderful day?" he called to them.

"No good for the rhubarb," the old paralytic called back mysteriously.

Before Ray could fathom this, Ralph had shot ahead and away, muttering, "From one extreme to the other. Are you going to talk to *everybody* now?"

They drew up to a new group, a crowd of loungers, scuffling boys and shuffling girls, all of them with great heaps of hair on their heads, arguing languidly over the cover of a movie fan magazine. He was so close that he could count the studs on the boys' jackets and see sky through the fragile teased-up birds' nests teetering above the girls' foreheads.

At the next red light two women stood waiting at Raymond's finger tips. Both were crammed into slacks, both smoked cork-tipped cigarettes, both pushed baby carriages. But only one of the carriages contained a sleeping baby, lolling bowlegged, framed by parcels; the other was packed with a week's load of frozen foods, steaks, vegetables, and beer. The mother was complaining. "He parks himself in front of the TV, he don't even let me clean around him. I tell him I wisht he'd take his sprained ankle and his Blue Cross to the hospital and he tells me to get lost, he can't see the ball game through my behind. And who do you think complains about the fluffballs under the end table?"

Her companion's reply was lost in the roaring blast as Ralph took off with the green, then threw the motor into second as it gained speed. The women were lost to sight and sound forever; but in the one moment he had been beside them Raymond felt, with a quick thrill, that he had learned something essential about them, as one feels that suddenly one has understood the intent of an artist.

He turned to say something of the sort to Ralph, but his brother foreclosed the possibility by asserting, rather curtly, "If we keep straight, we can get to Marty's by way of downtown Emersonville. If we bear right, we pass the cemetery. Want to pay your respects to the folks? And to Uncle Max, from whom all blessings flow?"

"Oh no," Raymond replied quickly, he hoped not too quickly. "I'm just getting used to the living. I'm sure the dead are in less of a hurry for me." He laughed nervously. "They'll wait, won't they?"

"Forever, if need be," answered Ralph grimly, and kept straight on through the shopping section of Emersonville.

It had once been an elite village. The postwar years had erased the family farms which formerly sheltered it from the city, and now it too was a suburb—but still of a serene amplitude which impelled its uneasy inhabitants to take legal precautions against its becoming another Happy Valley. Those in belated flight from the decaying city would have to look elsewhere; Emersonville's handsome wrought-iron gates were firmly closed.

The business area was not marred by the chipped, rusted, and dangerously dangling signs of declining drugstores. In fact, Raymond was fascinated to observe, there were not only no shabby stores, there were no overhead signs at all. The shops hid their wares modestly behind little greenish bull's-eye windows, shaded by the overhang of the half-timbered Tudor houses which discreetly sheltered them. Even the gas station made do without flags or flying horses. Its pumps, sunk partway into the ground, might almost have been hitching posts.

Safely away from the stores, Emersonville's homes resembled those in the older and statelier areas of the city which had resisted engulfment by the flood of projects and the rushing streams of arterial traffic. Determinedly unmodern, they held painstakingly aloof from one another (even after the finical niceness with which the occasional newcomer was selected) by means of sinuous roadways, head-high hedges of rambler roses, and stone walls sweetened with honeysuckle and wisteria. Tennis courts and lawns tightly trimmed for croquet and garden parties accented delicately the country-like atmosphere and reinforced the impression that the community consisted of modest estates (although it would have shrunk from that word). On these drives, roads, and lanes, none of which were ever called streets, even the children's voices were muted.

Amid all this emphatic understatement, Ray was bemused by the extravagantly colonial street names, apparently selected because they reverberated with the echoes of a history otherwise recalled only when a child, poking through the excavation for his family's new swimming pool or greenhouse, came upon an arrowhead or a spent bullet.

So he observed that Martin Stark lived in a rambling three-story pile almost completely buried in glossy green ivy, fixed like a chateau on a sweeping knoll at the corner of Flintlock Drive and Redcoat Lane. As Ralph cut expertly into the curving graveled drive, Raymond glimpsed the tiny iron nameplate, STARK, an inch or two above the pachysandra from which it might have been growing, and half hidden by the yews and junipers which bordered the drive.

"Looks like they've been living here forever, doesn't it?" It was the first time Ralph had spoken to him since the crossroads. "You'd never know that Dr. Stark was born in the old country just like Pop."

Ray could not resist replying, "It's a little late for jealousy, Ralphie," but he regretted it when he saw the stricken look come over his brother's face.

Ahead, at the end of the driveway, bulked the stone garage, its glass overhead door slung into the roof to reveal, in addition to yellow bicycles, green plastic hose, and pink wheelbarrow, the two Stark automobiles, a white Ford station wagon and a smaller white Mercedes convertible.

As his brother drew up the hand brake, Raymond heard the high almost wailing sounds of children's laughter. He climbed out clumsily, self-conscious under the stares of two girls in striped jerseys and shorts who were just leaving a blacktopped badminton court beyond the garage. The girls were only a year or two apart, the older perhaps eleven, but very unlike. The younger was dark and skinny, with huge knees like doorknobs, and much solemnity; she picked at her nose with her free hand as she swung her badminton racket. Her older sister was blondish, like Martin, but decisively fat and hospitable.

"Hi." She greeted them amicably by tapping the bird at Ralph, who snared it and slapped it back to her. "I'm Judy. This is Sarah. Sarah, take your finger out of your nose. Are you the men Daddy is expecting?"

"I imagine we are."

"Come on, I'll show you the way."

Ray hastened after her, very much aware of the unblinking gaze of Sarah, who had not uttered a word. But then, neither had he—and he was hoping that he could sit quietly in a dark corner while Martin and Ralph talked.

But not so fast. Judy was saying, in her bubbling, fat girl's voice, "Then you must be the Lands. I read all about you in the papers, the missing will, and the hidden money and stuff, and the guy that broke in, and everything. Gee, it must be exciting!"

Staring at them hopefully, as if at any moment they might do something outrageous, Judy held open the screen door of the carriage entrance for them.

"Mommy!" she called out loudly.

Silent Sarah stuck her racket into the umbrella stand of the cool dark carpeted hallway and wandered off, leaving Judy to produce their mother from the living room beyond.

Ellen Stark, a tall bony woman in her late thirties, came forward to greet them.

She wore a cashmere sweater set with pale beads at the neck, she was allowing her brown hair to turn gray and, when she shook hands, she put down, alongside the latest number of the *American Scholar* and a novel by Mary Ellen Chase, a pair of substantial tortoise-shell spectacles. Behind the pleats of her plaid skirt hid Abby, youngest of the Starks, and the only one who really resembled her elderly grandfather.

As she spoke to Ralph, in a softly modulated voice, Mrs. Stark picked up a pair of garden shears from the hall table and commenced to prune the late white peonies standing thickly in a vase.

"We've regretted that you and your wife haven't been able to visit us, but then it's been a difficult time all round. Perhaps after she returns from the hospital? I'm so relieved to learn from my father-in-law that she's doing well."

"Thanks to him," Ralph replied readily. "Now that I've had the pleasure of meeting your charming girls, I'm all the more sorry that we haven't gotten together earlier. But let me introduce—"

"Raymond, I assume."

Ray nodded dumbly. He was impressed by the ease with which his brother could manage this kind of small talk. It was one thing to know that Ralph had to do it all day long; it was something else to see him in action. As for Ellen Stark, she spoke so coolly, with such poise, that if this were San Francisco and he had just swum in from Alcatraz, he would have elicited from her, he felt, nothing more than a very polite, "You look quite wet, would you care for a towel?"

She murmured, "Now that you're getting about, you must come one day with your brother and sister-in-law."

"Thank you," was all he could manage, in a half-strangled voice. He wanted to clear his throat, but he was afraid it would sound even worse. If Laura were this poised, he would never have been able to speak to her.

"I know you want to see Martin, and he's most anxious to see you, so I won't detain you. Let me show you to his study."

They moved through the living room over faded Oriental carpeting, skirting a dark old Steinway with massive spooled legs, past prints of Venice labeled *Ca' d'Oro* and *Scuola di San Rocco*, past many bookcases crowding the long hallway, to a solid-looking door on which Ellen Stark rapped lightly before opening it. Imagine anybody in our family, Raymond thought, knocking on a door before opening it. Uncle Max had never bothered, even when Mama was still alive, to close the bathroom door. But at least Uncle Max was no hypocrite, in fairness you had to say that, especially when you sensed how anxious this very well-bred woman was to be rid of her two visitors.

"Come on in," Martin Stark called out, and arose from behind his desk, at which he had been stuffing a curved meerschaum from a large tin of Blue Boar tobacco. He had slung his jacket over the back of a leather chair, from which he lifted it as he approached them; he was cool but correct in a short-sleeved white shirt with a severe regimental-stripe tie. The hospitable haste with which he propelled his lanky frame forward made his limp more pronounced; it made you nervous to watch him, even though his self-assurance was absolute.

"May I bring you anything, Martin?" his wife inquired.

"Thank you, dear, no. I have all the needful."

"Then I'll leave you." Ellen Stark's brisk closing smile was almost palpably one more in her long list of well-managed household duties.

"What'll it be, gents?" Martin demanded, bending over a private bar which was so stocked with bottles, like the compounding alcove of Land Bros. Pharmacy, that Raymond was intimidated into denying his thirst.

"Nothing, thanks," he said quickly. He cursed himself; now Martin must know that he had no idea what to ask for.

Martin however, after remarking, "How about just some ice water, all right?" turned amiably to Ralph.

"Scotch and water, please. Yes, with ice. You have a beautiful place here, Martin."

"That's right, this is your first visit, isn't it?" And as if he had overheard Ralph's bitter remark in the driveway, and wanted to forestall another such, Martin added candidly,

"Sometimes when I glance around me I can hardly believe that only fifty years ago my dad was working his way through med school as a greenhorn candy butcher on the lake boats. Our history here is pretty brief, after all, isn't it?"

The lawyer served them, motioning Raymond to a brass-studded red leather chair before the bookcase, and Ralph to another, beside a three-legged globe. While the men sipped, Raymond, his back to the curtained window (he could hear the girls' voices outside, including Abby's, now raised to a whine, and uselessly soothed by a Negro maid), glanced about at these strange surroundings, so clean, so orderly, so carefully comfortable, and as Martin himself said, as stable as if the Starks had always lived like this.

Martin's fiddle, about which Ralph had spoken so often, lay in its case, alongside a cello and a music stand on which rested a volume of Schubert sonatinas. So he practiced here, away from all the females except his wife—his three daughters and their girl friends, the maid, and doubtless his mother-in-law. Above the desk at which he sat, drawing meditatively on his meerschaum, hung an oil portrait of Dr. Stark—"He broke down and let us commission it," Martin explained, "to commemorate his seventieth birthday"—painted by an artist who had not merely captured a likeness but had succeeded in seizing the doctor's inimitably rueful regard, half somber, half mocking, as he sat before a wall decorated with the bearded sketches of some of his illustrious predecessors in the medical arts.

The books at Ray's elbow were mostly histories, biographies, and travel books. He supposed that lawyers kept their lawbooks in their offices, where they were more impressive and probably more useful, although he did see here a number of volumes on aspects of the law by Holmes, Cahn, and Frank, and a fat tome entitled *The Wisdom of the Supreme Court*, a gift no doubt. The only novels that he noticed were *The Caine Mutiny* and *By Love Possessed*, both of them under a long shelf of multicolored back issues of *Commentary*.

"I hear you've got word for us from Mel," Ralph remarked.

How casually he said it! He might have been asking after someone's health.

"I don't mean to stall, but I think it would be best if you told me first how the two of you stand." The lawyer spoke gently, but there was something minatory in his tone; Ray felt the goose flesh rise on his arms, and waited tensely, as much to hear what his brother would explain as to learn what Mel had conveyed to the lawyer.

"Martin, you know that we can't go on. We've done things that we'd rather not remember. Now, finally, we're ready to settle up."

"I'm afraid it's not going to be quite that easy."

Ralph's hands were shaking. The ice cubes in his glass slid from side to side, clinking gently as they moved. "Better tell us, Martin."

The lawyer sighed. "If only you two had gotten together earlier."

No matter what reply Ralph would make to this, Ray saw, it would not do. He leaned forward and said eagerly, "But that's the whole point. It was Mel's coming, and his fight with Ralph, that brought things to a head. Without Mel, who knows when we'd have gotten together?"

Martin Stark contemplated his pipe. "Neither of you seems to realize what you're up against."

In the sudden silence that followed, little Abby's weeping voice was high and clear. "If they go, why can't I? Why can't I?"

"I think I told you, Ray," Martin went on, "Mel's nurse got hold of my dad at the hospital. He rang me up here just as I was coming into the house. Now, I didn't get it straight, whether she had delivered a message from you to Mel. I think she must have, but in any event her message from Mel was for me. I don't know whether it's any consolation to you, but he's not too sick to talk very tough indeed."

"How tough?" Ralph was on his feet. "That's what we want

to know. How tough? And why did he send you the message instead of us?"

"Because he doesn't trust you," Martin replied in his smooth, dark lawyer's voice. "Because he wanted to find out whether I'm the Land estate executor, the family lawyer, or what. To put it bluntly, he means to attack you with every weapon he can find. Both of you."

"Why both? And what does he want?" Ralph's voice rose. "For God's sake, what does he want?"

"He believes you have brainwashed Raymond. The nurse said she couldn't argue him out of it. He's convinced you betrayed him, Ralph, and you mean to chisel him out of his due."

"His due? Legally he's got no more coming than I do."

Martin Stark said patiently, "He's in a rage. He talks about legalisms, just as you do, but actually he's no more rational now than you or Ray were until this afternoon. He talks about morality too, just as"—the lawyer smiled coldly—"all of us do. No doubt he thinks he has a moral right to all of your Uncle Max's property."

"But that's preposterous!"

"Of course," the lawyer said with maddening deliberateness, "on the surface of things it's preposterous. It seems perfectly clear, A, that Raymond is the legal heir, B, that in a matter of days he comes of age, and C, that when the will is admitted to probate the estate will become his to dispose of as he sees fit. But you never know. Mel might claim that your father, or your Uncle Max, or both, were of unsound mind when they executed their wills. Certainly it would be foolish, especially when you're ready to give him a substantial share, but do you have any idea how many legal actions have been inspired by hatred? In fact, there are many other things he could do. Most of them would be self-defeating, but they'd be messy, dragged-out, expensive. If he's bent on making you suffer . . ."

Raymond arose. In his agitation he bumped against the globe and sent it spinning rapidly.

"I'm sorry." He bent down to stop it. "It's just that there's been so much suffering already. Too much."

"We're all agreed on that. But don't you find it odd, how so many of us think we can bring it to an end by inflicting more?"

Prowling restlessly, Ralph mumbled, "Now you sound just like your father. Let's get practical. What can we do in a hurry to finish this thing? Don't tell me we're doomed to years of litigation with that fanatic."

"Everyone uses that word about everyone else." Martin Stark pushed back his chair. "But you're right, I couldn't agree more. It's to everyone's advantage to move fast. The quicker you can bring Mel to reason, the quicker outsiders will lose interest. The less publicity, the less suffering for everyone— including Mel."

"I think he wants to suffer. But never mind. We ought to go see him as soon as possible, is that what you're saying?"

"It is."

"The thing is, Martin, I phoned the hospital earlier. The police say no visitors. Do you think you could get around that?"

"I already have." Martin smiled impartially at them both. "While I was waiting for you, I spoke to my father again. He's going to have Mel waiting for us, in the hospital pavilion. So whenever you're ready . . ." He glanced at a glass-walled, four-sided clock on his desk.

"I'll be damned. I'll really be damned." Ralph was staring at their host with unfeigned admiration. "No wonder your old man is proud of you."

But Ray could not still the uneasiness which the lawyer's words had aroused. It was not so much that Martin Stark had been planning for them while he waited for them—that could be accounted a kindness—as that he had his own plans, a parallel course which might be serving his own ends more than theirs.

Martin misunderstood, or chose to misunderstand, the hesitancy that Ray was unable to conceal.

"Don't worry, Ray, about the reporters and the police. I'll be right there with you. Just bear in mind that the quicker we can get to Mel, the better disposed he'll be to settle matters. The same goes for the authorities. The quicker the three of you state your relationship, the easier it will be for me to convince the district attorney that it's merely a family affair."

Is that the reason, Ray wondered, why he seems so eager?

The lawyer went on, "All the advantage rests with you if you take the initiative in making a public statement. It's rather wonderful, how quickly the media lose interest in you once you've shown that you have nothing to hide."

Ray said nothing. But Ralph, gnawing on a finger, demanded, "How can we give out a statement when we don't know what to say?"

"Oh, I didn't mean before seeing Mel. I meant after. What we might do would be to inform the authorities and the press —I could do it, if you'd prefer it that way—that Ralph and Mel hadn't seen each other since 'forty-nine, that Mel was trying to find his way around the house in the dark, that Ralph was naturally nervous about intruders after all the unfortunate publicity. What could be more understandable than a struggle in the dark? Or that now Raymond, who had been living in seclusion for reasons of health, should be concerned about his eldest brother to the point of giving up his seclusion and coming to the hospital? Then, if things work out with Mel, I can simply issue a brief statement on the way out, to the effect that the family has made private arrangements for disposition of the estate."

It reminded Ray of the pastel portraits executed by lightning artists at fairs and carnivals. Martin's construction was an excellent likeness, swiftly and cleverly sketched in but, precisely to the degree that it was a caricature of the truth,

it lacked humanity. The lawyer might have been talking of
anyone, and so in the end he talked of no one. Above him,
his father's face grinned, more sardonic than ever.

Was this what was troubling Ralph? His thick black eyebrows were drawn together into the familiar menacing straight
line.

"That's great as far as it goes," he said, "but it's full of
holes. Like, why did Ray put off having the will probated,
even though he was staying in the house? Or why didn't I let
on to anyone that he's been in the attic all this time that people have been supposedly looking for him? Or where has
Mel been all these months before he turned up in the dead
of night?"

"I don't mean to sound sententious, but the truth is always
your best spokesman. Ray hasn't acted on the will because
he wanted to consult with his other brother, who's been un-
available. You haven't disclosed his presence in the house
simply because you respected his wishes. As for Mel, since
it will have to come out anyway, why don't we just say that
he was serving a sentence in Pennsylvania under an assumed
name, since he didn't want to bring disgrace on his family.
I know that manliness is a word that's almost gone out of the
language, but I still feel that the public will respond to an
appeal to its sense of sportsmanship."

"Well, I don't. The public wants thrills and dirt. But I don't
see any way out of it. All I want to know now is, what do we
say to Mel when we walk in?"

Martin did not immediately respond. Ray felt anyway that
the question was really directed at him and not at the lawyer,
so he said, "Why don't we just listen to him, and then decide? Maybe that's what he really wants, for us to listen."

"You mean, go in there cold, with no plan at all? That's
typical of you. It means we're completely unprepared if he
tries to pull a fast one. Instead of acting, all we'll be able to
do is react." He turned to their host. "What do you think,
Martin?"

The lawyer said slowly, "I think Ray is right."

Ralph made one last tearing wrenching bite at the quick of his little finger. Then he looked up, measuringly, at Ray. "What do you say?"

"I'm ready to go."

Having surprised himself with his own forthrightness, Ray found that he was unable to meet his brother's tormented gaze. He bent down on one knee and straightened out the rug, near where the globe had fallen.

"We can all go together," Martin said. "I'll take the station wagon, it's very roomy."

"I wouldn't want to come all the way back here to pick up my car. Besides, I may need it for a fast getaway." Ralph laughed shortly, without amusement. "I'll hop out now and pull mine off to the side, so you can back yours out. Ray, you drive along with Martin and keep him company. I'll follow."

Ralph was gone and making for the driveway before Martin could say a word. Ray surprised himself yet again by extending his arm to bar the lawyer's way for a moment.

"I think he'd prefer to go alone. It's not just Mel. Or even the police and the newspapers, although he's been brooding about this moment for months. It's Kitty."

"And what about you? I didn't hear him say what a trying experience this is for you."

"He knows that. All this time, he's been trying to buck me up to face the outside world. But in my crazy way I have been facing it. And in his own way, he hasn't. Can you imagine how he feels, having to see his wife and his brother just as he's discovered that about himself?"

Seated in the car next to Martin Stark, Ray felt called upon to make a formal family apology.

"I'm afraid we're imposing on you, making you run all over town like this."

"Not a bit of it. Even if it weren't a professional obligation, I'd feel it my personal duty to go along and see you through it."

"Still, you're very kind."

"Well, if I am, you're very courageous. That strikes me as a superior virtue. So let's say no more about either."

The flies buzzed lazily in the summery air, the boys cruised languidly on their bikes, not pumping, in these last moments of freedom before supper and the family reunion. Even the voices of the girls who played hopscotch, and with their blue chalk marked mystic hearts and monograms on the sidewalk, were muted on the June streets.

Martin Stark glanced at him. "Ray, what are your expectations?"

"I don't know that I've got expectations any more. But I've still got hopes, if that's what you're asking."

The lawyer smiled his slow private smile. His eyes were fastened briefly on Ray before being recalled to the thickening dinner-hour traffic. "Want to tell me about them?"

Raymond twisted about until he could see the Triumph behind them, so that he could keep his brother in sight as well as in mind.

"They used to be pretty grandiose," he said. "Now, I'd just like for us all to be free to go on in whatever ways would be best for us."

"Do you know what those ways are?"

"Not even for myself. But finally I'm ready to find out. I think Ralph is too."

"Would it make much of a difference to you . . ." the lawyer paused to negotiate a left-hand turn in the face of oncoming traffic, ". . . if there wouldn't be much money forthcoming?"

"I've tried for six months to tell Ralph that I didn't need the money. After all, in my own way I've been living in the lap of luxury."

"But you weren't any more successful with Ralph than he was with you."

"He claimed all along it was the principle that mattered, but I always thought that with him it was the money. Does that sound unfair? I mean it was his idea of what the money would buy for him, that's what I think has driven him on all these months. We'd always lived miserably as children, not just shabbily like poor people, but miserably. Peculiarly. Ralph thought this was his chance to live it up, no matter exactly how, so long as it would be different. But it's frightened him, how desperately he'd come to want the money. I think now at last he really is more interested in principle than in money."

"Then what about Mel?"

"You'd think he'd be after the money, wouldn't you? Who could need it more? But it sounds like he's so set on his principles, whatever they are, that he's forgotten about the money."

"I must say, that for a person who has supposedly cut himself off from the world, you have more savvy than some trial lawyers of my acquaintance. If only my father, and your brothers, and everybody else who's mixed up in this, would worry less about you and simply concentrate on being reasonable, we'd wrap this thing up in no time."

The lawyer's words were flattering, but something about his manner was not. I've been telling him more than he's been telling me, Ray said to himself. It was not so much that you had to learn mistrust when you went out into the world, as that you had to teach yourself a prudence, a holding back.

"Well, there's the hospital. We'll take the emergency entrance, we're less likely to be observed there. Is Ralph still with us?"

Ray glanced back and then nodded. He squeezed his hands hard between his thighs to conceal their trembling. In a few minutes, he knew, terrible things were going to be revealed, things which no lawyer or family friend should hear or even know of.

Martin Stark swung the car deftly into an empty space,

and hoisted his long legs out onto the gravel, moving with grace despite his limp.

"This is about dinner hour, they eat early in hospitals, you know. So I don't imagine we'll encounter too many people. Still, let's go in the side door. If there's anything that has to be said, I'll take care of it, and you and Ralph can go on ahead."

He indicated the emergency entrance, a sloping ramp up which they scrambled, Martin hoisting himself with the aid of the railing, and found themselves at the end of the ground-floor corridor, already safely beyond both Information and Registration desks. They turned to the left, and suddenly Laura stood before them. She was radiant.

Ray had been trying to imagine her in this ambience which she had chosen for herself, but he could not, it evaded him. When he thought of her she remained obstinately as she had been before, determined but forlorn, in a cause that was wildly irrelevant to her own inner life and to those of the people who had passed her by without a glance.

But to see her here was to erase the earlier memory, to make her new, to make it marvelous that they should know each other. Her welcoming smile illuminated this dark place as if she bore a candelabra to light the way for him.

They did not greet each other. Instead she spoke in a rush, but shyly, as though she might be talking out of turn.

"I've been waiting. Dr. Stark told me to watch for you. We'll go this way."

He wanted to take her by the hand and go away with her, someplace where neither of them had ever been, where they could sit quietly and look at each other. Instead he had to say, "Laura, this is Martin Stark, the attorney, Dr. Stark's son."

Embarrassed, she shook the lawyer's extended hand. "I think you'd better go right on."

"Let's just wait one minute for Ralph." Martin seemed amused. "Here he comes now."

I almost forgot him, Ray thought, I almost forgot why we're here.

Ralph hurried toward them, his open jacket flapping with his quick nervous stride. His clothes hung on him, he looked more gaunt than he had only an hour earlier.

"Ralphie," Ray said quickly, "this is Laura."

Ralph nodded impersonally.

Laura said to him, "Mrs. Land is already in the pavilion."

Ralph closed his eyes for an instant. To anyone but a brother, he might only have been blinking. "And my—"

Martin Stark interrupted him, casually, but quite low. "Let's follow the nurse, shall we?"

Rumpled and defiant, but hot-blooded again—maybe he had swallowed some more pep pills in the car?—Ralph muttered curtly, "Come on."

They walked in twos, Ralph with Martin, Ray with Laura but not touching her. He had the sense of her at his side, the sound of her starched skirt, the sweet fresh smell of her, all through their swift passage down the lime-green corridor.

They turned abruptly to the right and were just as abruptly in the midst of the maternity receiving ward.

It was a zone which he would have thought would be serene if not sacred, tiptoe in tone and churchly in spirit, reverential at the arrival of new life. Instead he saw not only doctors but husbands and brothers-in-law, talking not in whispers but in loud assertive tones; and he shrank from the chattering women, no more glamorous than if they were going to the toilet—which in fact most of them were. They shuffled about in bathrobes, in wrappers, in hospital gowns; they bore their swollen postnatal bellies not like holy vessels but like goitrous encumbrances; they gossiped, they complained, they hardly troubled to give way to one of their sisters who was being wheeled to the labor room with her globe jutting like a basketball. Relatives hovered, noisy with felicitations and encouragement, bearing baskets of chicken wings, jelly doughnuts, and pizza. Surrounded by female flesh and smells, Raymond would hardly have been startled to see one of the harried nurses dumping a bloody basin of clotted slops into the jammed and odorous hallway.

He was even less prepared, though, to find here the detective who had come to the house in the morning to talk to Ralph. Shadowed by a summer straw, the detective's pale heavy face showed but little surprise.

Ralph drew in his breath audibly. Ray wished only that there were some way for him to protect his brother from this sullen stranger in the sport shirt and business suit.

Martin Stark stepped forward, coming between him and Laura, and said amiably, "If you people will just go on ahead, I'd like to have a few words with Lieutenant Karpinski."

How easy he made it seem!

Walking three abreast now, he and Laura and Ralph turned left, away from Martin and the detective, and were out of the female zone, back into the order of the impersonal clinic, where patients lay strapped or in traction as they were intended to, drooling quietly into basins behind half-open doors or staring patiently at the ceiling, waiting for the alternative releases of healing or death.

At the end of this corridor was their goal, the pavilion. Large-windowed, sunny, its glossy potted plants lightened by a sun now low enough to stream in through the glass, it harbored not merely the ambulatory, but outsiders soon to be told the most important news of their lives. Red-eyed wives awaiting the findings of exploratory operations sat beside expectant fathers who leafed aimlessly, their eyes unfocused, through tattered tracts of the Religious Information Bureau of the Knights of Columbus. Pregnant women virtually at term huddled into their distended housecoats, embarrassed by the false labor which had brought them here too soon, and glared with wretched envy at the convalescents in midpassage to the world of the well. One of these latter was Kitty, who was carefully made up, Raymond observed, despite her dressing gown and mules, and sat relaxed with a cigarette and a fashion magazine, her legs crossed, at ease.

Hearing them approach, she glanced up. Her poise vanished. She tried to rise, her legs caught awkwardly beneath her, the magazine fell from her hand, cigarette ash scattered the front of her gown.

"Ralph!" Her voice was lower, older, than Raymond remembered. "Ralph, Ralph, I'm sorry. Do you believe me, I'm so sorry!"

His brother was clutching her arms. He was crying. Ray turned away, stunned, but Laura had already left them and was hurrying off. He heard Ralph as all the strangers, grateful for the distraction, must have too.

"Please don't apologize, Kitty, I beg of you, please don't apologize."

"If you'll just believe me, that's all I want." Now Kitty was weeping. "The only reason I phoned for help after you told me not to was because I was afraid, I couldn't stop you. I didn't want it to end like this, I didn't mean for you to suffer too. I tried to make it up to you, I thought these few days would give you a little more time. I didn't want—"

"Who cares, who cares, who cares," Ralph was crooning as he rocked his wife in his arms.

The two were oblivious to all the hungry onlookers who watched, pleased with this passion, from every corner of the solarium. Ray, staring as frankly as any of them, learned of love from the rounded back of his weeping brother and the curled clasping fingers of his brother's wife.

Because he had been afraid to weep before others, he himself had sat out two funerals and a battle between his two brothers. What a fool I am, he thought, and turned to see Dr. Stark entering the pavilion with his familiar slouch, his arm extended in imperial but friendly salutation.

"Hello, Ray," Dr. Stark greeted him, as casually as if this were their customary meeting place.

Ralph and Kitty released each other abruptly. Suddenly blank-eyed and wary, they awaited news and instructions.

"Supposing we shove a couple of these chairs over to the couch. That way we can all relax and be by ourselves for a bit."

The doctor spoke then to Ralph and Kitty, ignoring the tears still damp on their cheeks. "Mel will be along any minute. Did you folks really think I wouldn't recognize him? I did deliver him, you know. Fortunately for everyone, his cranium is tougher now than it was then. Ah, here we are."

Laura was approaching their newly arranged corner, her face set to the task of pushing a wheel chair before her.

Ray stared at the man in the wheel chair. Swathed in a boxer's bathrobe that enfolded everything but the neck of his hospital gown, he held himself still in concealment to his very finger tips which held the robe together. To see his face was enough, though, and maybe that was what he wanted to insist upon.

Swollen and bloated, patched and scarred, it could have been the battered visage of some weirdly misplaced Roman gladiator—except that the eyes were the eyes of a Tartar. It was the eyes finally which drew Raymond forward.

He approached, trembling. "I'm Ray."

The eyes did not blink but narrowed even more, as if what they saw amused them beyond measure. The amusement was tormenting, unbearable.

Ray threw himself to his knees and buried his face in the folds of the robe, hiding from the dispassionate gaze.

"Mel," he cried, his mouth muffled against his brother's body, "forgive me, Mel."

13: KITTY

MEL MIGHT HAVE BEEN, Kitty thought, the central figure in some odd religious tableau. With his bearded repentant brother kneeling under the drapery of his sheltering arm, with his other brother and wife standing on his left, red-eyed witnesses to the benevolent scene, with the elderly family counselor soberly attending, with the young nurse in white like a representative from on high, it was practically all that the most spiritually-minded could have hoped for. It was a wonder that he didn't demand, just to round off the scene, that she and Ralph also kneel for his benison.

But if he was savoring his triumph, he was apparently in no mood to prolong the moment, for he gave a convulsive wrench to free himself from Raymond's embrace.

"This is a lot of crap," he said harshly. "Come on, Ray, get up. You're hurting my ribs."

Raymond backed away awkwardly. "I don't want you to be hurt any more. Or any of us."

"Very noble. But there's been too much melodrama in this

family already. Look at you, hiding behind that beard. What did you think you were doing, bucking for a monastery?"

"I didn't mean this to happen to you, Mel."

Mel gazed at him with weary distaste. Was this why he had been so insistent on seeing the boy, merely to make it clear that he found him a bore? Surely he must have something more subtle in mind. He was impassive as Raymond continued his plea.

"I'm not just a stooge of Ralph's. I was afraid for you both, but I couldn't see how to resolve it."

"So you let the two of them gang up on me. Maybe you were hoping that we'd beat each other to death, and leave you ruling the roost?"

"No! At least, not consciously. And besides, I was physically weak."

"The way I heard it from Dr. Stark, you're full of muscles."

Kitty held her breath. Although she held Ralph's hand, she dared not look at him while they waited to hear how much Ray would tell.

"For six months I struggled for you, Mel. If you don't believe me, ask Ralph."

"What a laugh!"

"Will you at least listen? I'll listen to you."

"You should have made that offer a few days ago. But go ahead."

Mel was drawing his brother out in order that Ray, tangled between denial and guilt, would accept anything just to obtain absolution. She was more sure of it every moment, but there was nothing she could do about it.

"Ralph wanted to give you nothing. I stayed in the attic, trying to think of some way to persuade him. I said we'd divide it three ways. He said no. I said I'd give you half, and him the other half. He said no. He was only interested in freezing you out, in punishing you. We were stalemated, like Indian wrestlers."

"But now the stalemate's broken."

"Right! It's got nothing to do with my being brainwashed. It was your coming back that did it, and you had to suffer for it. But now we're all paying the price. And maybe we can all be saved yet."

"Hallelujah." Mel smiled coldly, with one side of his mouth only. Kitty was astonished to see that Laura, the little nurse, had flinched. Why? And why was she moving, her face flaming, from behind the wheel chair to Ray's side?

"I didn't mean it that way, Mel." Ray wet his lips. "Ralph and I want to settle with you, right now, with Martin's help, on any terms that the three of us can agree on."

"There ain't no such animal."

"But there has to be! Nobody wants to win any more. Nobody can win."

"That's where you're wrong. I want to. And I can."

Ray hesitated before this decisiveness, and when he finally did respond, averted his head from Kitty and Ralph, so that he was barely audible.

"When Ralph and I still believed that, I tried to win by sitting tight. And he tried to win by cutting off first my books, then my mail, then most of my food."

"So you really were physically weak. Sounds like the old Ralph. But he couldn't have starved you without help. Kitty, you gave him a hand, no doubt?"

Dr. Stark sighed, not in judgment, but with the weary comprehension of the old. Hearing only that wavering drawn-out sigh, groping for the chair behind her, Kitty could not bring herself to look at anyone, but held her hand pressed to her eyes as she fell back in the chair.

"It's true," she mumbled, hating herself for crying all over again, "I did it for love."

"I'm getting awfully sick of that word," Mel said. "Aren't you, Ray?"

"Yes, I am."

Mel laughed. He laughed! And Kitty, clenching her husband's hand so tightly that she could feel him wince, took her fingers from her eyes and peered at Mel, who didn't really want the money, but only what he was getting now, at this moment.

"She brains me with a lamp, a vase, God knows what else. And all for love."

"But it's true," she heard herself crying, "I did it for love, why else? And what right have *you* got to hold that against me?"

Temporarily startled into silence, Mel allowed Ray to renew his plea.

"If I bear no grudge against Ralph or Kitty, can't you—"

Mel held up a bandaged hand, the first two fingers raised hieratically, in caricature of a Byzantine icon. "One saint is enough for the family, Ray. Let me cherish my grudges."

"But Ralph has given up his. He's ready for a settlement."

"That's white of him."

"It proves that he's changed."

"To me it proves that Ralph knows when the jig's up. Nothing more. I learned that about him when your face was still in Mama's titty. Don't kid yourself, Ray, you haven't converted Ralph. If he's got religion, it's Karpinski who brought him the Word, not you. He's practical, just like he was when he used to run to Papa saying that I was stealing cigarettes from the store, or when he ran away instead of helping me fight, or . . . when he ran me out of town."

Glancing up, Kitty saw that the color was bleached out of Ralph's face. Still holding her hand, he said monotonously, "It's not true. None of it. If Ray can't persuade you, I won't try. All I'm saying is, I want you to have a share now, and I leave the details to Ray. Never mind about my motives. I never admired yours, but they're not at issue. It's not easy for me to tell you that I'm sorry. The only way I can show it is by offering in good faith to settle."

"Bully for you." Mel would undoubtedly have said more, but just at that moment Martin Stark walked into the solarium. He came up from behind, placed one hand on the shoulder of the man in the wheel chair, and extended the other for a handclasp. The handshake was mere good form; what mattered was the coldness in his eyes.

"It looks as though you'll be out of here soon," he said to Mel, "but it doesn't sound as though you've been making much progress in other ways." The lawyer added, "I'd like you to clarify something."

"As long as you don't claim to be on my side too. Everybody else here is just a little too busy loving their neighbor."

"Love isn't my business. Settlements are. From what I just overheard, you sound as though you don't want any kind of settlement on any kind of terms."

"Not with Ralph I don't. He's not the heir—Ray is." Mel swiveled about swiftly and jabbed his finger at his younger brother. "Now's your chance, kid. You want to negotiate? Come on, speak up."

"On what terms?"

My God, Kitty thought, he has grown up.

"You and me. No Ralph, no outsiders. You want to get even, you want to make it up? Let's negotiate. Just you and me."

Ray had folded his arms. He bent his head toward the little student nurse, not to confer with her, but almost as if he wanted to indicate to everyone that there was an unspoken compact between them; and as he did so Kitty realized with a little thrill of surprise that somehow a connection had been established between these two. How? She could not imagine, but she found herself looking at the nurse with different eyes and so seeing her not as a mouse in uniform but as a tough and determined girl, worthy of a man's trust and confidence. Then Ray raised his head.

"I'm sorry," he said. "If I couldn't do that with Ralph, I don't see how I can with you. It's out of the question."

The nurse was breathing deeply, her bosom rising, her plain reddened hands clasped tightly before her. She was as transformed as if she were in love. And, in fact, what else could account for it? Wonderingly Kitty watched her as Mel returned to the attack.

"Okay. That tears it."

"Just a second." The lawyer ran his tongue around the inside of his mouth. "What difference does it make whether it's Ralph or Raymond who offers you what you came for, as long as you get it?"

"Correction. Nobody's offering me what I came here for."

"Which is?"

"Vengeance."

Once again Dr. Stark's heavy doglike sigh filled the air. The strangers in the pavilion had retreated to their private concerns, but the softness of Mel's tone—and particularly his final word—had served to draw his own circle so tightly about him that they all swayed forward, awaiting his next word with a silent breathless expectancy. All except Ralph, whom Kitty could not contain. Thrusting aside her restraining hand, he glared at Mel with congested eyes, and spoke in an unsteady voice.

"If you're trying to make me ashamed of having apologized . . ." Kitty could feel his trembling as if it were a wire vibrating against her. "If you're trying to make me regret that I didn't kill you . . ."

"I owe my life, such as it is, to Kitty's conscience, and to the cops. Not to you. So don't make me laugh. My head still hurts."

"What are you after?" Ralph pushed Kitty back into her chair. "You punished Mama, now you're punishing Kitty. Do you want to inflict suffering on the third generation, on her baby, is that your game?"

Mel said furiously, "You'd rather play to the doctor, to the lawyer, to your kid brother, to your wife, than face up to me. I'll tell you what I'm after, but I'll have to start at the beginning."

"I'm waiting."

"Do you want the rest of us to go?" Dr. Stark jerked his

thumb at his expressionless son and at the nurse, who was biting her lip but not budging from Ray's side.

"You might as well all hear what I've been up to during the last fourteen years. The history of my counter-punching has its moments. Running, mooching, hiding, covering, never able to straighten up, forced to let go of my own name—not because I was ashamed of it but because my own family was ashamed of me. Ralph was the one who was ashamed of the family, not me. Ralph was the one who went away and stayed away voluntarily. Ralph was the one who was too good for the town, for his uncle, his old man, his brothers. But every time I wanted to try again, I'd write to Max and he'd say, Not now, Roughneck, not yet. Not now, not yet. Now, when I finally do come back, when they're all safely dead, Ralph has beaten me to it. He beats me up to boot, and he thinks I'll sit here with my busted nose and settle for an apology."

His face shone with sweat as the words poured out, hot, gushing, blissful, in a sudden release.

"Everybody thought, including me, that I was a pretty tough kid when I left home. Tough? I was a baby. In Chicago I learned about double-dealing at the hands of a kindly Italian hood. He hired me to drive his hot cars, skipped before the pay-off, and left me to take the rap. In Iowa I learned about saying good-by, after detasseling corn with a Swedish philosopher who talked to me all the way out to the Montana wheat fields, day and night. Inside of two weeks he had chopped up his leg in a binder, and I had to leave him and his one leg in the hospital. He was my first friend. I haven't had many since.

"In California I learned about loneliness. I wrote Max and he said, No, not yet. On a bet I joined the Navy to save the world from the North Koreans. As good that as anything else, I thought. It was after boot camp, when I was halfway across the Pacific, that I learned Mama had died. I wasn't surprised that Ralph blamed me for it.

"I drew a chief machinist's mate who climbed on my tail at Pearl Harbor and stayed there all the way up to Pusan. He called me Chink, he asked me which side I was on, he explained how the Jews started up the war in Washington and sold it out in Seoul. Uncle Max sent word that if I behaved myself I could come home when my hitch was up and go to college, like Ralph and all the other good little heroes. But first there were six hundred million Chinamen to wipe out, and there was that C.P.O. on my back.

"I got everything you can get for slugging a C.P.O. When they discharged me in Algiers, Louisiana, without honor, my spineless father was back rooming with his brother as though he had never married and had kids.

"After that it was the same old story, trial and error, illusion followed by disappointment. New Orleans, Biloxi, Boston, Saratoga, Monmouth, Miami. You name it, I was there. In Biloxi a little old nurse gave me a lecture on germs and shooed me out of the Negro waiting room at the Trailways Terminal, where I was looking for a cup of coffee. It was before the days of the Freedom Riders, I had no message for the blacks or anyone else, not even for Uncle Max, but I made the mistake of telling the old lady to bugger off. She turned out to be the sheriff's aunt.

"I've forgotten more about Southern jails than any of you will ever learn. It was in Miami, after I got back from Cuba —never mind why—that I found a letter from Uncle Max. He was still proud of me, if I had lived fifty years earlier I would have been fighting the Czar. Et cetera. As for him, he was still in love with Ann Sheridan. A safe romance. I had no home to come home to, my father was busy with a project for promoting world brotherhood by filling in the Bering Strait and the English Channel with a plastic cement. Meanwhile, his sons were pushing their own notions of brotherhood in various ways, all of them phony.

"Myself, I was serving time in Pennsylvania for something I'm not defending. I did it in a fit of despair, that's all. It was then that I got word of Max's death, and of Pop's. When I read about the will, and Ralph being the only one here, I smelled more brotherly love.

"I've come to stake my claim. I'm not Lafarge any more. I'm as much a true son of the Lands as either of you two. Probably more."

He stopped, his chest working a little. He might have been having one of those nightmares in which you run, your heart pounding, trying to catch a train that is just out of reach. Not one of his little circle of listeners had made the slightest move to interrupt him. Ray sat hunched, elbows on his knees and fists digging into his cheeks, which were a little reddened. The pressure had forced his mouth open a bit, or perhaps he was simply filled with wonder. Laura, her fists clenched in her uniform pockets, did not seem to mind that her nose was red, nor that her eyes were watering as she gazed, not at Mel, but at Ray. Why are we women always at the mercy of our tear ducts? Kitty thought angrily. She turned away, toward her husband and the other men.

Ralph's eyes were closed and his jaw clamped tight. The mandibles worked steadily beneath his expressionless features. Martin Stark, his legs crossed at the ankles, maintained the fixed polite smile of a man watching an amateur entertainment in which his own children are not involved. He was looking at his hands, which he held before him, finger tips just meeting in an ecclesiastical arch; am I imagining things, Kitty wondered, or are his fingers the tiniest bit unsteady? His father had been slouched in the corner chair all this time, leaning on his hand, his face pushed somewhat out of shape by the pressure of his hand, like an old hound dog resting his chops on the hearth. His eyes were veiled by the drooping lids. Aside from his occasional mournful aspirations, it was impossible to tell what he was thinking. Not one of them, Kitty observed, was looking directly at the man who had just finished speaking.

"Well," Mel demanded impatiently, "no reaction? Fourteen

wasted years in forty different places. The least you can do is thank me for not disgracing the family name."

Ralph opened his eyes. They were cold. They bore no trace of either shame or misery. He said, "Maybe Ray is bleeding for you. I'm not. Who asked you to piss your life away?"

"Do you think I enjoyed it? Is that all it means to any of you?"

Ray muttered, "I don't understand."

"That's funny—I understand *you*. You locked yourself in because you didn't want what happened to me to happen to you. Right?"

Ray whispered, "Something like that."

"Then why can't you feel what I felt, creeping from place to place all those years, like a turtle with the wrong name scratched on his back, waiting to be turned over by anybody's toe?"

Kitty arose, pressing her palms flat against her hips, holding herself very steady. "If Ray doesn't understand, none of us does. Why blame your life on Ralph? If you liked it here, if this was the only family you knew or wanted, who forced you to leave?"

Mel pushed himself out of the wheel chair. Erect, he grasped her by the elbows; she could feel his pulse in the pressure of his spatulate fingers.

"My mother," he said.

"What a dirty lie!" Ralph, his face congested, lunged forward to pull her loose from his brother's grip.

Kitty shook her head at Ralph. "Don't make a scene." She turned to Mel. "The way you told it to me, you left for the noblest of reasons. To show your mother by your example what was in store for her."

"You misunderstood. Maybe you preferred to. I meant more than you thought." He was looking not at her but at Ralph. "Go ahead, tell her."

"He knocked up a girl. A Polish girl I knew in high school, I used to go out with her myself. Her big brother was a cop.

Mel was scared of him, he packed up and skipped town. He never came back, not when Mama died, or Papa, or Uncle Max. But now he's trying to blame everyone else, even his dead mother, for that cheap little seduction. He wants to make out that his life was a tragedy. He's probably done the same thing half a dozen times since, in one town after another, with one high-school girl after another."

"What's the use," Mel muttered. "What's the use."

He sank back into the wheel chair. "I didn't leave town of my own accord. Mama took me aside one day. Papa was too ashamed, he was too much of a coward. Mama said she and Papa knew about Stella. She said that if I didn't go I would have to marry a common tramp. That Stella's father was drunk at the saloon more often than he was sober at the mill."

"You were afraid of Stella's brother," Ralph said. "You were afraid he'd beat your brains out."

"Harold never knew. He still doesn't, or he would have made life even more miserable for the Lands."

Harold, Kitty said to herself, Harold! "Wait," she commanded. "Harold what?"

Mel smiled coldly. "Yes, Karpinski. He's worked his way up from traffic cop. But he wasn't the reason why I left town. And he's not stopping me now from what I intend to do. There was only one other person who knew, who told my mother, who turned her against me."

Ralph whispered, "I never said a word."

"Balls. You knew, Stella went crying to you, she even told me she did. You were jealous that she did it with me and not with you."

"That's true. But I never said a word to anyone."

Kitty was frightened to see how suddenly everyone was staring, not at Mel, but at her husband.

"I swear it," Ralph said. "From the day that Stella told me until this very minute, I've never opened my mouth about it. Not to Mama, not to Ray, not to Kitty. Not to anyone."

Mel seemed a little puzzled by this obstinacy. Or maybe, Kitty thought, he was uneasy that his brother just might be telling the truth—and then what would he be, deprived of the hatred that had sustained him all these years? He persisted: "Mama must have learned it from you. There was no one else."

Ralph replied, "There was someone else."

"I'm waiting."

"Where did you get the pills? You were dosing Stella with pills."

"From Uncle Max." Now they were all staring at Mel again. He added quickly, "But he was on my side. He was the only one I could count on."

"If Mama talked to you, if she really did ask you to go away, then she heard it from Max. And he must have put her up to it. Not me, not Papa. Uncle Max."

In the instant that Mel's face crumpled, Kitty said to herself, He loved the girl. And more than that, she thought, as she heard Mel delving into the past again, not venomously this time, but as though its meaning were only now being disclosed to him, He has always loved what he remembers of her.

"I was in a panic. Stella used to call me up and start crying over the phone. I was afraid if Harold found out, he'd have me arrested, slugged, killed. So I went to Uncle Max, the only one I could get around. I tried to be tough, I said, Max you dog, I've been stealing rubbers from the second drawer, and they're no good, they're stale, they're rotten, like everything else in your crummy store. Now I've got a girl in trouble, and you've got to make it good. He laughed, he showed me his little yellow teeth. He actually looked proud of me. Who is she? That was his first question. I said, a Polish girl, she's in Ralphie's home room, and he cackled like a rooster. We're getting even with the Polacks, he said, at last we're getting even!

"I had the feeling then and I still have it now, that he was proud of me for doing something he never had himself. I'd been with him a lot, in the store, in the streets, collecting his rents, and I'd seen how women could put him off. He was afraid of no man, but he feared the secret strength of women, their persistence, their staying power, their ability to do what one of them must have done to his own father—hypnotize him away from his sons. When he said that I was getting even, I don't think he meant just with the Polacks. I think he meant with women.

"But that was all right with me, I thought we understood each other. He didn't bawl me out, he gave me some pills for Stella. After that, when Mama told me I'd better go, I couldn't even say that it was going to be all right, that I had medicine for the girl, that she wasn't going to have any baby."

"But she did have one."

Mel turned blindly to Dr. Stark.

"What are you talking about?"

"I said she did have a baby." The doctor was absolutely imperturbable. Ignoring everyone else, he said slowly and precisely to Mel, "Max sent her to me, as pregnant as a girl can get. If he gave you pills, I'll bet they were only placebos. Max wouldn't take a chance on an abortifacient. He didn't tell me who was responsible, but he left me the impression that it was Ralph. That seemed dubious, especially since you were the one who had left town. In any event, I persuaded Stella's family, who could not sweat the name of the father out of her, to sign her into a nursing home. In due time I delivered her, and saw the baby through the adoption process. Her brother has always been grateful, which is one reason he's been co-operative through this whole mess—all I've ever had to do was hint. I can't say the same for Stella, who has four kids, last I heard, none of them delivered by me. But maybe it's understandable that she should have turned elsewhere for a family doctor."

Mel sat dazed and shuddering. At last he asked, "Why didn't you ever tell me?"

"Apart from the fact that you didn't ask, I don't volunteer professional confidences. As for your by-blow, it's never been a part of your life, and I don't think we ought to discuss it."

"So it was Max all along."

"I think he meant well. He couldn't turn you down, no doubt he was pleased that you came to him rather than to your own father. But he couldn't become an accessory, so he tricked you, and ran first to me to hint that I abort the girl, which he knew was out of the question, and then to your mother, to get you out of town in case the girl told on you."

"The old bastard," Mel muttered. "The old bastard."

Ralph said hesitantly, "I think Uncle Max wanted to play daddy, but he didn't know how to go about it any better than Papa. Neither one could admit to hating their father for his remarriage, after they'd sacrificed their youth for him. Max must have gotten a secret charge out of rearranging your destiny, the way his father had done to him."

The sun was slipping down behind the tall shrubbery outside the pavilion. As the light muted, it seemed to Kitty that the seven of them were becoming more isolated from the others in the spacious room, more self-contained. It was Mel who still held the rest of them; they waited intently for his reaction. It was not long in coming.

"Let's skip the philosophy," he said with renewed brutality. "If it was Max and not Ralph who did me in, then I'll take my vengeance on Max. I've got that coming to me. And I've got evidence."

The silence that bloomed in their quiet corner hung almost odorous in the air about them, as if his explosion had released some strange instantaneous blossom, exacting an awed silence rather than any exclamations of surprise, shock, or wonderment.

It was Martin Stark who broke the silence.

"You're not being practical. If you want vengeance, you can hold your brothers up for a substantial settlement."

"And you still don't see my purpose."

"As a lawyer I can assure you that you'll get no place if you attempt to exclude your brothers."

"As a lawyer you shouldn't make unsupported statements. And I should have known better than to get in touch with you today, just because of your father."

Dr. Stark growled, "For what it's worth, Marty is at least as disinterested and as honest as I am."

"Then why is he in such a hurry for me to toss in my hand, before he even sees my cards?"

"Just what are your cards?"

"That's more like it." Mel peered at each one in turn. "The issue isn't my father's will, it's Max's. Right? If it hadn't been for Max getting out and scuffling, Pop wouldn't have had anything to leave Ray but his best wishes."

"The fact remains that Max Land did leave everything to his brother."

"Except for letters. He left me some very interesting letters. He made me some promises in those letters. Anybody ever tell you that?"

The lawyer hesitated, and apparently in that instant Mel decided to take the plunge. Glancing obliquely at Ralph, he demanded of him, "According to the newspapers, you cleaned up the house. Ever come across any letters from me to Uncle Max?"

Ralph's reply was inaudible to everyone but Kitty. He cleared his throat and repeated the word.

"Yes."

"What did you do with them? Tell us."

"There's no reason for you to talk to Ralph like a district attorney," Kitty cut in. "He's under no obligation. Besides, he could just as easily have told you he didn't find the letters."

"I'll handle this," Ralph said. He turned back to his brother. "I destroyed them."

"Who gave you the right to do that?"

"You can't make a moral issue out of it. I was cleaning

out the junk, looking for a will. Uncle Max was dead. You were gone. Who needed your old letters?"

"Nobody. It's true. Still, you might have passed them around. Then these good people could have gotten some idea of what I went through during the years when Ray was living off old men and you were learning to swim with the stream." Mel raised his hand in a gesture of magnanimity. "But it's all right. I've got *his* letters. You're going to wish you could have destroyed them like you destroyed mine. Because anyone who reads them can see that I was his boy, I was the one he cared for, I was the one he wanted to provide for."

Martin Stark remarked neutrally, "They hardly supersede his last testament."

"That remains to be seen. I'm not showing you my whole hand yet. But I'm anteing up now for a moral claim to Max's estate."

Dr. Solomon Stark burst out laughing. It was more a carefree snort than a chuckle, and as such it was shocking. Even some of the few remaining strangers looked up from the other end of the room. Leaning forward from his stiff-legged position in the corner chair, the doctor tapped Mel on the knee.

"I think maybe that beating jarred your brain loose after all. Can you imagine how funny it would sound in a court of law if a wild boy like you, fresh out of jail, started pressing moral claims?"

"He who laughs last, Doc," Mel said. "Ask your son if maybe it wouldn't be wiser to wait until the evidence is in."

"Depends on the evidence," Martin murmured. "If it's going to be just talk and bluster . . . It's getting rather late, Mel."

The nurse stirred uneasily and glanced at her watch. But it was Martin himself who was most disturbed: despite his curt nonchalance, Kitty was sure that he was not happy with Mel's renewed self-confidence.

Mel glanced about him. He reached into the pocket of his bathrobe and drew out a folded sheet of paper. "All right, I'll ante up. Here's Max's last letter to me. Don't anybody

grab—it's a photostat. I came to town to show this to Ray.
Since he says he doesn't want to negotiate, you can all hear it
in the light of what the doctor has just told us about my loyal
pal, Uncle Max. Anybody who's bored can leave."

No one stirred.

"Dear Roughneck," he read, then interrupted himself. "Max
never called me Mel, maybe that's why the letter didn't identify me to Karpinski, when he went through my pockets.
Uncle Max always liked to call me Roughneck. He says:

> You might as well know. We are never going to see each
> other again. You are in your jail, I am in mine. You don't
> want people to know where you are, or who you are, OK,
> I have respected your wishes, now respect mine. I don't
> want people to know either. I don't think it is anybody's
> business that I am going to die. We have always under-
> stood each other on these things which is why I feel I can
> tell you what I wouldn't tell anybody else, OK? They
> always said you were wild, but it was like what they said
> about me. I don't like to boast but if it hadn't been for
> me what would have become of the family. When I ask
> that they can't answer. OK, just the same I have to look
> after my brother even after I have gone. Even his pride
> I have to think about. You get the point. To put it in plain
> English I have to leave everything to him. Don't think I
> am forgetting you. I am not. I will tell him this week that
> when it comes his time you are as important as the oth-
> ers. As far as I am concerned, more. I mean more like me
> and all of those who came before us who stayed in there
> punching so the family wouldn't fall apart. That's the
> way the human race makes progress. Not by daydream-
> ing or by trying to get into society. You have sowed your
> wild oats, OK, it is about time to straighten up and fly
> right. In my opinion you are the one who has the nerve,
> more than the others, and for that reason you deserve
> more. Maybe you will sweep the board yet. I wish I could

be there to see you show them, that is my only regret. But even though I will never see you again it gives me pleasure to think how you are going to knock them cold one of these days. You could do it on your own, I did, but if I can help you, why not. I am going to insist on that with my brother. That's my promise to you and my bequest, OK? Must sign off now because the pain is driving me crazy. Nobody else will, but I hope that you will always remember

MACK THE KNIFE.

Those were his last words to me—my nickname for him, these last years."

Ralph sat with his eyes closed against the sun, whose last probing rays were striking across his drawn face. But Ray and the nurse, Kitty saw, were staring at each other rather than at Mel, staring with a sad surmise, like children lost in the woods. For the first time she felt that her pregnancy had separated her from this young girl by an entire generation. The doctor rocked slowly back and forth, his large capable hands locked across his knee, a faint smile on his face. Martin appeared deeply perturbed by what he had heard; he chewed his lips and gazed at Mel as if trying to read his mind.

"There's no evidence in that letter," Martin said, "that your uncle ever actually communicated his desires to your father. And you understand that even if he did, they wouldn't have any legal force—not when Raymond is willing to do just what Max suggested."

"We'll let my lawyer worry about that."

"I know I sound stuffy. But I must point out that on a thousand-to-one shot such as yours, no reputable lawyer will go to bat for you on a contingency basis. Unless you have substantial backing, you'd really be better advised to settle right now, with your brothers."

"The very fact that you're so anxious, Martin, persuades me that I'm on the right track."

The doctor said impatiently, "You know what you guys remind me of, with all this sparring around? Those international conferences where they bicker so much beforehand about whose piece of property to meet on, what problems they should pretend to try to settle, and who's going to sit in what chair, that they break up before they ever get down to business. Instead of imitating grownups, who are intolerably irrational, why can't you behave like the kids who simply allow their hatreds to evaporate so they can go on playing? Mel, if you can't find a sucker to finance you in a hopeless struggle, why don't you just pretend to be converted by your brothers, and settle the damn thing right now? You know something? If you're bent on cherishing a grudge—to say nothing of making a fresh start, which I personally believe is impossible, given the nature of the beast—it's a lot more comfortable to do it with a pocketful of change."

The old man knew more than all the others put together. It was fascinating, Kitty thought, to watch Mel considering how to parry him.

Mel said carefully, "No one else but me is going to get his hands on Uncle Max's money. Especially not Ralph and Ray. If necessary we'll wash all the dirty linen in public. I'll prove that my father was not of sound mind, that he'd been cracked for years, when he willed everything to Ray. And that Ray was too, that the two of them were part of Max's private zoo. I'll—"

Kitty could not contain herself. "You'd do that to your own brother? After he struggled for you all these months? After he got down on his knees and asked you to forgive him for something that wasn't even his fault?"

"Look who's talking. The very person who starved him half to death. You know, Kitty, I don't see why we should keep that to ourselves either. Why shouldn't everybody hear how this respectable young couple mistreated a helpless half-cracked brother? Then we'll see which of us jokers is wild."

Kitty felt the blood drain from her face, even from her

mouth, leaving her lipstick greasy and stark, like some garish mask of healthy sensuality. She worked her lips, but no words would come out.

She heard Martin demand, "Is everybody all talked out now?"

No one replied, and he went on, "Before we call it a day, let me just add that something has come up concerning the estate that is going to affect all of you. I can't go into it here, I don't even have the entire picture myself, but I suggest that we meet at my office as soon as Mel can be discharged from the hospital." He turned to his father. "When will that be, Dad?"

Dr. Stark shrugged tiredly. His already sallow face had gone gray, and the spark in his eyes had died down.

"Judging by Mel's jazzy behavior, maybe I should never have had him admitted here in the first place. Suppose we say day after tomorrow."

"Good enough. Can you all be at my office at nine-thirty in the morning? The earlier—"

Mel waved his index finger like a flag. "I'm not coming to your office. If you've got anything more to say to me, you can say it at Max's house."

"That'll do perfectly well," Martin acquiesced. "I shall have to bring someone else with me. You'll understand why when we arrive."

Ray was already whispering good-by to the nurse. Kitty said to Ralph, in a voice that was much more unsteady than she had hoped, "Would you see me to my room, please?"

Dr. Stark put his hand to Mel's wrist, whether simply to squeeze it or to check his pulse Kitty could not tell, and said to him, "I'll pick you up here day after tomorrow to discharge you and drive you out to the old house."

"Don't bother."

"No, no, I want to." The doctor motioned to Laura that she might wheel her patient away, and with a farewell wave to Mel, strolled off with his son. He did not touch Martin any more than Ralph was touching her, or Ray, Laura; in his case, though, there was surely a paternal gesture of love that he dared not make because it might disturb the rhythm of the limp with which Martin moved decisively from objective to objective. Everyone to his private miseries. But suddenly they were all leaving, and Mel, she saw, was left alone with the little nurse, who was not even his, but had somehow been pre-empted by his little brother.

In the instant that Kitty glanced back at him, Mel, fixed and furious in his wheel chair, called out to all of them. "Hey! Just a minute!" And Kitty, far from being terrified once again, was curiously certain that this snarling lone wolf was calling for his family because he could no longer bear to be alone, with no one to threaten, no one to attack.

They all turned. Dr. Stark, with his hand at last where he wanted it, on his son's arm; Ralph, with his dark brow tightly knit and his arm tightly enfolding Kitty's shoulders, protecting her against any new revelations; Ray, standing apart, looking hopefully at his brother and the nurse.

Mel did not seem to mind who overheard him. "You forgot about my name. Since Ray doesn't want to negotiate, I'm taking my name back in another hour."

"It's already yours," Martin replied cheerfully. "Thanks for reminding me. While you were arguing with your brothers, I was having a frank talk with Lieutenant Karpinski. I must say he didn't seem particularly surprised. In fact, he's assured me that you won't be disturbed here until you're discharged. I'm off now to prepare a statement for the morning papers."

Mel turned savagely from them to Laura, who waited, starched and pale, offering him only the chance to get away.

"Come on, kid," he said to her between his teeth, "let's get out of here."

14: MEL

SEEN FROM THE WINDOW of Solomon Stark's car, Uncle Max's house was nothing at all like the spectral hulk that it had been the last time Mel had surveyed it, with beating heart, empty stomach, and a gnawing hunger to confront his brothers. Now, having breakfasted and dressed leisurely, if awkwardly, at the hospital, he could look at it as dispassionately as if it were simply a prison—which in a sense it was.

"You're a lot more quiet this morning than you were the other evening," the doctor observed, as he drew his car to the curb.

"I don't have to prove anything to you," Mel pointed out. And to make sure that the older man should not mistake this for an expression of confidence, he added spitefully, "Besides, you know as well as I do that your son is getting ready to shaft me."

Dr. Stark did not attempt to reply, and Mel, feeling a little guilty for his needless cruelty, shifted about painfully on the front seat and again turned his attention to the house which he would be re-entering in a moment.

315

Once you knew what you were going to find inside, Max's castle became simply prosaically shabby and more than a little ridiculous, with its overblown, billowing windows and pointless tiny porches embellished with curlicued railings, all impressive but meaningless, like the metal spikes that rose up here and there, pointing warning fingers toward a heaven from which no lightning ever struck. At least not until now. It had been different when it had loomed up before his bloodshot eyes the other night, a gloomy apparition in a menacing dream, a stage set for an unperformed melodrama that you knew in advance would come to no good end.

The chances were that the drama still would not end well, but the house's mysterious power to appall was quite gone in the June sunlight. Whatever ability he himself still had, though, to exert some control over the remainder of the drama would now be tested.

"O.K., let's go," he said to Dr. Stark, his bandaged fingers on the door handle. "What are we waiting for?"

The doctor restrained him gently. He gestured with his chin at a spattered and rusting Volkswagen parked across the street.

"Can't you make out the card in their windshield?"

"No." Mel squinted. "What about it?"

"It says Press. Even if we sit here and don't go on in, they'll be over in a minute. You'd better refer them to Marty and let him do the talking when he arrives—I don't see his car here yet."

"He's already talked to them. Today it's my turn." He opened the door and swung his legs out. "Coming?"

They were barely at the ragged fringe of Max's front lawn when the two men from the Volkswagen were trotting across the street, the shorter swaying on stumpy legs with the awkward rapidity of a monkey making for the trees. His camera was banging against his chest, wide like a gorilla's but covered with a floral-printed sport shirt, and even as he ran he tried to peer through it and bring it to a focus.

"Stand behind me, Mel," the doctor said.

"What for? Let him shoot."

The taller of the two approached, his long jaw hanging open. His eyes were watery and sad; he looked like a fish with a long Latin name that you stare at through the thick glass wall of an aquarium.

"Stanley Jenkins of the *Chronicle*, Mr. Land," he said.

"Tell me first how you knew I was going to be here. Martin Stark?"

"You can ask him that when he gets here. Do you intend to contest your father's will?"

"Ask me on my way out, not on my way in."

"Just one more, Mel," the little photographer said. "Thanks!"

"I'm going in now with my doctor for a family conference. I've invited some guests, so I can't say anything until it's over. But afterwards I may have a lot to say. Stick around if you want."

"We'll do that."

It was Ray who opened the door for them and closed it swiftly on the reporters. His brilliant blue eyes blinked out from the cool darkness of the front hall, which smelled of furniture polish and fresh coffee. In his white shirt and slacks, and with his woolly beard, he might have been an acolyte going off into the desert to do penance, but first making sure that his hair was combed and his shoes shined.

"I thought I'd try the front door this time, now that I've got a bodyguard with me," Mel said to him. "You're more sociable this morning than you were the last time I dropped in."

Ray blushed. "I must say something before we go any further."

"Say it."

"I didn't want the fighting to spread that night, I wanted it to be contained. That's an explanation, but it's not an excuse. The only thing is, how can I forgive myself if you don't forgive me?"

"I forgive you, I forgive you. As long as you don't keep whining about it. Now how's about some of that coffee I smell?"

"Let me ask Kitty."

Ray hurried on ahead of them into the living room, the furniture of which had been arranged in a loose circle. Ralph was seated before the fireplace and his wife was bending over him. Protectively? No, she was merely pouring cream into his coffee; at Ray's whisper she turned to greet him and Dr. Stark. Apparently she had decided, or had been instructed, to receive him correctly.

"Make mine black," he said to her. "No sugar."

"And you, Doctor?"

"Nothing. Trying to control my consumption of stimulants." The doctor raised his hand before his face and lowered himself onto the couch. "How are you feeling, Kitty?"

"Never better. But I'm not nearly as good an ad for your services as Mel. I think he's recovered amazingly fast."

"If I look beautiful," Mel said, "I do owe it all to the doctor. But he's sending Ralph the bill, not me."

Kitty laughed, a little too shrilly. The doctor was merely smiling wryly. Ralph was staring into his coffee cup, making no effort to be pleasant—or unpleasant for that matter. In his dark green summer business suit and tie figured with little signs of the Zodiac, he looked like a young professional man waiting uneasily for a client. Fair enough. Now was the time.

"I've got a little announcement," Mel said. "I've invited some reinforcements to Marty's meeting. I hope you'll have enough coffee for our cousins, Henrietta and Lillian. And Henrietta's husband."

Mel paused and cocked his head to one side so that he might have the pleasure of an unobstructed view of the anger rising to his brother's dark flushed face.

"What are you trying to pull?"

"Marty told me in the hospital that I couldn't buck you without substantial backing. Well, I've got it."

Kitty took her husband by the arm to restrain him, but he shook himself free. "I wouldn't put it past him to make a pact with those unspeakable people. You can't imagine how ashamed they were when he used to give Mama and the whole family so much misery. But now that it's a question of giving *us* misery, it's a different story. And he's not too proud to finagle with people like that."

"I leave the pride to you, Ralph," Mel said. "You're the one that wears the five-dollar ties and drives the stupid little English car. If Ray wouldn't negotiate with me, the Kadins will. That's good enough for me."

Dr. Stark growled placidly, "Damned if I can see why they should want to become involved. I thought all along they've been desperate to stay clear of the Lands and to keep clear of your troubles."

"It's too late for that anyway."

"If they go into litigation with you, though, they're just asking for it."

"They're going to get it no matter what they do. So why shouldn't they come in with me? At least that way they'll have a chance at a cut."

Ray was staring. "You mean you've offered them a share of the estate?"

Mel turned on him. "Not only are you slow on the uptake, you've got bad manners. You hurt the Kadins' delicate feelings. Here they went and kept your guilty secret, when they were the only ones besides the doctor and his son to know you were sacked out upstairs. And how did you repay them? Did you offer to cut them in, after the will turned up? Not you."

"What did they expect him to do?" Ralph demanded. "They never once showed up all the years he was living here. The only thing they ever did was to gloat over our troubles. It's no wonder neither Uncle Max nor Papa mentioned them in their wills. Why should they have? Why should Ray, why should I, why should you—"

"I already told you why I should. And if you think their motives are any chintzier than yours—"

The doorbell rang loudly.

"—why not take it up with them? That must be them. No, no," he said to Kitty as he started for the hall, "this one is on me. After all, I invited them."

When he got to the front door, however, Sasha tottered against his leg and growled stertorously, as if he wished to bar the way to whoever stood on the other side. Holding the hound by the collar, Mel flung open the door.

The driveway was now lined with cars. Before the latest arrival, a white Mercedes, Martin Stark and a broken-nosed stranger stood deep in conversation with the two journalists. A fifth man had just stepped away from them and was hurrying up the walk with the wind whipping his tie over his shoulder, to join the two women who already stood before Mel, panting and outraged as though indecencies had just been suggested to them. Until now the two Kadin sisters had existed in his mind not as specific human beings—despite his telephone conversation with Ben Lurie—nor even as generalized women, but merely as cousins of his mother's, and as such simply as emanations (not as savory as the odor of fresh bread and soap that she always gave off) of someone who had been surpassingly real for him. Therefore it had been easy to persuade himself that but for his mother, the indomitable Kadin who for love had driven him out of the Land house, these Kadins would have no objective reality of their own.

But here they stood in all their dumpy substantiality (which was Lillian? which was Henrietta? did it make any difference?), sending forth waves of face powder mingled with the honest sweat of fear arising from their meaty bosoms.

"Hello, cousins!" he cried. "Come in! You're in the nick of time! Revelations are the order of the day. Also threats, exposures, and reprisals."

"Can we wait here in the hall for my husband, all right?" This was the heavier one, who was therefore Henrietta, wife of Ben Lurie, the panting insurance salesman. As she and her spinster sister—who licked chapped lips beneath a disconcerting mustache—accepted the hospitality of Mel's outstretched arm, she continued, "Let's just hold the door for Mr. Stark and the other man too. He saved us from those awful reporters just in time."

"Hello, Mel, you're looking pretty good, considering. How do you feel," Ben Lurie said. To emphasize the fact that he did not expect an answer, he went on immediately, in a voice roughened by running, "We understood that a statement had already been given out. Wasn't this supposed to be a private meeting?"

"Well, it is, it is, at least inside." Mel shoved Sasha ahead into the parlor. "The reporters are just trying to live up to their movie image. When they nab you on the way out, either lie like hell about what went on inside, or tell them the absolute truth about everybody except yourself. That's what's always done at conferences like this, it's expected. Doesn't it always work like a charm?"

He raised his hand in greeting to the two reporters, the sad fish and the picture-taking gorilla, as they retreated to their Volkswagen. Then, fixing a glassy smile of welcome on his battered face, he attended the lawyer and his companion, who were mounting the porch steps, sober-faced.

"Good morning, Counselor," he said to Martin. "You know my cousins? You don't object to my having invited them to your séance?"

"Object?" The lawyer's smile was bland; Mel felt suddenly as though he had swallowed a heavy object. "If you hadn't, I'd have asked them myself."

Ben Lurie spoke up in his sharp nagging salesman's voice: "I was telling Mr. Stark that we want to try to help you young people."

As he took his wife and sister-in-law by their fleshy upper arms, two ball point pens and a retractible pencil glinted in the handkerchief pocket of his Palm Beach suit. When they had all trooped into the living room, Martin took over the introductions, identifying his broken-nosed companion, whose aging face was white and soft and withdrawn, as though he had been locked in a closet, only as Mr. Jesse Treadwater.

"O.K.," Mel said impatiently, surveying the coffee-sipping circle, eight of them, not counting himself. "I hear the rest of you know each other from condolence calls at the time of my father's death. We're here this morning on a happier occasion —to see that the right people get their hands on the loot—so let's get cracking."

"Now wait a minute, Mel." He had been a little blunt for Cousin Ben, who had to be both noble and aggrieved. "We only want to see justice done. The Kadin family has had nothing but grief from the Lands."

Ralph raised his eyes from his coffee cup. He smiled coldly. "Just be glad you're not a Land. We have nothing but grief from ourselves. And I don't recall that the Kadins ever offered to share it. So if some of us haven't offered to share other things than grief with you, that shouldn't be too hard to understand. Not even for a stranger like Mr. Treadwater."

Ben Lurie held out both arms to restrain his wife and her sister. "Don't put words in my mouth. We're accusing nobody." He repeated: "All we want is to see justice done."

"We all know what grief is," Ralph persisted. "But justice is a relative matter. What do *you* mean by it?"

"To me," the insurance agent replied stubbornly, "it's justice that your mother's only living relatives besides her sons should participate in the estate. When I think of what she suffered, I'm not saying at whose hands, it strikes me funny that Mel is the only one of you who should acknowledge even this much."

"I only wanted to carry out my father's wishes," Ray protested.

"Everyone for reasons of his own," Martin Stark murmured.

It made no difference to whom he addressed himself, Mel thought, whether to the strange white-faced man or to the others, he had to get everything said, no matter what the outcome, and quickly, for their faces were beginning to swim strangely.

"The story is that I left town and stayed away because I was a coward and deserter. Wrong. It was my Mama, your cousin Jenny Kadin, who pleaded with me to leave. I agreed because I thought some people might learn something from my going. Now it turns out that she was put up to it by the one member of the family who swore he was sticking with me."

Dr. Stark, who had been sitting in self-effacing silence in the furthest corner of the circle, now took hold of his long bulbous bologna of a nose and tweaked it. It made a soft dull sound that caught everyone's attention.

"I don't mind rehashing everything all over again," he said, "but aren't you guys a little embarrassed in front of a stranger?"

"When Mel has quite finished," his son remarked calmly, "Mr. Treadwater can explain why he's here."

"I don't know who the hell you are, Mr. Treadwater," Mel said, "but you must have gotten one version already from Perry Mason here. Well, from what I've heard I'm more convinced than ever that I'm entitled to Uncle Max's dough. Before, I felt I had a claim on Max's love. Now, after what they've told me, I want reparations."

"Can I butt in one last time?" the doctor asked. "I'm on Mel's side, but only because I'm on everybody's side. If you all took turns, each of you could recite a whole catalogue of suffering at the hands of both of the deceased. Ralph, who never had a proper home; Raymond, who was brought up by a committee of confounded men; even the Kadins, embarrassed by their family connection and pained by Jenny's unhappy life. Everyone has grievances. But why insist—"

"They've been working on theirs," Mel cut in. "I'm just catching up with mine."

Martin Stark squinted through the pipestem he had been

cleaning, as if it were a rifle barrel, and remarked offhandedly, "Mr. Treadwater is attached to the office of the district director of the Bureau of Internal Revenue. What he has to say may affect all this talk about grievances."

The stranger arose. Mel gazed at him speculatively, not startled by his identity, nor even wondering particularly what he was about to reveal (for it struck him suddenly that he had always known what the man was going to announce), but fascinated by the disjunction between his appearance and his official role. Standing soberly, indeed almost shyly, with his trousers bagging and his overlong belt strap dangling limply, he appeared unable to look any of his eight listeners in the eye despite the fact that the room had been engulfed in a roaring Niagara of silence. Mel, shrunk within the tender envelope of his hardly healed skin, could only marvel at the capacity of this frail, thin, already elderly man—who, to judge from his pallor, must for years have occupied without protest the nethermost desk in the darkest corner of his office—to impose breathless attention as if he were not a tired civil servant but a military commander about to order his troops to undertake a suicidal assault.

Ben Lurie was biting fiercely on his lips. They were not only redder than usual, they were the only spot of color in his face. Beside him, the Kadin sisters sat with parted thighs, stuck to the couch and sweating hard. Raymond perched in absolute silence, his hands hanging loosely between his legs; but a strange smile had come to his lips, a painful smile, as though he too had divined what was going to be said. Only on Ralph's and Kitty's faces, Mel thought with a bitter satisfaction, could you read clearly a terror that was so nearly uncontrollable that they clung openly to each other like two small children. It was impossible to read on Dr. Stark's countenance whether he already knew Mr. Treadwater's message. His hangdog chops were gloomy and eternally shaded by the immaculate but liver-spotted hand which supported them; his eyes were unamused but hardly ready to shed tears either. As for his son, he wore the self-satisfied look of alert interest that you see on the face of a chairman who has just delivered a witty introduction of the main speaker of the evening.

"I guess you all understand," the main speaker was saying in a voice rusty from disuse, "that my being here is a little unusual. We don't ordinarily do this, but then I don't turn down a friend like Marty Stark when he asks me to do him a little favor and help you folks to understand a peculiar situation.

"To put it bluntly, so as to save your time," continued Mr. Treadwater, looking at no one, "Max Land very seldom filed income tax returns in the last seventeen years. And when he did, he usually declared a net loss. If you went by his returns alone, there would be nothing for his heirs but some bad debts."

What was really confusing about this timid man, Mel thought, was his badly broken nose, which bespoke at least one moment of violence, of struggle, and at most . . . He turned, surprised that it should be Raymond who would interrupt with a question.

"How about all his properties? When they're sold—"

"Ah, yes, exactly. That's when my office became interested. If you liquidate the real estate as inheritor, you must understand that the charge would be on the estate, and that the federal government's claims for back taxes would have to be satisfied prior to those of any other creditors."

"Hold it." Ralph's command was cool and authoritative; how many people besides me, Mel wondered, can possibly realize how close he is to hysteria? "Tell us how much is owing in back taxes."

"That's just it." Mr. Treadwater raised his head for the first time. "It's a difficult case to estimate, partly because of the Lands' highly unorthodox bookkeeping. In addition to the capital gains taxes on the sale of the unreported real estate, there will naturally be penalties, plus accumulated interest, for false returns and blank years. But one reason I am here this

morning is to assure you that the Bureau is not a heartless
mechanism as it is sometimes depicted. In this case we do understand that the offenses weren't deliberately committed by
anyone now alive and in this room. Therefore we are prepared to be compassionate, to try to consider everyone's best
interests, to come to an amicable arrangement with the Land
estate. We want to be fair both to the public and to the estate."

"Mr. Treadwater, let me interrupt you." Ben Lurie was
whiney and frightened, but he was on his feet and determined
to be a man, or at least to do what he thought a man would
do in this situation. "I want to put a question to Mr. Stark."

Jesse Treadwater was so gratified to be relieved of the floor
that he almost toppled in his haste to sit down.

"Mr. Stark," Lurie went on doggedly, "maybe I can pre-
sume and just call you Martin."

The brother-in-law, the husband, the insurance agent, who
could supposedly compute survival percentages, likelihoods,
possibilities, chances, had found his voice. You had to admire
his struggle to put the best face on this compound humiliation, like a swimmer just rescued from drowning who, overcome by shame at the sea water belching from his mouth and
nostrils, attempts to pass off as nothing but momentary dis-
comfiture his public terror, his futile thrashing and floundering
against the annihilating sea.

Martin did not directly refuse this plea for familiarity, he
merely waited politely—which was eloquent enough in itself.

"My wife and my sister-in-law came here at Mel's request.
We were in hopes that we could do something to patch up
a bad situation before it got even worse."

"I think that's what we've all been after."

"Well, whether Raymond really wanted to is an open question. The fact remains that he didn't do anything. And we
offered to be helpful to Ralph and his wife when they got
here after Leo's death, but it looks like the only reason he
stayed on was to squeeze out his own flesh and blood so he
could get everything for himself. In those circumstances, we

felt we shouldn't turn our backs on Mel, like everybody else."

"That's laudable."

"Now I'm speaking not as an insurance man, but as one human being to another. The only person besides Mr. Treadwater who could have any idea about the value of the estate is you. So I think we're entitled to a frank statement, even if it's just a guess. What do you think the net worth of the estate will be after the government's been satisfied?"

"Nobody can say. The Bureau's preliminary investigation, in which I've been co-operating, to the extent I can without compromising the Lands' interests, indicates that delinquent taxes and penalties will be—Jesse, you'll bear me out on this, I think?—"

But the civil servant, steadfastly engaged in studying his shoe tips, only nodded slightly.

"—will be on the order of several hundred thousand dollars."

"I still want—"

"Say for the sake of argument that Ray decides, after liquidating the real estate, to divide what's left after taxes among everyone in this room. I very much doubt that there'd be more than a couple of thousand for each of you." He glanced about coldly and added, "If that."

The two cousins, come back to this house they despised and would gladly have wished out of existence if only it were possible, stared at each other wildly for an instant before they dropped their eyes in fright and confusion. It was as if in that moment each saw in the other's eyes the naked reflection of what was usually decently clothed in praiseworthy disguises, homely truisms: blood is thicker than water, God helps him who helps himself, nothing ventured nothing gained, you can't kill a man for trying.

Mel was overwhelmed by a guilty horror, as though he had been spying on a sixty-year-old woman who suddenly, almost by chance, had caught sight of herself in her brightly lit mirror. Not while she was busily and methodically adjusting her face to the vicissitudes of time with the aid of emollients, powders, and coloring agents, but before that, while she struggled clumsily into her undergarments, and beheld in all its collapsing horror, before she could drop her eyes in shame and misery, the ruined flesh, puckered and folded upon itself, discolored here, pendulous there, a corrupted betrayal of what seemed once—and remained, in the falsifying mirror of the mind—firm and incorruptible, without fault or fissure.

These two women had been betrayed not simply by cupidity, but also by its corollary, a wildly unrealistic assessment of their chances, which had entrapped them now in public contumely. Not only could they not have confessed to the collapse, which in a sense confessed itself in their faltering eyes and hands; they sat paralyzed, unable to scream, to cry, even to squeak. Martin Stark might just as well have wrapped his capable hands around their fat throats and squeezed the hope and the life out of them.

And I was thinking about Treadwater's nose, Mel said to himself. Noses! Martin Stark had brought them all to heel with such ease that it was laughable. But if no one was laughing, Mel asked himself, what do I hear? A terrible involuntary giggle was welling up within him and spurting out with the unbearable slow metronomic regularity of spasmodic hiccoughs.

Martin said swiftly, but quite smoothly, "Given what we now know, doesn't it make sense that everyone close ranks? Shake hands all around? Do what we can to work things out with Mr. Treadwater? And put the best front we can on it when we leave here to face public curiosity?"

"You don't give us much of an alternative, do you, Counselor?" Pushing back his chair, Mel groped in his hip pocket for a handkerchief and spat into it, choking and coughing. "You ring in your Mr. D. X. Machina, he makes his little announcement, we all collapse, and you wrap things up and move on to the next case."

"Mel, Mel," Dr. Stark cried in a strangely agonized voice, "what better answer have you got? What the hell is the difference how the torment stops, as long as it stops? And what more could any of us do?"

"Ask Ray. Look, he has tears in his eyes. Would you have believed it, Doc? All this time he's been saying he didn't care for worldly goods, but now he's crying because he hasn't got any to give away. Without the power to hand out money, what is he? And Kitty, she's shaking like a leaf, aren't you, Kitty? She went and made a baby on the strength of Ralph's promises, and now they're both stuck. Do you think it makes no difference to her?"

"Calm, calm," Dr. Stark implored him. "I warn you, the concussion . . . When wars have no object, you have to have peace."

"But aren't you shocked?" Mel swung on him.

The room spun, the white faces, tense and twisted, blurred into a swaying circle. Even Sasha, alarmed, had tottered into the room; as he lurched he collided with Mel's wrenching foot; although the impact was not severe, the dog lost his balance and fell sideways.

Mel shouted, "Look at us, still sitting up and begging for favors at Max's table. Arf! Arf! And there's Max, still laughing at us all, screwing us from beyond the grave like he screwed us in life. He couldn't trust you, neither could Leo, so they passed on the dirty work to your son. It's all been visited on the next generation. Are you listening, Doctor?"

Dr. Stark was on one knee before him. For a wild instant, it occurred to Mel that the doctor was kneeling to be knighted.

But he had not been concerned with himself or with Mel. Raising his head from Sasha's rickety carcass and glancing about him, he murmured, "I'm sorry. The dog is dead."

"Long live the rest of us!" Mel called to the staring distant faces, and, bowing to them all, he fainted.

15: DR. STARK

SOLOMON STARK KNEW why he enjoyed being recognized and greeted in public places. You do exist, we respect your title, you are important to us. Passing through the glass portals of his bank, he returned the stately declension of the uniformed doorman who, since the doors opened of their own accord, was really an armed guard in splendid disguise. He returned too the smile of the receptionist-inquiry clerk, who called out to him by name, and he proceeded to the counter behind which stood the cheerful young woman in charge of foreign accounts and traveler's checks.

"Where are you off to this time, Doctor?"

"Guatemala, just a brief winter holiday."

Starched and fresh in white shirtwaist, the newish wedding band glinting on her busy hand, she dimpled enviously.

"Imagine! I think it's wonderful to go to all those places the way you do."

He had his checkbook out now, to indicate that he was ready to get down to business, but he said, prolonging the human encounter for just another moment, "The most wonderful part is coming back. Sometimes I think that's why I go."

He was rewarded with an unbelieving laugh.

He endorsed the check and passed it on to her. She became businesslike: "What denominations would you prefer?" and he was free to withdraw into his own reflections once again, as he proceeded with the mechanical task of signing his name over and over until it became first comical, then meaningless. Solomon Stark, M.D. (Many Dollars, More Dough, Meaningless Digits).

As he signed, he considered the antiseptic nature of the transaction. Not merely the cool chatter; more important, the fact that you simply signed one crisp piece of paper in exchange for other crisp pieces of paper which, when countersigned, you conveyed to clerks in return for accommodations and presents for the grandchildren. All as bloodless and dispassionate as his son's little credit cards. It was a feeble climax, simply not commensurate with the sweat and striving that went into the getting of the money. A good thirty years had passed since the pit of the Depression, but he had not been a young man even then; he remembered, with considerable emotion, how his patients had paid him for a delivery or for setting a fracture with fifty-pound sacks of potatoes and crates of lettuce, and in one case even with some books of meal tickets for an all but bankrupt luncheonette. The direct sense of that exchange, service for service, value for value, had stirred him deeply, even though it had not helped him to pay his own bills.

This business was convenient, no doubt about it, but maybe there was such a thing as too much civilization. Packaged honeymoon trips, His 'n' Hers Steaks, quick-frozen semen—his countrymen were playing it mighty cool. Where was the passion, or even the plain pleasure, in flashing a credit card when you yearned to possess a pre-Colombian pot, or to reward an Indian kid for leading you through back alleys to the market place? Supposing it would have been the same money that the

Land boys had tried to press on him to pay for repairs for the assorted damage they had done one another? What value would it have had in such a transmutation?

When you thought of what Max and Leo Land had done for money! Still, he reflected as he watched the pretty clerk clip his bundle of signed traveler's checks into leatherette containers, Mel and Ralph and Ray had made their own passionate response to the money-hunger bequeathed them. And in truth it hadn't started simply as money-hunger even with old Max, any more than it had with Leo. The mania had begun, as many severe ailments do, with a series of seemingly benign semeiological developments. But by slow degrees successive ends—like running off with Ann Sheridan—had become so farfetched that they had been replaced by the crass means themselves.

What was funny, or maybe not funny at all when you thought about it, was how the displacement of the money-emotion had been carried to even wilder extremes by the next generation.

It was painfully evident that what Mel had really wanted was not his cut or his vengeance, but to be invited to take his name back. Raymond, on the other hand, had asserted all along that he hadn't wanted any part of the money, and no doubt he hadn't, at first, but how could you ever forget his face at the moment of his discovery that the Land fortune was really a misfortune, and that he was going to be gypped out of the opportunity to be generous?

Ralph was the only one whose libido had been at all in phase with objective reality, and yet look at the catatonic rigidity with which he had opposed even the most minimal sharing with his older brother, or the most logical compromise with his younger brother.

The doctor took one last gulp of the overheated air of the bank, nodding a second time on his way out to those who had greeted him on the way in. A strong wintry wind had come up. Despite his greatcoat and muffler, he felt himself taken by a sudden chill. He leaned for a moment against a parking meter, a concession he would have been ashamed of a few years earlier, until he should grow accustomed to the raw blast blowing up the street off the lake. Snow was overdue.

What a morning that had been! Even for himself, maybe most of all for himself, what an experience, what a revelation, when Marty had pulled off his little coup with the tax agent. Mel's wild brilliant outburst, half Homeric, half concussed, had been the most perceptive as well as the most immediate reaction, but even it had fallen short of understanding all the implications of the heritage—to say nothing of Marty's sleight of hand. And the others had been so stunned by the personal impact of the news that their responses had been more revealing of their own expectations than of any understanding of what had hit them.

Never mind the fat sisters and their spluttering consort, so far beyond their depth that the doctor had wished he could throw them a life preserver. But Raymond, sensitive as a bug feeling its way delicately across uncharted territory—the tears had started to his eyes as if someone had cruelly pinched the soft flesh of his upper arm, and he had spoken wonderingly not of his father or his uncle or of Marty, but simply of himself. "I'd just made up my mind, just now, to be a doctor, I know I could do it."

With Ralph, a twisted ashamed grin of relief, yes, relief, had spread across his face like a blush, even while his eyes darted sidewise in search of the wife to whom he must have made such grandiose promises.

And not one of them, after Mel's brief outburst, had challenged Marty, or really questioned his cool conclusion that, since their Pandora's box supposedly contained nothing more than a ghostly horselaugh, they had better make peace as quickly as possible.

The doctor shrugged himself down into his overcoat and walked on, pausing near the corner to drop another dime into the parking meter. (The cops never tagged M.D. plates, but he believed in being punctilious about small matters on the ground that it made the big ones more manageable.) Actually, he thought—it was something that he had not cared to probe from that day to this, now that he was making plans to go far away—there was nothing remarkable about the fact that no one had tried to carry on the fight against Marty's suspiciously convenient arrangement.

Quite the contrary. There were a number of excellent reasons (which a person like himself, pretending to an analytical bent, should have been able to foresee) for the Lands collectively to accept unquestioningly what any of them singly would earlier have considered catastrophic.

Had it not been for Mel's half-hysterical rendering of his autobiography, and Ralph's tortured self-defense, none of them would have been able to understand, much less to conceive, how their mother and their father and their uncle could have so arranged—or disarranged—their fortunes.

Take Max: It took a lot of doing to see the old boy. Not just to visualize him (striding along jerkily with his cocky little walk, dangerously digging wax from his ear with the end of a match, Sasha plodding along beside him to protect his rents), but to understand how he could dominate them all. Once they did understand this, though, it must have seemed all too appallingly logical that he should have tricked them one final time by slipping into the grave just one step ahead of the tax collector; by making sure, in short, that none of them would get any better use than he himself had out of the real-estate parcels that he had amassed like a kid playing Monopoly.

Besides, they were only hearing what in the bottom of their hearts they dearly wanted to hear. Marty had grasped, and boldly acted upon, what he himself had earlier hardly surmised: that the three brothers had mutually excited each other into a state of preparation for renunciation, and that they needed only the excuse of a supra-fraternal force to compel them to do collectively what they were incapable of doing separately.

Mel had raged, Raymond had cried, Ralph had besought the wife whom he had, after all, married for her strength, but none of them had balked, had said, Wait, there must be another way out.

But then, not one of them was in any position to defy authority. Especially not when their model was that very authority, flanked by Karpinski and Treadwater, one with a badge, the other with a brief case.

Even Mel, the defiant scorner of the bourgeois, whether it went by the name of Stark or Land, had been running so hard all these years from the Karpinskis and their kid sisters that he had breath left only for the wild bitter howl of the man who has known all along that he couldn't do it alone.

The doctor turned the corner, colliding with a Volunteer bell ringer, first of the season, timid and blotchy-faced beside her little cardboard chimney. "Sorry," he mumbled, even though he was not, and raised his head to see how far he was from his destination. The small neon sign of the Hazard Travel Agency (a poor name for almost any business, he had always thought) glowed in the dull winter sunlight, pale but encouraging because it was only two more blocks away. What he had finally to confront, he pondered with a queer sharp pang just below the sternal region (a bit like gastritis, but more ominous), was the home truth that if anyone should have known what Marty was up to, it should have been not the Land boys, but his father.

For he had known, from the moment Marty had exploded his ingenious device, not underground, but there before them all in the highly charged atmosphere, that it was a terror weapon. I was morally certain, he said to himself, that very day, that very morning, that Marty had cooked the whole thing up; and that Marty had used his etiolated friend Treadwater to browbeat them all into ending their battle by the absurdly simple but factually and humanly *untrue* assertion that there was nothing left for them to battle over.

And I, he thought, I went along. Was it because I was

ultimately the one responsible? Who else had saddled Marty
with a client who filed phony tax returns (when he deigned
to file at all)? No wonder Marty had been more concerned
than anyone else with cleaning out the whole mess as expe-
diently as possible, even if he had to resort to a transparent
maneuver. Now, months later, everyone knew what should
have been perfectly clear that very morning: for the government to make a deal, to accept a schedule of reparations, it
would have to make allowances, and let the estate realize the
best possible profits out of Max's properties.

Not that there hadn't been good reason for going along with
Marty's maneuver. The overriding consideration had been to
get the boys together, to impose upon them a pact which
they would be unable to breach no matter how things might
work out with the estate, the nominal source of their
trouble.

If Marty had had to be a little devious and lawyerlike, that
was his professional method—a small price to pay for such a
triumph.

But how small was the price? That was what nagged at the
doctor, and made his footsteps drag as he approached the
point of departure. Willy-nilly he was back in the very center
of the picture, when all he had wanted was to be an amused
and occasionally helpful spectator. What he knew, too, and
would never be able to say to a living soul, was that his son's
motives had been more mixed than anyone else could imagine,
and that the impulse to devise his theatrical stunt had sprung
not merely from that noble disinterestedness with which the
path to the Nobel Peace Prize is supposedly paved, but from
certain imperious demands of the superego.

Granted that Marty disclaimed any patience for psy-
chologizing. Granted even that for a peacemaker he had an
extraordinarily military turn of mind, ruthless, blinkered. What
stuck now in his father's craw and would stick there until he
had said his good-bys to this intriguing but infuriating world,
was that his son had driven swiftly through every roadblock,

and had attained an all but impossible goal, because he was ashamed of his father.

There it was. Why try to explain it away as an extravagant example of Marty's shrewd decisiveness? His son had passed his fortieth year, a decisive point in a man's life. He had come far, considering—or maybe because—he had been bequeathed a leg that would keep him off balance all his days (something for which no son could ever forgive a father). He had an intelligent wife, a gracious home, three lively daughters, a partnership in a lucrative law practice, a professorship at the Law School.

He also had a father who refused to move his office from its run-down neighborhood, and who plodded through the dull rounds of his general practice just as he had done twenty and thirty years earlier, drifting into flyblown drugstores to psychologize by the hour and to entangle himself inextricably with his friend's messy offspring.

Marty had never complained, not by so much as a grimace of distaste. He had cheerfully taken on the job of representing the crazy family with which his father persisted in being mixed up. But Solomon Stark knew, as he knew his own name, that Marty had despised it all from the very beginning, had hated the Saturday mornings at the Settlement House teaching sullen kids like Ralph Land an instrument for which they had no feeling, had loathed the sessions, before and after the Settlement School, in the pharmacy that stank of spilled medicines, rats' nests in secret corners, and the hoards and droppings of speculative eccentrics.

Then, years later, it had all come back from the outlived past to plague Marty again. The deaths of the old men had not finished off his father's connection with that dismaying tribe. Quite the contrary. The arrivals of the sons had given the reporters, the radio, the television even—with its cameras trained on the old house from the parking lot of the shopping center—the opportunity to make of them all a community joke and a community horror.

Specious to argue that a lawyer was no more labeled by the types he represented than by his father's patients or friends. The longer the battle dragged out, the more the name of Stark would be associated in the public mind with this tribe of crackpots, cranks, and castoffs. It was an intolerable situation for an ambitious man. With ruthless surgical skill, Marty had operated precisely as indicated: he had cut, removed the growth, sewed, bandaged.

And I don't dare even discuss it with him, Solomon Stark said to himself as he opened the door of the Hazard Travel Agency with his gloved hand and was met by a dizzying wave of heated air. Even if you did not take it upon yourself to preach at your children, you had to expect that they would do what you wouldn't. Marty had at best a kind of relaxed contempt for his father's dabbling in psychoanalysis (which he regarded as an overgrown jungle of poisonous metaphysical weeds choked with impossible verbiage). In turn the doctor himself had protected his own privacy by never telling his son of what he had gone through long years ago in deciding whether or not to specialize in psychoanalysis.

On the positive side had been his infatuation with the seductive possibility of being paid to devote all of his waking life (and his dream life too, for that matter!) to what could otherwise be only dilettantism.

On the negative had been his very practical fear of economic squeeze. He was no youngster, he had no father to whom he could turn. He was, rather, himself the father of a handicapped boy who needed, right away and for years to come, every advantage that you could possibly buy with money—music lessons, prep school, college, professional studies. The abandonment of his practice would mean that Celia, already afflicted with the multiple sclerosis that could have only occasional remissions, would be forced to scratch along on their dwindling savings while he spent years in training analysis and re-established himself. What was more, he would have to bow out of the lives of his old patients, some of whom he loved better than he did his own wife.

In the end he had lost his nerve. Persuading himself that his obligations to his wife, his son, and his patients outweighed his possibilities in a field which was perhaps not his vocation anyway, he had given up the idea. (No one else even knew of it but that sweetly impractical fool, Leo Land.) He had continued, always wondering, on his tiring way, only to see that now—so winded that he was compelled to lean against parking meters—his son was proceeding without compunctions to his own goal, apparently untroubled by the effect of his action on relatives, friends, or foes.

Besides, the doctor thought as he waited for Donald Hazard (who smiled a silent welcome at him and pointed despairingly to the telephone clasped like a violin between left jaw and shoulder), there was his own lifelong uncertainty about how far you had the right to intrude upon the lives of others, even when they invited you to trespass. At his age he knew that there was no answer, and yet it was a riddle that never ceased to intrigue him, and one that had also weighed in the balance against his becoming a psychoanalyst. Despite the intimacies that had been revealed to him in forty-five years of general practice, he never ceased to marvel at the nerve of the proselytizer, whether for party or cult, who blithely demanded of others that they quit their jobs or divorce their mates, stand on street corners in the rain, desert old friends or make new ones solely for the purpose of conversion, go to jail or to the stake.

True, you had to intervene, nobody lived alone, even Raymond knew that, and if there were any interventions more radical than surgery itself, the doctor had performed them too in his lifetime—telling a young father that he would soon die of Bright's disease, telling a young girl that she should have the baby even though the boy would not marry her. And yet he was painfully aware that a line had to be drawn. But where?

He was inclined now to think that it must be at the point where you stood to benefit personally from interference in the lives of your fellow men. You had to overstep the line with your parents, your wife, your children; indeed, every time a boy slept with a girl he would be breaking Solomon Stark's Law. And more power to him! Still, as moral laws went, it was worth striving toward.

But as he gazed around him, half-seeing, at Hazard's bright but cheap office displays, the cross-sectional aircraft, the snow-white cruise ships in replica, the posters of Scottish castles and Mexican sun gods, the absurd exotic dolls—all the little gadgets designed to prove that motion was pleasure, and to tempt people toward that pleasure—the doctor was ruefully aware that, even if it were possible to kid around with Marty (which it was not) about Solomon Stark's Law, his son would find it as tiresome as his dabbling in psychoanalysis.

He sighed, and turned his attention to Donald Hazard, who had finally hung up the telephone on his small cluttered desk and was approaching the counter. Hazard was a little old for such a pushing business, and was far from being the most efficient travel agent in town; but he was a patient, which meant that he was a kind of friend too.

Hazard could have used some of the sun he sold. His skin was almost as gray as his thin strands of hair, and his deep-set eyes were bloodshot as a bookkeeper's from reading time-tables by artificial light. But he had bravely given up the security of his railroad ticket agent's job to try his hand at this business, not to make a bundle for his children, for he had none, but because as an old-style Yankee he cherished his freedom.

"Sorry, sorry to hold you up, Doctor," he said.

"No harm done, Donald," the doctor replied. "Listen, you shouldn't hold the phone like that, it won't help your bursitis."

Hazard bent his grizzled head apologetically. "Say, say, it's a good thing you phoned me early. I booked you into a hotel

right in the heart of things. I know how you like to participate
in people's lives."

He laughed. "Hey, wait, using my camera isn't participating, it's the exact opposite. That's why I enjoy it. Just being
a spectator is a healthy change for me."

"I don't see that at all," Hazard protested. "When a man
like you takes all those pictures of people at work, you're participating in their lives. Maybe it only takes a second, but it's
the idea of the thing, the human sympathy. They look at
themselves differently afterwards. I can't explain it better than
that, but you know what I mean?"

Well, I'll be damned, the doctor said to himself. Who would
have thought fussy old Hazard had it in him? But then, how
many strangers divined the lovely flights of fancy which poor
dead Leo Land could conjure up for you, barricaded in the
dust and must of his old pharmacy? How precious life was,
and how beautiful, if only you could raise your head from
time to time, push yourself away from the parking meter, free
yourself for the unexpected!

He said confidently, "I know. I just want to be sure that
there won't be any hitch about my return flight. Am I all set?"

"Absolutely. Absolutely. You'll be home for New Year's,
Doctor."

"That's very important. For one thing, there's a baby due,
and a promise is a promise."

It was too wearing, delivering babies, and he had just about
given it up. But Kitty's baby was another matter. It was the
least—and the last—he could do for Leo and Jenny: to stand
by for the arrival of their first grandchild, a new Land to
usher in the new year.

He had to be at the hospital for the midyear nurses' graduating class anyway, to hand Laura her diploma. It was another promise he had made, not to Ralph and Kitty, but to
Ray. And, the doctor thought, if Mel was going to forget his
promise—which he undoubtedly would—to return for it from

whatever new plunge into the dark caverns of the western world, why should I?

On an impulse, he leaned forward across the counter to Donald Hazard, whose hand, wormy with protruding blue veins, was adding up the final figures.

"I want to tell you something, Donald. My son Martin is being appointed to the bench. He'll be sworn in shortly after New Year's. You can imagine how important it is to me to be home in time."

Hazard's sunken eyes, close to his of a sudden, were as innocent and wondering as Leo's had been. For an instant they seemed to be swimming in fluid.

"Doctor," he said, his voice quavering just a bit, "that's wonderful, that's wonderful. You must be very proud."

"Yes, in fact I am. It's a long hard row with children, but when they accomplish something, it makes you feel that all your effort has been worth while."

"My congratulations." Hazard set aside the proffered check, and clasped the doctor's outstretched hand in his own. "My congratulations," he said again. "Edna and I have been following him in the papers for years. In a way we feel almost like he's our own."

"I'll tell him what you said. He'll be pleased."

Hazard nodded after him, his hands resting flat on the glassed-in map of the United States, framing it, the check still ignored.

"Bon voyage, Doctor," he called out, his voice following him to the door. "And a Happy New Year. Now I'm sure you'll have one."

"Let's just hope that it will be better than the last one, Donald."

From the sidewalk Dr. Stark raised his arm in farewell to the travel agent, already somewhat blurred behind his window cluttered with the little flags of many nations and their excited assurances of fervent hospitality. What a foolish fraud I am, the doctor thought; five minutes after I formulated it, I violated my Law. Not only did I brag about my son and lie about my pride to a childless man, but by tonight I will have persuaded myself that the bragging and the lying were even praiseworthy, because they gave him a little vicarious happiness.

Catching sight of his distorted reflection, warped and wrinkled, in a shop window peopled with elegantly mustached dummies leaning on rolled-up umbrellas, the doctor struck a solemn pose and stuck out his tongue at himself. Then, chuckling, he squared his shoulders to the rising wind and strode on briskly through the frosty twilight streets.

ABOUT THE AUTHOR

HARVEY SWADOS was born in Buffalo, New York, on October 28, 1920. He took a degree from the University of Michigan in 1940, and published many short stories and articles while holding an unusual variety of jobs, including wartime service with the Merchant Marine.

Mr. Swados published his first book, *Out Went the Candle*, in 1955; Delmore Schwartz called it "one of the most remarkable novels in years." *On the Line* (1957), nine connected stories inspired by the author's experiences on the night shift of an auto plant, was described by James T. Farrell as "fair, honest, gifted with insight." Mr. Swados's second novel, *False Coin* (1960), was greeted by Granville Hicks as the work of "a writer who knows how to clothe his vision . . . in flesh and blood." *Nights in the Gardens of Brooklyn* (1961) is a collection of stories; Richard Gilman praised its "fine comic sense . . . and exact contemporary wit whose targets are pretension, blindness, and non-life." *A Radical's America*, selected essays and articles, appeared in 1962.

Mr. Swados continues to publish frequently in widely differing periodicals; six of his stories have appeared in *Best American Short Story* annuals; and he has been honored by a Sidney Hillman Award for an article, and by fellowships from the *Hudson Review* and the Guggenheim Foundation. He has taught at the State University of Iowa, New York University, and San Francisco State College, and is currently teaching at Sarah Lawrence College. Mr. Swados lives in Valley Cottage, New York, with his wife and three children.

THIS BOOK WAS SET IN

CALEDONIA AND BASKERVILLE TYPES BY

THE HARRY SWEETMAN TYPESETTING CORP.

IT WAS PRINTED AND BOUND BY

THE HADDON CRAFTSMEN.

DESIGN IS BY JACK JAGET.